T0357477

HOME HAS NO BORDERS

DON'T MISS

Magic Has No Borders

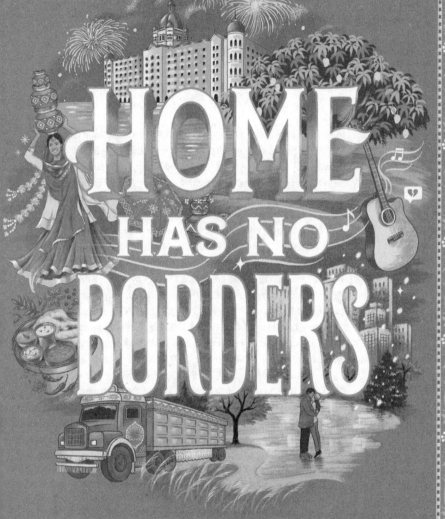

HOME HAS NO BORDERS

EDITED BY
**SAMIRA AHMED &
SONA CHARAIPOTRA**

HARPER
An Imprint of HarperCollinsPublishers

Home Has No Borders copyright © 2025 by Samira Ahmed and Sona Charaipotra
"Seven of Swords" copyright © 2025 by Fatimah Asghar
"we dine with our dead" copyright © 2025 by Kanwalroop Kaur Singh
"When Durga Devi Weeps" copyright © 2025 by Rajani LaRocca
"Simar, Aaron, and the Big Punjabi Wedding" copyright © 2025 by Jasmin Kaur
"You Can't Go Home Again" copyright © 2025 by Samira Ahmed
"One Island" copyright © 2025 by Tanya Boteju
"The Big Rig Blues" copyright © 2025 by Navdeep Singh Dhillon
"Lovesick" copyright © 2025 by Tashie Bhuiyan
"Love the One You're With" copyright © 2025 by Sheba Karim
"Star Anise" copyright © 2025 by Anuradha D. Rajurkar
"Kick Flips in My Stomach" copyright © 2025 by Nikesh Shukla
"No Taste Like Home" copyright © 2025 by Nisha Sharma
"The Way It Was Supposed to Be" copyright © 2025 by Veera Hiranandani
"Memories of a Mango Tree" copyright © 2025 by Sarah Mughal Rana
"Jahaji" copyright © 2025 by Rekha Kuver
"Rakhi & Roll" copyright © 2025 by Tanuja Desai Hidier
All rights reserved. Manufactured in Harrisonburg, VA, United States of America.
No part of this book may be used or reproduced in any manner whatsoever without
written permission except in the case of brief quotations embodied in critical
articles and reviews. For information, address HarperCollins Children's Books, a
division of HarperCollins Publishers, 195 Broadway, New York, NY 10007.
www.epicreads.com

ISBN 978-0-06-320831-5

Typography by Joel Tippie
25 26 27 28 29 LBC 5 4 3 2 1

First Edition

To the ones who paved the way.
To the ones who lifted us up.
To the ones who fought for our home to be free.
And to Thomas, Lena, Noah,
the heart of my home in the world.
—Samira Ahmed

Mama, say once upon a time . . .
To my Itsy Bit, Shaiyar Dhillon,
who always asks for stories so sweetly.
I can't wait to see what you write next.
—Sona Charaipotra

TABLE OF

CONTENTS

Dear Reader,

This collection of stories is the fruition of a dream. Years ago, Sona and I wanted to bring desi authors together to share our stories and the glorious and infinite diversity of South Asia and the South Asian diaspora. *Magic Has No Borders* and *Home Has No Borders* are cousins, and we hope when you pick up these anthologies, you'll see a piece of yourself in these pages.

I thought I'd be writing this letter as we were set to usher in our first woman president—a Black woman of South Asian heritage, the child of an immigrant. But that is not the world this collection is being published in. Instead, we see a rising tide of bigotry, racism, misogyny, homophobia, xenophobia. Over the last few years, we've seen a disturbing trend of book banning across the country—literally tens of thousands of books have been challenged, removed from shelves, their authors vilified.

What does all of that have to do with this anthology? In a word, everything. The stories in this collection are about young people finding home wherever they are. In these stories, teens are seen as they are, are known, are loved. Every person deserves that. And all of us need to build a world where that is possible. Let these beautiful stories remind you that you are enough. That you are powerful. That the world is your home.

In solidarity,
Samira Ahmed

Dear Reader,

I grew up a misfit and dreamer, a small brown immigrant kid in the thick of '90s New Jersey, always looking for myself on the page and the screen, but rarely finding that safe space. I wished for a book like this.

Samira Ahmed and I had the conversation a million times, and out of it, *Magic* was born. And now, we're *Home*. Never could I have hoped for a collection of this scope, where kids like me and you could finally find ourselves.

The stories here of the South Asian diaspora reach far and wide, both startlingly intimate and global in their scope. They are fun, funny, sweet, challenging, dark, and light. And now, they are more needed than ever.

In a world where we're fighting every day against censorship and book bans—where racism, religious intolerance, and bigotry are becoming normalized—we must protect kids and teens. And part of that must be sharing stories that might serve as windows, and especially mirrors.

It's critical for kids to see themselves on the page, now more than ever. It's critical for them to know that who they are—and who they want to be—is okay. They are to be celebrated. I hope they know that they can make their way through the world and find home wherever they go, like our parents did. Like we did, too.

So, dear reader, I hope you find reflections of hope and home in these pages. Thank you for reading.

With love,
Sona Charaipotra

SEVEN OF SWORDS

By Fatimah Asghar

It was the fourth time in the last two months that Sameera had visited Nabila, her tarot girl, telling her parents that she was going over to Nabila's house to study, saying her salaams to Nabila's parents and hot older brother, before sneaking into Nabila's room to ask her an unrelenting question—why was her best friend, Naadia, being such a raging bitch?

"Girl, don't you want to ask a different question?" Nabila sighed, turning the coal over in its holder as the bakhoor smoked throughout the room, the oud heavy, swirling, before floating silently out of the open window by Nabila's bed.

She'd met Nabila years ago; they both had attended the same mosque. And Sameera had stumbled across Nabila reading cards by the woman's wadu station, sacred geometry tattooed over her hands. Even some of the aunties trusted Nabila, sitting next to her at the wadu station to see what advice she might offer on their problems before prayer. Nabila was a few years older than Sameera—already off at college and home on weekends to visit family. It made the time she was home now precious; Sameera knew she only had an hour or so before Nabila's next client would come in. Sameera needed the tarot reading, a way that Allah could answer her prayers quickly without the humdrum of her own mind.

Fear flickered up Sameera's spine, her neck suddenly a bit clammy. Did her trusted tarot girl perhaps not like her? What did it mean that she was asking someone who found her annoying to divine on her behalf? Sameera took a sip of the mint tea that Nabila had put out for her, pushing the thought down. If she couldn't trust Nabila as a conduit for the cards, she was fucked.

"Yes, bitch, my heart is heavy and I need help. And maybe things have changed. So," Sameera countered, stubborn. Nabila pinched her brow, closing her eyes.

The light of the afternoon sun peeked through the blinds, spilling out onto Nabila's feet. She tucked them under her thighs, sitting crisscrossed, and took a deep breath in.

"Oh Allah, guardian angels, spirits who walk with Sameera Mahmoud and myself, Nabila Melek, I ask for your guidance and profound insight into Sameera's relationship with Naadia El-Khabir. Please offer my girl guidance so profound that it's enough to alleviate her heart, that she doesn't need to keep asking questions about the same shit over and over. Ameen."

"Ameen," Sameera echoed, leaning forward.

Nabila shuffled once and three cards flew out into the air, one banging into the incense holder.

"Damn, shit's hot," Nabila commented more to herself than to Sameera. Her brow furrowed as she considered, turning each card over in her hand to examine.

"Mmm. Six of Cups. Seven of Swords. Death."

She announced each card like it was a proclamation, a spell, a sentence in its own right. Silence filled the air. Sameera closed her eyes and held her breath, waiting for the tension around her heart to ease, to dissipate.

Nothing came.

"Okay, but what does that mean?"

Sameera opened her eyes to Nabila, arms crossed and annoyed at Sameera's question.

"All right," Nabila started, fighting the impulse to roll her eyes as she leaned forward. "Let me break it down for you."

SIX OF CUPS.

Set in the backdrop of a crumbling but well-loved village, a young child hands another child a golden cup filled with flowers. Behind him rests a bigger golden cup, also full with flowers. In front of them lay four golden cups, brimming with fresh flowers. The sun high in the sky.

Sameera remembered meeting Naadia for the first time. It was the first day of fourth grade, when Sameera threw a tantrum at home, insisting on wearing her favorite purple rain boots even though it wasn't raining.

"You're too old to be acting this way," Sameera's mom had said, annoyed at her daughter, before giving in to her wish so they wouldn't be late.

On the drive to school Sameera's mom had looked at her through the rearview mirror, wondering if Sameera was showing signs of developmental delays ever since Sameera's dad had left them without an explanation, a scandal that rocked the mosque they attended, making Sameera's head drop in humiliation before she eventually asked if they could just start praying at home. Sameera's mom wondered if part of her had become arrested, collapsed by a shame that wasn't hers, that she was incapable of holding and that was smothering her insides, coming out in ways that were understandable but annoyingly babyish. Namely, her inability to let things go, including the purple rain boots that Sameera insisted on wearing every day even though the sun was high, the sky was clear, and the heavens weren't threatening to break.

And here, we're introduced to the backdrop.

The crumble: a family in turmoil, separating, the tectonic plates moving under them rapidly while the rest of the world continued on, oblivious to the turmoil that was rocking them all, landing like a meteor blast on a small wooden shack.

The well-loved: Sameera's purple boots, which her dad had

bought her over the summer when they were coming home from a trip that all three of them had taken, spending an extra-long time in their car weaving through roads so they could look at the big houses upstate. The rain was relentless then, Sameera's socks and shoes had been soaked. So her dad had pulled over and gotten her rain boots, big and purple with a yellow plastic flower on the side of them. And then he left, and it became the two of them—Sameera and her mom, and the vast absence of her dad.

And the village: when Sameera and her mom had shown up at the mosque, the side-eyes that the other women had cast toward her mom as they walked in, the whispers that followed about how Sameera's mom was too busy working to be able to keep her man at home and happy. And then the way that the kids smirked at Sameera in Qur'an class, asking where her dad was.

"He's coming back," Sameera would say, and the kids would smile at each other but not her, like they knew a secret that perhaps she didn't, a secret that felt like the small glass armor she had been building around her heart had shattered into a million pieces, and that those pieces lodged inside her organs, splintering them, making it hard to move, and all she could do was learn to breathe through the splinters, to pretend that they weren't there.

It was then that she met Naadia, when they sat next to each other because everyone else had friends and they were the only two open seats left in the classroom, all the way to the back left. For most of the day they ignored each other, sitting forward, trying not to look at what the other one was doing, feigning disinterest.

It wasn't until their second subject—history—that Sameera started to hear the whispers. The kids glancing at her shoes and then laughing. Until finally, Mrs. Brenan, their new teacher, addressed the topic loud enough so that everyone could hear.

"Sameera, right? It's not raining today, why do you have rain boots on? Those shoes are bad for your feet if it's not the right weather."

The chorus of snickers. And Sameera, dropping her head low, unable to explain why she needed to wear the shoes just then, how important they were. After Mrs. Brenan walked away to consult the next student, Naadia turned to Sameera.

"I like your boots. Purple is my favorite color."

It was then that Sameera actually looked at Naadia for the first time though they'd been sitting next to each other for hours. Naadia's brown skin and big eyes, her curly hair pulled back into a ponytail. The softness around her cheeks, radiating warmth.

A small cup, brimming with flowers, being passed from one child in the village to another.

And Sameera felt it then, a single golden thread moving from the base of her navel, attaching to Naadia.

After that, Naadia and Sameera were inseparable. They went everywhere together, ate lunch together. Sameera's mom and Naadia's parents became friends—they had to, given the amount of time their children spent together, obsessed with one another. They started to dress alike. Their personalities were the same, almost so close that when one blinked an eye, the other did too, even if they weren't facing each other. And although they looked physically different, Sameera with her straight hair and thin face, Naadia with her curly curls and rounded face, everyone started to confuse them, calling them by each other's name.

Naadia shared everything with Sameera, including what Sameera needed most—a father, the overflowing cup behind the child in the village. Naadia's father doted on Sameera, like a long-lost uncle who spoiled his niece. Naadia gave generously, and through her giving, Sameera bloomed.

And for six years, six beautiful overflowing cups that remained in the front of them, everything was perfect, and seemed to Sameera like it could last forever.

SEVEN OF SWORDS.

At the backdrop of war, a man steals five swords, glancing over his shoulder as he leaves two behind. Betrayal.

Betrayal; the word that stung as soon as one thought it.

Betrayal: Naadia sitting at a table with the popular girls,

back turned toward Sameera, not even glancing her way. Halfway through their sophomore year of high school, Sameera found herself sitting by herself at lunch, while Naadia gossiped. Naadia hadn't talked to Sameera for weeks after Naadia's sixteenth birthday party. It had been slow, death by a thousand paper cuts. At first, Naadia stopped waiting for Sameera at the bus stop to go to school; she started to take the earlier bus.

"I have work to do!" Naadia exclaimed at her locker while Sameera stood, crossing her arms, the fourth time that she hadn't waited for Sameera at the bus stop to go to school and Sameera had finally confronted her. "I have to get here early so I don't fall behind."

"Yeah, but I could come with you," Sameera offered, the obvious answer.

"We don't always have to do everything together," Naadia said, rolling her eyes, slamming her locker.

Inside, something tilted inside of Sameera. Since Naadia arrived in her life, they'd always done everything together. So close it was as though they shared the same skin. The thought of doing something separate scared Sameera— who was she without Naadia? Who was Naadia without her? But she knew that she couldn't bring it up, that it would make her seem clingy and needy. And in high school, the worst thing was to be clingy and needy, especially as underclassmen.

"Okay," Sameera offered.

"Cool, see you around," Naadia said, shrugging her backpack onto her shoulders, without looking back at Sameera.

This was a few weeks after Naadia's sixteenth birthday party. Naadia and Sameera had been poring over the guest list for the slumber party, Naadia thrilled that Alicia—a junior who was in her art class—had agreed to come. Sameera had never understood the friendship between Alicia and Naadia; Alicia being older and definitely marked by all the trappings of coolness—on varsity soccer, dating a heartthrob hipster art boy, pretty in a way that skewed mean if you took resting bitch face personally. On the surface, it was clear why Naadia might want to be friends with someone like Alicia; the insight into the world she offered being so much vaster and thrilling than Naadia and Sameera's world, sophomores and still a little babyish.

But below that, Alicia seemed shallow. She binge-watched reality TV and often sounded like she spoke like those new-age inspirational Instagram posts with quotes about healing set against the backdrop of an overly saturated landscape. Sameera peeped that Alicia's last insta story was "if you change the thoughts in your mind, you can change the vibration of your future," which she had posted unironically. Sameera knew that the old Naadia would have laughed with Sameera about this and talked shit; the new Naadia lapped it up like it was a divine revelation.

Everyone knew that Sameera could be a judgmental bitch even though she tried to pretend she wasn't, but she just didn't understand Alicia. And the closer that Alicia got to Naadia, the less Naadia seemed interested in hanging out with Sameera.

Even though she was a sophomore, Naadia got into AP Art easily, just by showing the teacher her portfolio. And it wasn't long before she was a star in the class, everyone wanting to see what she was working on, as though by being in proximity to her work might give them some inspiration, as though her brilliance might rub off on them.

So, when Alicia started to befriend Naadia, it made natural sense to Sameera, who could see Alicia as the vampiric bitch that she was.

"Astagfirullah," Sameera would mumble to herself after she had that thought, asking Allah to correct her judgmental ways.

What was so surprising was that Naadia was geeked that Alicia wanted to become her friend and would not stop talking about Alicia. It was as though Naadia felt lucky that Alicia had chosen her, had deemed her exciting enough to be her friend.

"She's not even that cool," Sameera scoffed one day, when Naadia was gushing.

And Sameera was surprised that instead of agreeing with her, Naadia rolled her eyes, and looked at Sameera in a way that she had never before—like Sameera was the one who was dumb.

Naadia's dad was sick. Cancer, a faraway word that Sameera knew theoretically but had no previous lived experience with. Cancer, spreading through him. Naadia and Sameera watched as he went into chemo, his hair falling out, his body getting so thin and frail that the smallest amount of effort would exhaust him.

Naadia's paintings had turned dark. "You're in your nightmare phase," her teacher would say, though he didn't question what had turned his soft student to paint like that, the pain animating her brushstrokes. Nor did anyone in her class care about what was underneath the paintings, only that she had entered a new phase as an artist, one that they all envied because it seemed to elevate her, to make her a *real* artist, one that they all hoped to get close to.

"She has so much real suffering," Alicia would say, as though she was an art critic, never once asking Naadia what she was going through, just touting her grief like an accessory.

Naadia's mom refused to let anyone outside of her most trusted circle know. And so, Sameera and Naadia bore his sickness like a secret, unable to talk about it to anyone but each other. After visits from the hospital, Naadia would cry, lay on her bed for hours, looking at a point in the distance that Sameera couldn't quite see. And Sameera would gently rub her back, her hair, trying to coax the grief out of crushing her friend.

"It's a hard thing, jaanu. She doesn't want to attract any more attention to it. It's her choice how she deals with her pain," Sameera's mom told her as she kneaded the attah one day when Sameera asked why they weren't allowed to talk about it.

But what about Naadia's pain? What about Sameera's, who loved Naadia's baba like an uncle? Whose pain got to determine how things unfolded, were allowed to be talked about?

"Stop being selfish," Sameera's mom scoffed, back turned toward Sameera.

"You're the only one who understands me," Naadia said, when they were sharing a bed a week before Naadia's birthday party, her voice cutting clear.

Sameera squeezed her hand, and Naadia turned to face her.

"Thank you for being my friend," Naadia whispered, the moon catching her eyes, soft and brown, brimming with tears.

"In every lifetime," Sameera promised.

Naadia pushed her body closer to Sameera's, nuzzling into Sameera's neck. Her breath against Sameera's skin tickled, sending a jolt down Sameera's body. Naadia's fingers wove around Sameera's back, and before she knew it Naadia was pressing a kiss onto Sameera's lips.

Naadia pulled back, looking at Sameera. Sameera's heart pounding in her chest.

"Oh," she said softly, dazed, before Naadia smiled and kissed her again.

They never talked about their kiss. All of their kisses. But they didn't stop kissing either.

Sameera held it delicately, like a small balloon inside her chest. Most times they were just best friends, twins like they'd always been, maneuvering the world together. They'd go to school together, they'd sit at lunch, they'd hang out with each other's parents as they'd always done.

And then some nights Naadia would press her body against Sameera's and the lights inside her body would awaken. They would kiss, fingers slipping down each other's bodies, while the moon lay witness. Those moments Sameera collected inside the balloon in her chest, never taking out to talk about or think about until the moment came up again, until they were kissing, and Sameera felt alive in a way that she hadn't even known to be possible before.

For that week, it became almost like there were two Sameeras and two Naadias: the best friends. The lovers. And like those versions of themselves had to stay separate, as though they were guarding a secret that threatened to break them.

And then came Naadia's birthday sleepover: Sameera, Naadia, Alicia, and two of Naadia's other friends, April and Leila, all huddled up in Naadia's room, scrolling through Instagram and eating cookies that Naadia's mom had made.

"I feel like I'm in third grade again, it's like totally healing my inner child," Alicia said, legs up against the wall. Alicia had meant this as a compliment, but it definitely was not.

Naadia nearly choked on her cookie. Sameera knew what she was thinking: she had spent hours fretting about how she was worried a sleepover might seem babyish now that they were sophomores. Sameera envisioned punching Alicia in the face.

Instead, she reached out and squeezed Naadia's hand. Naadia looked at her and smiled.

Out of the corner of her eye, Alicia saw the hand squeeze and the smile. She flipped over onto her stomach and smirked.

"Oh my god, you guys are like . . . gay," she said, glee coating her voice.

"No, we aren't," Naadia refuted, pushing her hand away from Sameera's.

"Yeah, you are. It's totally fine, I mean if you're into that thing," Alicia continued, even though it was clear that it was the farthest thing she believed.

"I'm not gay," Naadia countered, standing her ground. "I mean, I don't know what she is, but I'm not."

Sameera was surprised when she heard it, the venom behind the word "she." The two of them, no longer tethered together as one, separated by Naadia's words. Sameera was so focused on Naadia's statement, on Naadia's back turned toward her, that she almost missed the whole room laughing at her, Alicia nearly screech-howling, and Naadia joining in.

And that's when it happened: the balloon Sameera had been holding so gently in her chest started to deflate, the air slowly seeping out.

"No, she didn't mean that," Sameera tried to assure the balloon, but it was too late. Denial couldn't save her now, not when the truth was right there.

Over the next few weeks Naadia stopped waiting for her at the bus stop to go to school. She stopped calling Sameera. She stopped sitting with her at lunch. Eventually, she stopped talking to her altogether; she just kept hanging out with Alicia, and painting.

What Sameera couldn't say, but felt in her chest: she would give back the kiss—all the kisses—if it meant she could still have Naadia in her life, if Naadia would stop ignoring her.

Sameera started visiting Naadia's baba in the hospital by herself, alone. Most days he was asleep. And then one day, he was gone.

DEATH.

Death comes as a skeleton in armor, riding a horse, carrying a flag that bears its symbol. Below him, a king lies dead and crushed, thinking he could have outsmarted death with his riches. A child pleads, a woman turns away, and another man stands upright, honoring the death that has come, embracing the change that is occurring.

When he walked through the door after years to announce his new family to his old family, Sameera's father stood upright, spine toward the heavens, without an ounce of shame on his shoulders. He came unannounced, strolling in as though he had just left the night before, not as though it had been six long years with no explanation of where he had been.

And of course, he came with the assumption that he would have a place to stay, that this house—even in his absence—was still his, that there would be warm meals and a doting daughter that would be ready for him. He came with the arrogance that only manhood could give a person, ready to receive, after already having taken so much.

Sameera's mom made up the bed for him and said she would sleep on the couch. Their meals expanded to include him, with no question. Sameera hadn't been used to seeing her mom like this—collapsed, like a mouse in her own home. It was then that she realized: that was the shape of her mother when her father had been around. But she had been too young to realize it then—caught up in her own love for him. After six years without him, when she had seen her mother cackle without abandon, strut around with comfort, talk shit to her stories on the TV, Sameera had gotten to know different shapes of her mother. The shape of her mother without a man, the shape of her mother in comfort.

And of course, Sameera was pissed. Furious at witnessing this weakness inside her mom, furious at witnessing this weakness inside herself. She'd always thought of what she might say to him if he ever came home, the stories that he might tell to justify his absence. "I was detained at the border of Pakistan," he might say, telling a story of how he had disappeared. "I was making money to be able to come back to you," he said in another one, and Sameera would tell him that they didn't need money, just him. The stories in her head went on and on, and yet, here he was, acting as though he had never left, no story in tow.

At dinner, Sameera and her mom didn't say much, just dragged their forks across their plates. Inside, Sameera felt a flame erupt inside her, a flame she had never felt before but she didn't know how to put out. It took all her concentration to not let the rage from the flame consume everything, the thousands of glass shards her father had broken inside her burning white-hot.

He droned on and on about brainless shit, Trump's prosecution and friends of his who had gotten into real estate, meaning that they were buying up properties to convert into Airbnbs. Sameera stabbed her daal viciously, suddenly overcome with the desire to punch her father in the face.

"Yeah, my second wife Raabia's brother is actually into it too. I think it would be a good way to save for our son Amir to get into school," he said casually, spooning daal onto his plate.

Sameera looked up, watching the color drain from her mom's face. Second wife? Son? The flame moved up from the pit of her stomach to consume her entire body; it felt like her very skin was on fire. The seconds slowed down as Sameera and her mom looked at each other, the news landing like her father had just taken a shit at the table.

And suddenly, her mom stood straight, and for the first time, looked him directly in the eyes.

"I divorce you, I divorce you, I divorce you. You can get the fuck out of my house."

The fire inside Sameera rejoiced. And out of their house he went, silently, as he had been for years.

"Wallahi, I don't understand men. Saying he has a second wife when he no longer even has a first," Sameera's mom said as they walked down to Naadia's house together, Sameera's mom carrying a Tupperware of goat curry and a basket of roti.

Sameera laughed. She liked seeing her mom like this. She had spent years missing her dad, being mad at her mom for whatever crime she had committed that sent him away. And then, seeing him in their house like that, she realized that she had the story wrong the whole time—it had been her dad who had murdered her family as she had known it, her dad's want to walk away.

The buoyancy she felt was enough to safeguard her heart from seeing Naadia again, after weeks of silence. The weeks of turmoil since the birthday party where she went to Nabila over and over, begging Allah and all of her guides to help show her what was in her friend's heart, the dissonance of the Naadia of the night—her moonlit eyes and soft lips telling Sameera that she was the most important thing in the world to her; and the Naadia who walked by Alicia's side, back turned toward Sameera at lunch, dangling as though she was a token on Alicia's charm bracelet without even realizing it.

Naadia's mom answered the door. They said their salaams, Naadia's mom hugging Sameera's mom extra tight.

"It's good you sent him away, no?" Naadia's mom said quietly to Sameera's mom, and the two of them burst out giggling like schoolgirls sharing a secret.

Sameera walked inside the house and saw a figure propped up watching TV.

"Salaam, Tariq Uncle," she said, surprised by how her eyes were watering at the corners. He turned slowly to see her and opened his arms.

"Sameera Jaanu. Aa jao," he said, his voice a bit hoarse. And Sameera walked over to him, collapsing in his arms, her tears spilling onto the cotton of his shirt.

"You thought I was going away?" he said, laughing a low rasp. And she clung tighter to him, unable to answer.

"I don't think Naadia is going to come down, beta," Naadia's mom said to Sameera later that afternoon, after Sameera and her mom had already been there for hours.

A lump hardened in Sameera's throat and she nodded,

turning away from Naadia's mom so she wouldn't witness her pain.

"That's all right. I have some homework so we should probably leave soon," she said quietly.

Naadia's mom watched Sameera's back noiselessly, wondering about the quiet rift that had been growing between her daughter and Sameera for weeks, the questions she had asked Naadia about Sameera only to be met with silence. How she had watched Sameera grow up like she was her very own daughter, taught Sameera and Naadia to ride bikes and make cookies, how she knew when not only her daughter was hiding something, but could see in the dip in Sameera's shoulders that she, too, was keeping a secret tucked in the deep layers of her heart. She sighed, not knowing how to broach the topic, the thing that was drifting them farther and farther away from each other.

"Okay, beta. Come over tomorrow? Naadia will be at an art seminar, but I want to take him outside by the lake, and I thought it would be nice if you came," she offered, and Sameera turned around and nodded.

It was quiet on the walk home, the birds filling the silences as they flitted about. Sameera's mom watched her daughter carefully.

"Sometimes you have to let people go and make their own decisions. It's hard when you hold on too tight to the past thing. You make a story so good that no living present can match it," she said softly.

Sameera's mom was unsure what prompted her saying that, other than she was thinking about the nights that she spent missing her husband, missing the way that he held her hand and would come home with fruit from the farmers' market. But how that version of him had been gone for a long time, how she hadn't seen that part of him for years before he left. And how she had been waiting, almost praying, for that version of him to come back home to her. But maybe that version of him no longer existed. Maybe it never did. Maybe she had filled in the gaps of his absence only with his sweetness, and forgotten the fullness of him.

The lump in Sameera's throat tightened, thinking of Naadia, the sun hitting her curls, her round cheeks. Naadia's hand in her hand. The pain of being left, again, by someone she trusted.

"It feels like dying," Sameera said, knowing she must seem dramatic, that only those who came close to death, like Uncle Tariq with his cancer, actually could speak with any kind of authority on what dying could feel like.

"It is dying. Part of you has to die. Part of them has to die," Sameera's mom said with such certainty that Sameera started to feel dizzy.

The pain inside her chest heightened, as though it was growing tentacles around her heart. The pain that she had been playing on repeat over the last few weeks, making her go to Nabila's to ask the cards how to go back to what it had been before, the feeling of love she had known so strongly in Naa-dia. And in their distance, in the silence, the pain had been the only thing that had been connecting Sameera to Naadia, reminding her that any of it was real.

Let it go, she heard something inside of her say, and breathed hard, feeling the tentacles loosen, then start to dissolve.

It felt as though all of the remaining air in the balloon she had been safeguarding finally released. The pain that had been creeping inside of her had been finally acknowledged, and she felt it moving through her body in a way that she had never known before, trying to release. And as it deflated, so did she, the gravity suddenly too heavy for her to keep herself upright, her body arching toward the ground.

When she opened her eyes, the sun was setting, the pink of it creeping through her room. Another death, the sun, closing its door to the night.

She was in her bed, unsure as to how she had gotten there other than the knowledge she had been with her mother when she fainted, and that her mother made her feel safe, and had made sure that she had ended up in bed. Her mom had seen the part of her that needed to die, made space for it, and then carried her home to safety.

Sameera sat up and looked around her room. Gingerly, she got up and walked to her desk, surprised by how strong her legs felt.

At her desk was a photo collage she had made throughout the years—littered with photos of her and Naadia, of her and her dad. She smiled, unpinned them, holding the memories in her hand.

And then, she tossed them in the trash. A gentle breeze came through her window, making her laugh.

we dine with our dead

by kanwalroop kaur singh

the cops don't take their shoes off inside the gurdwara, even though we all do. their big black boots leave unsettling imprints in the fuzzy carpet. hard, shiny leather, next to our soft, wrinkly, brown feet. biji says you can never trust a person whose feet you cannot see.

they are here to investigate they say—as if they don't already know what happened.

i used to love going to the gurdwara before. toddlers would run around the langar hall screaming. they weren't quickly shushed like they are now by their mournful moms and dads. the halls weren't lined with the photos of the freshly dead and the saturday weddings didn't seem like funerals then. the carpets were actually clean and, even if you squinted hard, you couldn't make yourself see the faint traces of spilt blood. i never felt trapped inside of tragedy then.

me and jassi came to the gurdwara to do carpet seva today. hoping the vacuum would suck out all the sadness from the gurdwara floor. jassi's here now, getting langar. today it's brown daal, mattar paneer, dahi, pakore, and cha. he fills his steel plate and comes to sit next to me. he eats in silence.

"why are the cops still here?" i ask. "it's been a whole week."

"they have to investigate, i guess." he shrugs.

"yeah, that's what they said. but seriously, there's nothing to investigate."

jassi ignores me and keeps chewing.

"why are they interrogating us when we're the ones who are the victims here?" i say angrily.

he side-eyes me. "why don't you go up to them and ask them why they're still here? seriously. i dare you."

"since i'm clearly a raghead, we both know that conversation won't go very well."

jassi sharpens his eyes.

"jivi, how many times have i told you NOT to say 'raghead'—it's offensive and racist." his eyebrows are wrinkled in exasperation.

"but i'm reclaiming it though," i say.

"you can't reclaim it because no one in this fucking country knows who we are anyway, until we get shot dead. we are NOTHING and we have NOTHING to reclaim."

he glares at me as he gulps down the last of his daal. then he picks up his plate in a huff and hurries over to the sewadar crouched in the corner of the langar hall to deposit his plate.

then. "let's go!" he yells from across the hall. i'm staring at the untouched cup of cha he left behind.

i slurp it down. the tea scalds my tongue. even the cha here used to taste like cardamom and warmth—now it just inflames.

in the morning, i watch jassi tie his pagh. he combs his hair like he's in love with it—wrapping it tenderly into a neat bun on his head, tucking his kanga inside. our parents taught us that sikhs aren't supposed to cut their hair. so far, jassi and i haven't. mine goes to my belly button. his goes until his elbows. no one has seen his hair down except me. it's his hidden treasure.

next, he ties his small keski, deftly layering one fold over the other. then he pulls out a long pink pagh from his closet.

"can you help me?" he asks.

"okay . . ." i mumble. he hands me one end and i slouch-walk to one edge of the room. he strolls to the other edge with the other end.

"are we just two people born into a family where no one cuts their hair?" i ask. the cloth is spread between us like a pink river. on the other side, he is distant and small.

last year, way before it happened, when i was waiting to get my yearbook photo taken, the white woman taking our pictures saw me and said, "you'll have to take off your hat. they usually don't allow those."

"it's a turban, not a hat," i said to her. "and i'm not taking it off."

she took my picture anyway, but the whole time my cheeks were hot with rage. so i wrote down what i wished i would have said to her then, when the words were caught between my teeth and couldn't escape. i realize i was excited about my dastaar then, about me then. but now it makes me sad.

"where is this coming from, jivi?" jassi clutches the left side of the cloth and neatly folds it into the center. i grab the right.

"nowhere. i'm just wondering. like don't you get tired of doing this every day? what's the point?"

i fold the right side in. he tucks in the remaining cloth. at the same time, we pull.

"the point is that this is who we are. yes, i get tired of looking hot every day, this takes a MINUTE. but people die for this. and we were born with it."

he gathers a foot of the folded cloth in his hands, arms moving in a zigzag motion. with each stop he gathers more cloth, gliding across the pink river between us, until he meets me on my side.

"what do you mean people die for this?" i ask.

he collects the last of the cloth from me and heads over to the mirror to tie his pagh.

"people are dying to be a part of something. to belong

to something sacred. a tradition. a history. a community. a movement. that's what we are. that's what *this* is," he says, holding up the bundle of pink cloth.

he places one end of the folded pink cloth between his teeth and starts to wrap the rest. he starts from behind his head, bringing the cloth forward, across his face, down to his ear, and around the back. he does it two, three, four, five more times. he is careful, precise, exacting with his wraps and rhythms.

jassi tucks the last of the pink cloth into the back of his pagh. he pulls out his salai and starts to refine the edges, straighten out wrinkles, ensure equidistant folds.

"i'm not sure if i belong," i say. "i just fake it until no one can tell the difference."

i watch him press and mold—like a sculptor intent on a masterpiece. when he's satisfied, he turns around.

"you do belong," he says. "one day, you'll see."

tea trickles down biji's throat. we are having cha-time. she's sitting on the couch and i'm sitting on the floor next to her tiny feet. she's tilted the mug too far forward again—a miscalculation, i think—but we both know she isn't as sharp as she used to be. i even doubt if she's noticed that i made the tea too watery.

"oh hohhhh!" she says it in the punjabi way, blowing out the hohhhh long and slow, like it's a puff of smoke, her mouth disappearing into a wrinkle as she says it, the lines of her brown face like the grooves on the trunk of an ancient tree. she chuckles at me and dabs at her neck with a folded napkin. no doubt she will say for the fifth time that the mugs in amreeka are like the damn country itself—too clunky and heavy, not dainty and light the way a teacup should be. meant for gulping and not sipping, they are slammed on tables by freakish peppy servers and not slid into your cupped palms by the shadow-eyed chawale of punjab.

"you amreekans don't know how to drink cha, because you drink tea!" she says, curling her tongue up to the roof of her mouth to spit that *t* out like it's a bullet. but biji doesn't know that "indian chai" is a fiction, an invention, like india itself. i read that tea-drinking was first introduced by the british for their commercial interests, that at first it was only the wealthy desis who wanted to be white that drank it. but in the end the joke was on them and on all the rest of us, because, as it turns out, tea might make you tan.

but i say none of this to her. instead, i say with a salty smile: "that's not true, biji, americans do drink cha now. you didn't know? all the cafés sell it."

she spits her cha out, almost choking on it, before letting out a raspy chuckle.

"ai hai! we both know that's not cha, that's packaged powder mixed with water and poured in a paper cup!"

i hug her knees and smile. we haven't smiled in days.

jassi drives me to school today. i think he doesn't want me to go alone, since it's my first time going back since it happened.

"i hate checking the asian box," i tell him. last night, i started filling out college application forms, but gave up ten minutes in.

"what do you mean?" asks jassi.

"you know, when they ask you your race on documents and forms and stuff."

"oh. why do you hate it?"

"cuz, who is gonna look at us and think we're asian? most of the time people think we're latinx or arab. so why do we have to check asian? it's a made-up identity anyway. and what is asia even? like fifty different countries with one hundred different languages and five different races of people. make it make sense."

"okay." jassi gives me that uncle-about-to-lecture look. "asians formed a coalition in america to advocate for change. they were split up. so they felt powerless. and they were made to feel powerless. so they joined together cuz there's strength in unity. but if it makes you feel erased, just don't check the asian box. just check 'other' or something."

"but if i'm 'other,' then i don't fit into any box. i don't fit in anywhere. that's the problem. i'm not white, i'm not black, i'm not latinx, i'm not indigenous, i'm not asian. i'm NOTHING. even you said it!" i'm yelling now.

"what do you mean 'even I said it'?" jassi asks, bewildered. he pulls over to the street corner where he usually drops me off.

"you said 'we are nothing'—at the gurdwara. you said nobody knows who we are!"

"i didn't mean it that way." he's trying hard to keep his voice low. "i meant that people generally don't know who we are. we're invisible. sometimes. but we're not nothing."

"well, until there's a box i can check that says SIKH, S-I-K-H, we ain't shit!" i slam the car door shut.

after jassi drops me off, the bell rings for first period: english.

ms. tran is at her desk when i enter the classroom. i pass her desk. she looks up and her smile warms me.

"hey jivi!"

"hey ms. tran," i mumble. i head to my desk in the back. people are still coming in and putting their stuff down, so i try to be low-key and disappear into the walls.

"wowwwww. jivi's not wearing her scarf!" eric shouts across the room.

shit. i was hoping they weren't going to notice i didn't tie my keski today. i should never have come. i quickly pull my hood over my head and stick my gutth inside so no one will see it.

"omg jivi!! can we see your hair?" says samantha, who sits a desk over from me.

"no. and it's not a scarf, it's a turban," i mumble as i slump into my seat.

"everyone please! let's stop talking and focus our attention up here. we have a lot to do today." ms. tran with the diversion, a queen. "as you may know, earlier this week a great tragedy occurred at the sikh temple."

ms. tran, the school counselor, and some other teachers

called my parents after it happened and told them i didn't have to come to school for a while. but i came back after four days, because if i missed a whole week of school, mom and dad were going to have a panic attack.

   you can't be a child of immigrants and miss school because you are "sad." that's not a valid excuse when your parents had to leave their families, escape a fascist genocidal state, fly across a huge ocean with 25 cents or whatever coin was in their pockets, and hustle at four different jobs so they could get a house in a nice-ish neighborhood so you could have a future. the only reason you can miss school is if you are dying, and even then you should probably die at school, or at least videocall in from the hospital bed. plus, mom and dad always say, "apaan sad-sood ni hunde," with that sideways hand wave punjabi parents always do. "apaan chardi kala ch rehne a."

   then biji always says, "koi na." and in a gruff whisper— "just pretend you went to class and no one will know the difference, not even you." sometimes, with a chuckle, she says, "these amreekans will not teach you anything worth knowing. all that—you're going to learn from me." her sunken eyes morph into a gentle wink and she cackles without her teeth.

   ms. tran asks if anyone wants to say anything about what happened. as if words matter.

   her eyes are on me. i keep my head down. i am not going to be the tragedy porn star of my people. there is silence for

33

a few seconds. then ms. tran says, "all right everyone, turn to page sixteen of *the invisible man*. i have extra copies on the bookshelf—"

i don't wait for her to finish. i pick up my backpack, swing it over my shoulder, and speed walk out the classroom door. i don't look at anyone. i don't say anything. i know my parents are going to get a phone call saying i ditched class. but i'm not going to stay here, and be normal, and leave the dead to be forgotten.

instead, i head over to the baseball field and find the hole cut in the back fence. some seniors are vaping. one of them looks at me and then looks away really fast. i climb through the hole to the creek on the other side.

i walk to the bridge over the creek that everyone writes on. there are a lot of hearts with initials in them scratched into the wooden boards of the bridge floor. BLACKLIVESMATTER is spray-painted in the center of one of the boards. cool. i look carefully for words that say white lives matter, but i don't see any. relief. they haven't made it here yet i hope.

i underline <u>BLACKLIVESMATTER</u> with a black marker. then i find a different board and i begin to write the names of the dead: JASWANT SINGH, SUCHA SINGH, HARPREET SINGH, GURPREET KAUR, SUBEG SINGH.

i trace the letters over and over and over until my hand moves automatically. the letters get darker and darker. i write until my tears stain the paint and i can hardly see what i have written. i wipe my snot on my sleeves.

when i'm done, i realize that people will probably walk over the names. they'll become the dust underneath our feet. like the bodies of the first sikhs who came here. they built railroads, worked in mines, labored in farms. dad always says—we've been here for a hundred years, we helped build amreeka. and yet. we're never treated like we did.

i do ardaas, as much as i can remember. in my ardaas, i pray that when they see the bodies and faces of our dead as they switch channels on their tvs and scroll down their feeds, it is not the first time they learn who we are. i pray that we do not die in silence when they shoot us at the gurdwara, at the gas station, at the store, at the street corner. i pray that our only memories of the dead are not hashtags and headlines. i pray for the day to come when everywhere they look, they see us and our power and they realize with dread that even their best efforts to destroy us will only make us bloom.

i start tagging the day after. i like the clack clack of the spray can, the smell of the paint, the hiss of the spray, and the beat of danger in the clear day. for my first time, i head to the side-walk down the street. i walk casually over, drop my backpack, bend over as if to pick it up, and tsssssss—leave a shiny brown swirly scribble on the concrete.

when i tag, i'm different. i never tie my keski when i do it. i imagine i'm a little girl from a rich family with sidewalk chalk in my hands, drawing on a street owned by my daddy. i shove down the dull panic inside me. i don't look scared over my shoulder to see if anyone is watching. a little rich girl never would.

i'm new at this, so i don't have a street name. the internet said i should be stylish. but i just use my nickname. sometimes i write my name with the i's as 1's like j1v1 or sometimes i write it in punjabi, cuz i know the cops are too dumb to read it—they'll probably think it's arabic and call the fbi saying it's a terrorist's sign. and the fbi will probably send in some translator who will tell them it's actually a girl's name written in punjabi, and then be pissed at the cops for wasting their time (or so i hope). anything that wastes their time is worth mine.

i never tag to post on the internet, not for tiktok or insta-gram or youtube. i like the anonymity of naming myself in public. it is something i can do invisibly, as a witch among the people, sneaky and sly, yet casual. i can walk up to a pole, a wall, a sidewalk, a bridge over the highway and just spray-paint my name all over it. my name can take up space in this nation like my body never can. it sneaks into corners or sprawls itself out, stands tall, spreads wide, immovable, unshakable. unlike me.

but things change on the day it rains.

this day, i'm bored and sad. mom, dad, and jassi have gone to the funerals. i stay home with biji. i stare out at the pour-ing rain from my window. on such days, those who dare to venture out into the rain are poised for greatness. they leave their silly warm homes for more serious adventures. this day is beckoning to me, so i get my brown spray paint cans from the drawer behind the clothes in my closet. (because that's the only place mom won't find them.) i mostly use brown for tagging, and sometimes blue and orange. never white though, because i'm not into whitewashing the streets.

this time, i decide i will bike to the highway underpass. i put on my boots, my jeans, and my navy blue khanda sweatshirt i got at the last nagar kirtan. i hold my breath as i slide open the screen door in the back, slowly slowly, so there's no screech. for brown daughters, disappearance and denial are the twin steps to freedom.

i grab my bike from the yard and wheel it out to the front. i ride down our side of the street, then cross to the other side when i get to the house of the old man who used to spit at me and biji on the way to school. then i cut through the park—empty swings swaying in the rain—pass a couple strip malls, one where i saw joti auntie pulling out of the parking lot. i almost crash into her, but i swerve at the last minute. after that, i bike deadly fast, pull my hood as far forward as i can, and wish her into oblivion. i wondered why she isn't at the funerals. but also, i don't really care. i'm not at the funerals either. she probably thinks it's more important to get her eyebrows done.

my sweatshirt is soaked by the time i get to the underpass and so are my jeans. i'm cold and wet and heavy. the underpass is dark and smells like piss. the screech of the cars passing by overhead is like metal death. shadows crouch and loom all around. i'm somewhere i don't belong yet can't escape. shivers and chills consume me.

still, i find an empty surface on the wall and take out a spray can from my backpack, finger poised on the trigger, about to spray—

dead. there, it strikes me, a horror. a few feet to the right, unmistakable, even in the dark. its four wavy white arms threaten to choke me. it seems enormous and supreme. next to it, my name means nothing. how can i take up any space here anymore? i pull out my phone to verify what i am seeing. i google "nazi flag" and there it is. in millions of tiny images that threaten to leak out of my phone and suffocate me. a swastika. complete with a circle behind it. a sacred symbol of divinity from south asia, stolen (like everything else) by white people who warp it into an omen of hate and death. without thinking, i press the spray can nozzle and start to draw a giant brown X over it.

"HEY!" a voice yells from the other side of the underpass. i turn. a blue figure steps forward.

"HEY!"

my frozen fingers drop the can. i get back on my bike somehow, i don't know how. everything is pixelated. then my twitching hands are opening the sliding door and i am falling falling falling over the doorframe, face smashed into the carpet. when I open my eyes, biji's wrinkled brown feet say hello.

it's the 1984 anniversary nagar kirtan today. it's supposed to be a sad week, but i love nagar kirtans. we parade through the streets like we own them. we wear our jutti with our kurta pajamas and our sunglasses. we wear our sneakers with our salwar kameez. we don't get nasty stares and narrowed eyes, because there are too many of us to stare at. we overwhelm.

among the gatka players spinning their chakkars and the floats strung up with photographs of bloodied bodies, there are children and smiles and strangers eating our samosas on the streets. a mix of terror and delight.

i walk behind the operation blue star float, trying to avoid aunties. someone's built a cardboard Akal Takht Sahib and underneath it says NEVER FORGET 1984. there's a gentle tap on my shoulder. i turn around. it's simran. she's my friend, one of the only other sikhs at my school.

we walk side by side, in sync with the sound of the kirtan.

simran sighs. she is withdrawn suddenly. "you know, i haven't been to the gurdwara since it happened. SUBEG SINGH was my dad's cousin."

i stop mid-walk, horror. "simran, i'm so sorry," i whisper. i wrap my arms around her in a death hug. her shoulders begin to shake with sobs. she melts into me and we are a blubbering pair, mid-street, locked in embrace, forcing the sangat to part ways and walk around us. a raft of sorrow lodged in the middle of a rushing sea.

as her tears wind down my back, for a second, it is only her and i, together in the terrible world.

i'm getting ready to go to gurdwara today. i bow my head. my kes falls before me like a waterfall. i take my kanga and start combing from the nape of my neck. its wooden teeth press into my head, scraping off worry, fear, exhaustion. i run my kanga through my kes again. the sesame oiled softness of the black strands graze the tips of my fingers. each time the kanga fills up with burs, lint, speckles of dust, and loose strands. each time i press harder into my scalp. more and more hair comes loose, more tangled pieces, more dust, more dirt.

when nothing else blocks my path and i can run my kanga quick and smooth through my hair, i tuck it in, grab the bundle of my kes together in my fist, twist it up and wrap it around. there it sits, curled up like a sleeping lion on top of my head.

i take the long cotton cloth of my keski in my hands. it is soft and nurturing, like a cloud. i tie one knot at the end and place the cloth on my head, beginning to wrap from right to left. folds and layers, wraps and tucks. when i'm done, my keski sits snugly on my head like a hug.

i haven't tied it since the shooting. i stare at my reflection in the mirror. i look like the descendant of sikh warriors. but is it really me, i wonder? can I be this?

at gurdwara, i wrap my chunni tightly around my head, take off my shoes, place them squarely in the cubbyholes. the chilled marble is smooth against my feet. i pass underneath the white dome, my chunni swishing behind me. i walk down the main hall with my back perfectly straight. i go down on my hands and knees to matha tek. the itchiness of the cleaned

40

carpet fibers is rough against my fingertips. as soon as i touch my forehead to the floor, i breathe in relief.

after divan, i sit in the gurdwara langar hall counting the pictures of the shaheed Kaurs and Singhs on the walls. sixty-four in total. some are women, their photos snapped on their wedding days. bridal bliss soon to be bloody ruin. some are laid back in lawn chairs, some in suits and ties, some in fresh ironed kurta pajamas, tied paghs crisp and layered. they were never allowed to grow old, instead their everlasting youth is a dreadful surprise—captured and framed forever in death por-traits hung in gurdwaras and homes across the world. i'm not quite sure how, but sometimes i think they are watching.

i'm waiting for jassi to come eat langar with me, so i google the martyrs' lost lives on my phone. i read about their families on neverforget1984.com. i screenshot one of their pictures on my phone and make it my profile picture.

i'm not sad about 1984 the way dad is. even mom isn't that sad. it's still distant for her, i think. but for my dad it's some-thing else. it's in the glazed loss, the lost look in his eyes when he remembers. it's in the mouth puckering and the struggling to even speak of it. it's in the words spoken at candlelight vigils, the screams of widows, and the prayers whispered with tight lips at dawn. all at once, it's always being invoked and never being spoken of. the specter of it haunts us at every turn. when our parents' voices get high pitched and start to crack. in the silences. in the stories. you can't even imagine, they say. masan bach ke aaye.

but we fight our battles in youtube comment sections and reddit pages now. we process our trauma on the internet, mostly. not like our parents. they relive it, stew in it, each time, the pain seams are torn anew. they were immigrants before they immigrated. they were turned into foreigners and terrorists in their own homes by their own nation. sort of like we are now, in america. each generation of sikhs, stuck in our own ceaseless spinning wheel of cruelty that reloads, again and again.

but mom says sikhs are like potatoes, they can grow anywhere, even in the most hostile soil. that's my job, she says. to grow. in spite of all the trauma. and because of it.

jassi's here now. i join him in the langar line.

"something weird happened," he says.

"what?" this can't be good. we're at the front of the line now. we grab our steel plates and hold them out so the sewadars can start pouring. it's rajma, rice, roti, dahi, kheer, cha, and samosas today.

"so there's a cop outside, and i heard him ask one uncle ji if he knows anything about a tag that they've been seeing around town in punjabi."

"really? what did the uncle ji say?" my muscles tighten and i almost tip my plate over. one rajma bean falls to the floor.

"he said all our kids are good. they don't do that kind of stuff." relief.

"oh okay." i hold up one finger to the last sewadar, for only one roti. he places one in my plate. i focus on the sound of dishes clanging in the kitchen. i grab my steel cup of steaming cha. i follow jassi and we weave through the buzzy cliques of uncles and aunties until we find a quiet corner.

"i don't think that's true though. i think maybe some kids are into tagging," jassi says, intrigued. we sit down together, cross-legged on the blue carpet, facing each other.

"yeah, well people are out there tagging swastikas all over the place, so what's wrong with us tagging in punjabi?"

"there's nothing wrong with it. it's about time we take up space in this town." jassi smirks, shoving a spoonful of rice in his mouth.

"i'm totally here for that," i say. i swallow a spoonful of kheer. it's my comfort food.

tonight, me and simran are tagging the underpass with our poetry. i take a sip of my cha. today, after a long time, the aftertaste is of cardamom and home.

WHEN DURGA DEVI WEEPS

By Rajani LaRocca

When I was little and upset about some injury or injustice, Mom would tell me, "Dry your tears, Isha. Durga Devi does not cry over small matters."

Legends say the goddess Durga was created to defeat a seemingly invincible evil. And I'm named for her—Isha, *the one who protects everyone*. I wish I could armor those I love against the cruelties of the world. I wish I could sprout 998 more arms, throw a discus, hurl a spear, then soothe my loved ones to sleep with a lullaby. I wish I could armor myself.

When faced with evil, Durga doesn't cry. She roars with rage, or sometimes with laughter. She defeats the bad ones and then goes home and does whatever she pleases.

So maybe that's why I am the way I am. I feel things as strongly as the next girl, but I'm not one for tears. At least, not when you'd expect them. When something hurts or disappoints me, my anger makes me quiet, turns me hard, pushes me into the physical. When I'm upset, I'm more likely to write an angry letter, channel my feelings into a poem, or clean my whole closet than fling myself onto my bed and cry into my pillow. I refuse to let hurt and disappointment be burdens. Instead, I use them as energy.

"Have fun tomorrow, Isha," Simone says as we stand at our lockers packing up to go home for the day. "Wave a flag for me."

I laugh. "It's no big deal," I say.

She pushes her heavy locs over her shoulder and smiles. "It *is* a big deal. That's why you're missing a day of school."

She's right, of course.

I was born in Bangalore and moved from India to the US with my parents ten years ago, when I was five. My little sister, Veena, is nine years old and was born in Cincinnati. I've lived in the US longer than she has, but she's a citizen, and I'm not. Not yet.

Tomorrow, my parents will become naturalized citizens of the United States. And when they do, I will, as their fifteen-year-old daughter, become a US citizen myself. I'm looking forward to it, but I don't think it's going to change much for me.

I've always been as American as I am Indian. The US has been my home for most of my life. I cheer for the Reds, even when they're bad. I go to an American high school, study

English literature, and take Spanish as my foreign language. I sing the national anthem and watch fireworks on the Fourth of July. The only thing not completely American about me is my passport.

That's not to say that everyone thinks I'm as American as I feel. Sometimes it's quiet: "Oh, yeah, that color looks so good with *your* skin tone," said with a slight curling of the lip.

"It's amazing how well your parents speak English," with a note of shock.

Sometimes it's silent: the invitation you never received, the group text you're not a part of, the social media posts that never include you.

And sometimes it's so loud that it makes you want to scream. Last year, when we returned from a summer trip to India, my sister, mom, and I traveled home in cotton salwar kameez, the soft fabric and drawstring pants providing the perfect comfort for the long flights home, while Dad wore his normal travel uniform of jeans and a tee. We passed through immigration at JFK airport in New York City, where no one batted an eye.

The trip was just fine. Until we got home to Ohio.

We were minding our own business, waiting for our suitcases at the baggage claim conveyor belt.

"Go back to where you came from," a red-faced, red-bearded, red-hatted man muttered to us.

I wanted to pull a lightning bolt out of the air and hurl it at him, ozone sparking.

But my family is well-versed in tuning out such words. My parents didn't react to him, just moved Veena and me away and continued watching the conveyor belt.

With no celestial weapon at hand, I spied one of our bags, grabbed it ferociously, and hauled it off the belt with a thump.

Dad and I gathered all four suitcases while Mom guarded our hand baggage. She stood with her arm around Veena, who curled against her like they were standing in a storm. Their clothes were rumpled, and tendrils of hair escaped from Mom's ponytail.

Then my parents led us to the exit without a word.

"Don't give them the power of making you respond," my mother once told me. "Ignorance should be ignored."

When I turned back, the man had disappeared into the crowd. So I said nothing and followed my parents out of the hall. After we staggered off the shuttle to long-term parking, I relished helping Dad load the large suitcases into our car.

"Let me take that one," Dad said as I began to lift the heaviest bag.

"I got it," I replied and swung it into the back of the SUV.

"My strong one," he murmured, and my back straightened with pride.

As we started driving home, Veena started sniffling. "Why did that man say that to us? We're from here," she whispered to me.

"He's dumb. Don't pay attention to him," I said.

"But why would he tell us to go home when we *are* home?"

I thought of all the things I could say about hatred and xenophobia and ignorance. But I wanted to protect my little sister from all that for just a little longer.

"Some people get their happiness by hurting other people," I said. "But we're better than that. We don't try to hurt them back, even if it's justified."

Veena nodded, wiped her tears, put her head on my shoulder, and promptly fell asleep. As I made sure not to move and wake her up, I let my anger course through me until it turned me to stone. Silent. Solid. Unyielding.

I went home and couldn't rest until I'd unpacked, done three loads of laundry, and put everything away. I smoothed my hands over bright lehengas, gauzy dupattas, and silk tops. I carefully placed glass bangles in a box and slid the *Amar Chitra Katha* comic books we'd bought for Veena onto the shelves of her bookcase.

I thumbed through the copy of *Tales of Durga* and sat down to read the whole thing—the origin of the goddess, how she defeated an evil that seemed unconquerable, how she is both beautiful and mighty. How she is the source of all power and strength.

I read this comic that I know like my own reflection, and finally, my rage dissipated.

The next day, I overheard my parents talking to each other as they sipped coffee in the kitchen.

"It's time," Mom said.

"I thought you weren't sure you wanted to," Dad replied.

"Our girls are here. Our life is here," Mom said. "I'm ready now."

That was the day my parents started their citizenship applications. They passed the tests and did their interviews. And now, nearly nine months later, they are ready to take their oaths.

"It's going to be a great day," I say to Simone.

After tomorrow, my parents will be able to do more than work and pay taxes and cheer at baseball games and celebrate the Fourth of July. They'll be able to vote.

And when I turn eighteen, so will I.

"You two coming to my house tomorrow night?" comes a voice nearby.

Carter Bowen looks at me as he opens his locker. He smells like pine trees under blue skies. Not that I've noticed. "The whole class is invited. First party of the spring. There's going to be a bonfire and everything." He smiles, revealing an annoyingly cute dimple.

"Sorry, I can't. I'm heading out of town," Simone says.

I shake my head. "My parents are going out, so I don't have a ride."

Carter lives way out in the country. Technically, it's a farm, but the house is way too fancy to be called a farmhouse.

"But it's going to be so much fun," Carter says, looking at me with liquid brown eyes that make my heart speed. "We'll find you a ride, Isha."

I glimpse Simone over his shoulder. Her eyebrows nearly fly off her face.

"Who needs a ride where?" Our classmate Amy sidles up next to Carter, her blond curls bouncing as she opens her locker. Amy and I used to hang out in middle school. Then we got to high school and she changed everything about herself—including her friend group.

"Isha needs a ride to my party tomorrow night," Carter says.

"I'm taking Steve and Laney. I can give you a ride, Isha," Amy says. She pronounces my name *ISH-ah* instead of *EESH-ah*, even though I've explained it a million times.

I consider her carefully. We were friends once, even if she can't get my name quite right. Even if she moves in different social circles now. I nod.

Carter shuts his locker with his shoulder and looks at me again. "Cool. See you tomorrow."

"See you," I say.

He shows off his dimple once more before he strolls away.

My smile lingers on my face as I turn to Amy. "I won't be in school tomorrow, but text me when you're on the way to my house. Thanks, Amy."

"You got it." Amy nods and heads off.

Simone leans close and whispers, "Carter seems very interested in having you at his party. Sounds like the perfect way to celebrate."

"You're a troublemaker," I say.

"That's why I'm your best friend," she replies.

I laugh again, but I have to admit for the second time in ten minutes that she's right. I'm looking forward to celebrating tomorrow like a typical American teen on a Friday night, going to a high school party where there will be music and dancing and talking too loudly around a fire. Where there's a cute boy with brown eyes and dimples. Maybe then, I can silence the voice in my head that says I'll never really fit in, no matter how long I've lived here. That no matter how much I feel this country is mine, others will never believe that I'm as American as they are.

Maybe I'll find acceptance.

Maybe.

The next day, my family and I wake early and get to the courthouse well before we need to. Mom is wearing a blue dress, and Dad looks distinguished in a dark jacket and star-spangled tie. Veena wears her favorite skirt, black with gold sparkles, and I'm wearing a white blouse and red scarf with my navy-blue skirt. My heart is full as my parents check in and we are waved into the courtroom to join other immigrants.

We file in. Light bounces off white walls and dark polished woodwork.

But I'm not prepared for what I see.

Families—moms, dads, children of different skin tones, eye colors, hair colors, speaking English and Spanish and Haitian Creole and Chinese and Romanian and other languages I don't recognize—all beaming with pride and anticipation. All ready to promise to be true to our country. To our United States of America.

My sister's dark eyes shine with wonder. "Look at all the people!" she says.

"I know," I say and press a kiss to her head. "It's awesome."

We are all here. We are all different, but we share one thing in common: we are all American.

Beauty is truth's smile, wrote Rabindranath Tagore.

Beauty is what gets me. The melody to that song I can't forget. My best friend's laugh, low and startling. A perfect line of poetry.

This true vision of the US that no one can take away.

My eyes start to burn.

The judge comes in and welcomes everyone. We watch a video from the president, thanking us for "believing that America is worthy of your aspirations." We watch more videos that depict what immigrants have done for this country and celebrate "America the Beautiful" and the flag and what it stands for.

India does not recognize dual citizenship, so my parents will need to surrender their Indian passports, surrender any allegiance to the place where they were born and raised, to the place they went to school and where they looked like everyone else, where no one looked at them and told them to go back where they came from.

Finally, my parents and all the others raise their right hands and take the Oath of Naturalization. I don't need to take part, but I say the words just the same. We promise: *I will support and defend the Constitution and laws of the United States of America against all enemies, foreign and domestic; that I will bear true faith and allegiance to the same.*

As they take the oath, my dad is beaming, a smile lighting his face; my mom is serious, reverent.

And I recognize with startling clarity why my parents are taking this oath today.

They're doing it for me. For my sister.

"Our girls are here," Mom had said last summer. "Our lives are here."

After the oath, the crowd murmurs with excitement and everyone gets their Certificates of Naturalization and voter registrations.

I take photos of my parents holding their certificates and waving tiny flags in front of the large flag outside the courtroom.

"You go, Isha," Veena says. "It's your day, too."

I can't argue with that, so I hold up my own flag and smile.

We drive home and have tea like it's a normal day. But it feels anything but normal. My parents are US citizens. And now, in the view of the law, so am I. We'll apply to get a separate certificate for me, but it doesn't matter. As of today, everyone in our house is officially American.

I didn't realize how much it would mean to me until it happened.

"Are you coming with us to Malati Auntie's house tonight?"

Mom asks. The Ramaswamys are our oldest friends in town and have two sons, Vivek and Rishi, who are near my age and Veena's.

"I'm supposed to go to a party tonight," I say.

"Who's going to be at this party?" Mom asks.

"The whole class," I say. "It's at Carter Bowen's house."

"How will you get there, and what time are you coming back?" Dad asks.

"Amy Billingsly is giving me a ride with some other friends," I say.

"That's nice. We haven't seen her in a while," Dad says.

"I'll either get a ride back with them, or I can Uber home."

"Don't Uber all the way from there by yourself," Mom says. She looks at her watch. "We can come get you. What time do you think it will be?"

"I'll text Amy and find out," I say.

I go to my room and message Amy: Hey, it's Isha. Looking forward to tonight. What time are you getting me and what time do you think we'll be back?

After a few minutes with no answer, I go to wash my face and get ready. I put on jeans and a cute white crop top and sweater. I apply makeup and tame my hair.

I stare at my phone, but Amy hasn't responded to my text. There aren't even any bubbles.

It's 6:45, and the sun is setting.

"Veena, get ready! It's almost time for us to go," Mom

calls from the kitchen. She's stunning in a midnight-blue sari. "Isha, what time do you need to be picked up? I want to let Malati know."

"Amy still hasn't answered," I say, looking at my phone again.

"Call her, then," Mom says. "We need to leave soon, and I want to make sure your plan is in place."

"Mom. No one calls anyone anymore," I say.

Mom raises an eyebrow. "We need an answer now. Unless you would like to come with us, I suggest you call her."

Mom doesn't need more than two arms or anything other than her Mom powers to make sure things are right.

I sigh. "Fine," I say.

I return to my room, not wanting anyone to hear me on the phone. But first, I decide I'll try texting one more time. Hey Amy, are you there?

No answer. No evidence that she's read either of my texts. Nothing. Maybe she's got her notifications turned off?

I sigh again. I'm actually going to have to call.

I tap my screen and hold the phone to my ear. It's funny how we hear a ringing like the old days that my parents talk about, but nothing is ringing anywhere.

"Hello?" Amy sounds confused, and I don't blame her.

"Hi. It's Isha. I've texted you a couple of times, but you haven't answered."

"Texted?" Does Amy not understand English anymore?

"Yeah. About the party at Carter's tonight. You said you were giving me a ride?"

"Oh, right," Amy says.

I breathe out. "What time are you getting me? I can help pay for gas or whatever. And . . . how long do you think we'll stay? I need to tell my parents."

"Oh, well . . . actually, I was meaning to text you. Steve and Laney invited Jeff and Audrey, and now I don't have any more room in my car."

My throat gets tight. "But you literally told me yesterday that you'd give me a ride," I croak.

"Oops. But you can Uber."

My parents almost certainly won't want me to take an Uber out that far by myself. And it would cost a lot. They'd probably offer to just drive me instead, which means they'd miss the party they've been looking forward to.

Amy's ghosting me just like she ghosted me when we started high school. She dropped me as soon as there was someone more interesting around. Which was always. So much for feeling like I belong. So much for believing I could feel like a normal teen tonight.

A spiky flower of rage blooms inside me. I long to scream into the phone.

Instead, I hang up without another word.

I tug off my shirt and sweater and change into a sweatshirt. I won't go to this stupid party. I won't go anywhere tonight. I'll just stay home, reorganize my closet, and then watch Netflix until I can't keep my eyes open any longer.

"Isha, Veena, we need to leave soon!" Mom's voice pierces the silence.

I practically sprint down the stairs, grateful for the chance to move, and stalk into the kitchen, where Mom and Dad are still waiting for Veena.

"Finally. What time is Amy picking you up, and what time should we bring you home?" Mom asks. She takes another look at me. "And why did you take off your nice shirt and sweater?"

I grab Veena's plate and water glass from the dining table and load them into the dishwasher. I take the sponge and start wiping down the already clean counter. "No one's picking me up. They ran out of room in the car. And it's way too far to Uber. So I'm not going to the party. I'm going to stay home," I say.

"We could take you—" Dad starts.

"No. You've been looking forward to going to Malati Auntie's house. You should go. This stupid party isn't even important."

"Can I stay home with Isha?" I hadn't noticed that Veena had entered the room.

"No," I say in unison with Mom and Dad.

Veena's voice rises. "But why not? I don't want to go to Malati Auntie's house, either."

"You're coming with us," Mom says.

"Rishi is looking forward to seeing you," Dad cajoles.

"How come Isha gets to stay home and I have to go?"

"Because I'm not a little kid who needs to go everywhere her parents do," I snap.

"But you're not even going to another party. You're going

to be alone. And tonight's a night to celebrate. We were all together today. I just want us to be together again tonight." Her words catch in her throat.

Something flares in my chest. I think about the sparkle in Veena's eyes earlier today, and now instead they're filled with disappointment. How for a moment, I wanted to hurt and reject her just like I've been hurt and rejected tonight.

Some Durga Devi I am. A goddess who uses her power to make her little sister cry.

My shoulders slump as I turn back toward the stairs. "Fine, I'll come. Let me go and change back into my sweater," I mumble.

I put my earbuds in as we drive to our friends' house. I refuse to look at Instagram and torture myself with the posts from my classmates at the party. Instead, I will spend another boring night with the people we've known forever, eat the same food and watch TV in their basement instead of in our living room. I don't know who else is coming or whether it will be anyone with a kid anywhere near my age. It's possible I'll end up playing pony rides with a bunch of preschoolers.

At least, though, I'll be with people like me, and no one will tell us with silence or in quiet ways or screaming in our faces that we don't belong exactly where we are.

We arrive at the house, and I'm surprised to see a dozen cars in the driveway and on the street. I turn off my music and pocket my earbuds.

"What's going on?" I ask.

"They've invited a few more people," Dad says as he pulls up to a spot in front of the house.

"Obviously," I say. "But why—"

"Enough questions. Let's go inside," Mom says. She climbs out of the passenger's seat and pats her hair to make sure it's still in place.

I shake my head and get out of the car.

Veena takes my hand as we go up the front path. Lights twinkle in the windows.

We approach the front door and instead of just going inside like we've done hundreds of times before, Mom rings the doorbell.

Really. What is going on? I think again.

But Mom doesn't wait for anyone to open the door. She grasps the handle and turns back to me. "You go first, Isha," she says.

I shake my head and go inside with Veena still clinging to my hand.

We step into a darkened living room. One step. Two.

The lights flick on. "Surprise!" thirty people shout at us.

We're surrounded by all our friends—aunties, uncles, kids from six months to eighteen. Everyone is dressed in red, white, and blue. A banner has been hung over the entrance to the dining room. It reads: "CONGRATULATIONS!"

Behind the banner, on the dining table, is a buffet full of our favorite foods: chana masala and chicken curry, greens and sambhar and potatoes. Festive pulao and heaps of fresh chapatis and puffed pooris. And at the center, there is a huge chocolate cake. It reads:

WELCOME TO THE USA
AMIT, REKHA, AND ISHA!

"We know you're not actually new to the country," Vivek says sheepishly. "I told them it was too goofy."

"It's perfect," I say as I hug him. Then I find Malati Auntie and Ram Uncle and Rishi and hug them. I squeeze Mom and Dad and Veena. "Did you know?" I whisper in her ear.

"Nope. I just wanted us to be together tonight," she says.

My phone buzzes. It's Carter. Sorry you couldn't make it.

I think about that other party, out in the country at a beautiful house with a cute boy. It would have been fun . . . but then I would have missed this.

There's no comparison.

Maybe next time, I respond.

We are congratulated by everyone, and I know that almost all of them have become naturalized themselves—or will soon. They're all on the same path we're on, moving away from the land where they were born to embrace the one that they've chosen. For their futures, and their children's futures.

And I think about how the power of Durga Devi—a power that isn't just about saving others. It's the power of community, of family beyond blood, of home beyond geography. It's the power to save each other.

I think about beauty, and how it lives here, with these people. My mom, incandescent with joy. My dad, smiling shyly as his friends clap him on the back. My sister, quivering with excitement. And me, here in the place where I will always belong.

My eyes burn, and I don't mind at all.

Here is truth's smile. Here is beauty that would make even Durga Devi weep.

SIMAR, AARON, AND THE BIG PUNJABI WEDDING

By Jasmin Kaur

THE JAAGO (NOUN)

A Punjabi pre-wedding party in which a family celebrates an upcoming marriage with lights, folk songs, and delicious food. Literally translating to "awakening," the jaago traditionally involves women dancing with brass pots on their heads, decorated with oil lamps. In modern times, oil lamps have been replaced with LED lights.

NOW

Simar's pissed.

And not the British kinda drunken pissed, which was on full display last night at the hall party where her chacha from England got all nostalgic about his childhood in Punjab. Simar's pissed because she's standing on the second-highest rung of a rusty ladder, balanced precariously against the back wall of Aaron's house, a garland of white flowers draped around her neck. Her little cousin Gavin is "holding" the ladder in place—"holding" in very cautious quotation marks. In a fight between the ladder and these two, Simar knows the ladder will emerge victorious. She doesn't tell that to Gavin, though. She simply rewards him with a "good job!" and a "you're so helpful!" and an "I couldn't do this without you!" The validation all little cousins crave from the olders at important family functions.

That August Abbotsford sun bleats through their stuffy party attire, while black-aproned caterers in a grand backyard tent begin setting out massive, foil-covered trays full of aaloo chaat and barfi and warm gulaab jamun. The heat has Simar sweating through her magenta salwar kameez. She suddenly regrets getting dressed for the jaago so early in the day. To be fair, decorating the flower arches isn't even her job. It's Aaron's. She specifically labeled it in blue on the color-coded wedding planning chart. Aaron, occasionally also called Arunvir when he's in a mood to embrace his legal Punjabi name, has somehow been more MIA than usual this week.

Somewhere on the grass, her iPhone buzzes with a phone call. A sliver of hope passes through her. "Gav, is Aaron Veerji calling?" Simar calls down the ladder.

Her little cousin blinks up at her. He stretches to see the phone, still trying his best to hold the ladder. Poor thing. "No, bhenji, it's Pamma Thaya."

"Oh," Simar mumbles. She wonders why she bothered with the planning chart in the first place. Or why she believed a massive family celebration would evoke the good old days when she and Aaron could effortlessly tag team on a project. Delegating isn't her strong suit, but she knew she couldn't handle everything for Amrit and Harman's wedding. It's not exactly a one-day affair. It's a weeklong festival. #HarAmrit-Fest, if you will.

As a bead of sweat drips down to the perfectly coordinated magenta bindi on her forehead, Simar weaves a garland of white calla lilies and wisteria through an elaborate metal archway, set next to another archway. And another. And another. And another. All lined up against the back wall of the house, to create a breathtaking backdrop for the party tonight. If Simar can get Aaron's job done, *his* older sister's pre-wedding party will be something out of a *Vogue* magazine dream. Emphasis on *his* older sister's party. Not Simar's. This isn't even her immediate family, and yet she's project-managing like she's been hired and paid for the gig. Leave it to the Dhillon family to try cutting wedding costs by guilt-tripping all the teenage siblings and cousins into forming a makeshift decor company.

Simar tries to focus on the tantalizing satisfaction of a gorgeous backyard before-and-after. On all the praise that will be showered upon her by the England relatives, by the Surrey aunts and uncles, even by her own parents. And, of course, Amrit will be grateful to tears when she sees how stunning the decor turns out. This is her motivation to get through the very long day ahead, perhaps all by herself.

This, and a dash of sheer, unbridled rage at her least favorite cousin.

SUNSHINE SANDS RESORT AND SPA (NOUN)
An all-inclusive getaway in Cancún, Mexico's Isla Mujeres, complete with two private beaches, award-winning waterslides, swimming lagoons, and wave pools.

YEARS AGO

Simar and Aaron stood at the very top of a winding hotel waterslide, grins so wide on each of their ten-year-old faces that their jaws would've been aching. Aaron had that sunshine-like glint in his chocolate saucer eyes, the kind that often preluded a daredevil-y activity that would've had their high-anxiety dads in an emotional frenzy.

"We're going down together," Aaron declared, smacking himself down at the opening of the cerulean tube. Water rushed down the slide, soaking his legs where he sat.

"Just one at a time!" chirped a blond-haired lifeguard, way too loud. She was done with the near-feral kids lined up for the slide, some of their snow cones melting on the stairs, others impatiently shoving those moving too slowly.

Aaron eyed Simar, egging her on without words, ignoring

the lifeguard's crisp instructions. Simar's palms were sweaty. Obviously, she wanted to jump on the slide with Aaron, but she wasn't one to seek out trouble.

A split second of hesitation. Then Aaron raised his wrist, flashing his half of the matching temporary tattoo they got at the snow cone stand. A smiling blue Popsicle stared expectantly at Simar. She glanced at the green Popsicle on her own wrist. A solemn vow to tag team on all their adventures that summer.

Simar was nervous, but there wasn't a chance she'd break the Popsicle vow. So, before Lifeguard Lucia could stop them, Simar bolted for the slide, grabbed Aaron's shoulder, and they both went tumbling down, down, down, heads and limbs and feet and hands clunking along the way, smiles still plastered to their faces.

THE JAAGO (NOUN)

A Punjabi pre-wedding party in which the family celebrates the upcoming wedding with lights, folk songs, and delicious food. Literally translating to "awakening," the jaago traditionally involves women dancing with brass pots on their heads, decorated with oil lamps. In modern times, oil lamps have been replaced with LED lights.

NOW

Simar and Gavin nearly make it to the end of the second flower archway when Aaron comes sauntering through the backyard gate, eyes so closely glued to a motivational TikTok about masculinity that he barely looks up to grunt some form of acknowledgment at Simar. He vaguely pats Gavin's head on the way to a catering table. Gavin stares saucer-eyed up at Aaron, forgetting all about the ladder at the sight of his older cousin.

Aaron notices little of his surroundings, besides what's directly before him. He pulls back the foil on a heated metal tray to find warm Shahi paneer. A rich aroma of garam masala, cinnamon, and cumin wafts across the yard.

"How long till we get to eat all this?" he shouts to Simar, still standing on the ladder. Not even waiting for the answer, he grabs a baby carrot from an elaborate vegetable platter and chomps down.

Simar shakes her head. Incredulous. "How 'bout you stop worrying about food and start worrying about doing your job?" It's been days of maintaining a cool facade, mostly for the bride's sake. Right now, her anger is unmasked.

Aaron arches a thick brow, pointedly grabs a few more carrots on his way to the flower wall. Two of the guys setting up the butter chicken trays glance at each other. Gavin, nervous, peers up warily at his two favorite older cousins.

"Not my job." Aaron takes another bite. "You'd know that if you checked the schedule."

Simar drops the flower garland clenched in her hand and it lands softly on the well-watered grass below. With every step down the ladder, anger rises just a bit higher up her throat.

She finds the clipboard on the ground, buried under a pile

of staple guns and pliers and damaged flowers that didn't make the final cut for the garlands. She flips past the first planning pages, labeled *Kurmai* and *Mehndi*, pre-wedding events they've somehow already handled without managing to claw out each other's eyeballs.

She finds the page labeled *Jaago*, taps her French-manicured nail on the section titled *Decor*. There, beside the instructions for the flower arches, in bold blue text, is Aaron's name.

She shoves the clipboard at him, ignoring the carrots in his hands. "What does that say?! Flower arches were yours."

Aaron fumbles with the carrots, tries to stuff them in the pockets of his metallic blue kurta pajama. He pulls out his phone, scrolls through Google Docs, and reaches the digital version of the same chart.

"We edited the Doc last night. Changed it to *you* doing the arches and me managing catering."

Simar's cheeks warm. "Aaron, did *we* edit the Doc, or did *you* edit the Doc without telling me?"

"Last night, right by the DJ table—you know what? Never mind. You aren't messing with my stoicism." Before Simar can ask what the hell that means, Aaron's phone lights up with a notification.

"Fuck, it's Pamma Thaya. He's bringing the Masala Taco Stand." He shifts uncomfortably, glancing at the gate as if their eldest uncle is about to pop up any minute. "I'm leaving before he comes. Not dealing with his shit today."

Pamma Thaya is notoriously annoying, but for all intents

and purposes, harmless. He never misses an opportunity to roast their atrocious, English-accented Punjabi, though. "You can't just bail 'cause he's coming. You're helping me finish this."

"Nah, I'm out. Tacos are handled. I've got other stuff to do." And with that, Aaron walks out of the backyard.

THE DHILLON FAMILY BBQ (NOUN)
An annual barbecue held at Bear Creek Park in which the Dhillon family gathers to make burgers and/or hot dogs, (badly) play volleyball, (skillfully) play bhabi, and sit around catching up about the year.

LAST SUMMER

Simar wiped red Flamin' Hot Cheeto crumbs on a napkin printed with the text *"Chillin' with the Dhillons."* The custom napkins were Amrit's idea. As per usual, the parents were highly impressed with Amrit.

To be fair, Amrit worked her ass off. She deserved all the praise the family showered on her. Across from the folding lawn chairs where Simar and Aaron were seated side by side, popping open their respective Fantas and Diet Cokes, Amrit was the center of attention with their aunts and uncles.

Deepi Bhua, their aunt, sipped on her virgin piña colada. "And—oh my goodness—you must be so busy! How's med school going, puth?"

Amrit twirled a straw in her strawberry-mango smoothie,

her pink sunglasses glinting in the summer sunlight. "Okay! My exams were rough but done now. So, onto the next thing—"

"Residency, hunna?" Pamma Thaya, Deepi's brother, tapped in before Amrit could finish.

"Hanji, Thaya Ji! Just waiting for a placement, hopefully somewhere in Vancouver," Amrit replied in flawless Punjabi, knowing Pamma Thaya wouldn't respond to anything in English. As far as fluency went among the cousins, Amrit was top tier, and they all went down incrementally the younger they got. Little Gavin could just about manage a bilingual greeting.

Of course, Pamma Thaya wasn't missing an opportunity to talk about the importance of their mother tongue. "Balle, mera sher puth! See that, kids! That's how you speak. Learn something." He was pointedly staring at Simar and Aaron. Simar weakly smiled. Aaron rolled his eyes the minute Pamma Thaya looked away.

Simar zoned out of their conversation, turned her attention to Aaron. "Wanna play volleyball?"

He pushed a dark-brown curl out of his face. It landed back in the exact same spot. "Mm, nah. Not into volleyball. How 'bout basketball?"

Aaron was pointedly good at basketball. So good, he was trying out for the team when eleventh grade started in the fall. Volleyball was another story.

"Court's too far," Simar groaned. "Who cares if you're bad? Not like I'm any better."

Something visibly tensed in Aaron's demeanor. "Who said I'm bad? My dad? Amrit?"

Simar cracked up. "No one said you're bad! It's just, like, a universal observation. I'm shit, too. It's cool."

Aaron glanced at his older sister, slunk deeper into his lawn chair. He spent the rest of the barbecue quietly simmering.

THE ANAND KAARAJ (NOUN)

The Sikh wedding ceremony, which translates to "Occasion of Bliss," held at a gurdwara, a Sikh place of worship. The main component of the Anand Kaaraj is the Chaar Laavan, in which the couple walks around the Sri Guru Granth Sahib, the divine Sikh scriptures, four times to signify their commitment to the Sikh way of life through spiritual hymns.

NOW

From the gurdwara stage, Daman Kaur strums an acoustic guitar as she sings the Sikh wedding hymn, her white turban artfully draped in a gold chunni that flows down her shoulders. A gray-bearded tabla player expertly matches her tune with an elaborate drumbeat. The effect, as they recite the third laav, is mesmerizing.

At the center of the gurdwara hall, before nearly seven hundred guests sitting cross-legged on the ground, heads covered with scarves or chunnis or bandannas, Amrit and Harman, Amrit's soon-to-be husband, walk around Sri Guru Granth Sahib Ji. The divine Sikh scriptures are draped in their own ornate cloths, placed higher than the guests on a canopied stage fit for royalty.

As Harman and Amrit walk slowly around Sri Guru Granth Sahib Ji's throne, gold embroidery shimmers on Amrit's powder-pink lehenga. Harman's pink turban perfectly matches her lehenga's shade. He walks ahead of his high school sweetheart, holding tight to a long pink cloth, a river flowing from his hands to his left shoulder to Amrit's mehndi-covered palms behind him. The palla bonds them together during the wedding ceremony, during their marriage, during what they both hope will be a long life together.

While the entire gurdwara hall is packed with guests (the Dhillon family invited every last distant chacha, thayee, and childhood friend they could think of), Simar is seated right at the front, cross-legged on the ground like everyone else, feet bare. Everything from her chunni to her salwar kameez to her jewelry is a combination of Tiffany blue and dusty gold, matching the rest of the bridesmaids.

Simar studies the details of her elegant older cousin's mehndi. The peacock drawn in dark-brown henna on her left hand. The dove drawn on her right. The dozens of red wedding bangles stacked on either wrist. Tears prick the edges of Simar's eyes—after the most chaotic wedding week, they've made it to the grand finale. A few hours late, albeit, but close enough.

Somehow, the jaago party last night was a hit with the Dhillon-Sidhus. Beneath a canopy of fairy lights strung across the backyard tent, both sides of the bride's family danced the night away to the sounds of Karan Aujla and Diljit Dosanjh and Jasmine Sandlas. Simar and Gavin managed to pull off the flower arches without Aaron's help.

The Masala Taco Stand turned out okay. Sort of. The tacos ran out quick, given that Aaron only ordered half the amount listed in the Wedding Planning Chart. The Google Doc is still a heated point of contention.

At the wedding, Simar draws her gaze away from Amrit's gold-dazzled lehenga. She peers across the gurdwara hall to the side where all the boys and men are seated. There at the front, a turquoise bandanna covering his head, eyes still glued to his phone, is Aaron. Gavin leans over his lap, straining to see the phone screen as well.

Simar almost shakes her head, but then remembers herself. It would be inappropriate on a normal day at the gurdwara to be scrolling through his phone like that. But during his own sister's wedding? That's beyond. What could be on his phone that's so important?

The laser-sharp heat of Simar's glare clearly hits Aaron because he glances up, catches her eye. He returns a fiery scowl of his own, whispers something to Gavin, continues scrolling.

BIBI JI'S BIRTHDAY (NOUN)

A family gathering to celebrate the elderly matriarch of the Dhillon family, Aaron and Simar's paternal grandmother.

Heartwarming in theory, the occasion is observed with Bibi Ji's favorite aaloo vale praunte and a multitier cake featuring her most ruthless quotes from the year.

LAST WINTER

Aaron, Simar, and Gavin were squished together, eyeing a massive Oreo-crumble cake on a granite kitchen counter. A cacophonous chorus of "Happy Birthday" filled the kitchen to ring in Bibi Ji's eighty-seventh birthday. Bibi Ji, grumpy to be away from her favorite La-Z-Boy recliner in the living room, watching the evening's Punjabi news broadcast, tried to act cheerful for the sake of her dewy-eyed children, grandchildren, great-grandchildren, and, well, the list went on, didn't it? She had her favorites and she was too old to feel bad about it.

Aaron sat directly across from her. He tried not to reveal his annoyance at the quote on the cake, but "Aaron? Who's Aaron? Isn't that a girl's name?" was scribbled around the cake's bottom tier. A lovely prize for not signing "Love, Arunvir" on Bibi Ji's Christmas gift. Pamma Thaya thought it was jokes. His parents laughed along, but he knew Dad was cringing.

As always, once the comments started, they didn't stop. At first, it was a playful family debate in the kitchen about whether Aaron was, indeed, a girly name. Then, everyone moved to the living room where Pamma Thaya dusted off a signature monologue about Punjabi kids who don't understand their roots. Before Aaron knew it, Dad was cussing him out for spending more time on TikTok than his calculus homework and Bibi Ji was yelling at everyone to be quiet. She couldn't hear the callers on Harjinder Bassi's live show.

Burning beneath the surface, Aaron did his best to maintain outward cool. His stomach knotted at the thought of looking corny before Gavin, whose gaze flitted just as easily from Aaron's unreadable face to the relatives gathered around, jokes ready to fire.

The noise from his family slowly became just that: meaningless, tinny static at the peripheries of his mind. He stared into the TV screen, absorbing little of Harjinder Bassi's opinions on haldi dudh, eyes glazed.

He blinked hard when Simar raised her voice, though. "Can we just leave the kid alone now? Change the topic. Bechara's always getting clowned. His marks aren't even that bad."

Aaron's dad shook his head. "Puth, his marks are okay because *you* do all his projects for him. Let him try working by himself, like his sister. Then we'll see what numbers he gets."

He wasn't sure what did it: the standard-issue comparison to his sister, Amrit; the insistence that he couldn't do shit independently; the fact that Simar always had to come running to his rescue, like he couldn't handle his own. But he stood without thinking, pulse pounding in his jaw, shoving past his dad on his way out of the living room.

For a moment, the whole family went quiet. Simar glared across the room. Gavin stared nervously at the now-empty doorframe, wondering whether to follow behind him. Then, Harjinder Bassi revealed a new desi remedy for diabetes involving sugarcane juice and the Dhillons erupted into a brand-new debate, forgetting all about Aaron.

THE LIMO (NOUN)

Short for limousine. A critical component of any Punjabi wedding. Transportation of choice for immediate family and close friends to travel to and from the wedding and, at times, additional wedding functions. Bonus points if it's a stretch Hummer.

NOW

Simar and Aaron are seated as far as humanly possible in a darkened, otherwise empty limo. Simar can palpably feel the tension, despite her cousin's physical distance. It could be as thick as all the barfi they've been force-fed this week. Maybe thicker? God, she hates barfi. And, God, she hates this. She shuts her eyes, visualizes the three-course reception menu, just to dissociate from the awkward silence.

Blue light illuminates Aaron's face. His awkward-silence coping strategy seems to be scrolling through his phone. Unluckily for Simar, hers is dead.

Just when she thinks she should go get some air, Aaron speaks up. "I'm gonna go see what's taking everyone so long."

"Yeah, cool," she mumbles.

When Aaron jumps out of the Hummer limo, he leaves his phone behind on a black leather seat. Simar watches him cross the length of the parking lot toward the gurdwara where the rest of their family is taking way too long to leave. She glances down at his iPhone's home screen, still unlocked, his background some bearded TikToker she vaguely recognizes. Who has a TikToker as their background, anyway? Objectively weird, in Simar's not-so-humble opinion.

Curiosity tugs at her. She knows it's wrong. Knows she should leave the phone alone. That he could be back at any moment. But he stares at this thing day in and day out, ignoring their entire family for whatever he has going on in there.

She won't go through his WhatsApp or IG DMs. That would be an excessive violation of his privacy, right? Instead, she opts for TikTok.

She scrolls through his *For You* page. A prank video in a grocery store pops up. Nothing interesting. Simar scrolls past. There's a video comparing different types of motorcycles. Another video pops up about motorcycles. Maybe the algorithm senses that Aaron wants a bike? Still, not exactly spicy. She scrolls further, swiping away a WhatsApp notification from a group chat simply called "ALPHA 🫤."

After generic videos about MMA fights and WWE takedowns, she encounters a bearded face that makes her pause: the TikToker Aaron's saved as his phone background.

The bearded man doesn't seem to blink as he speaks. He talks into a podcast-style mic, staring at someone off-screen.

"All of us know this," he says, brow furrowed. "As a man, you're going to be tested. You're going to be told you're not enough. And it's up to you to decide whether you're going to listen to that noise or tap into your true power. They're going to tell you what you should be. They're going to tell you to shut down your primal instincts to dominate. To be on top. They're gonna try to take your power from you. Call it *toxic masculinity*. Tell you to sit down. Do this. Do that. Make you listen and obey like sheep—"

As the man drones on about reclaiming masculine power, something coils tight in Simar's stomach. She clocks the red heart—Aaron's already liked the video. How does *this* appeal to him?

The coiling snake in her stomach freezes when a figure approaching the limo catches her eye. It's Aaron, several yards away, his massive strides drawing him closer and closer by the second. Heart pounding, Simar taps out of TikTok, clicks off his phone and drops it back on the seat where he left it. She races over to the other side of the limo, tripping over her way-too-elaborate salwar, the pins in her chunni popping out as she fumbles with the tikka dangling from her forehead.

Seconds before she makes it to her seat, gold jewelry in disarray, Aaron peels open the door.

"The fuck happened to you?" he mumbles, eyes narrowing.

ULTIMATE GYM (NOUN)

As its name implies, Ultimate Gym is the ultimate gym for both new and seasoned bodybuilders. Everyone who is serious about bodybuilding in Surrey has considered an annual Ultimate pass if their wallet allows it. The scent of dedication (see: pungent sweat and a lack of ventilation) is free. Don't worry, you'll get used to it.

LAST SPRING

Aaron knocked back the last of his protein shake, wiped a bead of sweat from his chin, sat solidly in the disappointment of another failed lift. He was hunched over the edge of a bench, staring intently at his phone. If someone was waiting impatiently for him to get up, he didn't notice. He was caught on the blunt edges of Gordon Smith's words. The bitter truth of them.

"You're failing, again and again, because you aren't ready to taste greatness. You're cosplaying as a man but you're still just a weak little boy who gives up and walks away when shit gets hard. Grow up. Stop complaining and just do the damn thing. Get your ass back in the gym and go again."

He used the split second of motivation to lie back down, fix his form, and push a barbell off his chest. Gordon's words rang loud in his brain: he was done playing the role his family wrote for him—the weak little boy who couldn't do shit on his own. His anger was a tool, a blessing, a source of power, and he forced it all into his arms, into that lift, held it right there and refused to succumb to the burning tear of his muscles.

When he finally put down the bar, the rush of dopamine hit from all sides. His phone buzzed with a WhatsApp notification: another motivational video posted in the ALPHA 🗿 group he joined from that Masculinity subreddit. That night, he would lie awake, eyes red with exhaustion, watching video after video until the words blurred into one another.

THE DOLI (NOUN)

A component of many South Asian wedding traditions in which the bride ceremonially departs from her parents' home to begin her new life with her partner, traditionally at her in-laws' home. Often involves crying and a team of wedding videographers awkwardly zooming in on the bride's sobbing face as she leaves the house.

NOW

It's only at the doli, standing outside Aaron and Amrit's house, that it finally hits Simar what this wedding means: Harman's from Calgary, and Amrit's moving there with him. Three days from now, Amrit will be packing up her bedroom and making the nine-hour drive out to her new home.

Simar's used to rolling her eyes during dolis, where the brides' families collectively cry it out, as if their daughters aren't just moving to the other sides of Abbotsford or Surrey. As the Dhillon-Sidhu family gathers on the driveway, walking Amrit to a flower-laden vintage Corvette where Harman is waiting, Simar swims in memories of her eldest cousin that meant everything: sleepovers where they'd do each other's nails, late nights on the weekend playing *Mortal Kombat* with her and Aaron, impromptu trips to White Rock Beach where Amrit would always buy her little brother and cousin lavender-vanilla ice cream.

Nothing will be the same without Amrit around. Nothing is the same *now*.

Not even Aaron, present and absent in his own way.

Simar doesn't realize she's ferociously crying, until tears pool around her gold necklace. She doesn't bother to wipe them. Somehow, there's something soothing about her family going through this moment together, their collective emotions honest, shameless, welcomed instead of hidden the way they usually are. Amrit's dad holds her in a fierce goodbye hug, his body plainly shaking with his sobs. Her mom rests her head against the back of Amrit's pink wedding lehenga. She struggles to let go. Nearly all of Amrit's aunts and some of her uncles sing along to a boli about a daughter leaving her parents' home.

Simar's breath hitches when a large shoulder brushes against her. Was Aaron standing there the whole time? She sneaks a glance at his face while his gaze is momentarily averted: his Adam's apple quivers with an almost-tear, but there's something tense and conflicted behind his flitting eyes.

He quickly throws on a pair of Ray-Bans, not fast enough to hide a tear that slips down his stubbly cheek. He wipes it away with his kurta sleeve and moves through the pastel sea of wedding guests standing on the driveway until he disappears into the house.

"Where'd he go?" Deepi Bhua sniffles. "He needs to push the car away when they leave . . ."

Simar's back straightens. Her wedding planner duties take precedence over her discomfort with Aaron right now. "I'll go get him."

She searches the kitchen, the backyard, the basement theater. Then she heads upstairs to Aaron's bedroom. Still, nothing. On her way to the bathroom, she swears she hears someone blow their nose in Amrit's bedroom. So, with a deep breath and a mental affirmation that she can handle this, she slowly opens the door.

There's Aaron, sitting on a feathery beanbag chair facing the window, as he bounces one of Amrit's championship tennis balls back and forth between his hands. She'd won first place in the local high school league three years in a row.

"You, uh, you good?" Simar startles Aaron, who practically jumps out of his skin at the sudden sight of her.

Fear quickly solidifies into irritation. Aaron turns back to the window, still wiping his face with his kurta. "How hard is it to leave me alone? Don't you have an Excel sheet to laminate or something?"

The words aren't surprising, or even unwarranted, but they still sting. Something blue and heavy fills Simar's chest as warm moments return—of times when Simar and Aaron did just about everything together: abysmal soccer tryouts at school, roller-coaster rides together at Playland every summer. That joint presentation about Malala Yousafzai they did for Social Justice 12 back in February.

Where did everything go so wrong?

"We—we need you outside. You have to be there when the car leaves."

Aaron half-shrugs, remains quiet.

A stretch of silence. Simar clears her throat. "You know it's okay to cry, right? I'm upset Amrit's leaving, too. Everyone is."

All he says is, "It's really not."

Simar takes a step forward. "I don't exactly know what you're feeling, or what's going on with you, but I just want you to know that it's normal to not have it together all the time. It doesn't make you weak, or something. You get me?" The words are as much for Aaron as they are for herself.

Perhaps because she's sparked something in his chest, or perhaps to make her leave, Aaron slowly nods. "I get you. Gimme me a minute, please? I'll be out in a sec."

Her pulse settles as she closes the door behind her. She exhales.

THE RECEPTION (NOUN)

The culmination of every Punjabi wedding party. Typically held in a desi hall where every last distant relative can grab a seat and a plateful of mouth-watering garlic naan and saag paneer from a never-ending buffet. In order to qualify as a notable reception, there must be a smoke machine and neon lights on the dance floor, and, maybe, a dancing robot.

NOW

Simar's growing as a person. She can feel it. Instead of emceeing the reception, she resisted her usual refrain of "if you want to do something right, you have to do it yourself." Kamal and Dimple, identical twins and two of the middle school cousins, are currently behind the podium, adorably fumbling through the dinner buffet announcement, cue cards slipping from their hands.

Is it perfectly polished? No. Did they forget to thank the England relatives for flying down? Yes. Does it all kinda work 'cause they're cute and little? It does.

Simar glides between tables full of guests she either instantly recognizes or pretends to. If she doesn't know names, there's usually an aunty at the table, who unprompted breaks into a round of introductions.

Beneath a decadent crystal chandelier, Amrit and Harman sit at the center of a long table decked with white peonies and ultra-realistic electric candles. It's something out of a Kardashian birthday dinner and Simar's here for all of it.

As Pamma Thaya comes over to congratulate Simar for all her hard work on the decor, Gavin comes bolting toward her, his forest-green patka cloth in one hand, his topknot all lopsided on his head.

"Simar bhenji! Simar bhenji!" her little cousin shouts over a Mankirt Aulakh song. "Can you tie my patka again?"

"What the fu—HECK happened to your patka, Gavin? You literally just got here."

Gavin explains something about an Undertaker tombstone smackdown on the dance floor while Simar scans the crowd for his parents. They're busy talking to the groom's Nani Ji. Then she spots Aaron standing around by the bar, doing just about nothing. She waves him over.

"Mind redoing his hair?" Simar asks. Aaron tied a patka

until he cut his hair in high school, so he's much better qualified for the task than her.

Aaron disinterestedly shrugs, nods, guides Gavin away from the dinner tables, toward the much quieter lobby.

"Oh shit . . ." Simar murmurs, as she sees what's coming before either Aaron or Gavin do:

Gavin, practically jogging to keep up with Aaron's strides and clearly preoccupied staring up at his #FamilyFave, doesn't see the glass door coming right at him. His face hits the door with a definitive thwack, and he tumbles to the ground. For a moment, he's in a disoriented daze. Then shrill shrieks erupt from his throat. Simar runs over, helps him off the black marble tiles.

"He's fine," Aaron gruffly says. "He can get up on his own. You're fine, right, Gav?"

The shrieks continue. Aunties at a nearby table look back, worried. There's clearly a bump on his chin, swelling by the minute.

"Chin up. Okay, bud?" Aaron taps Gavin on the cheek. "You can handle it. No girly shit."

At this, Gavin tries his best to stifle his tears. Something about his older cousin calling his tears "girly" seems to stir something. He brushes the dust off the shoulders of his black kurta, leans on a potted plant bigger than him as he stands back up.

Before Simar can get a word in, Gavin runs off toward his dad.

Aaron is already walking away when Simar says, "What the fuck is your problem?"

He turns back. "What?"

"No, seriously, what is your problem?" Her heels clack hard against the marble as she strides toward him. "Just 'cause you're in this weird-ass phase, it doesn't mean you need to shove it down Gavin's throat as well—"

"Phase? What are you talking about? What, 'cause I told him to stop acting like a girl? Guess what—he's gonna have to toughen up 'cause the family—everyone's gonna walk all over him otherwise—"

"He fell! He got hurt!" Simar claps back. "How do you go from *that* to some philosophical shit about life?!"

Deafening bass from *Rail Gaddi* fills the banquet hall, drowning out their voices to everyone besides the tables nearby, but they've still managed to draw attention, aunties and uncles tapping each other's shoulders, sipping cha as they try to figure out what's going on.

"Obviously you don't understand. He has to start thinking about this stuff now," Aaron says. "Things are different for guys. You and Amrit aren't gonna face—"

"Face what?! Our family roasting you *and* me for being shit at soccer? Or not getting As? Not knowing how to read Punjabi? Have I not been right there with you?!"

"No—no you haven't. Because after all this time, you still haven't got it through your head that I'm not your little pity project. I don't need you to come fix everything—"

89

"I'm not trying to fix everything! I'm—"

"And Gavin doesn't need you to baby him, either. I won't let him become a bitch."

The Uncle-Aunty Whisper Network™ has clearly notified the entire banquet hall that there's drama because Amrit's staring at them from the dance floor, mortified. A massive, neon-clad robot wielding a smoke gun fist pumps behind her, unbothered.

In what feels like a recurring theme these days, Aaron turns his back to Simar and stoically walks out the banquet hall doors. Simar, at a loss for words, at a loss for answers or solutions, heads to the dance floor, puts on her best wedding planner smile, and tells everyone that he's just grabbing a charger for the dancing robot.

YOU CAN'T GO HOME AGAIN

A LOVE HATE & OTHER FILTERS SHORT STORY

By Samira Ahmed

Is it messed up that a doorbell buzzing is forcing me to rethink all my life choices?

Fine, maybe not *all* of them. NYU film school was still one hundred percent the best idea for me because I wanted to get out and stay out of Batavia, Illinois, my hometown, where everybody knows your name and your business. I wanted to leave (almost) everything behind, and I'd done it (sorta). *Good on you, Maya. No regrets.* But my entire hometown isn't standing on the street in front of my building ringing my bell, Phil is. And it doesn't escape me that his arms were the one place that ever truly felt like home to me.

The doorbell rings again as I stare at the fuzzy black-and-white image of him as he looks into the camera and smiles, his dimples still beyond adorable. My heart squeezes. I take a deep breath and I buzz him in. I squeeze my eyes shut. I have three flights to prepare myself to see the first and, so far, only love of my life. I never told him that, but I stopped lying to myself about it.

The streetside door of my building shuts with a thud. And I hear the slow jog of his steps as he gets closer.

I wipe my clammy hands on my jeans and wrap my right hand around my doorknob. I haven't seen Phil since we said goodbye when we both left for college. We'd texted a bit, but that fell off, too. Then last week he'd texted. *He'd* gone home for Christmas. I hadn't, using my job at Sullivan Street Tea and Spice Shop as an excuse. He was flying through New York and had a few hours to kill before catching a bus back to Vermont. Would I maybe want to hang out if I was around, he'd asked.

I texted, Yeah, sounds fun, before I could talk myself out of it. Before I wondered if it would dredge up old feelings that I didn't want to revisit. After analyzing approximately one million hours of film, one thing I've learned (besides the fact that overly dark lighting on-screen is apparently how dude filmmakers want to convey that their work is Gritty and Serious and Art) is that clean breaks are hard to achieve, and Phil and I had done the seemingly impossible in breaking up without breaking each other. So maybe I was screwing it up by agreeing to see him, here in New York. He's part of my life, of course, but the past—the part that I left in Batavia, not the now that is New York. I might not be a physicist but I'm pretty sure my two worlds colliding could cause a rift in space-time continuum. But I don't have time to worry about that anymore, because I'm ten seconds away from opening the door to the past and letting it step right into my present.

Breathe, Maya. Is it normal to have to tell yourself this? No. But it's also not normal to feel the flutters of my high school crush roaring back to life in my belly and making me want to throw up. Or, maybe it is. I take a huge gulp of air, wrap my fingers around the doorknob. Open sesame.

Phil takes the final turn on the stairs that lead to my apartment and when he looks up at me and smiles that gorgeous smile that lights up his eyes, this warmth spreads through me and for a moment, I am a senior at Batavia High School again, tutoring him at the bookstore I used to work at, my crush burning so brightly you could probably see me from space. It's like all of time has reversed and the last eighteen months of my life in New York have been erased.

"Hey, Maya," he says, his voice low and as soothing as I remember it.

I clear my throat. "Hey," I say with a small smile. "Welcome to New York."

Phil takes a step closer to me and then leans in and I inch closer lifting my cheek to him for a kiss, but he reaches his arms out in a hug and bonks me in the corner of my eye with his nose and I step back in surprise. Oh my God, I thought I'd left the awkward back home, but I guess I was wrong.

Wherever you go, there you are, a mindfulness teacher once said to me and at the time it made no sense, but those words come crashing back into my brain with an *I told you so*.

He chuckles his deep, warm laugh as I lead him into the apartment. He drops his backpack in the corner of the small entry hall and slips off his shoes before stepping into the living room. Why am I so moved that he remembers that visiting a desi means taking your shoes off? I mean it's basic manners, but also more. Phil whistles as he looks around the living room. It's exactly the reaction I had when my friend Anjum told me I could crash in the other bedroom in this apartment that her parents own. It's on the edge of Washington Square Park and impossibly expensive and furnished with actual adult furniture. She refused to let me pay rent because her parents don't need the money and she said this is her way of making them support the arts. Yes, I'm absurdly lucky.

"Yeah, I know," I say. "I love how much light this room gets. The winter light in New York is different than Chicago's. It's brighter and sharper with a subtle, almost bluish hue but it's, like, deceptive because there's no real warmth to it. You know how in Chicago it's more gray and dreary?" I continue without letting him answer because when I'm nervous I blather on and on. "You should see the light in September. It's so amazing. And oh, Manhattanhenge. You have to experience that sometime; it's when the setting sun aligns perfectly with the grid and the entire city is golden and the light almost has a physical quality to it and—"

Phil spins around to look at me, a wide smile on his face. "I forgot how much you love light."

"What do you mean?"

He steps to the window taking in the view of the park and the Washington Square Arch. "You were always talking about the quality of light and how light filters through leaves and how it changes with seasons and how every city has its own kind of light. And how it felt impossible to capture on film. Honestly, you were obsessed. I guess some things don't change."

I laugh, trying to ignore the butterflies that are going wild in my stomach. "You remember that, huh?"

"How could I forget?" he says softly, and I feel my cheeks warm. I haven't seen him in so long and we've barely talked since we left for school and yet, here we are, like no time has passed at all. And I don't even want to admit how comforting that all is even though it's also totally head spinning. I stare at him for a second—his shoulders are broader than they were in high school and now he has real stubble on his face and, dammit, he is somehow even hotter.

We gaze at each other, smiling. One second. Two seconds. Oh no it's getting awkward. Three seconds. If I look away first does that mean I lose? Four seconds.

I step forward, closing the distance between us and whisper, "Is this a staring contest?"

"I would kick your ass."

"Wow. Are you this competitive with all your ex-girlfriends?"

I press my lips together but too late—that ridiculous question is already out there now, between us. We never used labels and were only together right at the end of senior year and the summer after.

"Only the ones I still like," he says, his grin widening, dimples creasing his cheeks. "So . . . since you love New York more than anything—"

"Well not more than *anything*."

"Not more than chocolate cake, right?"

Not sure why it's surprising that he remembers these rando details about me, because I remember a million tiny things about him, too. "Not more than chocolate cake," I say with a soft smile.

He clears his throat and repeats, "Since you love New York more than anything—besides chocolate cake—what are your plans for me?" He pauses. "I mean, for what we're going to do this afternoon."

"Well, I thought we'd wander a bit and I also have an iconic NYC moment in mind."

"A hot dog in Times Square?"

"Absolutely not. Times Square is the *worst*. And street dogs there are strictly for tourists. Besides no NYC dog can beat a classic Chicago dog. There aren't even sports peppers here."

"No sports peppers is a tragedy but I *am* a tourist."

I sigh. In the year and a half since I've lived here, a couple friends from high school have visited and my aunt and a cousin and they all wanted New York's greatest hits, tourist edition. And who am I to deny them? It's not like I'm a real New Yorker either, not yet. This city feels like the place I was meant to be, but I've barely scratched the surface of everything I want to see and do in this city.

"Okay, I'll consider allowing a hot dog, but do not blame me for any possible outcome." I grin.

Phil laughs as he follows me when I gesture him into the kitchen so I can get him a glass of water. "Why aren't you filming?" he asks.

"Huh?"

"I mean, like 99 percent of the time that I saw you, there was a camera in your hand."

"Yeah. I guess because I wasn't in film school yet, maybe? Maybe because that's how I was documenting my life?"

"And you don't want to document your life anymore?"

I hand him the glass of water. "That's funny. I hadn't really thought of it in that way before. I mean, I do want to document my life, but I also have other stories I want to tell. I guess maybe now that I'm actually studying film, I'm less inclined to want to be constantly filming because it gets in the way of observing."

"Of being present."

"Something like that." My mind floats to something Kareem, my first kiss, told me—about how I had to get out from behind the camera because I was the main character in my own life story. I guess those words stuck.

Phil sets his glass in the sink. "Are you going to tell me

what iconic New York experience I'm about to . . . uhh . . . experience?"

"It's a surprise!"

Phil scrunches his eyebrows together. "You're not going to tell me where we're going?"

I grin. "Yup. Exactly like when you didn't tell me about taking me to the pond the first time you dragged me into that freezing water." My mind wanders back to the swimming lessons Phil gave me at that hidden pond, at the hours we spent lazing around under the sun, our bodies nearly touching, the air electric around us. I pull my head back to the now.

He laughs. "So, this is payback?"

"Absolutely."

We walk back toward the front door, and I pop into my room to fix my lipstick and to grab the new red-and-blue plaid cashmere scarf and red beanie that my aunt sent me. Phil is waiting for me, leaning against the door in that easy way he has, not even looking at his phone, like he's just comfortable with himself. I always envied that.

I bend down to lace up my Doc Martens and my necklace slips out from behind my cream cable-knit sweater. When I stand back up, the pendant rests in the collarbone notch at my neck. Phil locks eyes with me and then reaches out to touch the silver gingko leaf—the necklace, a gift from him, is one of my favorites. He presses the tip of his index finger against it and the heat of his skin sears into mine.

"You still have that?"

"Yeah, it's in the necklace rotation." I don't know why I said that. Why didn't I just tell him I wear it almost every day, that it's like my talisman.

He nods, quirking his lips in a half smile, then stuffs his hands into the pockets of his peacoat.

The air is brisk, the sun bright as we step onto the street. The area around Washington Square Park and campus feels less busy than usual. Most kids won't be back for another week. This time between Christmas and New Year's is kinda dead but I like the quiet. I like exploring without having to sneak out of my house or ask my parents for permission. Last year, when I first moved into the dorms, it felt so weird— maybe even wrong—staying out past my parents' curfew or watching movies that I knew would make them blush. I still occasionally hear this tiny voice that wonders, What would your mom say? Like when I'm climbing onto the subway at midnight with friends. I don't know if that voice will ever go away—the one that questions my choices, and maybe it's not just my mom's voice. Maybe it's partly mine.

I lead Phil to the subway at West Fourth Street and as soon as we hit the platform, we see a giant rat scuttle across the tracks. "Ta-da," I say. "Now that is a real New York experience."

"That is the hugest rat I've ever seen." Phil shakes his head. "I mean it's the size of a small cat."

"I thought you liked nature and wildlife and stuff—isn't that your major?"

Phil laughs. "Outdoor education does not include a field study of rats. It's more like expedition canoeing, outdoor emergency care, mountaineering."

"Well rats are part of the outdoors!" I joke.

"Except in New York City where they're too busy grabbing leftover pizza boxes to get out of the subways."

I start laughing. "I have no idea why I'm caping for rats. They're the grossest thing ever."

"I think you like an underdog. Or, under-rat in this case."

I nudge Phil with my elbow. "Dad joke!"

Before I can pull my elbow away, he gently cups it with his gloved hand. Not gonna lie, when we first broke up—or moved away from each other—I thought about him a lot. We emailed but that eventually petered away and in the last year, he was only the occasional fleeting thought. I was over him. I'd gone on some dates, left him and everything about Batavia in my rearview, but now it's all speeding back to me. He's speeding back to me.

He gives me a lopsided grin and before I can say anything, the B train swooshes into the station, drowning out any words I could've possibly mustered.

We take two seats next to each other in a car that's only half full. The doors shut and the train jolts forward, jostling me into him. Our knees touch and neither of us moves away.

"So this is the subway." Phil scans the car.

"Don't make eye contact with anyone," I whisper.

"Is that a rule? Like does it mean there's going to be a rumble?" he whispers back.

"Yes, if you're a character in *West Side Story*," I deadpan. "It's just a thing like not eating stinky food on the train or clipping your nails or manspreading."

Phil's mouth drops open. "People clip their nails on the train? I thought New York City was supposed to be glamorous and sophisticated or something."

"It is. Except when it's totally not."

"And that's why you like it so much more than Batavia?"

I shrug. "I don't hate Batavia. There are some things I will probably always love about it. But it never felt like the place for me. I hated sticking out like a sore thumb. I hated being the only desi girl in our entire class. Here, I'm pretty much anonymous. I don't stand out."

Phil turns his head and locks eyes with me. "You stand out no matter where you are." He gives me a little smile.

We're quiet the rest of the way to our stop. Rockefeller Center. I grab his gloved hand and head up the stairs and outside.

"Okay. I figured out the surprise," Phil says as we emerge on the sidewalk next to Radio City Music Hall. "You're about to tell me you're a Rockette and I'm going to see one of your shows."

"Ha! Right. The Rockettes are now looking for dancers with limited flexibility and zero dancing talent."

"You can dance." Phil nudges me. "I've witnessed it."

"I don't think slow dancing counts," I say, feeling my cheeks flush as I walk a bit farther down the street and end up gazing at the giant Christmas tree at Rockefeller Center.

"Whoa. It looks even bigger in real life."

"Yeah, and surprise! We're going ice-skating."

Phil turns to me and raises an eyebrow. "I thought you didn't like to do touristy things."

"That's not what I said."

"I'm pretty sure it is."

"I don't like Times Square touristy things. But c'mon, skating here is classic. Haven't you seen *Elf*?"

"You like *Elf*?" Phil asks, incredulous.

"Why is that so shocking?"

"I mean, it's pretty low brow for a film studies major."

"I am not a snob."

"You totally are." Phil reaches out and wraps his arms around my shoulders. Initially, I tense, but then let myself lean into it because it's so familiar and cozy. "Total movie snob."

I sigh. "Well, this snob is taking you ice-skating."

"You know I can't really ice-skate. I thought I'd mentioned that a million years ago."

"Really?" I say, letting the sarcasm drip from my voice. "I had no idea."

Phil throws his head back and laughs. "Liar! This is all part of the payback plan for the swimming lessons."

"I play the long game." I wink at him.

"Fine. Let's do it. I'm ready to fall on my ass on the hard, hard ice of Rockefeller Center in front of about a million people. As opposed to the pond where I taught you to swim that was totally private and hidden in the woods."

"Like the lair of a serial killer."

"There are no serial killers in Batavia," Phil says.

"I guarantee you that small-town life has driven plenty of people to murder."

"Speak for yourself." Phil squeezes my shoulders.

"I totally am."

I glance over at Phil as we lace up our rental skates. He might not have skated much before, but he has the ease of an athlete around all things sports—probably because that's what he was. "Do you ever miss it? Playing football?"

He finishes tying his right skate, checking to make sure the laces are taut, then sits up. "Yeah, I kinda do. I miss the team. I miss game day. I miss—"

"The cheerleaders?" Oh God. I just resorted to snark and a vague reference to his high school girlfriend—the one before me.

He gives me a knowing smile but doesn't respond.

"Do you regret not taking that football scholarship?"

"Nah. I still love the game, but I was never going to go pro. So, I left it all out on the field of Batavia High School."

"Go Bulldogs," I say, my fist raised in the air.

"Go Bulldogs," he replies, then stands ready to walk out on the ice.

I stand with a little wobble. I've skated before, lots of times. Does twenty count as a lot? Just not this winter. Phil takes my gloved hand and loops it through his arm. "Let's go embarrass the hell out of ourselves."

We step onto the ice—this rink is way smaller than Wollman Rink in Central Park and significantly smaller than the large pond at the Depot Museum that my friends and I skated on in Batavia and about a million times more crowded with tourists. It takes me a minute to get my legs under me but then muscle memory kicks in and I begin to glide forward—still near the edge of the rink so I can grab the wall if necessary. Phil follows me but when I turn my head over my shoulder, I catch him losing his balance, flailing his arms, and falling on his ass. I turn around and skate back to him, weaving my way through the onslaught of other skaters. "Are you okay?" I ask, coming to a stop next to him.

"I meant to do that," he says and winks at me. I offer my hand to help him up, but when he takes it, I'm thrown off balance, my left skate slips out from under me, and I land on top of him, my forehead knocking into his chin.

"Ow!" we say in unison. Skaters glide around us, barely paying attention to our romcom-esque accident heap.

"Sorry," I say, rubbing my temple. "Are you okay?"

"I played football, remember, I'm used to being hit on the chin and tackled."

"I did not tackle you!"

Phil extends his arm, still on his back on the ice. "I'm pinned under you. I'm pretty sure you planned that."

"Ha, you wish," I say as I roll off him, onto my backside, and then push myself to standing.

"Maybe I do," he says, his eyes twinkling in that way that I always found totally disarming. Ugh. His charm still works on me, and I want to be madder about it, but I'm not.

He pulls himself up with the help of the low wall around the rink.

"Ice-skating is mainly about balance and control," I say. "You just need to bend your knees a little so they're just over your toes. You're less likely to fall backward that way."

Phil lets go of the wall and takes a position like a skier. I put my hand on his chest, gently correcting his posture so he's not leaning over quite so much. "Now you basically have to shift your weight from side to side when you skate. So, when you move your right skate forward, shift your body right and then repeat on your left side."

"Got it. It's just transferring your weight and keeping your center of gravity kinda low." He tries it, pushing off and skating forward, right then left, then again. He's totally getting it. Of course he is.

"You got it!" I clap.

Then he turns to grin at me and totally, comically, wipes out. I raise a mittened hand to my mouth to stop myself from laughing. I skate up to him. "Try, try again?"

He pushes himself to his knees and then to standing, rubbing his backside. "Really wish I had a tailbone protector."

"Is that an actual thing?" I ask.

"Totally, for snowboarding, skiing, falling on your ass in front of all of New York City. Or at least the tourists peering down at us." He nods to the people above the rink who are laughing, snapping selfies, and not all that interested in us, it seems.

I tilt my head to the side. "C'mon, drama queen. You can do this," I say, offering my hand.

"If I can make it here, I can make it anywhere."

"Oh my God, more dad jokes. This is painful."

He laughs as we successfully skate around our first turn. About ten minutes later, we've made it around the entire rink hand in hand without falling and with only a few little wobbles. And soon we are in a nice, slow rhythm, the sounds of holiday music and the swoosh of the ice under our skates filling the space around us. There's laughter from people falling down and getting up on the rink, there's the excited voices of little kids marveling at the giant Christmas tree and asking for hot cocoa. It's not lost on me that Phil and I are holding hands or that the familiar buzz of electricity is running from his fingers through mine.

"I can see why you think this place is so magical," Phil says, breaking the comfortable silence between us.

"Yeah. I don't have the same rose-tinted lenses on about it, though. Not like when I first got here. I mean, this city is amazing. It's more than I ever imagined, but there's also major income disparities, some neighborhoods clearly get way more benefits than others, housing is basically not affordable for regular people, and public schools are totally underfunded."

Phil looks at me, a wide smile on his face.

"What?" I ask.

"Nothing. I just missed you, I guess."

I raise my free hand to my eyes, trying to rub away my embarrassment. It's late afternoon and it's already darkening, the lights of the buildings popping against the deep blue and orange skies as dusk descends. I can feel that slight temperature drop in my bones and I shiver. We skate to the wall near the golden statue of Prometheus next to the rink.

"You're freezing," he says. "We should get off the rink."

"I'm fine. I'm not really that cold."

"Your lips are practically blue," he says.

"Stop looking at my lips," I blurt before I can stop myself. Once a blurter, always a blurter.

He inches closer to me. "Impossible."

I look up at him and he holds my gaze. I feel wet on my nose and when I cast my eyes upward, I see that it's starting to flurry. There's shouts and whoops from the rink.

"What did I say about this city being magical?" Phil chuckles, gently brushing the snowflakes from my nose and cheeks.

"I ordered it from the universe," I say softly. "I wanted to give you the ultimate New York winter experience."

Phil unbuttons his peacoat and inches closer to me on his skates, opening his coat and wrapping the sides around me. His body is like a furnace and I'm warmed as I snuggle into him. He smells like fresh laundry and crisp winter air and it's all so familiar and comfortable and before I know it, his lips press against mine, whisper soft, and I kiss him back. And he tastes like home.

It's not like our first kiss and it's not like the last time we kissed when we purposefully didn't say goodbye. It doesn't have that sense of wild curiosity, of abandon, but maybe it's something softer, quieter. It's like your favorite sweater that you've outgrown or the stuffie that you can't get rid of even though it's seen better days. Being in his arms is easy and warm and something I can't quite put my finger on . . . Nostalgic. Maybe that's it. Maybe there is a tiny part of me that's homesick, only not for a place.

We slowly pull apart. "I didn't come to New York to kiss you," he says, "but it's a major bonus."

I laugh. "Why did you come to New York?"

"I dunno. I kind of asked you if I could visit before I even thought of why. I guess it's what I said before, I missed you. And we never . . ."

"We never had a real, real goodbye." I swallow, suddenly so aware of what this is and who he is to me but then correct myself. "I mean we said goodbye, but a little bit of it never seemed over?"

"Maybe something like that."

I nod. "Something like that."

"Does one of us skate off into the sunset now?" Phil asks, pointing to the stairs where we entered.

I look down at the ice, then lift my head back up to see him waiting for my response. "Impossible," I say. "Because that's east and your backpack is still at my apartment."

He looks at me and starts to laugh and then I slip my hands out from inside his coat and we head over to the rental booth to return our skates. As we sit on a bench slipping on our shoes, Phil says, "So, part of the reason I'm going back to Vermont early is that I'm leaving for Costa Rica in a few days. Doing a semester abroad."

"Phil, that's awesome."

"Yeah, I'm going with a couple other students—we're studying rainforest conservation and spending some time at volcanoes, too. Should be cool."

"Amazing. Love this for you," I say, straightening up after adjusting my Docs.

Phil chews on his lip, a bit uncharacteristically. "I think I'm actually a bit nervous about it," he admits after a heavy exhale.

"Why?" I'm genuinely perplexed because Phil always had this easy kind of confidence in high school. Not swagger, but just like he trusted himself to know what to do or to figure out how to do it. Not that he was perfect.

He shrugs. "Honestly, I'm not sure. Maybe the distance? I haven't really been out of the country ever. And there's this girl, she's one of the other students going on the trip."

My eyebrows shoot up. "Do not tell me you just kissed me when you have a girlfriend."

"No. No. I don't. Not at all. I wouldn't do that to you. It's just that I think maybe I might be interested in her."

My chest tightens. Not that I have any right to be jealous. I have barely spoken to Phil in over a year. But there's a part of me that feels possessive of him, or maybe, protective?

"And you want me to pass her a note asking her if she likes you?" I ask, my snark rising.

Phil gives me this look that I can't quite interpret and then takes his gloves off and presses the heels of his palms over his eyes. I see him take a few deep breaths. So often in my life, I've witnessed what was happening to me like I'm an outside observer, like I'm not in it. And I'm watching us now like we're in a movie, the camera zoomed in on my confused face then panning out to capture both of us. My heart thuds in my ears. I'm not even sure why. Am I mad? Should I be mad? Or hurt? My thoughts are all muddled.

"Phil," I say, hesitatingly touching his shoulder.

He turns to me and says, "The thing is I kinda still love you."

My jaw drops and my heart thunders in my ears. This is not what I was expecting. I don't know what I was expecting.

He continues. "You don't have to say anything. I know we never said the L word."

I raise an eyebrow at him because he just used the phrase *L word* like we're in seventh grade.

"I am so bad at this," he says, shaking his head. "I think maybe I was in love with you and I never told you and then time passed, and we stopped talking and I figured that's how it goes with high school girlfriends and then this other girl at school happened and I wanted to ask her out, but I kept not being able to and I realize it was because of you."

"Because of me?"

"Yeah, you. And that's when I realized, I kinda still love you and I'd never told you and it didn't feel like I could move on even though we said we were moving on and . . . damn. I'm babbling. It's just weird, you know, and I thought maybe seeing you, maybe telling you and now I've told you and—"

"Phil," I say in a quiet voice. "I still kinda love you, too. And I don't think I realized that until I saw you coming up my steps today."

Phil smiles, revealing his dimple. "So what happens now?"

I breathe in and out, my heart feeling like someone's reached into my chest and is squeezing it. If this were a rom-com, we'd realize that we should still be together. If this were a French avant-garde film from the 1960s, I'd probably slap him then kiss him madly. If this were a superhero movie, there would be an earth-shattering catastrophe right now. But it's none of those things. It's just us. Me and the boy I loved for a little while when I was in high school. The boy who made a fake prom for me when I couldn't go to prom. Who taught me how to swim in stolen moments at a hidden pond. The boy whose arms feel like home—one I love but am not going back to.

"I think now," I finally say. "You go on an adventure in

Costa Rica with a girl you really like." I give Phil a soft, sad smile. "I think now, we're good."

"We'll always have the pond." Phil winks at me, echoing something he told me a million years ago.

"We'll always have the pond," I laugh.

We stand up and Phil wraps his arms around, kissing the top of my head. "You're the first person I could ever really be myself around."

Together, we turn away from the rink and the crowds at Rockefeller, we walk down Sixth Avenue, past lit-up store windows, and the holiday market at Bryant Park, the Empire State Building rising just to the east of us. We walk past couples and families, by people with their collars up and chins down against the cold rushing into the subway. I don't think I was ever really aware of how much Phil was just always with me. I've been on dates, but maybe the memory of us held me back from really thinking of anyone else seriously. Maybe the door I thought I'd closed was actually slightly ajar.

As we continue the long walk back to my apartment, mostly in silence, darkness enveloping us, the wind chaps my cheeks and I snuggle in closer to Phil and I feel like there's a sort of understanding between us. An awareness of what we were to each other. Then. And what that memory is to us. Now.

I think of something one of my film studies professors said—he's approximately a million years old but when he talks about storytelling, his eyes dance: "How lovely it is to be young and to have a heart that can still be broken."

These final moments play out like a movie in my mind. I set up the crane shot:

The sky darkens on a New York street, strangers hurry by, a taxi honks. But the couple only gaze at each other, knowingly, a bittersweet smile on the boy's face. The girl holding in a small sob as she smiles. Snow falls and muffles the sounds around them, softening the light of the streetlamps. Together they walk the final steps to the girl's apartment building. They understand that this moment is The Goodbye. A door closed, so others could open. The girl gazes up, briefly, at the camera, then out at the world that awaits. Music swells over the dying din of the city as the edges of the frame fade to black.

ONE ISLAND

By Tanya Boteju

Sithara frowned. At the DJ, who had better change the music from trash Top 40 to bhangra ASAP. At the adults who forced this event. At the tension in her shoulders and neck.

She hadn't wanted to come tonight, but her parents insisted, since the whole event was their idea. Sithara's mother was the president of the Sri Lankan Friendship Association, her father on the board. They'd wanted to bring the younger generation of Sri Lankans together more—or at least, *appear* like they did after receiving backlash about catering too much to the Sinhalese component of the association. So they'd organized this youth dance for "all Sri Lankans," called it "The One Island Dance," and made Sithi and her friends decorate in an island theme.

Sithi had grown more and more annoyed with each crepe paper strand, each string of yellow and green lights.

Finally, the music switched to something Sithi could work with. She grabbed her friends' hands and pulled them onto the floor, ready to sweat out her irritation and stress. As Sithi started to move her body, her jaw relaxed, her frown lifted. She tried to lose herself in the beats.

Her eye caught on a group watching her from across the floor, though—Iyla and her annoying friends. The kind of people—Tamil people, mainly—that Sithi's parents were trying to appease with this dumb dance.

The association included all Sri Lankans, technically—Sinhalese and Tamil, Buddhist, Muslim, Christian, and more—but as long as Sithara could remember, she'd heard her family talk about the political strife in Sri Lanka, about the Tamil Tigers and the war, the bombs and deaths. Her grandparents had lived through the thick of it, but the stories and traumas had been passed down and distilled into one clear message: Singhalese and Tamil people are not the same. They could share space if they had to, like at the association, but their histories were too fraught to get too close. Maybe it was different elsewhere, but here, this was what she knew.

Sithi felt her forehead crease again and tried to refocus on her stomping feet and pumping arms. *Just move, Sithi.*

From the other side of the hall, Iyla's eyes lingered on Sithi. She hated giving the girl any of her attention, but Sithi was a strong dancer. She moved with confidence and hit each beat hard—with no hesitation, it seemed. Unlike Iyla, who loved to dance, but had always been self-conscious and worried about what others would think of her. She had good reason to be. She'd never had a personal vendetta against Sithara or her friends, but they seemed to have one against *her*, so Iyla responded by keeping her distance—more out of self-preservation than anything else. She knew a lot about self-preservation—from her parents and their experiences as Tamil refugees coming to Canada, but also as the only girl in a family of four Sri Lankan sons. She'd learned to stay quiet and polite—fly under the radar. Things were simpler that way.

But she *wanted to dance.*

When the floor became crowded enough, she finally allowed her friend Jeffrey to coax her into the mix. And once she was there, tucked among her friends, her worries diminished and she could focus on that feeling she would sometimes get when she was dancing—of being at home in her own body, of a kind of calm—even with the music blasting.

Only once did the feeling falter—when she caught a sharp poke in her hip and turned to find Sithara glaring at her, as though Iyla's hip had somehow ambushed Sithi's elbow. Iyla's chest pinched at Sithara's irritation, but also at her proximity. How had they gotten so close together on the dance floor? She turned away quickly and merged back into the safety of her friend circle.

At the end of the dance, two aunties approached Sithi, dragging Iyla behind them.

The good feelings summoned from dancing all night seeped away from Sithi, and Iyla, too, grimaced.

"Sithi baba!" Aunty Bell shouted. "We have exciting news!"

Shit. What's this about? Sithi thought.

"We've decided you and Iyla will teach the harvest dance to our children's group for the Sri Lankan New Year's Celebration!" Aunty Caryl chimed in, pulling Iyla up beside her.

Sithi held in a curse. "Pardon?"

"We all saw you two dancing tonight," Aunty Bell says, indicating a group of aunties in the corner, "and decided you would be the *perfect* instructors!"

"Yes, such *wonderful* dancers! Who knew?"

Sithi knew. She'd been dancing hard since she was three. Her gaze shifted to Iyla.

Iyla caught Sithi's eyes and immediately focused on the ground. She wasn't any more excited about this idea than Sithi was.

Sithi had known Iyla for almost four years, since they were twelve. Iyla was quiet—even shy at times—but she didn't have to say anything for Sithi to resent her. Not just because Iyla was Tamil, either. Sithi also just thought Iyla was too pretty, too perfect, too polite. She was sure Iyla was full of shit, though. No one was that nice.

"But—" Sithi began.

"No buts!" Aunty Bell proclaimed, with finality.

Sithi sighed. Once the aunties had spoken, there really were no buts.

"What does this entail, exactly?" Sithi asked.

"You'll meet with the group on Tuesday and Thursday evenings this week and next, and then one final time the night before the celebration. That works for you both, no?" Aunty Caryl asked without really asking.

Sithi looked at Iyla again. This time, Iyla met her eyes and shrugged.

They were stuck.

"Control your kids!" Iyla heard Sithara bark behind her as Iyla tried to wrangle the group of eight five-year-olds rampaging around her. She closed her eyes and took a breath. She'd already decided that this would be a lesson in patience. She would remain gracious and calm. She would not let Sithara get to her. This, Iyla knew, would be the best way to annoy her.

But when Iyla turned to face Sithara, who'd just arrived, she was momentarily caught off-guard. She'd only ever really seen Sithara in jeans or maybe a sari now and again. But today she wore tight blue leotards and a yellow tank top with looping armholes—her full curves on proud display. Her long straight hair sat in a high ponytail. She was vibrant and glowing. Iyla had to blink herself out of her surprise and the annoying tingling sensation in her stomach.

Iyla tried to reply with confidence, but her voice trickled out. "They're *our* kids . . . and *you* try to 'control' them."

Sithara smirked. "Let me show you how it's done."

Iyla almost rolled her eyes, but managed to refrain. She watched as Sithara strode into the middle of the fray, slapped her hands together in an aggressive pattern of claps, and then waited for the kids to—presumably—stop their madness and clap back the same pattern. Iyla had seen this tactic work in classrooms. It did not work here. The children continued to run rampant. One small boy even ran into Sithara's leg as he barreled past her.

Sithara placed her hands on her hips and turned to Iyla somewhat deflated. "What the hell?"

It was Iyla's turn to smirk. She came up beside Sithara and they stared at the whirl of small hooligans. She was surprised by Sithara's defeated posture. Sithara always seemed so bold, so in control. This discrepancy made Iyla a little more brave.

After a moment, Iyla went to the stereo and put on a baila song. She came up to Sithara again and held out her hands, trying to hold them steady despite the nerves vibrating her body. "Here," she said.

Sithara looked at her hands. "What?"

"Let's just start dancing and see what they do."

"Like, you want me to waltz or something?" Sithara did not waltz.

"Yes, I want you to *waltz*." This time Iyla let her eyes roll openly. "I was thinking more along the lines of a silly dance? For the kids?" She braced herself for rejection.

Sithara pushed her lips out, considered the lawless children, and then shrugged. "Fine." She took Iyla's hands and they started in on some random steps, but found themselves out of sync.

"Just move with me a little, okay?" Iyla said.

Sithara's muscles tightened, her skepticism grew plain on her face, but she told herself she just needed to get through this and tried to loosen into Iyla's movements. They started swinging around, hands gripping each other's tighter and tighter the faster they spun. Their feet worked quickly to keep their bodies rooted but in continuous motion, and Iyla couldn't keep from smiling. She glanced at the kids and was happy to see them stopping to watch.

"It's working—keep going!" Iyla whisper-shouted under the music and into Sithara's ear. Sithara flinched at Iyla's closeness, but kept dancing and noticed that a couple of the kids had even begun to spin around on the spot, too.

"Okay, let's see if we can figure this out," Iyla said, and she and Sithara let loose each other's hands to turn to the children.

Half an hour later, Sithi was surprised to find she wasn't *hating* the session with Iyla or sick of trying to get their group of eight mostly uncoordinated kids to learn the dance. She was even more surprised to find that Iyla had turned into a balanced force of firm and goofy, keeping the young dancers focused on the task at hand, but using ridiculous faces or gestures to make them laugh, too. She seemed to have a bit more patience—maybe a lot more—than Sithi did. Sithi had wanted to teach them all the steps at once, but when she'd tried, Iyla suggested they work on one piece of the dance at a time, which pissed Sithi off, mostly because it made sense.

"Fine," Sithi had said through gritted teeth, trying to keep a smile on her face, trying to show the children—and Iyla— that she could be flexible and fun, too. She wasn't about to let Iyla show her up.

So they'd proceeded to work through the dance in small chunks, until one of the kids—a tiny human named Bartholomew—had asked, "Why do we have sticks?"

Sithi had sighed, annoyed by yet another interruption— kids had so many *questions*—but Iyla had just grinned and said, "That's a great question, Bartholomew!"

Sithi had wanted to strangle them both.

As Iyla responded to the boy, though, bringing the sticks together to create the jubilant clacking sound and demonstrating how they kept the beat for the rest of her body, Sithi's irritation lost its strength. She would never admit to it, but she was actually drawn into Iyla's demonstration—the well-timed thump of her feet to each strike of the sticks, the way her eyes crinkled at the corners when she smiled, the powerful flex of her arms.

Christ, Sithi, get a grip. They're just sticks, for God's sake. She folded her arms and waited for Iyla to finish.

"Any questions?" Iyla asked a few minutes later. Four hands went up. Iyla could practically *hear* Sithara's impatience, but didn't react. She took each question one by one, feeling like a schoolteacher and kind of liking it.

"Can I wear a hat?"

"No, Dilly, we won't be wearing hats."

"Can I wave to my parents?"

"Maybe you can wave to them when we're taking our bows?"

"How do I bow?"

"What if I drop my stick?"

"Who will hit play on the music?"

"*Okay.*"

Sithara was suddenly at Iyla's side and her voice came out shrill enough that it startled Iyla. She noticed a couple of kids' eyes widened, too.

"Can we get back to dancing now?" Sithara continued, staring at Iyla with straight lips and a hard jaw.

Iyla didn't want to argue, so she bit her tongue and said, "Sure. Yes. Good idea." She looked at the kids, who were silently watching her and Sithara, a few small mouths open. "Children, let's answer more questions later and get back to moving our bodies!" She grinned big so the kids would know everything was perfectly fine.

Everyone scrambled up and they all continued to work through the dance. Iyla did notice that as they got moving, the anger seemed to fall from Sithara's face, the hunch from her shoulders. Iyla filed that fact away for future reference. *A dancing Sithara is a more pleasant Sithara,* she thought.

"Geezus, that was exhausting." Sithi lay flat on her back by the stereo, chest rising and lowering, pits sweaty, eyes gazing up to the ceiling. "Why do people even *have* kids?"

Iyla huffed a laugh. "Good thing they do, or we wouldn't be here."

Sithara propped herself up on her elbows and cocked a suspicious eyebrow at Iyla. "So what you're saying is, you *liked* this?"

Iyla was leaning forward over one leg to stretch and Sithi had to avert her eyes from the opening in Iyla's T-shirt, the cleavage presenting itself to her.

Iyla sat up, shrugged, and then switched to the other leg. "It wasn't the worst thing I've ever done."

Sithi snickered. "Oh, and what's the worst thing you've ever done?" She couldn't imagine Iyla doing anything interesting enough to be the "worst."

Iyla gazed at Sithara. She could tell Sithi thought she was naive . . . or worse—boring. She wanted to prove her wrong. "Oh, I don't know . . . maybe dealt with your bullshit?" she said, forcing her eyes to stay firmly on Sithara.

Sithi's eyebrows bounced up and her mouth opened. Iyla's eyes gleamed and the start of a smirk appeared. Sithi couldn't help but let out a huff of laughter, more in surprise than amusement.

"Wow. Okay," she said. "You're an asshole, you know that?"

"Said the pot to the kettle."

"Said the what to the what now?"

"You've never heard that before?" Iyla asked. "The saying, 'That's like the pot calling the kettle black'?"

"The fuck? Why would a pot call a kettle anything?"

Iyla laughed into the knee she was still stretching over. "It *means* you're being a hypocrite. It's like a cast-iron pot calling a cast-iron kettle black, when they *both* get black over a fire."

"Okay, so we're living in olden times now? We're cooking over fire?"

They stared at each other for a few moments. Sithi was the first to crack up and then they were both laughing.

Sithi fell onto her back again and laid her hands over her belly. "God. I must be more tired than I thought."

Their next two rehearsals were no less exhausting, but to Iyla, they still didn't qualify as the "worst" of anything. Sithara continued to be ornery every time a kid asked too many questions, or farted around too much, or actually farted (which happened more often than Iyla would have thought), but a couple of the kids seemed to grow attached to her, and if Iyla wasn't mistaken, Sithara actually seemed to like the way they cozied up to her or absentmindedly took her hand while Iyla explained something.

It was cute.

Midway through their third rehearsal, the dance was

starting to take shape. They would definitely need all the rehearsals they had, but if they were to perform that very day, they wouldn't be terrible.

Iyla didn't think Sithara would be satisfied with "not terrible," though, and she herself wouldn't mind proving to the aunties and the association that they knew what they were doing. Part of her even wanted to show them—and maybe Sithara and all their friends—that they could work together to produce something wonderful.

Iyla shook her head at herself. *Such a romantic, Iyla*. People had told her that before—when she was little and she drew hearts on anything she could find, or as a preteen who wrote awful love poetry. She didn't mind it, though. Better a romantic than a cynic, in her books.

Iyla brought herself back to the room, where the kids had mostly been nailing the routine to that point, but were getting muddled over the final section of the dance. Iyla turned to pause the music, but found Sithara already pressing the button on her phone. At the door, a tall man in a business suit and an equally tall woman in a beautiful sari stood.

Sithara's parents.

Iyla recognized them because they'd belonged to the Sri Lankan Friendship Association for as long as her own parents. But where Iyla's parents stayed mostly with their group of friends and the more social events at the association, Sithara's parents seemed to be involved at every level and branch.

Iyla's parents didn't have good things to say about these two, but that was the norm—everyone gossiping about everyone, especially if the individual, pair, or group was part of "those people." And Iyla's Tamil parents and their Tamil friends certainly did not like it when a Sinhalese person was in charge, so Sithara's very commanding, very prominent parents were always a target of ire.

Iyla certainly found Sithara's parents intimidating, especially as they just stood there, checking on Iyla and Sithara's progress, Iyla guessed. They probably didn't want this endeavor to be an embarrassment and Iyla wondered if they approved of her and Sithara working together. She shrunk a little at their appearance, but then tried to pull her shoulders back again.

Sithara, however, stiffened. Her features became serious, her body rigid, like she was going to war.

"Kids!" Sithara said, loud enough for the sound to echo in the open space. "We only have two more rehearsals! You need to get this last part down *perfectly*. Do you want to look silly up there?"

Iyla couldn't ignore this. "Whoa," she said, her voice soft but firm. "Sithara. We still have time. We'll get it."

Sithara's jaw worked like she was chewing up her next words to spit them out at Iyla. Iyla braced herself. But then she was surprised to see fear, rather than frustration, in Sithi's eyes. Without really thinking, Iyla reached out and placed her fingers around Sithara's forearm. Sithara pulled away immediately, shooting a glance at her parents by the doorway, but they'd already left. Sithara's body slumped a little—in relief or disappointment, Iyla wasn't sure.

They proceeded with the rest of rehearsal without incident, but Iyla was hyperaware of Sithara's energy—somewhere between tense and timid, like she was suddenly petrified they wouldn't be able to pull this off.

As soon as the last child had been picked up by their parent, Sithara left quickly with a terse "Bye." But Iyla wanted more than that. She scrambled to grab her things and followed Sithara down the hallway and into the large foyer of the association building. A few people milled around at the reception area and Iyla could hear the muffled, busy sounds of the small café attached to the foyer.

"Hey," she said in a neutral tone as she caught up to Sithara. "Hey!" she said again, louder, when Sithara didn't react.

Finally, Sithara stopped, paused, and turned. "What?" Her face was mostly impatient, but also . . . guarded?

"What?" Iyla repeated, cocking her head sideways. "What was that about today?"

"What was *what* about, Iyla?" She didn't have time for this.

"You acted like some kind of drill sergeant, when you know the kids are doing fine."

"Fine?" Sithara scoffed and folded her arms, jutted a hip. "'Fine' might work for *you*. Some of us aim a little higher. Some of us aren't aiming for *pathetic*."

Iyla's heart pinched, and for a moment she didn't know how to respond. Before she could open her mouth, the moment was interrupted by a loud "Yo!" from behind her.

She and Sithara both twisted their heads to see a group of Iyla's friends coming toward them from the café.

"That's my girl you're dissing!" Ben said, as he, Jeff, and Hemi approached.

Oh God, Iyla thought, *this is bad.*

Oh, Christ. This was all Sithi needed. Iyla's irritating friends. Her hackles rose even further.

"Beg yer pardon?" she said to the tall, lanky boy who'd just spoken.

"I *said*, back off."

Sithi quickly glanced around, hoping no one who knew her parents was around. They preferred to do their quarreling in private.

"Ben, chill out," Iyla said. She put a hand on his arm, like she had with Sithi, and Sithi wondered if this was just a thing she did—to anyone.

"I'm chill, I'm chill," Ben said, looking at Sithi. "I just don't like people talking to my friends that way. Especially a certain *kind* of people, you know?"

"Oh, for fuck's sake," Sithi snapped. "This isn't *West Side Story*, asshole. Get over yourself."

"Whooaa! Someone's riled up!" Ben said, laughing and nudging his friends, which pissed Sithi off to no end.

She took a step toward him, which brought her closer to

Iyla, too. Iyla tensed beside her. "What kind of person did you mean?" she asked, glaring at Ben. She wanted him to say it.

He grinned and said, "You know what kind."

Sithara's fingers squeezed into fists. "Tell me to my face, asshole." She kept her voice low, but her fury came through in every word.

"Okay, okay"—Iyla stepped between them and placed a hand on Ben's chest—"this is unnecessary."

Ben said something in reply, but Sithi barely heard his words, because she hated that Iyla's hand was on his chest.

She stiffened her jaw and said, "Whatever. This is a waste of my time." Then she turned to go.

At home later that night, Sithara's phone buzzed just as she was spitting out her toothpaste. She'd spent the evening avoiding her parents, trying to focus on her homework, trying to ignore the fire in her chest—the burn over the interaction with Iyla and her friends, but also over the look on her parents' faces. She knew that look. It said, *Not good enough.* It said, *Don't embarrass us.*

So when she glanced at her phone and saw Iyla's name, that fire flashed hot, but with it also came a twist of something both painful and pleasant. Sithi frowned—at the feeling in her chest, but also in confusion. She and Iyla had followed each other on Instagram, just in case, but why the hell was she messaging at 11 p.m., and after what happened today?

Iyla: Hey

Sithi's frown deepened.

Sithi: Hey?

Iyla: Sorry, I know it's late. Just wanted to check in?

Wtf? Like you care? Sithi wasn't about to let Iyla have the satisfaction of knowing she was still pissed.

Sithi: Why?

Three dots hovered, stopped, hovered again. *Christ.* Sithi just wanted to go to bed.

Iyla: Sorry . . . nothing. Night.

Sithi watched the little green dot indicating Iyla was online disappear, and that twist of whatever was in her chest coiled tighter.

Thursday's rehearsal was a shambles. Sithara arrived twenty minutes late, and by then, the kids were practically feral. Iyla found it impossible to get them focused.

Sithara couldn't care less. She leaned up against the wall, scrolling her phone. She barely even responded when Bartholomew asked her what she was doing. "Research," she said.

By the end of the hour, they were no closer to a tight performance than they were two days ago.

"Thanks for all your help today," Iyla muttered to Sithara as she collected her things.

Sithara didn't even look up from her phone. "You're welcome."

Iyla straightened up to stare at Sithara. "Wow. Really?" They were only two feet apart, but they may as well be on different planets. "What exactly do you have to be so pissy about? I'm pretty sure it was *you* who called me *pathetic*, wasn't it? You're mad because my friend defended me?"

Sithara still didn't look up but scoffed. "Well, I *am* a 'certain kind of people,' you know."

That deflated Iyla a little. She knew what Ben meant and she didn't like it. But she also hadn't addressed it. But then, hadn't Sithara *also* treated Iyla like a "certain kind of people," too? She stepped closer.

"You're really going to act like Ben is the only one judging based on ethnicity here?"

Sithara's fingers paused for a moment, but then kept moving. She shrugged.

Iyla wanted so badly to swipe the phone out of her hands. Instead, she took out her own phone and opened Instagram. She found the DM thread with Sithara.

Iyla: You know you're being a super duper asshole, right?

Sithara's eyes caught on the notification that sprung up on her screen. Iyla watched as Sithi read it and her eyebrows rose a touch. Iyla braced for impact, but the tiniest smirk appeared on Sithara's lips. Sithara's thumbs swiped and tapped. Iyla glanced at the message that popped up below hers and couldn't help but smirk herself.

Sithara: Sounds like a potty kettle thing.

"I am *hardly* in the same category of asshole as you," Iyla said, looking up.

Sithara looked up, too, and couldn't maintain the coldness she'd carefully cultivated before walking in late for rehearsal that night.

"I don't know," Sithi said, "it takes a special kind of asshole to let her friends gang up on someone, doesn't it?"

Iyla's small smile fell a little, and Sithi bit her bottom lip in response.

Iyla shook her head. "You're right. I'm sorry."

The apology felt nice, though it didn't give Sithi the satisfaction she thought it might. So she tried. "I'm sorry, too."

"For?"

Sithi rolled her eyes. "You know what."

Iyla cocked her head and an eyebrow. "Oh, you mean for basically hating me because I'm Tamil?"

Sithi flinched. But she rallied. "Well, I also hate you for other things, if that helps."

Iyla's mouth dropped open. Sithi had a wild impulse to close it with her own.

She forced a grin instead. "Kidding. Kind of. It's more like a skeptical dislike for your annoying optimism and dedication to politeness."

Iyla placed her palms on the back of her hips and narrowed her eyes, but a smile laced her lips. "Wow. Okay. Well, if we're being honest now, you should know I can't stand how impatient you are, or that you have the judgiest face on earth."

Sithara contorted her features into judgment and gave Iyla a slow, deliberate once-over, down to her feet and back up to her face.

By the time her eyes reached Iyla's, Iyla was no longer smiling. Her face was flushed and her eyes were on Sithi's lips. And then it was Sithi's turn to let her mouth open in surprise. And Iyla's turn to close it with her own.

The kiss started with a certainty that had been missing from so many of their previous interactions. It began with open, hungry mouths and searching tongues and turned into a long, slow exploration. Neither was even sure how much time had passed before their lips finally parted, both of them breathing heavily, their arms still wrapped around one another.

With their foreheads pressed into one another's, Sithi said, "Holy shit."

A breathless "Yeah" was all Iyla could manage alongside a thumping heart and pulsing body. She was keenly aware of

Sithi's hands pressed into her back, their stomachs pressed into one another's . . . her own fingers now resting against Sithi's collarbone.

"Okay, so . . . I guess we're friends now?" Sithi said, and they both laughed into the small space between them.

Their final rehearsal wasn't perfect, but it was a heck of a lot better than the previous night's practice. Iyla and Sithi were somehow wholly in tune with the kids, and with each other. Glances, light touches, a firm squeeze now and again—it was definitely the most fun of all their rehearsals. After running through the performance twice with only the smallest mistakes, Iyla and Sithi agreed it was time for a dance party, and they'd spent the last ten minutes rocking out to *Bananaphone* at the kids' request.

And then Iyla and Sithi had driven to Iyla's favorite park and spent the next couple of hours walking and talking and kissing and other things far away from the Sri Lankan Association and any prying eyes. They didn't talk about those eyes or the judgment that would come with them. Instead, they pretended it was just them and the soft, shifting moonlight.

"Oh my God." Iyla's eyes widened. "This is a disaster."

"A *fucking* disaster," Sithi agreed, next to her.

They were standing stage left in the wings, watching their little group of eight fumble their way through the performance that they'd completed almost perfectly the night before. Now it was as though they'd never danced before, and their brains were obsessed with their parents in the audience. Two of them had barely even moved since the music started.

"Maybe we should have practiced with an audience?" Iyla said, watching the fiasco onstage.

"Maybe. Or maybe they're five years old and just living their best lives?"

Iyla and Sithi looked at each other. "What should we do?" Iyla asked.

Sithi put a hand on Iyla's hip and shrugged. "If you can't beat them . . ."

Iyla's eyebrows popped up and then she grinned. "Really?"

Sithi shrugged again and grinned back. "I mean, what've we got to lose . . . besides the approval of our elders and friends, our reputations . . ."

Iyla finished Sithi's sentence with a kiss, not caring a bit who else was backstage with them, watching. She grabbed Sithi's hand, and they jogged onto the stage together. When the kids saw them, they hopped up and down and squealed with excitement. The group held hands and spun and danced ring-around-the-rosy and did something like the do si do and tried the five-year-old version of breakdancing, which was really just snow angels on the stage.

Sithi and Iyla didn't notice or care that some of the audience was scoffing or frowning or gossiping.

But they heard the clapping that started, and the whistles. They sensed expectations shifting. And they felt the firm grip of each other's hands in their own.

THE BIG RIG BLUES

By Navdeep Singh Dhillon

The ground rumbles beneath us as we drive past walnut groves and vineyards. Outside, the sky turns all kinds of hues of orange and red, the sequoia mountains so clear in the distance you can see snow on their peaks like uneven scoops of ice cream. Mom and Dad couldn't drop me off, that much was obvious. The Liquor Store. Always *The Store*, a great big albatross around our necks. Still, I was surprised when my sister, Jyoti, offered to drive me to the Military Entrance Processing Station—MEPS—a hundred and sixty miles away in Sacramento. Technically, she's dropping me off across the street at the Holiday Inn the night before I ship out.

I got a text from her a couple of hours ago. I'll drive you. No yoga pants or flip-flops in your overnight bag.

Like that's even my vibe. Then she had to add, It's on my route, making it clear this wasn't really a favor, or a way to spend quality time with her little brother before I start Basic Training. As usual, I'm an errand.

My sister drives trucks now. Big Rigs. And when I say Big Rigs, I mean humongous mechanical beasts that eat up the entire highway and are so large time slows down when she's going through an intersection. The size of one of the eighteen wheels that keeps this demon moving is larger than my entire existence. They should be called Ridiculously Ginormous Rigs.

I roll down the window and get blasted with light debris and hot wind. It feels nice against my face. "Do I need to put the motherfucking child lock on? Roll your window up," Jyoti snaps. She seems anxious. Agitated. We haven't seen each other in months and this is our first real interaction that wasn't her just barking orders at me on text. Slowly and with much irritation, I roll up the window. She breathes a sigh of relief, like some wild animal was about to come through.

Jyoti's nose ring glistens as she merges onto Highway 99, the material of her turquoise Puma hoodie creasing as she uses her core to turn the steering wheel, her eyes glancing toward the rearview mirror. Her hair looks like she's had it recently done. Wavy, expensive. In the midst of her multitasking, I have that sibling urge to roll down the window again and let the wind and dust and dry heat wreck her hair. But I'd rather this not be the day I die.

We were never what you'd call close. Our dynamic has always been in extremes. One time she told Mom and Dad about my stash of stolen beef jerky from *The Store*—all because I used her strawberry-scented bodywash and said it made my butt smell so fresh and clean. That same day she tripped one of my cousins who was bullying me for my Pokémon obsession and proceeded to shame and threaten him if he ever messed with me again. Of course, then I was terrorized even more, especially after she left. Still, it was a nice gesture.

I didn't even get to tell her I enlisted. She found out in the worst way possible: through Facebook, when Dad decided it would be a great idea to use Jyoti's boot camp photo and my high school graduation photo to post something corny about how proud he is both his kids are serving our great country—like he didn't throw a fit when he found out. Then, for good measure, he tagged a million people, including me and Jyoti, like a spam bot.

Jyoti told me she enlisted a day after she signed everything and had already gone to MEPS. I didn't know it then, but I was the first one she told. We were setting up for the Diwali party at home. I was thirteen and didn't understand most of what she was saying—*being part of something bigger, a true institution of meritocracy.*

She used the word again when she had an argument with Bubbloo, our first cousin. I don't even know his real name. Probably something boring like Gurbachan. Anyway, he was making a point he probably stole from an alpha bro podcast about how war is a necessary part of life, but men are predisposed to war and women are predisposed to being mothers.

She took a crumbly yellow ladoo into her hands and threw it right at his head, sending an explosion of tiny sweet grains all over him. Then she added something about meritocracy as he rolled on the floor, shaking ladoo granules out of his hair and beard. It was only after she left for boot camp that I realized how big of a deal the ladoo Diwali incident was beyond shutting up Bubbloo. She set fire to the path laid out for her by everyone, choosing to write her own story.

Her iPhone is locked in place on top of the ugly yet elegant mahogany dashboard, which has fourteen gauges embedded into it, like we're in the DeLorean breaking time-travel protocol. It lights up and I hear a million dings as people start commenting on some kind of stream.

"You're livestreaming our drive?" I say, in disbelief. "You better not be recording me for clout. I do not consent." I see chuckles in the form of laughing emojis.

"Move your gigantic head out of the way so people don't immediately switch it off," Jyoti says.

I peer closer. "Fifteen viewers? That's pretty . . ."

I'm in the middle of a stellar burn when she cuts me off. "Humme ghar ghar mein mashoor hone ki koi zaroorat nahin," she says dramatically. Viewers on the stream start sending heart and firecracker reactions and comments start pouring in, saying, "Vah, vah."

"Is this a bit from one of your soap operas?" I ask.

"It's from *Heeramandi*," one of the viewers comments.

"I don't need to be famous in every home," Jyoti translates. "The rest of it doesn't apply, but as the great philosopher Bruce Lee says, 'Absorb what is useful, discard what is useless.'" She smiles at the camera. And like clapping monkeys, everyone on the stream also laughs. And claps. Nonsense is what it is. I bet even that quote is unfinished.

"Hey, Jyoti's little bro," people start writing.

"Yo," I say suspiciously. Who are all these people?

A woman appears on the stream. "Ayyyy. Now we can get started," Jyoti says.

A co-streamer? She is speaking Punjabi with an old school straight from the pind accent, complaining about forgetting to pack ginger and fennel for her trip.

"That sucks. It's the absolute worst," Jyoti says. "One time I brought everything except my Wagh Bakri and let me tell you, that was a miserable drive."

"Why don't you just google Indian stores and pick some up," I say, trying to be relevant. "Boom. Problem solved."

"Such a boy. Trying to solve the world's problems one cha da cup at a time," Jyoti says, and I realize this is one of those moments my ex told me about, where sometimes you talk not to solve a problem, but just to be heard. "Routines, huh?" Jyoti says. "Sometimes they help. Sometimes they just seem pointless. After I drop my little bro off at MEPS, I'm going all the way to Lodi to pick up my next load just for something familiar."

Comments flood in, latching on to the routine thing, and not one of them recognize that I was just trying to help this poor woman with her ginger and fennel situation.

"Load," I say. "In Lodi." I slap my knee and laugh. Jyoti looks at me the way she used to when I would loudly sing Punjabi songs at her as she would try sneaking out of a family party with an Irish goodbye. *Balle Balle, Jyoti!* is one of my personal favorites. It roughly translates to *Hurray, Jyoti!* but you know, nuances. Five minutes go by and her co-host isn't saying anything and nobody is commenting. Jyoti stretches out her arms as she eases off the accelerator on a long stretch of highway. Is the livestream over? No wonder she only has fifteen viewers. That was an abrupt end. Imagine if people just ended conversations like that.

"So. Navy, huh," Jyoti says, turning her attention briefly toward me.

"So. Truck, huh," I say, as long as we're making obvious statements to each other.

"Don't disrespect the rig. You know what I'm saying."

I can't tell her she inspired me to join. A little anyway. Or that I failed the physical for the Marines, that I don't have the grades or the money for college, that I don't want to be stuck in Fresno working at The Store and hearing about Neelam Auntie's son who got a full scholarship to Stanford, or Rana Uncle's daughter at Berkeley, or Bubbloo, who's running two of his dad's gas stations.

"Well, there are a lot of reasons, but mainly I wanna serve my country."

She quirks a brow at me. "Oh. We're all patriotic here." There is some LOL emojis on the stream. Which is not a fun way to learn the live isn't over. Was our conversation meant for her audience? She looks at me and I know she can tell I thought we were having a real moment.

Her co-host starts speaking again. "One thing I will say though is that maybe one of the reasons I never freaked out when I was in it is there was always something to do. Push-ups, sit-ups, drive here, drive there. And staying fit wasn't even something I needed to think about."

"Dude," Jyoti says in agreement. "I used to run three miles in under sixteen minutes like it was nothing, smoking every-one, and never got or expected any acknowledgment. But now I feel like I'm owed a standing ovation when I walk around the rig two days in a row. My therapist suggested doing any-thing to ventilate the brain. Crochet stresses me out and I get too competitive when I work out. Walking will do the trick for now."

I sink into my seat, my eyebrows furrowing at the casual-ness of her mentioning therapy like it's a totally normal thing. And what the hell happened to her? Why does she need to "ventilate" her brain? She wasn't in any war zone.

"Don't do that with your brows. You'll get frown lines and make your face even more lopsided," Jyoti says, not even turn-ing to look at me.

I scoff. Loudly. But quickly return my eyebrows to their normal position on the off chance she is right. "Actually, my face is super symmetrical," I mumble.

I wish we had the kind of relationship where she could be this open, and I could be all, "So, therapy, huh?" And she could just explain it. Brown people don't do therapy. That much I know.

"All right all. It's that time. My newest poem, *dimag de taare*." She starts reciting a poem in Punjabi, which is definitely not the direction I thought this live was going to take. It sounds like she wrote it. I'm no poem analyst, but it's got nice imagery and you know, good words. A starry night in her head and a dark sky outside and then a twist where the starry night is outside and the dark sky is in her head. I don't know exactly what the poem means, but it's not a happy poem. It sounds sad and beautiful.

"Cool poem. You running a Punjabi poetry coven?" I say in a hushed voice when she finishes. I'm thoroughly confused about what's happening.

"It's actually a Punjabi kudiyan-identifying veterans' coven," Jyoti replies, staring straight ahead. "Hoo-rah, churails."

Everyone chimes in with fire emojis and exclamation-laden comments, and gifs. Finally, the live ends. I peer closely to make sure.

"I'm friggin' hungry," I say. "Take the next exit. There's a bunch of food options there."

"Yeah, right, Mr. Money Bags," Jyoti says.

I gulp like a cartoon character as we pass by what was probably the last food mecca for miles. "We are most definitely not stopping at any of these overpriced roadside restaurants. I thought your generation was supposed to be smart."

"I am smart. You're just a curmudgeon. How is McDonald's overpriced?"

"Here." She reaches behind her seat and grabs a white box, throwing it at my feet.

"From my last delivery," she says. "I have a box cutter in the glovebox."

"Of course you do," I say and proceed to stab the box.

"This looks like a mangled internal organ. Like the innards of a turkey," I say, staring at a bunch of grotesque produce.

"Dragonfruit. You know how expensive this is? You're looking at a $4,000 box. Maybe $400. At least $40. It's the latest superfood."

"I bet it's a laxative," I say as I carefully peel the bright red skin and cut the humpbacked fruit into slices. "It looks like a defiled kiwi that's had all its color sucked out." We both take a bite.

She looks over at me. "This is terrible," she says. "Tastes like Styrofoam."

"Worst thing I've tasted since water," I say.

We both beam with pride that, despite us growing up without a lot of money, we still manage to behave like spoiled first-world brats.

"What other things do you transport?" I say, curious. Could be a trailer full of endangered animals or Froot Loops for all I know.

"Depends." She looks at her face in the massive side mirror.

"On what? The wind? The stars aligning?"

"The dispatcher," Jyoti says.

"So, if the dispatcher in Lodi told you to pick up some elephants, how many you think would fit?" I ask.

"What are you, five?"

"Just say you don't know because you're not good at math," I say.

"I'm great at math. Maximum overall weight limit is eighty thousand pounds and there's also maximum axle weight limits to consider in this dumb situation you've concocted. And if we're talking about Asian elephants or African forest elephants. That's a difference of thousands of pounds. Plus, if the elephants are on pallets, you gotta account for the extra weight, as well as the fiberglass body on top of the trailer."

"Why would you put an elephant on a pallet?" I ask quizzically.

"Same reason you put her in my rig. To waste my precious time."

The first few years after she enlisted, she'd come back home for leave pretty often. Once, she came during my first year of high school and let me take the day off so she could take me to the range, where she attempted to teach me how to shoot the Beretta M9 and the M18. I didn't hit any of my targets and ended up watching her shoot bull's-eye after bull's-eye as she talked about how amazing it was being in the Marine Corps. She had so much energy and so much to say, it almost felt like she needed to take me to the range just so she could get everything out.

"Why'd you join?" I blurt out, turning toward Jyoti.

She looks over at me. "To serve my country," she says. "Because who needs the VA to approve my claim when I have national pride and people thanking me for my service one day of the year on social media?"

"Yeah, okay. Very funny." Even though we both know she isn't joking. "Still think the *military* is a meritocracy?"

She smiles. "You remember that?"

"The only time in history that Bubbloo had nothing to say. Now he's taken over two of his parents' gas stations, rearranged the junk food aisle, and thinks he's Elon Musk."

She grips the steering wheel and exits at a sign for a weigh station, driving over a little bump. An electronic sign flashes up, reading, "OK to bypass." We get back on the freeway.

"You still hungry?" she says, not actually answering my question.

"I've been hungry for like a hundred miles. You better not make me open another box of weird-ass fruit."

She takes the next exit and starts filling up the diesel-hungry beast, which takes forever. I look around the gas station. No restaurants. Nothing but darkness. This better not be a trick. If she hands me some jerky and says, "Bon appétit," I am going to lose it. We get back in the rig and she starts driving on a bumpy dirt road behind the gas station. We drive past a small patch of land and park in a makeshift lot—basically in the middle of a wheat field.

"Dude, this is creepy. Can we get out of here? It looks just like that horror movie you made me watch as a kid. *Children of the Wheat*," I say, my voice shaking a little.

"*Children of the Corn*, fool. I can't believe how uncultured you are. It's a classic."

"Think *He Who Walks Behind the Rows* gives a padh whether it's corn, wheat, or juju berries that are growing?" I say.

The gravel crunches under our feet as we make our way in the dark. We're definitely ripe for slaughter.

"It's a good thing you're joining the Navy," she says and walks on ahead.

"Oh. Really?" I squeal. "Just how many wheat fields have you done combat in?"

"You've got to be kidding me," I say, shaking my head when I see what we're doing here. Glowing lights flicker from the fields. There are string lights hung around a "restaurant" with a sign that reads, "Happy Best Punjabi Restaurant," along with the words, "truckers welcome," and a printed photo of a man with his arms folded, standing next to a huge truck decked out with garlands and paisleys and two colorful peacocks just above the windshield.

Using the word "restaurant" for this place is being very generous. It's a food truck. Barely. "We couldn't have gone to any of the thousand burger joints or taco places we passed?"

"Trust me, you're gonna miss Punjabi food the most if you ship out," she says, her pace quickening. "This is the closest you're gonna get to a home-cooked meal. Come on, let me introduce you."

"Wait. What do you mean if?" I stop walking. "I knew it. This is an intervention. I know it's too much to ask for you to say you're proud of me, but not even some support? You made your own way and now . . ."

"I'm in therapy. And not in like a cool Gen Z way. In case this is my fault," she says slowly, "I just want you to know you can still dip. Just do a second swear-in and don't sign shit. It's still an option."

Before I can register what Jyoti is saying to me, I find myself speaking very loudly. "Who's the narcissist now? Unbeliev-able. Like I have no . . ." I struggle to find the right word. "Brain." My eyes widen and I knock on my head for some kind of effect. Brain is definitely not the right word.

My stomach rumbles, reminding me I'm hungry, and I power walk toward this food truck, wanting to be at the hotel already. Jyoti catches up to me with ease.

I take in a whiff and smell the familiar aromas of home: the roasted hing, jeera, dhania, and that super secretive blend of garam masala that's unique to every desi kitchen. The menu is handwritten on a small chalkboard on the side of the van in Gurmukhi script.

"Dude. This isn't even in English," I say with much annoyance.

"Well, maybe you should have paid more attention in Punjabi class."

"Do you know how to read it?" I ask.

"No," Jyoti admits without an ounce of sharm. "But I have an app." She whips out her phone to scan the handwritten menu for the app to translate.

I look at her incredulously.

My stomach croon-croons as I smell the deliciousness. She passes me her phone.

"Great," I say. "What the hell is boona? This just says chicken boona, lamb curry, okra boona. What even is a curry?"

"A baqwas word," a large Punjabi woman wearing an apron says, stepping out of the truck. To my alarm, she and Jyoti do a mini gallop and hug as they scream "bhena" at each other. Sister.

A burly mustachioed Punjabi dude with a tattoo of a khanda on his neck and a receding hairline attacks me with a very aggressive handshake. Even though he's super old—early forties at least—he looks like he should be wearing a monocle and riding on a unicycle. He peers at Jyoti's phone. "I get a kick out of AI's white supremacy no matter how many times I see your app translating our menu." He holds his belly and laughs.

"Gulabo and Happy," Jyoti says.

"Hello, Happy . . . uh . . . Uncle. Gulabo auntie," I say awkwardly. I'm terrible at addressing my elders, more so when they think they're young and cool and have gender-neutral nicknames.

They both smile.

"I'm actually Gulabo," Gulabo Uncle says.

"Because he's delicate," Happy Auntie adds.

"Like a rose." Gulabo Uncle laughs.

"She was on the stream earlier," Jyoti explains.

"I'm there for your sister's beautiful poetry," Happy Auntie says. "Livestreaming is beyond me."

"We were both truck drivers and met on CB radio before this whole streaming thing," Gulabo Uncle says. "So, curries and boonas for everyone then?"

"Thanks, British Raj," Jyoti says, punching a fist in the air.

I look longingly at plates being carried out to other tables by two young dudes wearing jeans and stylish fitted dress shirts. "Oy, mundeya," Happy Auntie calls to one of them. "Platter le ke aa. One of everything." That settles my stomach a little although I'm ready to commit murder at this point.

"Cha vi le ke aayi," Gulabo Uncle says.

"Me and Jyoti are going to catch up," Happy Auntie says, leaning on the food truck, so me and Gulabo Uncle head toward the seating area—plastic chairs and stolen park benches.

"So. You used to be a truck driver," I say as we sit down. "And now you're—"

"Living my dream," Gulabo Uncle says.

I feel terrible as I realize how condescending that sounded. Just because I'm about to flip the script on my life by joining the Navy is no reason to shit on this man's small dream.

One of the fashionably dressed waiters brings us our cha and I can see the other dude carrying a platter in the distance.

I take a sip of my piping hot cha, which hits the spot. The kick-in-your-pants ginger and cardamom flavor makes its way through my body. He takes a big swig, like it's tap water.

"It's funny how life works. I was a truck driver for years and loved the open road and freedom, but one night I jack-knifed my cab and trailer. By God, I thought this is the end. But like Shah Rukh Khan said in that one film: picture abhi baaki hai, mere dost."

"There's still more to this story, my friend?" I say, guessing on the translation.

"More or less. Anyway, it was a miracle I survived. It was surreal. Like an out-of-body experience. And all I could think is what a dumb obituary this could have been. I was on my CB radio just before the crash and Happy was on it. We were talking about food and getting so hungry. We'd never met in person and then I hear the kharr-kharr of the CB radio come on, so I risk death and climb in through the window just to talk to her. She decides to drive almost a hundred miles to see me. So nice na?"

Both waiters come armed with plates piled high with steaming hot rotian, large crispy samose, juicy chicken and lamb dishes roasted presumably in a tandoor and simmered in oniony masala. I was ready to destroy it all. Jyoti and Happy Auntie walk over as the platters arrive, absolutely smoldering. Me and Jyoti go feral, ripping up roti and lathering it with chicken and lamb, scarfing down skewered paneer fresh from the tandoor, and barreling sabji into our mouths like we're street urchins in a Charles Dickens novel.

"So," I say, "Uncle Gulabo was telling me about the origin story of this restaurant and how you all met."

"It was a nightmare that turned into a dream," Happy Auntie says. "I was telling him someone should open a dhaba to feed our Punjabi trucking brothers and sisters. So strange it doesn't exist. So two hours later, I finally get to the crash site . . ."

"Right there," Gulabo Uncle says, pointing past the wheat fields, toward the gas station. "And first thing she says to me: *So go do it then. I'll help you.*"

"Definitely the wildest thing I've ever done, and I did two tours in Iraq. Just up and quit my job driving." Happy Auntie smiles. "I still get stress triggers. Insomnia, crowds. A whole bunch of other things, but the freakouts aren't as often and I know I got a little slice of paradise right here. Bonus is listening to your soul-revealing poetry every week," Happy Auntie says, putting a hand on her heart.

The magnitude of what they're saying hits me. This is not a small dream like I thought. This is an immeasurable, colossal one.

An hour later, we waddle back through the wheat fields toward the Big Rig and things make even less sense than they did at the livestream. Jyoti points up at the stars. "The Central Valley has the best stars. I don't know the Milky Way from Orion, but no other place in the world I've been to has a sky like this."

"Yeah," I say. "It is a good sky." Even though this is the only sky I know.

"It's not just a livestream," Jyoti says still looking up at the stars. "It's a support group. For female vets with . . ." she pauses, "PTSD."

"Oh," I say, like I get it. "Were you in," I move some of the gravel around with my shoes, "combat?"

"I've been in combat my whole life, little bro."

Jyoti looks up at the stars, then looks at me. "My whole life, everyone's been telling me who I'm supposed to be. A good wife. A good mother. I wouldn't give a shit if people told you you'd make a good husband or father when you were eleven."

"Dude, that's so weird," I say.

"In middle school, I got a warning because a boy snapped my bra. And obviously, I should have known better than to have it visible underneath my sweater. No showing legs. No showing arms. All for the boys, who get to dream bigger than being dads and husbands. In the Marines, I'm smoking all the dudes in my platoon in push-ups and pull-ups, and I still get written up for wearing leggings to physical training because I'm more distracting than the dudes in their short shorts. Or a commander who told our entire platoon that we just put ourselves through hell not to do our jobs, but to find husbands and boyfriends and be good moms and wives."

I look at Jyoti and she's shaking. Post-traumatic stress disorder makes it sound like there's something broken. Is my sister broken?

"I sound so frivolous compared to Happy. I wasn't in a war zone. I was a POG—Person Other than a Grunt. I've never even seen an IED, got no issues with crowds or fireworks or insomnia."

"Or wheat fields in the dark," I add.

"No." She smiles. "Know what I got an issue with? Someone rolling down my window. My Big Rig is the one space I feel like I control. If even one thing is out of place, I start to lose it."

"That sucks. I'm sorry," I say.

"One time, I freaked out at a gas station because I thought I wasn't breathing. I still don't know why. The smog. Ate too many corn chips, had a belly full of soda. I couldn't tell you. For so long I just did what I was trained to do: embrace the suck, muddle through, and things will work out. You know the funny thing is the breathing thing wasn't the thing that made me go battle the VA to approve my claim and find a therapist to finally help me. It was when I freaked out in my Big Rig because I forgot my Wagh Bakri. Like a full-on meltdown. That was when I wrote my first poem and streamed it to exactly one person."

I feel a pang in my stomach. I reach over to give her a hug and she immediately recoils and elbows me, barely missing my eye. "What the hell was that?"

"Sorry. Gut reaction. What were you doing?"

"I was trying to give you a hug, you maniac," I say, my hands up defensively.

"That was a hug?" She mimics me, moving her arms stoically toward me like a murdering robot.

"That is wildly inaccurate," I say.

"Let me show you how it's done."

We awkwardly hug and I cling tightly to her.

It feels like we've been saying goodbye to each other our whole lives. But this feels different. A reintroduction. I realize this is not an errand for her and it's not an intervention. She's just being a good sister.

We climb back into the Big Rig. The highway is empty, and we're not far from Sacramento now.

"I don't think I want to get out of joining," I say. "I already did the duck walk."

Jyoti slowly turns to look at me to gauge whether I'm being for real right now. She raises an eyebrow. "Well then you should definitely do it," she says. "I mean that's how our greatest warriors made the important decision to enlist. *I did the duck walk.*"

"Remember that time you came home for leave after boot camp," I say, changing the subject, "and farted at The Store?"

She snorts at the road. "Did you already fall off your boat and get hit in the head by an anchor? My body is a temple and it's incapable of doing something so crass."

"I bet it was all the MREs you were eating. You would not

160

shut up about it. It was like you were getting paid every time someone would ditch actual food and get a Meal, Ready-to-Eat, which is not even a meal."

"Actually," she starts, "they are super nutritious, delicious, and very filling. Totally a meal."

"A fart-making meal," I add. "Mom quietly put hing into your seabag. I always wondered if you used it."

She laughs. "It got confiscated. What do you think happens when airline security finds a small stinky bottle filled with a white powder and Hindi instructions scrawled on the outside?" Jyoti taps on the steering wheel and fiddles with the controls. "Remember when you kept saying oorah to everything?"

"What? Why would I say hooyah?" I say.

"Still not even saying it right. It's pronounced Oorah. I'm a Devil Dog. We invented the word. Hooyah is something you sailors do when a big wave splashes your cute white uniforms on your little boats."

There it is. The interservice ragging, even though I haven't earned it yet. I purse my lips tightly. "Why would I have ever said oooooooohhhh-raaaaaaaahhhh?" I elongate every syllable, so I pronounce it correctly.

"Oorah. And you totally did. Completely disoriented all the aunties at Jassi chachi's party. You kept saying it without realizing. Someone came up to our table and asked when I was getting married, and before I could get all snippy, you thought she was asking if you wanted more naan and said, oorah. And she just sputtered around and then awkwardly left to harass some other unmarried girl minding her own business, stuffing her face."

We both burst out laughing at the absurdity of it.

I doze off for what feels like hours, but was only about fifteen minutes. I wake up with a jolt at the thought of tonight being my last night as . . . me. It's making me queasy. I can't tell if it's in a good way or bad way yet. We're off the highway and pulling into the parking lot for Holiday Inn. It felt like me and Jyoti had all night to reconnect and now we're here.

"Think you'd do it again?" I say as she turns the engine off.

Jyoti is silent for a beat. "Probably," she says. "Out of respect to eighteen-year-old me. That chick had guts. She's the reason this version of me exists. She's pretty great too."

I smile at Jyoti and have every intention of saying something solemn, but instead I pat her shoulder slowly, like I'm swatting a really stoned fly, and say, "You're both really full of yourselves. At least neither version of you is doing hard time in the brig for possession of hing."

"You're such a dork," she says.

"Guess I should go check in," I say.

"Guess I should go get that load in Lodi," she says.

She climbs back into the Big Rig. The lights turn on and she rolls down the window. "I'm proud of you," she screams at me.

"I'm proud of you, too," I scream back, my eyes welling up.

If I didn't know better, I'd think she was teary-eyed, too.

162

I start walking toward the hotel, past the MEPS kids milling around outside, way too excited about tomorrow.

Jyoti starts up the Big Rig and pulls up next to me.

"You know you're gonna have to get up at three anyway. You could just stay up," Jyoti says.

I climb up into the passenger seat. "Wagh Bakri?" I confirm. She nods and hands me a mortar and pestle.

LOVESICK

By Tashie Bhuiyan

Even after inhaling four pints of ice cream and watching a shitload of trashy television, I still feel like a truck ran me over. Actually, I think I might feel even worse than I did before.

I toss the latest empty carton of strawberry ice cream into the trash can and set my spoon down in the sink. Instead of washing it, I stand there for a minute, staring at the drain, wondering how my life came to this.

I mean, I know how.

It started with a love confession.

It ended with a broken heart.

I groan and turn on the faucet, grabbing the sponge from the side of the sink. I can't think about this anymore, or I'm going to need to make another run to Baskin-Robbins.

I'm washing suds off my hands when my phone starts ringing. I glance at the screen, which reads *Celine Wan would like to FaceTime . . .*

I sigh, drying my hands off before sliding my index finger across the screen to answer my best friend's video call. "What? What could possibly require my attention on this godforsaken Monday evening?"

Celine has an unimpressed look on her face. "I can see your Spotify activity, Ava."

I wrinkle my nose. I had it set to a private session this morning, but I forgot those run out after six hours of inactivity. "So?"

"What do you mean 'so'? You've been listening to breakup playlists ever since spring break started. You said you were feeling better!" Celine throws her hands up, which dislodges half a dozen things on her desk, although she doesn't seem to notice. "You know *she* can also see what you're listening to, right?"

"Good," I say, jutting out my bottom lip, even though my heart skips an uncertain beat. "Maybe she'll get the hint and stop trying to talk to me like everything is normal when I'm literally withering away."

Celine's face grows dark. "Is she still messaging you?"

I stay silent, moving to my bedroom so my father doesn't overhear our conversation.

"Ava," Celine says again. "Is Haley still sending you messages? It's been like three days since she rejected you."

I set my phone down against my laptop and climb into bed, pulling the blankets up to my chin. Maybe if I pretend I don't hear her, we can avoid having this talk.

Celine hisses like an angry cat. "Avika Shah, answer me right now."

I groan, pulling one of my stuffed animals over my head. "What do you want me to say?"

"I want you to tell me whether or not I should go out and steal my dad's shovel from the shed."

"Don't," I say emphatically. "She's not a bad person, Celine."

"Of course you're going to say that. You're still in love with her!" Celine starts pacing on the screen. "What Haley's doing is shitty, Ava. If someone confesses their love to you and you reject them, the least you can do is give them time and space, neither of which she's affording you. Fuck her."

I press my lips together. Celine isn't wrong. Every time Haley texts me or tags me in an Instagram post or sends me a silly Snapchat like things are normal, like I never confessed, like my heart isn't broken, I want to curl into a ball and drown in my tears.

"She was—is," I forcibly correct myself, "one of my best friends. She's just trying to make things normal again. She's not intentionally trying to take a sledgehammer to my heart."

"That's bullshit, dude," Celine says. "If she was really your best friend, she'd know to leave you alone for at least five to seven business days. It's just fucking common sense. If you confessed your feelings to me, I wouldn't—"

At the same time, Haley sends me another TikTok, the notification appearing at the top of my screen.

My eyes begin to prickle, and I turn away from the camera.

Celine sighs quietly. "Whatever. Forget her."

"Forget her," I repeat hoarsely. "How?"

Several beats of silence pass as Celine considers her next words. Though both Haley and Celine are my best friends, they've always been in two different friend circles, which rarely overlapped with the exception of birthday parties. It's easy for Celine to write Haley off when she's only ever known Haley through me, but it's a lot harder for me to do the same when I've been half in love with Haley since we first met during sophomore year, though I spent a long time convincing myself it was platonic.

"Come out with me tomorrow," Celine says. "Let's have a self-care day, like we used to back in middle school. Get a mani-pedi, go to the bookstore, get some boba. I let you wallow by yourself for the whole weekend but clearly, it's not helping anything."

"My mom and dad aren't going to let me go out with you on a day's warning," I say, but I roll back over to face her. "You know how strict they are. Hell would freeze over first."

"Yeah, but your parents love me," Celine says, which is fair. It helps that she's a straight-A student, president of the speech and debate club, and first in line to be valedictorian at our high school graduation.

They'd much rather I take after her than spend my afternoons with our school's baking club, but I would sooner shave my head than sign up for speech and debate. Celine is well aware of that fact and has never tried to tempt me otherwise.

"If you want to convince them, by all means," I say, sighing as I tuck my stuffed elephant close to my chest.

"I've got this," Celine says, flipping her dark hair over her shoulder. "I'll see you tomorrow morning. And stop with the sad music, it's only going to make you feel worse."

I wave her off. "Let me mourn my only chance at love in peace."

"Oh my God," she says under her breath. "This is not your only chance at love."

I laugh weakly. "Isn't it?" A pause. "It's fine. I'm just going to be alone forever. I'll never date anyone. I've accepted my future as a lonely spinster. It's clearly what fate wants for me."

"You sound ridiculous," Celine says, flicking the camera. I almost smile. "We're only seventeen, dude. We have all the time in the world for fate to intervene. Love is out there somewhere."

"We're seventeen and you've had three boyfriends already," I say. "And what do I have? Nothing except for a broken heart. You know what? Maybe love doesn't even exist. Maybe we've all disillusioned ourselves. Maybe this is all some kind of cosmic joke."

Celine gives me a flat stare, too used to my dramatics.

Except, now that I'm saying it aloud, I can't help but wonder if I'm right.

Is love real? And if it is, is it even in the cards for me?

With each passing minute, it feels more and more like fate is playing a sinister joke on me.

"Love is real, Ava."

I give her a tight smile. "Yeah. Whatever you say."

Celine grumbles something under her breath, too quiet for the microphone to pick up. Before I can ask her to repeat herself, she says, "You can't give up on your future just because one small thing sets you back."

"It's not a small thing, Celine," I say, my voice quiet. "You know how scared I was to tell her about my feelings. You know how much it terrified me to be that vulnerable with someone else. I put my heart on the line and . . . now it's broken. The way I feel right now—I don't ever want to feel this way again. I think being alone might be better than ever loving someone again."

Celine's mouth curls into a frown. "I'm sorry, Ava. I really am. Haley would have been lucky to have you."

I exhale deeply and look away. There's an uncomfortable lump in the back of my throat. "Yeah. Well. Here we are. Listen, can we talk in the morning? I kind of want to be alone right now."

She nods slowly, even though it's obvious she wants to say more. "I'll see you tomorrow, okay? I'll have my parents talk to yours."

I give her a thumbs-up, unable to pull together any more

coherent words. I think if I tried, I might burst into tears again.

God, I was really, really hoping I was finished with the waterworks.

"Good night, Ava," Celine says quietly. "I love you."

"I love you, too," I say, the words choked, and hit the end button before she can see a tear slip down my cheek.

There's a knock on my door and I wipe my face hastily, hoping to smother any other awful emotions attempting to rise to the surface.

Baba pokes his head into my room. He falters when he sees me. I imagine that I must have puffy eyes and a red nose, but I'm hoping and praying he won't ask.

If he does, I don't know what I'd say. Dating is forbidden in my house, and I imagine trying to date a *girl* is asking to die by my desi parents' hands.

It's been hard these last few days, having to keep up pretenses in front of both of them. There's no way to tell them about my heartbreak without telling them *why* I'm heartbroken. It doesn't help that neither of them ever really liked Haley.

"What's wrong, Avika?" Baba asks, his thick eyebrows furrowed. "You don't want to watch any TV tonight, either?"

"I'm really stressed about my pre-calculus test next week," I lie, and it's a miracle that my voice remains steady. "Maybe once I'm done with it."

He frowns at me. Usually, on nights when my mother has a late shift at our local grocery store, Baba and I sit together in the living room and watch a movie until she gets home safely. The two of us don't usually talk while we do it, content to let the movie run its course.

In theory, it should be fine to lounge on the couch silently with my father and pretend to focus on the television screen, but in practice, I haven't been able to go even half an hour without wanting to cry. The only solace I have right now is that I don't have to sit beside Haley in physics class and pretend to be okay until spring break is over.

But what I didn't expect is that I'd also have to pretend at home. I didn't even consider how I'd have to put on a brave face in front of my parents until I got back to my house an hour after confessing my feelings, on the verge of a panic attack, and Ma asked if I needed my asthma inhaler.

I've always been too sensitive, and people can often read me like an open book. I have no idea how to hide this gigantic crack down my middle, so I'm stuck shoveling ice cream down my throat when I think my parents aren't looking and hoping for the best.

"If you're sure," Baba says. There's a suspicious light in his eyes that makes my skin prickle. "Is there anything you want to talk about?"

"No," I say as cheerfully as I can manage. "Good night, Baba. Turn the light off when you go, please."

He keeps frowning at me, but he reaches out and flicks off the light switch. "Good night, Avika."

As soon as the door closes behind him and I hear his

footsteps carry down the stairs, I turn my face into my pillow and *scream*.

Falling in love with your best friend should come with a warning sign and a handbook for beginners. And the first chapter should be entitled: *DON'T*.

As Celine drags me around a bookstore, that's all I can think about. She's shoving self-care books at me like they're going to help, and I don't know how to tell her that I have no intention of reading them unless they can teach me how to time-travel to the past and stop myself from even considering shooting my shot with Haley.

"You know," I say, idly flipping through the pages of the last book she handed me. "The real problem is that I miss her. I used to be able to talk to her about anything. I'd tell her about the stupidest parts of my day, and she'd be happy to listen. But now . . . I don't know how to talk to her anymore."

Celine stops browsing through the shelves to look over at me, the sharp lines of her face softening. "I know I've been giving you a lot of shit, but you can talk to her if you want to. It's natural to miss her."

I shake my head, setting the book down. My fingers tremble and I curl them into fists. "I can't. What am I supposed to say when she asks how I am? What I've been up to? Oh, I'm awful, thanks for asking! *As if.*"

Celine sighs, taking the book from me and walking back to the correct shelf to put it away. I follow her mindlessly.

"She obviously misses you, too, otherwise she wouldn't be messaging you every ten minutes. Which I still think is shitty, by the way."

"Yeah, well, no worries. I haven't been answering them," I say under my breath.

After Celine and I hung up last night, I got a text from Haley saying, I miss you:((let's hang out tomorrow? like old times?

I haven't confided in Celine about it, mostly because I'm certain I'd have to bail her out of jail afterward. Ever since Celine and I met in first grade, we've stuck to each other like glue. She's less of a friend, and more of a sister to me at this point, but I don't think that would hold up in court if she was charged with Haley's murder.

I also haven't told Celine because I don't even know how *I* feel about Haley's text. I don't understand how she thinks we can go back to old times. The way we—or at least, the way I—acted had romantic undertones, and returning to "normal" would be the same as battering on my already bruised heart.

I think that's the worst part of falling in love with your best friend when you're both girls. The way things can catapult so far without meaning anything.

I hate it.

Is this just affection? I'd wonder. *Is this love?* Is she making a move or is she just being friendly? Is she flirting with me or just joking around?

With boys, it's so much easier to tell when they flirt with intention. With girls, it's an endless question of: what does this even mean?

My throat is dry, as a handful of instances pop into my head. Celine doesn't seem to notice, stretching on her tiptoes to grab a book from the upper shelves.

She said I looked pretty when I did my makeup differently. Did she mean I look *pretty* or was it just a regular compliment?

She saw flowers in the park that reminded her of me, so she left some in my locker. Did she do it because I'm *always on her mind* or because she wanted to do something nice for a friend?

She slept over and in the dark, she whispered that she wanted to live in this moment with me forever. Is it because we're best friends or because she's in *love* with me?

Am I delusional? Is this all in my head? Am I reading too much into things? Or could she be sending me a sign?

Not that any of my overthinking mattered in the end.

"Celine, I want to go home," I say, throwing myself at her back, burying my face in her hair. "I don't want to be here anymore."

"Hey!" Celine turns around, pushing me away from her with gentle hands and firmly gripping my shoulders instead. "No crying in public. I know this is hard, okay? I'm sorry I can't make it all go away. But avoiding it isn't going to help anything."

"So what am I supposed to do?" I ask miserably.

"Lean on me," Celine says, squeezing my arms gently. "Ask

for help when you need it. Don't hide away and hold it all inside."

"Are you sure I can't just ask the earth to swallow me whole instead?" I ask, giving the ground a considering look.

Celine sighs. "Yes, I'm sure. Come on, I have a mani-pedi booked for us across the street."

I groan but let her lead me out of the bookstore after she pays for her books at the counter. As we walk down the sidewalk, I can't help but be hyperaware of our surroundings. The last thing I want is to bump into Haley after ignoring her texts.

Thankfully, we manage to evade her for the rest of the day, though that doesn't stop me from being paranoid and continuously checking over my shoulder like Haley might appear any second.

When I finally get home, I'm still afraid I'll have to face her somehow. I imagine the horrifying prospect of Haley showing up at my house, and my parents, none the wiser, letting her in.

I glance around my living room nervously as I toe off my shoes. A figure appears in the kitchen doorway, and I nearly collapse on the spot until I realize it's just my mother, wiping her hands on a dishcloth.

"Why are you so jumpy?" she asks with narrowed eyes. "Did something happen?"

"No," I say quickly. "I just didn't expect to see you there."

Ma doesn't look like she quite believes me, but she nods

at the dining table. "I left your food out. Warm it up for two minutes before eating it."

"I'm not that hungry," I admit and then regret it a moment later when her expression turns even more suspicious. "I ate with Celine," I rush to add.

"Ate what?" she asks.

"Just this and that." The real answer is that I don't have an appetite and the world lacks any true meaning, but if I say that, she's actually going to bite my head off.

When she places a hand on her hip, clearly waiting for more of an explanation, I decide to improvise.

"I think I still have some room," I say, forcing a bright smile onto my face. I pick up the plate of food, a mix of bhat, dal, rui macher jhol, and dharosh bhaji, and set it in the microwave.

Ma doesn't take her eyes off me, unconvinced, but there's no way for her to know *why* I'm acting so strange if I don't tell her. She doesn't stop staring at me, even as I return to the dining table with a plate of steaming food.

"Will you mix it for me?" I ask, hoping that'll distract her somewhat.

Her posture loosens somewhat at the familiar question. "Give it here," she says, and I slide the plate down the table toward her.

She begins mixing it all together with her hand, dissecting the fish and getting rid of the bones as I contemplate banging my head into the wall repeatedly.

"Are you sure you don't want them separately? You won't get the taste otherwise," Ma says, grimacing at me.

"All together is better," I say, despite knowing it's not the answer she wants. It's what I would say normally, though, and it seems to further convince her that everything is all right.

My phone lights up with a text, and I know before I look at it that it's going to be Haley. There's a new knot in my stomach when I turn my phone over, facedown and away from me.

I wonder if this is how it's going to be for the rest of the school year. Will I have to keep living with this ache in my chest and pretend it doesn't exist? When will it go away? Will it ever?

I look up at my mother and wonder if she's ever had her heart broken. I don't think she would tell me if she had. As far as I know, until my parents were arranged to be married, neither of them had been in a relationship before. Once again, it reminds me that *dating isn't allowed.*

When Ma finally passes me my plate, I shovel down the food in less than five minutes, wanting to be done with it. It tastes like nothing in my mouth, and I have to keep drinking water to actually make myself swallow it down.

Once I finish, Ma tells me to leave the plate in the sink, and I do. I contemplate taking the new carton of ice cream I bought out of the freezer and then decide against it. I can't afford to make my mother any more curious.

After I brush my teeth, I go upstairs and lie in my bed,

staring at the ceiling. My phone buzzes again but this time I don't even look at it.

It's going to be Haley. Who else would it be?

Slowly, I fall apart. Quiet sobs escape me and I turn my head into my pillow to drown out the noise. My chest feels so heavy and I'm so *tired*. All I ever wanted was for Haley to love me back.

In the darkness of my room, I feel devastatingly empty and alone.

I keep crying until my eyes burn and my face is wet, my head foggy with exhaustion. With the sleeve of my shirt, I wipe haphazardly at the tears dripping down my chin, but there's no point. It's not like anyone is going to see me like this.

A part of me aches to go downstairs and tell my parents everything. To lay this burden at their feet instead of mine.

But that's not possible, and even if it was, they wouldn't sympathize with me. They would be angry that I broke their rules and their trust.

I allow myself to briefly imagine a world where I can be honest with them—where I tell them about Haley and they hold me in their arms and try to soothe me. Where dating isn't so taboo, and being sapphic isn't a crime, and my parents love me unconditionally.

Then I laugh bitterly because that's never going to be my reality. Love is a myth, in more ways than one.

The next few days are a blur of tears, sad music, and copious amounts of junk food. The morning after spring break ends, I'm halfheartedly stirring my cereal. Baba is reading the Bangladeshi newspaper, his glasses perched low on his nose, and Ma is making chai in the kitchen.

The last thing I want right now is to go to school. Celine already promised that she wouldn't let me suffer a single moment alone with Haley, but it's not enough. I'd rather spend the day curled up in my bed, listening to a breakup playlist that doesn't even really make sense since Haley was never my girlfriend and we were never dating. Not that the lack of real labels makes it hurt any less.

I have a pounding headache and I'm so impossibly sad.

My phone buzzes with a notification and I flinch. Baba looks up from the newspaper with a curious look, and I hurriedly grab my phone to avoid dealing with any questions he might have.

Instead of a message from Haley, it's a series of texts from Celine.

Celine Wan: just checking in on you <3
Celine Wan: I know you're still beating yourself up abt everything but pls don't
Celine Wan: what you did was brave and being vulnerable is worth it even when it hurts
Celine Wan: plsplspls let me know if you need anything!!! I promise it's ok to ask for help
Celine Wan: I love you forever ava (which is proof that love IS real even if it's not the ideal kind LOL)

"I'm not feeling well," I say suddenly.

Baba folds his newspaper slowly. "What's wrong?"

"I have a stomachache," I say and let go of my spoon, letting it slip into the bowl of cereal. "Maybe I caught a bug or something."

Ma comes out of the kitchen and presses the back of her hand against my forehead. "You are a little warm," she says, frowning at me. "Why didn't you say something earlier?"

"I thought I could manage it," I say, and it's truer than they know. "But I don't . . . I don't think I can."

Ma and Baba trade a look over my head, and it lasts for longer than it should. I don't know what kind of conversation they have with just their eyes, but Baba nods at her, picking up his newspaper again.

"You can stay home today," Ma allows. "But if you're still sick tomorrow, you have to go to the doctor. Do you understand, Avika?"

It takes me a moment, but I do understand. They're letting me have this one day to gather myself, but if I'm still like this tomorrow, then I'll have to sit in a doctor's office and prove that I'm as sick as I claim.

Celine was right. Maybe all I had to do was ask for a little grace.

"Yes," I say and stand up, tugging my cardigan tighter around me. "Can I go back to bed?"

"Go," Baba says, cocking his head toward the staircase. "Do you need any painkillers?"

"I'll grab some Tylenol on my way," I say and bite my bottom lip. "I'm sorry."

"What for?" my father asks, but I don't have an answer. He must know that because he gestures toward the stairs again. "Go on. Try to get some more sleep."

"I'll come check on you soon," Ma says, already handing me two Tylenol pills and a glass of water. "You better not be on your phone when I come."

"I won't be," I say, swallowing the pills in one go. "I promise."

Then I turn around and leave the dining room to head back to my room. As I'm climbing the stairs, I can hear the two of them whispering to each other in Bangla, but I can't make out the words. I decide not to question it too much. I don't want to look a gift horse in the mouth.

Back in bed, I pull a stuffed animal to my chest and lie on my side. There's no end in sight to my heartbreak, but I knew this was a possibility when I confessed my feelings. I wish it didn't hurt this much but maybe that's the cost of honesty.

Today is the last day I'm going to let myself wither away like this. Tomorrow, I'm going to hold my head high again. Maybe I won't be smiling, but I won't allow myself to keep crying, either, even if I know Celine will be there to wipe away the tears.

Ma and Baba aren't asking questions now, but they will if I keep this up. Already, they've been more gracious than I expected.

I don't think I'll heal from this pain overnight. I don't know if I'll heal from it over an entire lifetime.

But at least I'm not alone in this. There are people on my side, looking out for me, knowingly or not. If I can be brave enough to confess my feelings, I can be brave enough to ask for help, too.

I set aside my stuffed elephant to grab my phone again and send Celine a quick text.

Ava Shah: not feeling up to coming to school today but can we ft later pls?? maybe we can figure out a game plan that isn't just avoid looking haley in the eyes lol

Ava Shah: I love you forever celine (your love IS the ideal kind, thank you always)

And then I close my eyes and will myself to go back to sleep.

LOVE THE ONE YOU'RE WITH

By Sheba Karim

The day he encountered the devil, Ali was with his sister. He'd brought her along on his Apple store errand, a decision he quickly regretted because Naz spent most of the time ranting. It was a family joke that his sister had been born fist-first, but ever since she'd turned fifteen, everything seemed to piss her off, their mother most of all. While it was true that Ammi was harder on Naz than she was on Ali, and that Ali was allowed more freedom, in Ali's opinion, Naz's constant rebellions and knee-jerk anger responses only exacerbated the situation. He didn't dare say this, though, because then she'd turn her ire on him. Instead, he nodded his head and half-listened as they left the Apple store and wove their way through the shutter-happy downtown tourists. It was a surprisingly cool evening in early September, but you wouldn't know it from the bachelorette party dressed in hot pink crop tops and denim cutoffs, striking a pose in front of the "Love the One You're With" mural. The mural was of two hearts on a forest path, holding hands. As they walked past the rowdy bachelorettes, Naz took out her new favorite gloss, a blue-black shade called "Hickey XX," and applied it to her lips. Ali was always impressed by her ability to put on cosmetics while in motion. He hadn't worn lipstick since he was seven, when Ammi kicked him out of her closet and told him he was officially too old to play with her saris and makeup.

They reached an intersection and he instinctively reached for her. She pushed his hand away and kept ranting.

"Ammi told me she doesn't want me on social media because she's scared I'll get *kidnapped*," Naz said. "Can you believe that?"

"No," Ali said. "Whoever kidnapped you would quickly regret it."

Naz elbowed him but he could tell she was pleased. "I mean, if you're going to be scared, at least be scared about things that are likely to happen."

"I don't think that's how fear works," Ali said. "Let's go down Hagarty. There's a store I want to check out." As the tourism downtown grew, the city had started developing the brick warehouses that lined the riverfront. Though most of it was live-music venues and chain restaurants, Ali had heard about a denim store that sounded cool. One of his goals before heading to college next year was to up his style game.

On the next corner was a building that used to be a gay bar. Ali knew this because when he was a kid, they'd driven by it and Ali's mother had told his father, "That's a bar for the gays." Though this was before Ali knew he was gay, he remembered turning around and looking at it until it disappeared from view. Jungle Jim's, it was called. Now, it was an Urban Outfitters.

"She's like, why can't you be more like Ali? He hardly uses social media. I swear, if she asks me to be like you one more time—what are all these people lined up for?"

Ali shrugged. "Maybe a new mural?"

A dozen or so people had formed a line alongside a large, brick building. Above the entrance was a large sign featuring a hooded grim reaper. *Horror on Hagarty*, it said, in letters that dripped blood onto the long, curved blade of the grim reaper's sickle.

A tall devil with pale red skin and golden horns worked the line, chatting up people and calling out to passersby. As Ali and Naz approached, he stepped in front of them, leaned on his pitchfork, its prongs twisted like snakes, and regarded them with his striking green eyes. Ali couldn't get over his elaborate, black feathered wings, which shimmered ethereally in the light of the setting sun. He was suddenly conscious of his drab prep school uniform, khakis and a sweatshirt emblazoned with the Sebastian Oaks crest and motto: *Athlete. Scholar. Citizen.*

"Would you two young souls care to journey to the depths of hell?" the devil said.

"Already been, it's called high school," Naz said.

The devil laughed. "Touché. Might I tempt you with 10 percent off?" He swept open his cape, removed two coupons from an inner pocket, and handed them one each. "We're open every evening Thursday to Sunday."

"I really like your wings," Ali blurted out.

The devil looked at Ali. Ali swallowed and dared himself to meet the devil's curious gaze. Freshman year, the PE coach had taken him aside and said, *Ali, whether you're trying to make a friend or fight an enemy, you gotta be able to look them in the eye.*

"Do you need a weekend gig?" the devil said. "Because we're hiring."

"Me? Really?" Ali said.

"Yeah right," Naz said. "He'd be too scared. He won't even watch scary movies."

"That's not because I'm scared," Ali said.

"Even if you are," the devil said, "my momma once told me, every day you should do something that frightens you. You can apply on our website if you change your mind." He flashed Ali a smile, his teeth a brilliant white, and went back to entertaining the line.

"I'm gonna use that quote in my next spoken word," Naz said as they walked away.

Ali couldn't stop thinking about the devil's comment. It would be easy enough to convince his parents he needed a part-time job; he could argue that he'd save some money for college next year, that the college counselor said work experience looked good on college applications. His parents would not, however, approve of him working at a haunted house. This meant that he would have to lie. Putting aside the whole in the closet thing, Ali rarely lied because he rarely did anything he needed to lie about. He also had no idea what it was like to work in a haunted house. What if he hated it? If he hated it, he told himself, wide awake in bed at night, well then he could quit. What if he wasn't good at it? Then he'd either get better or get fired. What if his parents found out? He'd make up a story—he needed material for his college essay about something unique and different. By midnight, Ali had thought of every possible objection and countered it. It was settled. He'd lie to his parents, work at the haunted house.

This was all assuming, of course, that the haunted house would want him. But he'd gotten a good vibe from the devil, and something about it felt like fate.

Sebastian Oaks Academy had been founded in 1841 to transform wealthy Southern boys into wealthy Southern gentlemen. In front of the dining hall was a statue of a Confederate soldier, a musket in one hand, a book in the other. The statue was removed the spring of Ali's freshman year, after the Black student group, called African American

Achievers, started a petition. Suffice it to say that Sebastian Oaks Academy, despite recently including "sexual orientation" on their diversity statement, was not the easiest place to be a minority of any kind. Though he'd struggled at first, Ali had found things to like: his small group of friends, the academic rigor, a lot of his teachers. His mother had sent him there because it offered a serious education while still emphasizing physical fitness. Both of her parents had heart disease, and her father had died when Ali was just a baby, of kidney failure due to diabetes. Good brain genes, his mother liked to say, bad body ones.

All students at Sebastian Oaks were required to do a sport. Ali played Ultimate Frisbee. He was the second worst player on the team, the worst being his friend Edwin. On the sidelines at practice, he thought of telling Edwin that he'd applied online for a haunted house job. *What is your availability now until November 1?* Fridays and Saturdays. *Have you ever worked in a haunted attraction?* No. *Do you have any theatrical experience?* No. *What attributes can you bring to the Horror on Hagarty team?* Enthusiasm and my strong work ethic.

He decided against saying anything to Edwin. Given his lack of experience, he doubted he'd even get the gig. During practice, he D'ed an end zone pass without even meaning to, preventing the other team from scoring and eliciting hearty cheers from his teammates, a high point of his day. Later, he waited for the locker room to clear out so he could shower, and obsessively checked his email. Still no response from Horror on Hagarty. He was halfway through changing when he heard Evan come in with Nico and Brooks. Evan was a Sebastian Oaks dream student: National Merit Scholar, tennis captain, and one of the riflery team's sharpest shooters. He was what Naz called HUTOTeM, which stood for "hot until they open their mouth." Evan could also be pretty mean, the kind that made fun of you then slapped you on the back like you were in on the joke.

Ali was relieved when they stopped one row over.

"What girls do you want to add?" Evan was saying.

"Definitely Huntley," Nico said. "She's got a sweet ass."

"Can't say the same for her attitude," Brooks said.

"What about Claire? She was looking good at the last game."

Hoping they'd be too distracted by their obnoxious conversation to notice him, Ali quietly gathered his stuff and made for a swift exit.

"Hey, Prince Ali," Evan said. He'd started calling Ali that after he watched *Aladdin* with his little stepsister. He pronounced it Prince Ally, even though he knew perfectly well how to say it right. "You want to add anyone to the list?"

"What?" Ali said.

"MFF," Nico said. "Most Fuckable Finns."

Finn was slang for girl, specifically a Finlay Hall girl. Finlay Hall was the private girls' school with whom they shared mixers and a few academic activities in order to encourage coed socialization. Girls from Finlay Hall were also the cheerleaders for the Sebastian Oaks football team.

"No thank you."

"Come on, there must be someone you have your eye on," Evan said.

Ali gazed at his feet. If he said nothing, pretty soon Evan would get bored and move on.

"He probably thinks it's misogynist," Brooks said. Brooks was a stocky wrestler who'd spent part of last summer in rehab. His parents had had a nasty divorce that made the local news when his dad rammed into his mom's parked car while she was on a date. Of the three, Brooks was the most physically intimidating, but also the nicest.

Evan snickered. "Guess what, Mr. Offended? The girls have their own list for us. Claire showed it to me."

Ali nodded, wishing they would hurry up. He was supposed to meet Edwin and Sumit in the chem lab.

"And you're on it," Evan said.

"Excuse me?" Ali said.

This set all three of them laughing. "Just kidding," Evan said. "But if you lost some weight and shaved your back, you'd have a fighting chance."

"I don't know," Nico said. "Some women like a hirsute gentleman."

"Ah, leave the poor kid alone," Brooks said.

With that, they returned to the list on Evan's phone, and Ali walked as fast as he could out the door. He wanted to scream, punch Evan in the face, call him names, do all kinds of ungentlemanly things. He hated that Evan made him feel this way, hated that he was always too scared to speak up, hated his hairy back, hated how he cast his eyes downward whenever Evan and company teased him.

His phone buzzed. An email from hiring@horroronhagarty.com.

Congratulations! it said. *We think you'd be a great fit for the Horror on Hagarty team.*

Ali whooped out loud in the hallway just as Mr. O'Grady, his Latin teacher, exited the classroom.

"Having a good day, I take it?" Mr. O'Grady said.

Ali smiled. "I am now."

His first night at Horror on Hagarty, Ali was told to observe the cemetery. He put on his outfit, a long-sleeve black shirt and black pants, and was introduced to a young woman named Gemma, who played the cemetery's ghost bride.

"Horror on Hagarty has ten rooms, each with its own actors and theme-specific scares, and the cemetery comes second," Gemma explained. Her skin was painted pale white and her wedding dress had an eerie blue tinge. She pointed to a man in a skeletal mask and dark robes who was currently in downward dog. "That's Rick, our graveyard ghoul. He likes to warm up with stretches."

Rick waved. "Pleasure to meet you," he said in a thick Southern accent.

"Me, I like to warm up with voice exercises." Gemma tilted her head back and let out a yodel.

"Wow, that was good," Ali said.

"Thanks! I used to sing on a cruise ship. What else . . . everyone is expected to bring their own flair to the role, you know, play to your strengths. Rick, anything to add?"

Rick swung one leg up on top of a tombstone and bent forward until his head rested on his knee. "Don't touch anyone," he said. "And try not to let them touch you."

"Yes," Gemma agreed. "Sometimes, when people get scared, they react by acting out, trying to hit or push you."

"A guy tried to kick me once," Rick said. "But he ended up falling on his ass."

"So get close, but not too close," Ali said.

"Exactly," Gemma said. "It's a tough job but scaring people has its perks. Whatever you're frustrated about in your own life, you can just channel it and let it all out."

"We call it scare-apy," Rick said.

Gemma threw her head back and released another yodel.

As Rick switched legs, Ali read the epitaph on a tombstone.

IMOGENE GRAY, 1841–1854
VICTIM OF THE BEAST

A shrill bell rang.

"Ten minutes till showtime," Gemma said. "I have to test the zip line."

The rest of the night Ali observed from a dark corner of the cemetery, as tendrils of mist curled around dimly lit tombstones and a creepy soundtrack played through the speakers—the cawing of a crow, an ominous wind, ghostly murmurs, a graveyard bell. The audience entered the room in groups of six to seven, walking single file. The cemetery featured two impacts, or scares. When the fourth person in line reached the cobweb-laced tree, Rick came out howling from behind a giant cross. Then, when the fourth person reached the tomb of the dark angel, Gemma came hurtling across on a zip line, reaching out her ghostly arm and crying, "Marry me!"

Rick always got some screams, Gemma even more. After Gemma's impact, the group would rush forward, following the path into the next room, and Gemma and Rick would quickly return to their starting positions, ready to do it all over again. It was hard work, Ali realized, tough on your body and your voice, but there was something exhilarating about your and the audience's combined anticipation, especially when only one of you knew what was coming next.

The following weekend, Rick was assigned to play Scary Monk #1 in the medieval dungeon and Ali was promoted to graveyard ghoul. When he put the costume on, he felt like a different person. He tried out various ghoul personas: the ghoul who moves like a zombie, the ghoul with an unsteady gait. People were startled, but no one actually screamed. As a baby, he'd been early to crawl and late to walk, so he decided to try vengeful crawling ghoul. He remembered what Gemma had said and channeled his frustrations. He thought of Evan, of college application stress, of the fact Edwin was spending all his time with the new girlfriend he'd met at a Vietnamese Cultural Day. On cue, he came out on hands and knees, surprised by his own speed, and punctuated his spidery movements with bellowing moans. To his delight, two people screamed. Toward the end of the night, when one woman yelled, "Oh hell no!" and ran the opposite way, toward the entrance, Ali had to stop himself from laughing. Afterward, Gemma congratulated him on getting his first runner, and he couldn't remember the last time he'd felt so proud.

The worlds of Sebastian Oak and Horror on Hagarty were so opposite it was surreal, but in a strange way, the fact they were so different made it easier to move between them. They were also kind of simpatico; any annoying thing that happened at school he could take out at the haunted house. Scare-apy was legit.

So far, he'd only told Naz about the job. His parents thought he was working at the Gap in the outlet mall. Between his own shyness and this shroud of secrecy, Ali thought it wise to maintain a cordial distance from the others at his work. Anyway, with the exception of one person who attended the public high school for the arts, the actors were all older than him, with a myriad of life experiences, like traveling with the circus or spending a summer being a metal band groupie or going viral for a sword-swallowing video. A lot of them were veterans of the haunt industry, had spent years working in scream parks or seasonal haunted attractions. He was the only one without some combination of septum piercings, dyed hair, and copious tattoos, and, he guessed, probably the only one in the closet.

Initially, Ali had worried the people at Horror on Hagarty would see through him, that they'd call him out, say, hey, you're not like us, you don't belong here. He quickly realized this was unlikely to happen, because most people assumed if you'd found your way here, you belonged, simple as that.

One Sunday, Ali came home with a cheesecake for the aunties. Ali's mother hosted a monthly card afternoon, when the aunties came over to play Choi Dai Da, a game that Auntie Riffat, who'd grown up in Hong Kong, had taught them. Ali had spent the day cleaning up Wegner Park with the Environment Club, and half of the parking lot had been taken up by a farmers' market.

"Ali, guess what?" Auntie Farida said when he entered the dining room. "We are going on a hot-air balloon!"

Ali looked at his mother, who had a fear of heights. Ammi responded with a slight shrug. Since gambling was haram, the auntie who won the most games got to make everyone do something. Most of them chose an innocuous activity, like going to see the latest Bollywood movie, but spirited Auntie Farida liked to pick something that took the ladies out of their comfort zone. Thankfully for the other aunties, she rarely won.

"That's exciting," Ali said. "I brought you all a cheesecake from the farmers' market."

He set the cheesecake, decorated with fresh, glistening berries, on the dining table and the aunties oohed and aahed.

"Naz, beta," his mother called out, "would you get us some plates?"

Naz, who was in the living room reading on the couch, didn't respond.

"I'll get them," Ali said.

As he headed into the kitchen, he heard Auntie Riffat say, "You're so lucky, Mashal, to have such a good son."

Ali didn't need to look at his sister to know she was rolling her eyes.

The following weekend, Ammi found one of Naz's spoken-word poems that had the word "labia" in it, ordered Naz into the living room, and began to admonish her.

"What is wrong with you," Ammi said, waving the poem in front of Naz's face, "that you think it's okay for you to say dirty words into a microphone, in front of so many people?"

"It's not a dirty word!" Naz said.

"Don't shout," Ammi said. "It's rude."

Ali, who was on the couch opposite, looking over the MCAT workbook his father had bought him the other day, turned the page, pretending to be absorbed by the practice questions. Though he knew Naz wanted him to come to her defense, he took after his dad and preferred to avoid conflict unless absolutely necessary. Plus, he doubted there was anything to gain by entering the fray; Naz still wouldn't get what she wanted, and it would just make Ammi more upset.

"If you want people to respect you, you have to respect yourself," Ammi was saying in Urdu. "Ali, can you explain this to your sister?"

Ali tucked the MCAT book under his arm. "I gotta go," he said, "I can't be late for work."

Naz glared at him, mouthing, *What the hell?* He made a sad face back and left the room. Whenever Naz got a major dressing-down, Ali, always remorseful for not sticking up for her, usually bought her something, food or a gift, which Naz would then grudgingly accept as his apology. Tonight, he decided, on the way home from the haunted house, he'd pick up her guilty pleasure, Taco Bell.

Ali had his ghoul costume on and was waiting for makeup when the haunted house manager, Mr. Rodinger, a petite man with a handlebar mustache who liked to scurry around the dressing room barking orders, said, "Ali! You shadowed Psycho, didn't you?"

"Just once," Ali said.

"Ready for a promotion?"

Ali blinked. "Sure."

"Fantastic. Go back to wardrobe and switch outfits." Mr. Rodinger gave Ali a high five and called out to Erin, the head makeup artist who was currently blow-drying latex onto a zombie's face, "Erin! Ali's on Psycho tonight."

When Erin was done with him, Ali couldn't stop staring at himself in the mirror. He'd been transformed into an old lady, complete with a gray wig in a tight bun, a pearl choker, and a long, high-collared dress, dark gray with black flowers. An off-white crocheted shawl was draped over his shoulders and pinned at his chest. His face was heavily powdered and at his request Erin had added a touch of rouge. Deep down, he'd always wanted to try drag, see how it felt. This wasn't exactly the type of drag he was imagining, but it felt exciting, and surprisingly comfortable.

"You look magnificent."

Ali looked up to see the devil's reflection in the mirror. The devil had a name—Lawrence. In the dressing room a few days before, Ali had admired the cute freckles along his sharp cheekbones. Ali hadn't gotten to talk to him much yet because he was usually working the line outside.

"Thanks," Ali said shyly. "I definitely prefer it to ghoul."

Lawrence smiled. He leaned toward the mirror and snapped his fangs into his mouth. "Psycho is a big promotion. Congrats."

Makeup was almost empty, most people off to have one last smoke or go to the bathroom before the haunted house opened. Something about the quiet and the fact that he was in costume gave Ali the courage to ask, "That day on the street, what made you think I'd be a good fit to work here?"

Lawrence cocked his head. "I don't know. I guess it was because you liked my wings."

"They're beautiful."

"Farrell spent two weeks making them." Farrell was the head of costume, a gay man who wore a ring on every finger and bore a striking resemblance to Robert Downey Jr. "I'll let you try them on, next time."

The ten-minute warning bell rang.

"I should get back outside," Lawrence said. "By the way, do you know anyone who'd want to play an evil mime?"

"Sure, let me think about it," Ali said. Later, over 1 a.m. soft taco supremes, he'd relay this exchange to Naz, and they'd laugh about how casually he'd answered, as if the contact list on his phone was rife with evil mime potential.

The Psycho room was one of the smallest at Horror on Hagarty. Upon entering, the first thing you'd see was a haphazard collection of decaying objects gathered along the left side, a rusty candelabra atop a decrepit piano, empty barrels, a rotting bench, a menacing coil of wires, a dead, thorny plant, all blanketed in cobwebs. As you continued farther, you'd notice the staircase on the right. On the top step was a wheelchair, tipped forward like it might fall, and on this wheelchair was Norma Bates, a wigged skeleton wearing an identical outfit to Ali.

When the first guest entered, Ali would move into the dark doorway. To set the mood, he'd hit the Audio FX button, and the demented hoots of an owl would echo throughout the room. Then, when the third guest reached the staircase, he hit another button, which sent Norma's wheelchair hurtling to the bottom of the steps, the first big impact. Then he'd come running out screaming, a knife raised over his head, and chase the terrified group out of the room. Sometimes he'd scream, "I'm Norma Bates!" or "I'm your Momma!" or "Who wants an A in chemistry?" or whatever else he felt like on that particular night or in that particular moment. The words were more for him than them, since no one could really understand what he was saying.

For the first time in his life, he was in a space where no one expected him to be straight, or obedient, or a gentleman. Known as the quiet kid his whole life, working in this room made Ali realize just how loud he could be. There was something truly cathartic about screaming; by the end of the night, he felt wiped out but lighter, less burdened.

One evening, as Ali emerged to scare a group, he recognized Bilal, a kid from the community, and was instantly worried—what if Bilal told someone else in the community, and it traveled the grapevine to Ali's parents? But Ali could tell from the way Bilal yelped with fear, his hand flying up to the Quranic verse on his necklace, that he'd had no idea it was Ali. After all, Ali thought as he returned to the doorway to wait for the next group, why would he? The Ali Bilal knew was the courteous kid at the community parties, the one who watched from the sidelines as the boys played basketball in the driveway, who lost at video games, who the aunties praised because he always helped clean up, not a knife-wielding, costumed young man in a dress, who'd learned from Erin how to fix his own wig and layer color corrector, concealer, and powder on his face to cover his five-o'clock shadow.

When he got home that night, he was surprised to find Ammi awake in the living room. "Ali, you're home," she said.

Ali walked over to her, relieved that he was so diligent about his makeup removal, first soap and water, then cold cream, then makeup remover wipes.

"You look tired. Here, come lie down." She shifted to the end of the couch so he could stretch out, his head resting in her lap.

"Why are you still up?" he asked.

"I'm worried about your sister. She's always fighting with me and I don't know what to do. You never gave me any problems. What am I doing wrong with her?"

Ali thought of what Naz might want him to say in this moment, versus what he felt comfortable saying. "Maybe she needs you to listen to her more."

"I do listen. But maybe I can try harder." Ammi ran her fingers through his hair. After seven hours of wearing a hairnet, this felt amazing. "Gap keeps you working so late. Are you sure you want to keep doing this?"

"I got promoted, which means I have to stay and close up. But I'm going to quit in a few weeks anyway."

"Good. Should I make you a snack?"

"No, I just want to rest." Ali closed his eyes and relaxed against his mother's body. He'd always been his mother's favorite, and Naz their father's. He wondered if it would stay this way after he came out. He didn't think his parents would disown him, but they would struggle. The last time he'd gone to the masjid, the imam had given a lecture about how marriage could only be between a man and a woman, that if someone was a homosexual and could not change, the only way to live an Islamic life was for them to not act upon their homosexual desires. He hadn't been back to the masjid since. But he couldn't stay in the closet forever. One day, he'd have to tell his parents the truth. Until then, Ali thought as he drifted to sleep, he might as well enjoy these tender moments.

The two weeks leading up to Halloween, the haunted house became increasingly busy. Ali told his friends about it. Sumit, who couldn't watch horror movies, was too scared to come, but Edwin brought his girlfriend and the deranged clown almost gave her a heart attack. Naz came with her best friend Bella and had been duly impressed. "I can't believe it," she told him. "You're finally cool."

Horror on Hagarty was now open six evenings a week and Mr. Rodinger was putting pressure on everyone to work more shifts. Against his better judgment, Ali agreed to work the Friday, Saturday, and Sunday right before Halloween. It would be exhausting, but it was also his last weekend at the haunted house. Might as well go out with a bang.

On Thursday, at the salad bar, Ali overhead Evan saying something about Nico being scared by a doll. Curious, he slid his tray down so he could eavesdrop better.

"It wasn't a doll," Nico said. "It was an evil monkey with cymbals. I thought it was an animatronic, and then suddenly it leapt at me. I've never been so scared in my life."

They were talking, Ali realized, about the doll room at Horror on Hagarty.

"It wasn't that scary," Evan said, putting three boiled eggs on his plate.

"Oh yeah?" Nico said. "Let's talk about you in the Exorcist room. Evan got so scared he started crying like a Finn."

"That's not cool," Ali said.

Evan looked at him across the salad bar. "What?" he said.

Ali couldn't believe he'd spoken aloud, but he wasn't going to back down now. If he could terrify people on a regular basis, he could at least look Evan Montgomery II in the eye. "How you used Finn just now. It's not cool. Also, a man is just as likely as a woman to cry in a haunted house, so get your facts straight."

As Evan crossed over to Ali's side of the salad bar, Ali held his breath, bracing for whatever was coming next. Evan put Ali in a chokehold and gave him a noogie on his head. "Look who's finally grown some balls!" he cried. Then he let Ali go with a slap on the back, grabbed his tray, and went off with his friends.

Edwin came up to him. "Hey, what happened with Evan? Are you okay?"

"Yeah, actually," Ali said. "I am."

On his last night at the haunted house, after finishing the last touches of powder, Ali decided to experiment, adding a little more rouge and a smoky eyeliner along his top lash line. Then he went to the break room to grab one of the energy drinks Mr. Rodinger had left out for them as a treat, careful to only have a few sips because once the show began, bathroom breaks were few and far between.

"Hey, Ali!" Gemma said. She'd taken a jar of honey out of the cabinet and was squeezing some into a giant Carnival Cruise Lines thermos. "We're going to Dusty's tonight after work, wanna come?"

"Who's Dusty?" Ali asked.

Gemma laughed. "Dusty's is a lesbian bar. It's eighteen and over karaoke tonight, not that they ever card. In my personal opinion, they also have the best nachos in the city."

As someone who was tone deaf and couldn't carry a tune if his life depended on it, karaoke was a lose-lose situation; if he didn't participate, people would think he was a bad sport; if he did, he'd embarrass himself. "Me singing is scarier than anything in this haunted house."

Gemma squeezed his shoulder. "Then you definitely have to come. I gotta go—make 'em scream."

Ali cut through the morgue to get to his room, pushing through symmetrical rows of synthetic cadavers hanging by metal hooks from the ceiling. He was glad they hadn't put him in the morgue when he'd first started; it was freezing and he hated being cold and he might have quit. He couldn't decide if he should go to Dusty's. He was curious to go to a lesbian bar but was loath to sing. All the world may be a stage, but some stages were more forgiving than others.

Sunday night was slower than Friday and Saturday had been, but the groups were still coming through at a fairly steady pace. A lot of people were in costume, which made for a weirder, more festive atmosphere. Tonight, Ali had decided to be Norman Bates the murderous nerd, who planned to celebrate getting into Columbia by killing everyone. Before every group, he imagined getting the acceptance email, and came out screaming in mad ecstasy. He scared one guy so much he yelled out, "I just peed my pants!" His friend laughed, and Ali heard him whisper, "No, for real."

Ali grinned. He had his first pee-er. He went into the hallway and did a quick stretch, gearing up to do it again. The next group entered, and he cued the deranged owl hoots. Then, as the group approached the Norma on the staircase, he heard a voice say, "Oh I know! It's that movie, with the motel."

The voice reminded him of Auntie Farida. He brushed it off; even if it was her, which was unlikely, if Bilal didn't recognize him, she wouldn't either. He sent Norma hurtling down the stairs, raised his knife, and ran out screaming, "My first choice is your nightmare!"

The group screamed back. Ali saw a pirate, a Superman, an angel, and four aunties.

Auntie Farida. Auntie Riffat. Auntie Shahnaz, and his mother. His eyes widened, his knife suspended in the air.

"Let's go!" Auntie Riffat cried, pushing Auntie Shahnaz ahead.

Ammi, last in line, looked back at him. He thought he saw a moment of recognition in her eyes, but then she shook her head, turned around, and hurried after her friends.

Ali stood frozen, imagining what his mother must have thought.

This weirdo has eyes like Ali. How odd.

Ali retreated to the hallway, his hands shaking. The encounter had jolted him out of character and he couldn't see a way back. He couldn't breathe, he needed fresh air. Every room had an emergency intercom, and he pressed his and said, "I feel really sick, I have to go outside." He ran down the employee access hallway that connected the rooms, his panicked footfall accompanied by screams and nervous laughter from the other side of the walls, until at last he burst through the side door into the crisp, moonlit night.

When he got to his car, he saw Naz was calling.

"I just saw Ammi," he gasped into the phone.

"I know, I texted you. Auntie Farida won cards again and made them all go to the haunted house. I'm almost there, where are you?"

"In the parking lot." He leaned against the car hood. He'd parked under a tree, its dark leaves crackling in the wind.

Bella's ancient Honda Accord pulled up. The passenger door opened and Naz came rushing toward him.

"I ran off set," Ali said. "I abandoned my post."

"I'm sorry." Naz rubbed the back of his dress. "I tried to warn you. Do you think she recognized you?"

"I don't think so. It was too far out for her to comprehend."

"Well, it is a pretty big leap. For her," Naz said.

Still, it had been too close a call. The haunted house had made him braver, more confident, but he wasn't ready yet for his worlds to merge.

They got inside Ali's car. Ali pulled off his wig and hairnet and closed his eyes. His clothes were still in his locker. Thankfully, he kept a set of extra clothes in his car. Tomorrow, he'd have to drop off his costume and apologize to Mr. Rodinger. For now, though, he just wanted to be with his sister, somewhere they could safely process what just happened.

He looked over at Naz, who'd put on his wig and was making funny faces at herself in the vanity mirror. It hit him that in less than a year he'd be in college, and would go weeks, months without seeing her. He'd miss her laughter, her snarky sense of humor, her advice, even her rants. Then he remembered what Lawrence had said to him when they first met.

Every day, do something that frightens you.

"I'm sorry," he said, "that I haven't stuck up for you more. I didn't do it because I was scared of getting in trouble, but that's not a good excuse. I'll try to be better."

"Wow," Naz said. "I like you in a dress."

Ali laughed. His stomach growled. He was starving. "Hey, how would you feel about going to a lesbian bar for some nachos?"

"Uh, yes and yes," Naz said.

Ali pulled up directions to Dusty's and they exited the parking lot. The line for Horror on Hagarty wrapped around the block, and the devil was taking a selfie with a bachelorette party. The moon was nearly full, and inside the haunted house, people were screaming. He imagined the Psycho room, a group passing through ready to be scared, instead being greeted by cobwebs and quiet, skeletal Norma suspended at the bottom of the stairs. He drove away slowly, watching as the haunted house disappeared from the rearview. *I'm sorry,* he said to it, *and thank you for everything.*

STAR ANISE

By Anuradha D. Rajurkar

I was deep frying pakoras in the kitchen, trying to forget the fact that I'd blown up my life, when Maa dropped the bomb.

"Damon? I have great news." She grabbed me by the shoulders, hope in her eyes. "Kalina will be staying with us this summer."

I froze. Kalina, my cousin in India whom I hadn't seen in years. Kalina, who spent hours with me on the tennis court the summers we'd visit and who took no shit. Who'd see through my walls into my soul and never forgive me for what I'd become. "W-why?"

"She's been admitted into UW–Milwaukee as an international student! Seeing that we're her family in the States, she'll stay here until her fall courses begin."

I stared at the lumps of batter browning too quickly in the hot oil. "What'll she study?" As if that mattered.

"Engineering," Maa said, after a beat. "But maybe also film."

With a slotted spoon, I began rescuing the pakoras from the hot oil. *Kalina. STEM-brained movie buff. Chatty, charming, funny as hell. Outraged over everything while being duty-bound. UWM. Staying with us. Will unearth my secret in no time.* My brain tried to compute. Adding more lumps of chickpea-spinach-chili batter to the pan, a dot of oil splattered onto my forearm, burning like an omen. "Shlugh."

I'd been counting on a summer of heaving compost bags into minivans at the garden center by day, cooking with Maa by night. A summer of evading my teammates, and Talia. Of trying to forget the choices—and consequences—of that night two months ago at Hubbard Woods.

Maa's eyes softened in a way that couldn't conceal the truth—that she felt deeply, desperately sorry for me. "It'll be a good thing, beta," she said, "having her with us."

"Shhhhit." The new pakoras I'd plopped in were already burning. Everything was maddening. Including and especially a mother's unreasonable love.

"Yaar. What is up with you?" It was pretty much the first thing out of Kalina's mouth. She'd arrived like a warm summer storm, carrying too many bags, wearing too much makeup, and yapping incessantly, which ordinarily I'd find amusing but only set my jaw on edge. "Your vibe is weird."

"Cool to see you, too."

She studied me. I watched her take in my handlebar mustache, my too-long sideburns, my stained Strokes tee, and general aura of malaise I never seemed to be able to shake. But she punched my arm with a grin, embracing me in a tight bear hug. Her hair spewing from the back of her head like a shiny black fountain, she plopped herself at the kitchen counter.

I slathered ghee on a fresh gobi paratha and placed it before her. "What—is this madness?" she breathed. She ripped off a shred and took a bite. "Wait—I see what this is: distraction by feeding." She chewed, her eyes half-closed. "Whoa, man. Best gobi paratha I've ever tasted. And I'm from Mumbai."

Maybe having her here would be okay.

"But, yaar? This whole thing you've got going on?" She twirled a finger at me, her eyes wide with concern. "Is Coach okay with this?"

I added a dollop of spiced cauliflower filling to a circle of flattened dough, folded it like a potsticker, rolled it out, and tossed it onto the hot tava. I had no response.

Brow furrowed, she waved at the cooking mess. "Also? I'm confused. Where'd you learn all of this?"

"Maa. YouTubers. Experimentation."

She stared at me. "But I don't understand. What about tennis? Aren't you teaching it this summer? You always said it helped you stay in tune, have a better season."

I flipped the gobi paratha and rolled out a new one. "Needed a break," I said finally. I tried not to remember the hours Kalina and I spent on the court by her parents' place in Mumbai. How tennis had been what had connected us—she the kite, I the spool—and how that was over.

She stared out the open window, folding her hands. "Look. Your cooking serves me *way* better than tennis ever did. But sweating it out on the court I kind of miss."

"Sorry to disappoint." I rooted through the fridge for stuff I didn't need, trying not to imagine what Kalina would think if she knew everything.

She regarded me, then tapped the table with her palm, twice. "Okay. I've an idea. Come." She moved toward the back door. "And I've not yet gotten my license, so you're driving."

Nowadays, I avoided driving. But I was determined to not have her see that.

Before I knew it, I was turning the key in the ignition, both of us pretending not to notice that my hands were trembling.

"Where are we even going?" The whine in my voice was decidedly not cool, but Kalina was being so bossy that it was my only defense.

"On a tour of Milwaukee's culinary scene, led by an emerging chef. I want to taste Milwaukee."

"Gross. Also, I'm no chef. I'm just tooling around Maa's kitchen passing the time."

"Don't be self-hating." She peered at her phone.

"How is that self-hating?"

"Look at you: Other than being brown, you *are Milwaukee*. I mean, you are sporting a handlebar mustache. Be proud of your city. And your culinary skills."

"This," I gave my mustache a twirl, "is not Milwaukee. It's just cool."

She smirked. "It's *quintessential* Milwaukee, yaar. I'm not even American and I know this." She studied her phone. "I'd like you to take me to a beer garden, please," she said slowly. "A Milwaukee specialty, apparently."

I bristled. Beer gardens are usually mobbed, but I drove her to the one at Estabrook Park. I watched as she inhaled a bratwurst and a pint—which she acquired thanks to her stupid fake ID. Amid the din of a live polka band, kids slid down a bouncy house and ran through the playground amid picnickers. Along the western edge of the garden, the Milwaukee River cleaved through a forest, swift and silent. I pulled my hat down low, fighting the ever-familiar nausea rising within me, trying to forget the last time I was this close to beer—and the river.

She glanced around. "So, who do you hang with nowadays?"

"People from work, kids from school," I lied. "So, are you going to tell me when you decided to apply to UWM, or . . . ?"

She took a huge bite of her brat and gazed at the sky,

waggling her head like she was formulating a critique. She chewed, swallowed, shrugged. "It's good. Gristly. But good."

I wanted to yell: *Gristle is, by definition, never good. And what's with all the beer?* Instead, I said: "So you're not going to share why you decided to attend school here, huh?"

She inspected her brat. "Does my presence offend you?"

"What? No. Of course not." A group nearby toasted a guy in a bow tie, pints raised in the air while he conducted the birthday song. "It's just weird that I had no clue."

"Is it, though? Was *I* the one that decided that WhatsApp wasn't worth taking up space on my phone?" She gazed at me, eyes blazing with a ferocity that had shame burrowing into me like a rat. It was true—after my life bottomed out, I'd dropped WhatsApp and other modes of communication without a thought.

Her phone pinged. As she glanced at its screen, the fire in her eyes gave way to impenetrable smoke. She looked up at a group dancing in front of the band, but her gaze was unseeing.

"Who—is everything okay?"

But she ignored my question, scrolling through her phone. "Tomorrow's the State Fair."

"No."

She set her phone down and grinned. "Yes, cousin-brother."

"I draw the line."

"You can't *draw lines*."

"I can."

"Bloody hell. I'm in your country *for the first time* and you won't show me the sights?"

"The State Fair is not a sight, but rather, hell on earth."

"Well, take me to hell, then!"

Several cut their eyes in our direction. "Maybe you don't live here," I said, my voice low, "but I do."

"Oh, for God's sake, Damon. You sound like my parents. Who *cares* what people think?" Her eyes flashed. "And in case you weren't aware," she said, sniffing, "I *do* live here now."

At the State Fair, Kalina insisted on cream puffs, fried cheese curds, and corn on the cob dipped in a vat of butter. This along with the dizzying rides, searing August heat, and smell of manure did nothing to contain my rising panic and nausea. Not to mention the odor of Kalina's skunky, ever-present beer. Every swig caused a twitch of worry in my throat and a roil in my stomach. "When did you become such a beer hound, anyway?"

"Around the time you became insufferably judgmental."

As if this wasn't enough, Kalina dragged me on a Milwaukee culinary expedition: Mader's for German pancakes, Milwaukee Brat House, and Kopp's for frozen custard. She insisted that we take the Milwaukee Historic Brewery Pedal Bar Bike Tour, which meant four hours of pedaling a human-powered party bike from Brewer's Hill to downtown, with stops at various breweries to learn about captivating beer history.

For an underaged kid who can't drink, it was beyond annoying.

We biked to Milwaukee Ale House for a fish fry, past the Summerfest grounds and Milwaukee Art Museum, through hipster Brady Street, ending with a tour at Lakefront Brewery. I sipped specialty sodas designed for the under-twenty-one crowd, irritation scraping at my insides as everyone in sight—including Kalina—got sloshed. I clenched my jaw, trying not to think about how the last time I went to the city was for volunteering alongside Talia.

"So. Fabulous," Kalina said, downing her fiftieth beer sample of the day.

"What—Milwaukee eats?" I could sense a noxious grin creeping across my face. It's like I had no control over the urge to dismantle her joy, a joy that—let's face it—felt aggressive. "I believe that is the beer talking."

"You don't have a monopoly on what is or isn't delicious, Damon." She took a selfie of us then, tongue out, cool-girl fashion, me cocking a brow. She studied it. "Nice. Considering."

"What's remarkable is how you can find pleasure in the fine dining options of beer, brats, and cheese, is all."

"What can I say? I'm remarkable." She wiped her mouth with a napkin and drummed her fingers on the table. "Okay, yaar. Your turn."

"My turn to what?"

"To take me someplace. Since you're being such a weird snob about *your own city*, show me your Milwaukee. Forget the cheesy stuff. No pun intended." Her phone lit up again. Her eyes dimmed as they flicked over the words of a text. This time, to my surprise, she turned it fully off and tucked it away.

If last year hadn't happened, where would I have taken this kindred spirit—this brazen cousin whom I'd always looked up to?

And then, it struck me. The one spot I'd felt peace. Where there was no chance of running into anyone from school. A place that felt—at one point in time—like home. I swallowed the dregs of the cloying cream soda I'd been nursing, trying not to think about the fact that the last time I'd gone there was with Talia, who had brought me there in the first place. "Let's go."

Twenty minutes later, we pulled up in front of Amaranth Café.

Kalina had been silent as we moved through Brewer's Hill and Brady to I-43, speeding past the old row houses that stood tight together facing the highway. When I took the exit for Walnut Hill toward Milwaukee's west side, she'd stared out the window, her face averted. I thought she sniffled and could have sworn she wiped at her face.

"Hey. You okay?"

"I'm fine. Just jet-lagged."

This section of Milwaukee was gritty, with less-than-optimal crime statistics and several boarded-up buildings. But past the vacant lots and blank storefronts were timeworn Queen Anne–style duplexes with wide front porches painted in bright colors, parks featuring garden art flags created by elementary students, and a community garden bursting with kale and cucumbers.

As we passed a city park with a huge mural painted along its brick wall, something dormant shifted inside my chest. Here, gentrification's rumblings had begun, but it was the neighborhood's history that had its grip on me. I tried to ignore the fact that this place was filled with memories of Talia and me, where possibility first took root.

Inside, Bennie, the owner, greeted me with a handshake-hug. "My man," he said, his eyes shining. "What took you so long to come see us again?"

As I had no good answer to that, I introduced him to Kalina, whose gaze moved in wonder over the cinematic indigo walls plastered with art from around the world. As she shifted into documentarian mode with Bennie over Amaranth's history, I settled into a curvy bentwood chair near one of two bay windows flanking the front door where Talia and I would settle after a tutoring session. The café's oak floors gleamed in the late summer light and the place smelled of cloves and oranges, a tea I remembered Bennie simmered as much for its flavor as its scent.

Bennie told Kalina how Amaranth was the product of a

revitalization plan, how patrons and donors contributed art from their own collections, and how highlighting cuisines from around the globe was a goal. I watched the cars putter along the main thoroughfare. I hadn't been here since before that night I slipped on the black ice of my mind and blew out my integrity, the night I observed the team—and Talia—lurch toward their fate. A young couple sat in the corner sipping coffee and sharing a scone. The place was warm and cheerful and filled me with shame: I no longer belonged there. As Bennie went to tell his partner, Kya, that we were there, Kalina studied a flyer tacked to the door. My eyes flitted over the words.

CALLING OUR NEXT CHEF OF THE DAY!
SHARE YOUR CULINARY TALENTS WITH
YOUR COMMUNITY BIMONTHLY BY CREATING
A SPECIAL PAY-AS-YOU-CAN MEAL. ALL
PROCEEDS GO TO HELPING WITH HEART,
BELOVED AFTER-SCHOOL TUTORING CENTER
NEXT DOOR. INQUIRE WITHIN!

I could practically hear Kalina's thoughts.

When we got into the car, I looked at her squarely. "No."

"Already told Bennie you'll do it," Kalina said, shrugging.

Beads of sweat materialized across my forehead. "What?"

"The next one's August sixteenth. Leaving plenty of time to develop a menu."

"That's *two weeks*."

"Exactly."

A group of teens strode by, backpacks slung over their shoulders. They filed into Helping with Heart. "So, you just . . . volunteered me. Without asking."

"It's not like I'm going to *film* you."

"How thoughtful." I closed my eyes. "I'm not doing it. You'll have to tell Bennie."

"You want me to tell Bennie you won't do it?"

I simmered in silence.

"For what it's worth," she said, "he was very, very excited. Said you were a regular. That it'd mean a lot to him and Kya to have you as featured chef. 'That kid got shine.' His words."

I gazed out the windshield, suddenly seeing images of that night: silhouettes weaving toward the car, the exchange that replayed in my brain like a ragged reel, Talia's eyes meeting mine moments before our lives switched tracks. I cleared my throat, where my heart seemed to be beating.

"Consider it an intervention. And this brooding-Mr.-Darcy-chef thing? Oddly, it works. Despite the Milwaukee-maharaja mustache." She playfully mime-boxed my face.

My hands gripped the wheel. I was lightheaded with rage.

"You'll thank me later." She rested her legs along the dashboard. Her toenail polish was chipped and the skin on her heels was cracked—details that didn't fit the impeccably groomed Kalina that I knew. There were bags beneath her eyes, black makeup smudged along the creases of her lids. She drummed her fingertips on her thighs. "Trust me."

I couldn't tell her that the reason I brought her here was because it signified a lightness of being, an era of ease and possibility, but that it was no longer mine. I couldn't explain how the thought of preparing a special meal for people in a place filled with goodness felt like a boulder in my chest.

The next two weeks were a blur of obsessing over the menu, dreading the notion of human beings, and arguing with Kalina. I tried channeling the many Amaranth community meals I'd attended after working next door with students at Helping with Heart alongside Talia. The café's windows would fog up, the aromas of Ethiopian, Argentinian, or Thai cuisines filling the atmosphere as people—Walnut Hill locals to hipster suburbanites to friends of that day's chef—crowded the café. They were memories from another life, a dream.

As I sifted through some of Maa's family recipes, cross-referenced with YouTube, and experimented with spices, Kalina filmed me using her phone.

"You'd better not post those to my account." The last thing I needed was social media visibility after that night.

"Like your account would make any kind of dent. It's literally five posts."

"Which reflects that I'm busy living, not posting."

"Whatever you say," she said, uploading videos to her computer. "But we do need to spread the word."

"People will come." But saying the words got my stomach storming. The truth was, the most memorable Amaranth events featured great food, but also a chef that drew a crowd with their charisma. Who'd emerge from the kitchen to mingle with customers, charming and humble.

How could I pull that off? And who would come out for me, after everything?

"Breathe, Kriya-style." Kalina leaned over me, her eyes dark with worry.

It was the morning of Chef of the Day, and we were at the Indian grocer's getting ingredients. One moment I was selecting onions and garlic and the next I was fighting an invisible boa constrictor that was successfully squeezing my chest walls closed. My back against a cooler of chili peppers and curry leaves, I slid down to the floor.

"You're having a panic attack." Kalina said this quietly and in a way that made me wonder if she knew a thing or two about them. "Breathe through your gut."

I shook my head, sweat pouring down my face. I had no idea what that meant.

"This day," she said, "will be amazing. I mean, you're serving your gobi parathas."

But the thought of doing anything made me want to lie down and perish. As I gulped for breath, the owner of the store leaned over from the side of an aisle to peek at us. Kalina waved. "All good!" He went back to stocking the shelves, humming to the Bollywood tune jangling through the store. I wondered if customers had panic attacks in his shop on the daily.

Twenty minutes later, I was on my feet and Kalina was checking out—buttermilk, tomatoes, coriander, star anise, kokum, and jaggery powder.

"Star anise," she said, reading the package. "Pretty." She fingered the outline of the star-shaped pods that I planned to include in the kadhi. "Don't even know what that is. Genius." She smiled at me encouragingly but her eyes were dark, affected. "Time to kick ass in the kitchen."

When I stepped inside Amaranth, my airways seemed to open and the nausea vanished.

With the car unloaded, the cast-iron pots arranged, and the garlic peeled and chopped, things began falling into place. Maa arrived, and soon, she and Kalina were rolling paratha dough into balls, their palms shining with oil. After chopping vegetables for the chicken curry, buttermilk kofta kadhi, tomato chutney, and raita, I stir-fried onions with red chili peppers. Soon, I was in the zone.

It wasn't until Kalina glanced into my face with an expression that said, *Ready, brother?* that it hit me: this was happening.

People began ambling in, and by noon, the place was packed. Bennie took orders that Kya relayed to me, Kalina, and Maa, who heaped food onto plates, trying to keep up. What had Kalina gotten us into? She didn't even like cooking—it's one of those old-world expectation-duty things that made her bristle.

After an hour and a half of serving up plates, a few customers wandered near the kitchen. One man asked about ingredients and where he might get them. A woman wanted to talk about her late mother who loved to make saag paneer and how this lunch stirred up memories. A young couple asked if they could watch me cook and if I'd be hosting another Chef of the Day.

"If they'll have me," I heard myself say.

"Oh, they'll have you. Your food is the best we've had in the city." The guy shifted his gaze to Maa, addressing her. "You must be proud."

To my surprise, Maa's eyes filled with tears. "Yes."

We soon ran out of raita, so I chopped cucumber, onion, and tomatoes, folding in yogurt, salt, pepper, and sugar in record time. There was an undeniable high from feeding the masses. At one point, Kya flashed me a huge smile. "Doing good, baby. Keep working that magic. This food is beyond. Helping with Heart will be so happy."

And suddenly, I sensed the atmosphere shift. I looked past the counter to the front doors, and there it was: my old teammate Justin with Talia, two people I hadn't spoken to since that night. The two I'd been closest to, who'd sat in the car as I wrestled with what to do, their back-handed shots and my unforced error, resulting in a loss we wouldn't recover from.

"Dammit, Kalina." Blood rushed to my face. I turned, staring into her confused, troubled eyes. "What have you done?"

I often thought about how that night would have been different had we not won state.

After congrats from our coaches, the varsity team rode in TJ's minivan to Hubbard Woods, where, in a clearing along the river's edge, TJ's brother had left two coolers filled with icy cans of Old Milwaukee brew.

I'd won the best match I'd ever played, and the high was real. We moved from the parking lot through a short tunnel that ran beneath the Oak Leaf Trail, our laughter echoing against its domed walls. We were cutting up, the relief sweet after months of training and matches and tournaments. We settled upon the trunks of two fallen logs beside the coolers as the river rushed past, swift and silent. The night was warm, the scent of pine heady as we relived the highlights.

And in the way that that day held infinite possibility, Talia and Janey appeared. Both tennis players themselves, they had watched our entire tournament, sharing stories of sideline happenings. Soon enough, one cooler was empty. We started on the next.

Most of us avoided drugs for fear of their impact upon our game, or were study hounds that were gunning to get into a good college. Most of us had little opportunity to work on our alcohol tolerance.

TJ—our team captain—was heavily inebriated, obvious to me as I was pretty much sober. I was the weird one: I just wasn't into ingesting stuff that made no sense to my taste buds.

I grabbed the keys off the ground before we made our way back to the Jeep. I would serve as the designated driver. Obviously.

Approaching TJ's car, I settled into the driver's seat. Others clambered into the back.

Everyone except TJ.

What the fuck do you think you're doing? TJ stood just outside the driver's window. His words were slurred and his eyes were glassy, trying to focus on my face.

Driving, man. Get in.

He stared at me for a moment. *Like I'm letting* you *drive* my *car.*

I smiled, uncomprehending. *Um, what?*

But TJ leaned in and slammed a hand on the car door. *Get out, you terrorist.*

I froze. I took a deep breath.

You're drunk. I'm driving. Get in. I said it evenly despite the electric current in my blood.

You think you're better than everyone. But you're a terrorist like the rest of them.

A deadly calm expanded in my chest.

Sure. Drive everyone home. Have fun. I threw him the keys and climbed out.

Damon. It was Talia, her words almost as slurred as TJ's. But I barely heard her amid the blood roaring in my ears.

I'm out. My words hung in the air. Over the sudden growl of the engine, I heard TJ calling after me.

Yeah you are.

The Jeep sputtered to life as TJ turned the key in the ignition. I glanced through the car's window into the front seat, locking eyes with Talia. The car slammed into reverse. It peeled out of the lot, lurching up the sharp curve of the road and roaring out of sight. Moments later, the sickening screech of metal on metal

Then silence.

They had T-boned a parked car, totaling the Jeep and shattering Talia's right hand, along with her chances of ever playing tennis again. TJ got a DUI and lost his tennis scholarship, I got shunned by the team, and consequently I quit, receding into the dark folds of regret, escaping into my mother's kitchen as self-loathing slowly began to devour me alive.

Talia and Justin settled at a table as Bennie took their order.

"Go," Kalina said. "Whatever it is, just go."

"How did you manage to pull in the two people I am least prepared to see?"

"I can't help that my social media skills led us to capture our ideal viewers—which," she said, aligning her face so that I had no choice but to look at her, "are those who want to see you." She shoved me lightly. "Damon. You'll tell me everything later. Go."

They were seated at our old table, Talia's and mine. As I

walked toward them, my eyes locked with hers. A kaleido-scope of butterflies took flight within my chest. "Hey."

"Hey." Talia's hair was cut short, a new style that involved longer strands falling into her eyes. I tore my gaze away, bumping elbows with Justin. "It's cool to see you two," I said, as though running into them was completely chill. "How's it going?"

"Working Summerfest, practicing my problematic back-hand, the usual," Justin said. At this last part, his smile faded; he regretted the mention of tennis. I tried not to think about our evenings volleying, the dinners at Culver's, our dreams of making it to State . . .

Kalina ambled up, introducing herself. As she and Justin chatted, I stood, attempting the breathing routine Kalina had taught me that morning and praying against another panic attack .

"H-how are you?" I asked.

"Good, I guess." She smiled. "The big news is that I am now a PT Queen." Talia cupped and waved her right hand—her damaged one.

"Congratulations." I cringed. Way to be sensitive.

"I have physical therapy three times a week. It's helped. So much that I've decided to become a physical therapist myself." Her eyes shone.

"You'll make an amazing physical therapist."

She flashed a nervous smile that I knew well. She cleared her throat and gestured toward the room. "Look at this.

Who'd have guessed back in our tutoring days that you'd one day be Chef of the Day at Amaranth?" She smiled. "Serving Indian food, no less."

I considered this. "I wouldn't have. It turned into some kind of obsession—learning to make my comfort foods, maybe even improve upon them. But I kept coming up against the lack of . . . precision, I guess you'd say, in Indian cooking. Cooking with my mom was basically watching her toss stuff into a pan with zero measuring and nonexplanations."

She grinned. "Sounds fabulous. And so frustrating."

"You have no idea."

"But still, wow. You had this in you." She looked at me in a way that reminded me of old times, of our easy connection.

"I realized that subbing a spice or vegetable for whatever's on hand is part of Indian cuisine. Practically every aspect is flexible. It's like you can't really mess up."

Talia's eyes were soft. She touched my hand with her injured one, sending a shock wave through me. "Speaking of messing up: I should have spoken up that—that night."

"And I should have stonewalled the team captain and driven everyone home—even if it meant leaving him there."

"It wasn't your fault, and I don't blame you. For what it's worth," she added, her voice quiet.

The early wave of diners began filing out, the bell jingling on the door. "The others do."

"Them taking out on you the disappointment they feel in themselves? Not your problem."

233

"But I had no business leaving them—you—in that car. I didn't think—"

"That we'd get into a crash, no. None of us did. But we're all accountable for what happened. And not standing up for you in the face of TJ's hatred? It's unforgivable, actually." She hugged me as a wave of grief and relief rose inside my chest. "I hope you'll forgive me anyway," she whispered.

After I spent a few minutes talking to the guests, Justin and Talia got up to leave. Justin gave me a quick hug. "Good seeing you, man. And hey—incredible food."

Watching them go, a strange realization hit me: Maybe pain forces us to discover our hidden dimensions—new aspects of ourselves that allow us to survive. Maybe even thrive.

As the final customers left the café, Kalina was nowhere to be found.

I checked the kitchen, front walk, and car, fretting that she'd wandered off to interview random people for a new film project or something.

But soon I found her on Helping with Heart's back stoop, chatting with a girl who looked to be in middle school.

"You're moving here from *India*?" I overheard the girl ask. "Bonkers, huh?"

The girl considered this, her braids gleaming in the sunlight. "I mean, *yeah*. Why'd you leave your family for this place? Or any place, really?"

I'd have expected Kalina to laugh and say, *good question, kid*, or *why do any of us do the dumb things we do?* But in a gravelly voice I didn't recognize, she said: "Sometimes we need to escape old versions of ourselves. Sometimes we . . . hurt, and it's best to just start fresh. With new family. In a new home."

I paused in the doorway, a thali of food balanced in one hand, ashamed that it was only through eavesdropping that I could see how self-involved I'd been; I had no clue what was going on with the one person who got me. I had no idea that maybe she came here partly because she needed me.

I introduced myself to the student just as her mom texted her home for dinner. Handing Kalina the plate of food, I settled beside her.

After several beats of silence, she said, "They'd selected someone for me back home." Her voice was hoarse. "A really nice, kind someone. But I couldn't do it."

I sat, listening.

She turned to me, her eyes red. "What if I don't want to get married, ever? What if I just want to make films?" Her eyes welled. "What if what I think I want, I'll later regret?"

"What about deciding now that you don't believe in regret?"

"Damon, walking away from the guy and his family brought a lot of shame upon my parents, and even our extended family. The entire community felt—well. It's been rough."

I thought about how Kalina's parents—Sheila Mami and Vikash Mama—would shower me with their attention during my infrequent visits to India. I thought about how little beneath that surface I knew about Kalina's life. How little any of us know about the battles we fight.

"I get it," I said, though I didn't, really. "Do you think that maybe there's shame in living a life that doesn't align with who you are?" I knew I was out of my realm and a total hypocrite. "That maybe it's your right to figure out what you want, on your timeline?"

"Nice American advice," she said, grinning. "But shame? We know it too deeply, too intimately." Her smile faded. "And it can eat you alive."

I took a breath. "Yes." Kids on bikes whizzed by, a collective human rocket. "But may I point out that you're eighteen, sorely uneducated, and way too immature to promise yourself to anyone? I mean, you still sleep with a stuffed elephant."

"Ay." She shoved me. "Leave Mambo out of this." We breathed in the odor of gasoline and garbage baking in the heat. "Is now a good time to tell me what happened?"

So out it all came. How I should have stayed in the driver's seat, steady despite the taunts. How that decision led to an accident that derailed several life paths, including my own. How seeing Talia tonight was both amazing and a reminder of all I'd lost—my friendships, my team, my dignity—none of which I could imagine fully getting back.

"Hey. This wasn't your fault. Punishing yourself for the decision you made while being attacked is cruel. And speaking of cruel: Did TJ ever apologize for what he said?"

I shook my head, swallowing at the lump of charcoal in my throat.

"So instead of taking responsibility for his part," she said, her voice low, "he takes the coward route: he blames you. And as a result, *you* blame you."

"Something like that." We stare at her thali.

"It's bullshit. It also appears that Guilt and Shame are our long-lost sisters."

I broke into a grin. "I'd no idea that having sisters would suck this bad."

"Ay, sisters don't suck, man. *I'm* your sister." She spooned the kofta kadhi over the basmati rice and took a bite, the worry lines on her forehead disappearing. "Home. Right here," pointing at our meal with her spoon.

Maybe home is your family history, your country, your birthplace. Maybe it's a dish inspired by your mother's cooking, or a memory.

Or maybe it's where you hang your heart, which can be anywhere, with anyone. Maybe sometimes you forget where you put it, and just need something—or someone—to help you remember.

"Damon." She arranged three soggy star anise pods in the center of her now-empty thali. "Do you think you got your artistry from me?"

I got her into a headlock the way I did when we were kids. "Ah. A trick question."

She wriggled out from under my arm. "You did, yaar. Pretty sure." She did two kicks into the air like a Rockette, quick and dainty. Her face looked tired but her eyes gleamed in the burning afternoon light. "So, I mean, you're welcome."

KICK FLIPS IN MY STOMACH

By Nikesh Shukla

I don't know what prompted me to say "nice board" to Uzma as we passed each other in the corridor. Perhaps it was because I hadn't spoken to anyone all day, and I longed to reach out into the world and say, hi guys, I exist. Perhaps it's because she just transferred to the school a few weeks ago, midsemester, from another school, and everyone treated her like a freak.

Maybe she just looked super cool, walking toward me, dressed all in black, her skateboard hung through her backpack straps so it jutted out either side of her elbows, like wings. And it scrambled my brain. Maybe I didn't think she'd hear me, or maybe even, I meant to say it in my head and the universe decided to switch my brain voice and throat voice around.

"Nice board," I whispered.

She stopped and grabbed my arm.

The world stopped. She stared down at me. I looked up at her, though my head was bowed, as it tended to be, staring at the few inches in front of my trainers.

Feeling the intensity of her gaze scared me.

I had watched her every day since she'd started. Like me, she was always by herself. We had French and English together and we sat on opposite sides of the classroom. I would spend lessons stealing looks at her. Every now and then she'd notice I would be looking and my eyes would water with embarrassment.

She was beautiful, so quiet and still and with a serious, concentrating face. There was something about her I couldn't shake. Something I longed to get to know more. Someone who seemed as lonely as me.

"Nice board," I said again. What a cringey cretin.

"Do you skate?" she asked, an eyebrow raised, half in hope, half in elation.

I hesitated, admiring the wrecked nature of her board. Its edges splintered, the grip tape a distant memory, the wheels ground down to the axle, the design on the back of the board scuffed and plastered with stickers that had also been scuffed.

She was waiting for an answer.

"Errr . . . not really," I replied.

"Right . . ." she said. "Gotcha . . ."

She sighed, *how disappointing*, and started to move on again, toward her destination. And something in me just leapt up out of my chest, I didn't want this to end. I didn't want her to stop looking at me.

"But I've always wanted to learn . . ."

She stopped and turned to me. She looked me up and down, appreciatively. Sizing me up?

"You'll do," she said.

"What do you mean?"

"I've been looking for an apprentice. I definitely have skate master vibes, and I could do with someone to show the ropes. A willing participant. You up to it?"

She leaned in close to me. I met her eyes. Her long eyelashes, a butterfly's kiss away.

"Yes," I said. The most unequivocal yes I could give. I was caught in her tractor beam.

She looked around. Conspiratorial.

"It involves cutting. You got the stomach for that?" I nodded. "Okay, cool. Let's do it . . . You know, if you want, and you're serious or whatever . . ."

"I am," I said. "I definitely am. My name's Nish."

"Uzma," she said. She held out a hand. It was cold, cracked black nail polish holding on for dear life. "Okay, cool, so tomorrow . . . meet me at campus at 10:30 a.m."

"Oh wait. We have school . . ." I said, before regretting it immediately. I didn't want her to think I was a square. Everyone else did. She was yet to discover who I was.

She laughed. "That's what cutting means . . ."

I was embarrassed. You know when you think a thing and then you say the thing and it shows you working it all out in your head.

"I know, sorry, yes, I was just trying to work out the last time I cut," I babbled. "I don't want to establish a recognizable pattern of cutting that they can give to my dad. Say this guy is always in the wind Tuesday mornings. Where is your child? You know? It was to be erratic. A surprise. Convincing. Plausible deniability."

I was just saying things I had heard on television shows at this point.

"Sure that time's okay with you?" she asked. "It's just always really quiet at that time. And I can just concentrate, you know? Unless it establishes a pattern for you."

I stammered. "Oh, yeah, you know . . . it's . . . I had other plans to cut school later this week . . . with some other people. I guess, they won't mind if I cancel . . . Leave it with me. I'll move some things around." Oh god, lies upon lies. I had never cut school before. Dad would kill me.

She laughed, her entire face changing, suddenly, so light and easy. "Great. It's a date."

I showed up early at the skatepark. It opened at 10 a.m. and I was there at 9:55 a.m., waiting for the guy to open the door. I figured if I showed up early, maybe there was a lost property board I could borrow. Last night, I went online to find a starter skater kit and it was . . . more than double the balance in my bank account.

I dressed in my school uniform, as normal, ate two slices of toast as normal, made Dad's tea as normal, and lit a candle for Mum as normal. Everything was normal. I was normal.

Pretending at being normal made me more paranoid. Every single thing anyone said to me, I assumed was them letting me know I had been found out.

Dad asked, "You going to school today?" as I filled up a water bottle.

I panicked, a cold sweat stinging at my hair, like nettles all over my scalp.

"Of course I am, what a stupid question," I said. I pointed to my school uniform. I had a backpack with my coolest T-shirt (an Indian Spidey bootleg) and smartest jeans (black, worn once, at Mum's cremation).

"Just making conversation," he said, annoyed with me. "You've been so quiet all morning."

On my way to campus, I stopped to buy doughnuts for Uzma. I'd seen her eating a doughnut every day she rolled into school on her skateboard.

The doughnut seller asked what school I go to. I flinched. Why? Were they going to call my principal and do me in for bunking?

I made a noise like I chose not to answer, and I thought he must have assumed I was one of those sullen teenagers who did not give out information to grown-ups unless under pain of death. He gave me two doughnuts. I opted for ones with a mango and passionfruit filling. I could trade off not going to school with a nod to something resembling nutritional value.

Everything in Bristol is two buses away. Even if you live close. Two buses later, I was standing in front of campus, my body flooded with nostalgia.

It used to be the swimming pool I had learned to swim in when I was six years old. It had fallen into disrepair and then closed. Eventually it was bought by a famous skater who grew up not far from here, in Easton, and had learned to swim at this very pool, like me. Now it was a skatepark using the old pool as the bowl.

It felt jarring walking into such a familiar space and it feeling so different. I recognized photos of parts of the city that I had walked past, but not paid much attention to. In Dean Street, under the M32, out by Hotwells, like a different world existed in these same streets for skaters. There were posters of skaters, and stickers for brands, and graffiti and signs that used all this language and jargon I had no clue about.

What was a kick flip?

What was an ollie?

What were trucks and bearings and C-clips and wheelbases?

I wanted to leave. This didn't feel like a place I belonged. At all.

I closed my eyes and breathed, trying to picture a happy place, like the therapist told me to.

That's when it hit me.

For months, my happy place image was coming here. With

Mum. Forty-five minutes every Monday after school where I could feel free in the morning and Mum could take a paperback, and read it, guilt free, by the side of the pool. It's like she always knew when I was looking for her, because she would look up from the page at the exact right moment every single time and smile at me.

"You skating?" the person behind the counter asked. They wore all black, black T-shirt, black trousers, their right arm was tattooed in a black block of ink, their left had a grapevine from wrist up till it disappeared under their sleeve. Their hair was black, their eye makeup and lipstick was black.

"Buddy," they said again. I nodded. "Why don't you go get changed out of your school clothes. That way you look like you should be here. Do you need pads and a board?" I nodded again. "Cool. You don't need to give me a real name for the liability waiver but I do need it to be convincing."

"Nish Ganguly," I said. I didn't have the imagination to give a fake name. There was something in their demeanor that felt like perhaps I wasn't the first kid to do this.

I smiled and backed into the changing room.

I changed quickly, marveling at how the changing rooms had been gutted and replaced with toilets and a long bench and a couple of lockers but it still felt like the same cubicles my brother and I used to use. We were the only boys in that lesson and so had the run of the changing rooms. We'd sing and shout and play-fight and all sorts knowing we were under the radar at all times.

I emerged from the changing room and the person who'd signed me in was waiting for me with a board that looked pretty beaten up, and pads.

"Your first time?" they asked. I shook my head, vigorously. "I tightened the trucks on this for beginners but I can loosen them if you want." I shook my head again. What were trucks?

They watched as I padded up before returning their interest to their phone.

All that was left to do was wait for Uzma.

I stood, in the entrance to the empty bowl, the music thundering trap beats that echoed off the dull concrete behind me, and I held the skateboard in my hands, then clutched it to my chest, till the grip tape was catching on my T-shirt, and I waited, anxiously, padded up.

She showed up at 10:20 a.m., strode right into the park, with her long straight hair down, she wore a black T-shirt over a white T-shirt, short sleeves over long sleeves, and the T-shirts were both long and baggy. She had fingerless gloves on, and oversized khakis. Her trainers were duffed-up Vans that looked like they'd been through the wars.

She looked amazing.

It was like she walked into the place in slow motion, like she owned the place, she spudded the receptionist, said, "What's up, Sam," and took one look at me and smiled.

"You ready?" she asked.

There was an ease to her in this place that I hadn't seen in school. An ease I had not found just yet. The fact that she was so relaxed here made me more nervous.

"I am," I said, my stomach pounding. "For sure. Would you like a doughnut?"

"I love doughnuts, yes please," she said.

I pulled the paper bag out of my backpack and held it open for her to take one.

"Did you punch it?" she asked, holding up a very squashed doughnut.

"I couldn't find a stress toy," I replied, and she laughed.

She bit into the doughnut and walked past me into the bowl and beckoned for me to follow.

The concrete of the bowl was gray and the walls had been covered in murals of local skating legends. Everything about this place was of its own world. It made sense to those who knew. I didn't get the rules. How to navigate the ramps or how much I could walk or who the guys on the mural were.

"You good?" she asked me, and I nodded. I clutched my board so tight I was losing feeling in my fingers.

"I'm good," I stammered. "You do your thing. I just want to watch for a bit."

She nodded. She dropped her board onto the ground and it glided away from her. As if she was stamping, she stood on the board and pumped her foot, sending her speeding off around the perimeter of the bowl. She looked back at me, upright, straight back, straight leg to pump, arms by her sides, useless. She broke into a smile. Her arms out by her sides like wings. Like she was floating. She swayed from side to side, closed her eyes for a second before meeting my gaze and winking.

It made me realize that I hadn't had anything in my life that made me feel this way since I stopped going swimming with Mum.

Uzma suddenly jerked her board round at a right angle, and she was flying down a ramp, with abandon, her smile dropping into a concentration. I assumed she was concentrating. I studied the way she moved through the bowl and then up one side, pausing the board on the edge, clamping it down before coming off it and flicking the board back onto the side.

She carried on, dropping in like this, and cruising around the park with the utmost ease, like she was born with wheels on her feet. Glorious and exquisite. I loved watching her. It didn't matter that I was doing nothing except spectating.

I wanted to drop in, but I was scared. I knew I would fall.

I watched as two men in their forties watched her, with admiration. They were past it, gray-haired codgers, the types who still wore cool T-shirts with interesting graphics on them to show that they were still young or something. They were both padded up and one was more confident than the other. He did a ramp and then encouraged his friend to do the same thing. He even held his hand. He was patient and encouraging. I could tell they were both dads and I could tell they both were most unlike my own dad. The overweight guy was a desi, too. I loved the thought that the majority of people in this place were brown. All the photos I'd seen the night before, as I googled how to skate, were white guys in their twenties.

Uzma came and sat next to me.

"I love this place," she said. "You ever have a place that you walk in and everything in you relaxes. You just breathe a huge sigh of relief?"

"Not your bedroom?"

"I share my bedroom with my sister," she said. "It's a lot. I feel like she's watching me always. Like I'm squatting in her space."

"I learned to swim here," I said. "I haven't been swimming in so long. I remember my lessons here were like an hour away from the world, you know? It was magic. I'd jump in and then seconds later, they'd be telling us to get out. I'd realize an entire hour had passed."

"How come you don't swim anymore?" she asked, turning her head toward me.

"Look at those two guys," I said, fleeing from her gaze. "I want to be them when I grow up. They're so creaky."

She laughed.

"At least they're doing it! You ready for your first lesson?"

"I'm happy just watching today," I replied. "I'll build up to it."

"Listen, as your skate master, I will be forcing you to get on your board at some point. No arguments."

"Okay," I said, excited by the idea, terrified at the reality.

She picked up her board and held it in front of her, like we were examining a piece of art.

"This was my brother's," she said. "He saved up for ages to buy it and then injured himself pretty badly. He was supposed to get rid of it. It was banned in our house. But I grabbed it and he taught me. My sister knows I have it. She keeps threatening to tell my mum."

"Oh man," I replied. "I'm sorry. What happened to your brother?"

"Oh, he just dislocated his knee and it never healed right. He did that classic thing of just pretending the pain wasn't there for ages. He needed an operation but by the time he admitted he needed it, and got it, well, the doctors did the best they could."

"Damn, so you're carrying on the tradition?"

"Not really, this is just a good place to be in my head without being alone, you know?"

"How do you mean?"

"I grew up in a household that was so noisy. Three brothers, a sister, and me, the baby, and there was always sports on and play fighting that became real fighting and loud stereos and instruments, one of my brothers was a drummer and my parents just yelled between rooms. And since all my brothers moved out, and I'm still there, with my sister, who looks at me like I'm a spare part, it's just too quiet. I find it so unnerving being at home."

"I feel you," I said. "My house, hardly anyone speaks and

the television is always on low, with subtitles on, and my dad is listening to music in headphones."

"I overheard someone saying your mum died," Uzma said. Her knees were close to mine and I put my hands on the ground between us. My fingers brushed her fingers and she moved her hand closer to mine. I wanted to grab her hand and pull it to my cheek. Everything in me was on fire.

She put her hand on mine and I flinched, immediately pulling my hand back. I didn't mean to, but something flinched in me.

"Sorry," she said. "That's too intrusive. I shouldn't have said anything."

"Why did you ask me to come here?" I asked. Maybe it was our hands touching. Maybe I just wanted to push away anything that seemed nice. "I don't skate, we've never spoken, this is your space. Why me?"

"Why did you say 'nice board'?" she asked. She shrugged. Took a deep breath. "When you reached out, you know you were the first person to speak to me that week? Maybe ever. It was nice being seen, I guess."

"I wish I could walk the corridor like you do. Like you don't care."

"I do care," she said. "Maybe too much. I dunno, it was just nice . . . you know? To be seen by someone as sad as you."

We fell into another silence.

"Mum died last year," I confessed. "Some days it feels like it happened a lifetime ago, some days seconds ago. I keep waiting to get to that point where I don't feel as sad about it, but it never comes. She was in a lot of pain for a long time, and this just feels better than being in pain. She was never going to get better. That doesn't make me feel any better."

"It's okay to feel sad," she said.

"Yeah, I know," I replied. "The things I miss are so stupid. I miss her picking me up from school and us chatting about soccer. She loved the Premier League. Or when I'd just woken up, and she'd sweep me up into a hug like I was still her baby. Or the smell of her home-cooked food."

"I'm sorry," Uzma said. "If you ever want home-cooked food, my mum still cooks like there are three strapping boys in the house."

"Thanks," I said, laughing. "My dad's useless. He can only make omelettes. I'm so sick of omelettes."

I mimed a retching sound.

We watched the two old men try the big ramp. The less confident one tried the ramp for the first time and he nailed it. He whooped in delight, so happy, so pleased.

We watched him try it again and again, he nailed it and was happy. Uzma grabbed my hand and squeezed it.

I stood up, pulling her up with me.

"I want to drop in," I said.

"Oh, just like that?" Uzma replied. "The apprentice has become the master."

"Just like that," I said, smiling. "The apprentice is ready to learn."

"Sure?"

"You make it look easy. He makes it look achievable."

She laughed and skated off, taking a steep ramp and then attempting an ollie at the bottom. She landed right and the board was flipped but there wasn't enough air between her and the board, so her landing clamped it down. The board shuddered and she stood off it. She skated it back toward my direction.

I approached the ramp and waited patiently. One of them gestured to me.

"Go for it, boss," he said. And I shook my head. I needed to see him do it one more time.

Uzma was next to me. She held my hand. When she let go, I held the board in front of me and got ready to place it on the ground and stand on it.

The confident old man took the ramp and shouted "Boom" at the bottom, before swinging into a circuit of the entire bowl, back up to his friend. The friend looked at me and then at Uzma and smiled encouragingly.

He stepped onto the board and took the ramp, going down with speed and confidence. At the bottom he pumped his fists in the air, and was going so fast, he approached a mini ramp at the bottom. He clipped the side of it and in order to steady himself, he stepped his back foot off the board. Except he missed the ground and stepped back onto the board.

He fell.

He fell bad. He bounced three times, first on his side, then on his hip, and then on his bottom, slamming into the concrete, the cruel gray concrete that holds no prisoners.

It looked painful. He was on his back and still. Spluttering.

It was terrifying. If he wasn't wearing a helmet, he would be dead. He would have smacked his head into the concrete.

"Yo," Uzma said.

"Damn," I said, a sudden urge to sit down, my entire body heavy.

The man started laughing, shifting onto his side. In pain. A lot of pain. But he was laughing at the whole thing. With utter joy. With abandon. Like a child being tickled by a loved grandparent.

I turned to Uzma. "I saw they do pizzas next door. Shall we go eat?"

"Definitely. Pizza and skating, a perfect date," she said, and everything in me lilted and lurched. It was a date! A date! She called it a date!

"Wanna drop in one last time and then we go?" I said.

"Sure," she replied.

I stood watching her, smiling. I looked around the swimming pool. I could see the opaque windowed ceiling above us, letting light in. I remembered swimming here all those years ago, staring at those tiles and feeling completely at peace. It was nice to see they were still there.

I placed the board on the floor, watching it rolling away from me. I stood on it, one Bambi leg then another, pushing down with all my weight.

I stood on the board. I was standing. It swayed forward and I stood still, getting used to the motion beneath me. I felt unsteady but I was firm. I looked up, expecting Mum to look up from her book at the exact right time to smile at me.

She wasn't there.

Uzma, instead, cruising through the middle of the bowl, punched the sky and cried out "woo-hoo" in my direction. I punched my hand in the air back at her.

I wobbled, falling backward, shouting "woo-hooo" as the ground raised up its hands to catch me. I lay on the floor, listening to Uzma's laughter echoing around the pool.

I laughed too. Joy coursed through me, reminding me of a long-forgotten feeling.

NO TASTE LIKE HOME

By Nisha Sharma

The Hartceller University post office was a fifteen-minute shuttle ride from the west campus freshman dorms. Located above the bookstore, the facility was way too small to support thousands of full-time students.

Based on the advice she'd read on campus message boards, Reet Kumar had shipped her online textbook order to her parents' house. But Reet had gotten a notification before her first day of classes that a package was waiting for her to pick up, so now she had no choice but to join the serpentine line that stretched across the entire second level of the Davis Building.

The whole expedition wouldn't have felt like such a waste of time if Reet knew what was in the package. Her parents had apparently sent the box three days ago, the same day as her flight. When she'd called them on FaceTime and asked what was inside, they refused to tell her.

"Reet, your packing lists were comprehensive, but we realized there were some things missing from them," her mother had said, her accent softened with years in her multigenerational, multicultural Seattle community.

Her father had to lean down to fit in the video-call frame. "We wanted to make sure you had everything you needed, beta."

Her parents' words were ridiculous because Reet already *had* everything she needed. She'd been looking forward to college since she started high school. She'd applied early decision, then after securing an acceptance to her number one school, she watched every YouTube video, read every Reddit post, checked every hashtag. She memorized campus maps, and purchased everything for her room, her classes, her new life almost two full months before her move-in day.

Which meant her parents had sent something they *thought* she needed instead, rendering this whole mail room experience a total dud.

Because, obviously, they were wrong.

As the line inched forward, she tried to guess what her very practical, very *westernized* mother could've mailed her. Reet was a proud third-generation latchkey South Asian kid. She had zero delusions when it came to her parents. They weren't the coddling type.

Well, her mother wasn't the coddling type. Her father had

subtle ways of showing his affection. He was probably the one who came up with the idea to send her a package her first week of college.

Maybe it was a fat check so that she didn't have to find work study for extra cash.

Reet snorted absently. Like her parents would send her cash. They believed that she had to earn everything she got.

"Kumar!" a voice called out from behind the long desk at the far end of the mail room.

"Present!" Reet responded just as another voice yelled, "Here!"

She whirled around and came face-to-face with a very tall, very gorgeous desi student wearing a backward hat that said *Hartceller U Tennis.* He had a long, lean frame with wide shoulders covered with the thick straps of his black backpack. His chiseled jaw was model-like, and he had flecks of gold in his deep brown eyes.

He looked down at Reet, his crooked grin revealing a small dimple at the corner of his mouth. "I don't think I've ever been confused for another Kumar before," he said.

Reet shrugged. "I'm from the Seattle suburbs. In my class, I was Kumar number three."

"Well now, you're only Kumar number two."

"*Excuse* you, I am Kumar number one now. You are Kumar number two." In reality, they were probably Kumar numbers 76 and 77 considering they were in New Jersey, but in this moment, she was claiming her title.

"Why do you get to be one?" he said, crossing his arms over his chest.

Holy cow, even his forearms had definition. She wondered what it would be like to trace the curve of muscle even as she replied, "You just said yourself that you've been the only Kumar because this has never happened to you before. I deserve the chance to be number one now."

"What if there are more Kumars at the school than just the two of us?" he asked, one dark brow arching almost to the brim of his hat.

"I've factored that in already, and they don't matter right now," she said. It was a ridiculous thing to say, and she knew it from the grin on his face.

"There is a package for a second Kumar!" the attendant behind the desk shouted. He had two almost-identical boxes in Hartceller University bags sitting on the counter in front of him.

Reet and Kumar number two raised their hands again.

"We should probably retrieve those," Reet said.

"Agreed. I'm Kavin by the way."

"Kah-veen, like Kavita?"

His dark brown eyes widened. They were as rich as the deep color of his skin. "Yes! Exactly. Family is Tamilian. You?"

"Reet. My grandmother told me it means culture or something. I'm Punjabi. Third-gen."

"No way," Kavin said with a grin. "First. Moved to Ohio when I was three. This is my first year."

"I'm first year, too," she said, smiling. She didn't recall seeing him at orientation the week before, and was about to say something to that effect, but they'd finally made it through the crowd of waiting students who had already signed in to receive their packages.

"IDs please," the attendant said. He was a burly bald man wearing a blue vest and sporting a sheen of sweat on his forehead and nose.

They slid their IDs forward. The attendant scrunched his nose, as if he was trying to make sense of the names.

"Yeah, these are you two," he said. "Kevin and Rit."

"It's Kavin."

"It's Reet."

The attendant didn't respond, and instead slid both boxes forward without further explanation. Reet grabbed the box closest to her and stepped to the side so she could get out of the way. Kavin did the same.

Before she could ask him where he was staying, what his major was, anything to keep the conversation going, a sharp, shrill ringing blistered the air. He dug into his short pockets and retrieved his cell phone.

"Shit, it's my dad," Kavin said. He smiled in her direction and waved his phone at her. "Nice meeting you . . . Kumar number one."

"Likewise, Kumar number two," she said. And then he was gone with a phone pressed to his ear and the large Hartceller bag in hand.

"What are you even thinking?" Reet mumbled to herself, then shook her head. A few days in and she was already struck speechless by a guy. If she wasn't careful, she'd lose sight of everything that she'd worked so hard to achieve. No, Reet thought to herself. She was going to make her family proud. She was going to make *herself* proud.

And that meant that she had to steer clear of anyone who could get in her way.

Kavin was still thinking about Reet Kumar when he walked into his dorm room twenty minutes later. He wished that his father hadn't interrupted, but since Kavin had been waiting all day to find out if his mother needed another round of chemo, he wasn't going to ignore the call.

In retrospect, he should've sent it to voicemail, so he had time to brace himself for the news.

The cancer isn't gone yet, Kavin. But they're hopeful. I am, too.

Damn, he wanted to be home in Ohio. He planned on deferring a semester, but his entire family had sat him down for an intervention and told him he was a fool to pass up a tennis scholarship at one of the most prestigious tech schools on the East Coast.

Now he looked down at the plastic bag and rubbed at his chest to ease some of the ache. Just what he needed. A reminder of what he left behind.

Kavin slowly removed the bag and froze when he saw the hearts drawn around a mailing label.

His Tamilian mother had never drawn hearts on a cardboard box in his life.

"Uh-oh," he muttered to himself. Then he examined the label closer and saw that he'd picked up the wrong care package.

REET KUMAR.

He'd retrieved Kumar number one's package. He grinned as he remembered their interaction. Kumar number one. At least he had the opportunity to see her again.

Because he definitely needed to swap the packages. He didn't know how many care packages his mother had in her, and he wanted to enjoy every single one while he still had a chance.

"Was it crowded?" Reet's roommate Maria said from her cross-legged position on the twin bed pushed up against the far wall. She was tying her long brown hair in twin French braids, a calculus textbook laid open in front of her. "I ordered some more books online and I just got an email that said they're ready for pickup."

"I was waiting about ten minutes once I checked in," Reet said as she dropped her care package on her desk across the room. She immediately pushed the plastic bag away and retrieved her scissors from the top drawer. "I met a guy."

Maria's eyes widened. "I mean you need to girl boss your way through the comp sci program here, but that doesn't mean you can't look. Tell me everything."

"There isn't much to tell. We were both called up to the desk at the same time. We have the same last name." She quickly slid one of the ends of her scissor blades along the side of the box to cut the tape, then did the same along the top. "He was wearing a Hartceller University Tennis hat. Very tall. Lean frame. Broad shoulders. The kind of jaw that they talk about in books. Gorgeous dark skin."

"Ooh," Maria said with a sigh. "I can already picture you two together. You'd . . . fit."

"Well, stop because that's where things ended. His dad called, and he left."

"Family man," Maria said. "I appreciate that." She tied the end of a braid, closed her textbook, and then slid off her bed. "As much as I like a meet-cute, I appreciate homemade snacks even more. Do you think your mom sent you some delicious stuff? What did you get?"

Reet was still thinking about Kavin's smile when she pushed the flaps back to reveal neatly packaged jars, bags, and containers.

What in the world?

"It smells great," Maria said, taking a strong sniff of the contents.

"It does, but it also doesn't smell . . . right." There was something about the combo of spices and contents that was both familiar yet unfamiliar to her.

She picked up what looked like a hard snack in a spiral shape. She'd seen it before, but at a family friend's house.

A South Indian family friend's house.

"Oh no," Reet said, dread pooling in her gut. "Oh no, oh no, oh no." She dropped the bag of snacks back in the box and closed the flaps so she could check the mailing label.

KAVIN KUMAR.

"What's wrong?" Maria asked, glancing at the label. "Oh, yikes. You got the cute guy's box instead of your own. *And* you opened it."

"Maria, this is technically mail fraud, right? I mean, this is definitely mail fraud." She gasped. "Oh my god, I could go to jail."

"Don't be so dramatic," Maria said, rolling her eyes. "You have his name. Just look him up in the student directory and send him an email. Let him know it was an accident. It's not like you *ate* his snacks."

Reet shook her head, her long ponytail whipping back and forth. "God no! Then I'd definitely go straight to jail." Though she was tempted. Would he notice if just one tiny little snack pouch was missing? It smelled so good.

Because the temptation was intense, she carefully closed the box, wrapped it in the mail center bag, and moved it to the floor so she could access her computer. Reet had just pulled up the school portal when she got a new email notification.

Incoming message from Kavin Kumar.

Maria leaned over her shoulder to look closer at her screen. "Looks like he beat you to the punch. What does his email say?"

Reet could feel her heart beating faster and she had absolutely no idea why. She glanced back at the box, and then at the email notification. Did he open up her care package by accident, too?

She clicked on the notification, and the email window popped up.

Kumar Number One,

You have something that belongs to me. Until I get it back, I'm holding your care package hostage. You have until 0-800 hours tomorrow to return the contraband, otherwise I'll be opening your mail and keeping whatever items you've received from this Seattle address.

Sincerely,

Kumar Number Two

"He has a sense of humor!" Maria said, her voice filled with excitement as she patted Reet on the shoulder. "Tell him that you'll meet him, and then you'll take him out to dinner or something afterward."

"What happened to girlbossing?" Reet muttered.

"Girl boss later. Right now, you have a meet-cute to follow up on, Kumar number one."

After a moment of hesitation, Reet hit the reply button. "Okay, Kumar number two. Let's try this again."

Kumar Number Two,

Let's meet in the quad. That way we can exchange goods out in the open without any funny business. Seventeen hundred hours. Below is my phone number in case that time doesn't work for you.

Reet

Kavin stood at the edge of the large green park space in the middle of campus. It was surrounded by the student center, the library, and the computer science buildings. The student government committee was setting up for the activities fair scheduled for Monday afternoon, and a few upperclassmen were lying in the grass under the brilliant early September sun, propping their book bags behind their heads like pillows.

He could see himself doing the same thing.

He wondered if Kumar number one, with her shiny black hair, big brown eyes, and compact dancer frame, was the type to lie out in the sun. She vibrated with so much energy, he could see her getting impatient and moving on to do the next big thing on a list.

But then again, he'd only spent a minute in her company. He could've read her all wrong. The question was, did he want to get to know more about her? Between tennis and worrying about his family and keeping his grades up, he didn't exactly have a lot of time for something serious. At least that's what he'd told himself before school started.

"I'm sorry I'm late!" a rushed voice said from behind him. He turned to face Reet, her face flushed, ponytail sliding over her shoulders, holding a large box in her arms. She placed it gently at their feet next to the box he'd brought with him, then she dropped her backpack to the ground. "I'm on the west side of campus in the freshman dorms near the river. The shuttle wasn't working, so I had to walk the twenty minutes here with the box."

"Shit, I'm sorry," he said as he looked down at the box and back up to Reet's face. She was out of breath from the trip, and he hated that he hadn't considered how far she was located from their meeting spot. "I could've come to you."

She waved a hand. "I need to get used to it. I have a feeling it's going to happen again. And it was my penance."

Kavin raised a brow. "Why do you need penance?"

He saw the guilt painted all over her expression before she spoke. Tugging at the hem of her tank top emblazoned with the university logo, she said, "I didn't read the mailing label before I opened the box. I'm so sorry! I didn't take anything out. Well, I mean I saw one of the snacks and then knew right away it wasn't from my mom and I put it back."

The thought of snacks from his mother had his mouth watering. "What kind of snacks?"

Reet shrugged. "I'm not exactly an expert in South Indian snacking."

Well, he definitely was, Kavin thought. He hunkered down, flipped open the box that she'd secured with a thin strip of regular masking tape, and immediately found the murukku.

"Score!" he shouted and popped open the baggie so he could remove one of the crispy fried disk-shaped treats. He immediately bit the end, savoring the salty spice that he'd loved since he was a kid. He pictured his mother using the small, metal cylinder with a crank handle to squeeze out thin strips of dough in a spiral pattern before carefully lowering them into hot oil. She knew she shouldn't be on her feet so much, but she made these for him with love.

He'd never missed home as much as he did right at that moment on the quad in New Jersey, hundreds of miles away from his hometown in Ohio.

"Try it," he said, and held out the murukku for Reet. He wanted to share this taste of home, and maybe the burden that came with being so far away from those he loved.

Reet hesitated for a moment, then reached in, and retrieved the smallest end of a single piece. She tossed it into her mouth and her eyes went wide.

"Good, right?" he said.

"Oh my god, I bet you can get addicted to these things," she said after chewing and swallowing.

"If I'm not careful, I'll finish off this whole box within the next two days."

"Oh yeah?" she said, and then peered over the open flap. "Is the whole thing snack food?"

He grinned. "You really didn't look?"

She shook her head. "Kumar number two, that's technically illegal."

"It's not if I let you," he said.

Her smile brightened her whole face, and it made sharing his precious murukku worth it. But when she leaned over to inspect more of his mother's care package closer, he immediately slapped the flaps closed.

"Wait a minute, Kumar number one," he said slyly. "If I show you mine, you have to show me yours, too." He motioned to the second box that sat next to them. "I, unlike yourself, checked the mailing label so I have no idea what's inside."

"To be honest," Reet started, "neither do I. But we can fix that right now."

She picked up her box and bag and moved off the path at the edge of the green and into the sun. Then she dropped her things and folded her muscled legs into a pretzel as she sat down. He'd joined her just as she removed a set of keys from the hook on her bag and used the sharp edge to cut the tape.

"Does your mom always draw hearts on mailing labels?" he asked once she'd cut through most of the tape.

"She doesn't," Reet said softly. Then she paused to look at the drawings, running her fingers over the edge of one of the tiny little signs of love. "This is the handiwork of my dad. He used to draw hearts on my napkins for my school lunch. He's usually as practical as my mother, but I wondered if he'd have a difficult time adjusting to my move across the country."

"Why did you choose Hartceller?" he asked. "There are a ton of great schools out west."

"Hartceller has a comp sci program with a ton of alumni who work in government and innovation. I also got financial aid and an opportunity to join the fusion Kathak dance team. I studied Kathak my entire life, so I wanted to go to a school where I could dance, too."

"I got a tennis scholarship," he said as he rested his fore-arms on his knees. He'd sat next to her on the grass, a few inches away. "My family is in Ohio. I have a feeling I'll be getting a few more of these boxes from my mother when she's thinking of me since I can't visit as often as I want. It looks like you might be in the same boat."

Reet pushed back a crinkle of blush-pink tissue paper and picked up a slim white card.

Her name was written in her mother's no-nonsense, impa-tient handwriting.

"I guess both of my parents are in on this," she said, amused as she touched the dried ink. "This is so unlike them. They're just not . . . sentimental."

"If they're not the sentimental type, then why did they send you a care package?"

Reet shrugged. "Mom went to college in Chicago. That's where she met my dad. My parents probably saw their friends get care packages when their immigrant parents never sent them anything, so they feel like they should do the same." She held up the card, as if debating whether or not to read it at all.

"Do you want me to go so you can read that in private?"

"Stay," Reet said, her voice going soft. "I feel like this is just as much your note."

Kavin looked at his box, wondering what his mother would tell him if she wrote him a note, too.

It would probably only include two simple words.

Eat something.

Translation: I love you. I miss you. I hope this reminds you of all the times I've fed you with my own hands, and you think of me while you enjoy it.

Reet lifted the envelope flap and removed the card.

She scanned over the scrawled text, and she tilted her head back, bursting out in laughter. The sound was like music. A few neighboring groups of students turned to look in their direction with smiles.

Kavin was just as enchanted. Reet, on the other hand, was completely oblivious to his reaction. She turned the card to show him what it said.

Don't forget to eat.

This time he laughed. "North or South," he said. "It doesn't matter which type of desi mom, they're always preoccupied with making sure we eat. What did you get?"

Reet looked inside the box, and then paused. A slow smile spread across her face. "Want to play a game?"

He grinned. Who was this sunny, yet serious girl? She was full of discovery, just like the items in their boxes. "I'm always ready to play a game."

"I show you one treat from my North Indian household, you show me one from the South."

"Deal," Kavin said immediately. "I know my South Indian snacks are going to kick your snacks out of the park."

"We'll see about that," she said with a snort. Then she shifted in the grass so that she was facing him. They positioned their boxes at their hips and reached in at the same time.

"Ready?" she asked.

"One, two, three, draw!"

Reet should have been back in her room, finishing homework for her first day of class. There was also an Indian Association welcome party at one of the Greek houses later that night she was thinking about attending. But right now, she wanted to spend more time with Kavin.

At the sound of the word "draw," she reached in the box and removed a bag filled with a brown powder with cashews and raisins.

He removed a bag filled with puffy fried donut-shaped food.

"Panjiri!" she said with a smile.

"Medu vada," he replied with equal excitement. He looked down at the bag and touched it reverently. "My mother must've overnighted this or something. It lasts a few days but gets soft. This is still pretty crispy."

There was something about his face that had her pausing. As much as she wanted to tear open the bag and pour the panjiri straight into her mouth, she waited a beat, then nudged his knee. "What is it?" she asked.

He shook his head. "My mom shouldn't be on her feet for so long. Making all this food takes time and energy that she doesn't have."

Reet wanted to ask, but they'd just met a couple hours ago. She didn't have a right to his secrets yet. "We can stop . . ."

Kavin took a medu vada from the pouch and tore it in half. The daal stuffing smelled rich and spicy as Reet took the piece.

"My mom has cancer," he finally said. "She just finished her first round of chemo, but they didn't get it all. They're going to change her treatment and do something a little more aggressive. She's lost her hair, and she's losing energy. She is also going in for a double mastectomy in a couple weeks."

"Kavin," she said softly. "I know this is the most useless thing to say, but I'm so sorry you're going through that."

"I am, too," he said. "And it's not useless." He reached out and tapped his half of the vada against hers. They both bit into the crispy fried dough's outer layer and the rich soft daal filling at the same time.

"Your mom sounds amazing," she said, her mouth full. "But holy shit, is this spicy."

"Yeah," he said, swallowing. "Too spicy?"

She popped the rest of the vada in her mouth, chewed and swallowed. "It's just enough to burn my tongue, so no. And it sets us up for some meethi panjiri."

She took his hand, feeling the strong fingers underneath hers as she shaped his palm into a cup. Then she poured a small mound of panjiri into the makeshift cup.

"Toss it back," she said, then poured herself some of the mixture before she opened her mouth wide and slid the contents from her palm onto her tongue. It melted exactly like the sweet, toasted brown sugar should. She got the crunch of cashew and the chew of raisins in the mix, and she was in heaven.

"Oh my god," Kavin groaned after he licked his palm clean. "Vada and panjiri? This is like the perfect snack mix ever. Do Indians know this?"

"I'm sure they do," Reet said with a laugh. And then she looked into her box again. "Ready for the rest?"

"Sure," he said, dusting his hands off into the grass.

One by one they revealed the contents of their boxes.

More North and South Indian snack mixes.

Then there was chaat masala and rasam powder.

Instant idli mix with freeze-dried daal makhani.

Mango thoku and mango achchar.

Reet looked at the mason jar, wrapped in Saran wrap, then in another layer of protected plastic. The memory of different pickles lining a pantry shelf flooded her heart and squeezed her lungs.

"Reet?" Kavin's voice was gentle, as soft as the subtle breeze that blanketed the quad.

"My parents may not be sentimental," she said softly, "but they always know when I need to be. Is it weird that I'm already homesick?"

Kavin hummed. "Mango pickle will do that to a person."

Reet looked up at his smiling face, then hugged the jar to her chest. "I thought it would be easy saying goodbye. I've waited for this for so long. To just leave, get started, be my own person. I felt . . . stifled at home. I don't even know why. I thought that by coming out here, I would have the freedom to just be whatever I wanted. But my family is so much a part of who I already am . . ."

She put the jar back in the box, chest tight at the thought of her parents sitting in front of the TV, watching the latest episode of *Jeopardy!*

Kavin reached out, palm up. On instinct, she placed her hand in his, and tried not to blush when he flexed his grip in reassurance.

They sat in silence, their care package goods strewn between them until finally Kavin clasped his other hand over their joined ones. "I have an idea," he said. "Well, I have two."

She worked up the courage to squeeze his hand back. "Tell me."

"The first one is that we tell our moms that our roommates absolutely loved the snacks in our care packages."

Reet raised a brow. "Okay. Why?"

"Because that will guarantee that we will get more of these. Then we can schedule a monthly quad meeting where we do a North and South snack exchange. That way, when we start to feel homesick, we can support each other. But don't tell my team that, otherwise they'd be pissed that I didn't lean on them, too."

The thought that he wanted to see her again, so much so that he'd schedule it out in the future without an end date in sight, was . . . thrilling. She pulled her hand out from between his before her palm started to sweat.

"What's the second idea?" she asked.

He turned his hat backward, and smiled at her in such a cheerful way that she knew that he was purposely trying to be charming. "I think we should pack up our care packages, drop them off at our rooms, and go out for Indian food tonight. To celebrate, I don't know. Something new. That is, if your boyfriend or girlfriend doesn't mind?"

She had to sit on her hands to stop from flapping them around like an idiot. Had she ever been asked out before? And had anyone this kind ever done the asking? She was pretty sure the answer to that was a no.

Well, there was that one time in kindergarten with David Chang, but he moved away right after the first grade.

"What kind of Indian food?" she asked. "North or South?"

"There is actually a Sri Lankan place that my roommates raved about yesterday. Want to try different desi altogether?"

"Yeah, that sounds like neutral territory," she said, then

began packing up her box as he did the same. "I am still hungry even though we've been sampling everything."

"Me too," he said. Then he reached down to help her to her feet. Even though she didn't need it, she accepted his help anyway.

They both started walking in the general direction of the shuttle stop.

"Hey, is your girlfriend or boyfriend going to mind if you have dinner with me?" she asked.

He gently bumped into her arm. "I wouldn't have asked if I had a girlfriend, Kumar number one," he said.

Reet smiled, and listened as he started to talk about all his favorite foods he hoped he'd find in New Jersey.

When they got to the Sri Lankan restaurant an hour later, they were still talking about the places they loved in their hometowns, and their mothers' cooking.

"Can I ask you a question, Kumar number one?" Kavin said as he held open the restaurant door for her.

"Yes, Kumar number two," she replied as she walked through. "I'll even keep it in the Kumar code of conduct if you want."

"No need," he replied casually. "I just wanted clarification. Is this our first date?"

Reet stopped in her tracks, aware of his hand at the small of her back. She looked up at Kavin and realized that for the first time since they opened their packages and he mentioned his mother, he wasn't smiling at her.

"Do you want it to be?" she asked.

"Only if you want it to be."

She thought about everything that she had planned to do once she reached college. She had made zero room for distractions. But then again, her mother had always told her to plan for surprises, too, and Kavin was most definitely a surprise.

Thanks, Mama.

"Yeah," she finally said, her words slow and cool. "I really want this to be our first date."

"Great," Kavin said, letting out a breath. "That's awesome." Then he linked his fingers with hers. "I'm so glad our packages got mixed up."

"Me too, Kavin," she said. "Me too."

THE WAY IT WAS SUPPOSED TO BE

By Veera Hiranandani

THE END.

It wasn't the New Year's Sita was supposed to have.

She expected to be watching the ball drop on TV with her parents and her brother on the living room couch. Instead, she stood in the Taj Mahal Hotel in Mumbai, seconds before midnight.

THE BEGINNING.

Lisa wasn't the friend she was supposed to have.

Sita had a few other close friends before Lisa. There was her first best friend, Dana. They met in kindergarten. But things got sticky when Dana turned out to be a pathological liar.

After that, she became friends with two girls in her neighborhood, Amy and Suki. They were also their own brand of misfits, and for Sita, this was starting to become a familiar space. They all joined the math club together even though Sita wasn't very good at math. Then there was an incident in a math competition freshman year when Sita didn't prepare very well and they lost. So Amy and Suki decided they were smarter than Sita, which they probably were, and moved on to bigger and better math competitions. Sita spent tenth grade in a soupy blur of a few almost-friendships and many weekend nights watching movies on the couch with her parents.

Sita met Lisa on a particularly lonely Sunday at the beginning of her junior year after she decided to take an uncharacteristic walk. Her parents had both cars, her father driving Vikram to swim practice, her mother at the tennis bubble. She had watched way too much TikTok and her eyes felt like they were spinning around in her head, so she pulled on a hoodie and left her phone at home.

The late September sun felt warm on her back, the wind cool on her face, and she was glad she managed to tear herself away from the grip of her phone. At the end of their long driveway, she made a left onto the main road instead of a right in order to avoid walking past Amy's and Suki's houses. Lisa lived about a half-mile down the street in the opposite direction. When she was friends with Amy and Suki, they never considered trying to become friends with Lisa, who wore her shiny blond hair in a high ponytail down her back, whose family owned a stable of horses, who had an older brother and a younger sister who were also golden-haired and popular.

She could see the horse ring from the road and Lisa was riding a white horse, gently bouncing up and down in the saddle. Sita stopped near a tree to watch, hoping Lisa wouldn't notice her. Lisa pulled up on the reins and positioned herself in front of one of the jumps. Then she squeezed her heels into the horse and it cantered toward the jump, but Sita could tell something was off the way it kicked out its back legs and flicked its tail. Still, the horse barreled forward. She heard Lisa call "Whoa," but the horse didn't slow down. Then, just before the jump, it stopped short. Lisa, however, kept on going. She flew over the jump, landing hard on her side. The horse bucked and ran off to the other end of the ring, finally coming to a stop. Lisa lay still on her back. A few seconds went by and then a few more, but she didn't move.

"Hey!" Sita called, stepping out from behind the tree, her heart speeding up. "You okay?"

Nothing.

She felt an electric panic jolt through her body. What if Lisa was unconscious? She didn't even have her phone to call 911. Sita climbed over the fence and ran the hundred feet or so to where Lisa lay in the middle of the ring. She glanced back at the horse who was peacefully chewing on its bit in the shade of a large oak tree. It was only when she stood over Lisa that she saw the smile on Lisa's face.

"Are you all right?" Sita asked, now more confused than panicked.

"I think so," Lisa said, "but the sky looked so blue. I just wanted to stay here."

Sita was surprised that a girl with such a sunny life, at least from the outside, cared about a blue sky. It always seemed to Sita that the people who noticed things like blue skies or pretty views were trying to cheer themselves up.

Lisa lifted her head and propped herself up on her elbows. "Penelope is trying to kill me," she said.

"Who's Penelope?" Sita asked.

Lisa pointed over to the horse who was now eating grass like a cow in a pasture. "That bitch," she said. "But I love her anyway." Her voice lowered an octave and her eyes narrowed. "It was nice of you to check on me. If I had been really hurt, you might have saved my life."

Sita felt her cheeks get hot, from both the praise and the embarrassment of being looked at so carefully by Lisa Harvey.

"Do you live on this street?" Lisa asked. "Or are you my guardian angel?"

Her heart sank. *I've lived down the street from you my entire life,* Sita thought.

"Yes, about a half a mile that way," she said, pointing. "Next to the Rothchilds' house."

Lisa nodded, but didn't seem surprised. Sita wondered what aspect of her had made her invisible to Lisa all these years. Her brown skin? Her Indian name? Not belonging to any of the local churches? Her years in the math club? All of the above?

Lisa held out her hand. "Help me up?"

There was a part of Sita that wanted to say no and walk away, that someone like Lisa didn't deserve her friendship after ignoring her all this time. And yet, here Lisa was asking her for help, inviting her in, the sun only making Lisa's hair shine more. Sita couldn't turn away. No one turned away Lisa Harvey. She looked into Lisa's eyes and did what she thought she was supposed to do. She smiled and reached out her hand.

SEVERAL WEEKS LATER.

The red-and-black dress wasn't the dress she was supposed to have. On a trip to the mall with Lisa, she saw it on a mannequin in Macy's. She saw it way before they reached the store. It felt like the mannequin was beckoning to her. She started to walk faster.

"Wait up," said Lisa as she tried to finish her shake, but Sita kept walking.

Now that Sita was sixteen, her parents said she needed an after-school job for extra spending money. Occasionally her mother would give her $20 for snacks at the mall and she did buy Sita a pair of Lululemon leggings last year for her birthday, but normally it was only approved clothes from T.J. Maxx or Old Navy. If Sita wanted unapproved clothes or makeup— she needed her own money.

When Sita showed Lisa the dress, Lisa said she had to try

it on. They rushed over to the saleslady and asked for her size. Finally, in the dressing room she looked at herself in the big mirror. The fitted shimmery red bodice and the black satin miniskirt flattered both her long legs, slim shoulders, and smaller chest in the most perfect way. Sita felt like she could transcend high school in the dress.

Lisa froze when she emerged from the dressing room, her eyes opened wide.

"I can't believe how good you look!" Lisa exclaimed.

"Don't sound so shocked," Sita said, trying to sound playful.

"I'm not," Lisa said, but it seemed to Sita like she was. That's the way Lisa always said nice things to her, these little backhanded compliments that Sita felt forced to thank her for. Lisa tended to take on a new best friend every year and teach them how to be popular. Last year it was the Italian foreign exchange student, Lucia. Now *she* was Lisa's new project and Lisa toured her life with a strange fascination that made Sita feel both special and uncomfortable.

"You have to buy this for Winter Formal!" Lisa said, as Sita spun around in front of the mirror.

She stopped twirling and sighed. "I don't have the money. Or a date."

"I'll buy it for you and you can pay me back whenever," Lisa said, holding out her mother's credit card. "And you'll totally get a date."

It was tempting, but she wouldn't be able to pay her back. She didn't want to feel like she owed Lisa anything.

"That's so nice," Sita said, "but I'll talk to my mom about it." She took the dress off and left it hanging on the back of the dressing room door.

A few weeks later, Sita invited Lisa over for dinner. Her family had ordered takeout from the Indian restaurant in town. Lisa said she was excited to taste Indian food for the first time. Sita wondered how anyone got to be sixteen and never tasted Indian food especially since there were two good restaurants nearby. Lisa sat at their dinner table gobbling up the samosas, the palak paneer, the aloo gobi, the onion naan. Then she sat back and announced that it tasted much better than she thought it would. Sita saw her father raise his eyebrows to her mother when Lisa wasn't looking, but Sita ignored it. She wasn't giving up on Lisa. She wasn't giving up the chance to finally see what it was like to be in the center of things.

After, they watched a movie and baked cookies. It got so late that Lisa ended up staying over. Sita hadn't had a sleepover since she was in middle school, but it was fun to snuggle under the thick comforter on the pullout couch in the den, feeling safe and close. They lay in bed scrolling through people's feeds, gossiping about who they liked and who they didn't. Sita noticed that Lisa liked to critique people's clothes, body types, and had makeover ideas for everyone. Lately, she had started giving Sita advice on what to wear, too. Lisa put her phone down and turned on her side facing Sita.

"Do you feel more Hindu or Jewish?" she asked as if she was talking about some secretive crush.

"Um, I'm not really sure," Sita said, taken aback by the topic change. She moved away a little from Lisa's face. "We're not that religious. We celebrate holidays with each side of the family, like Passover and Diwali, but that's about it."

"It must be so weird," she said.

Sita blinked, now wishing she could pause the conversation or better yet, fast-forward over it entirely. "Weird how?" she asked.

Lisa just kept staring at her, not seeming to notice Sita's discomfort. "Weird to not know who you are in that way," she said. "Like I know I'm Presbyterian. It's just what I've always been."

"I know who I am," Sita said, sitting up now, pushing the hot comforter off.

"Yeah," Lisa said. "But I mean just about this. It's probably really hard for you."

"Are you saying there's something bad about having two religions in my family?" Sita finally said, her mouth feeling dry. She did sometimes feel confused, but she thought everyone felt confused about something. Maybe someone like Lisa never was confused, never did actually wonder who they were and who they were supposed to be.

"No, of course not," Lisa said, her eyes even wider. She sat up too. "I think it's really interesting."

"Oh, okay," Sita said, her shoulders relaxing.

"I'm sorry, I didn't mean to upset you or anything. Maybe I shouldn't have asked," she said and turned away slightly, as if she was the one who was upset.

"No, it's fine. Really," said Sita, trying to sound comforting, and they got back under the covers again. "I'm just so tired," she said, though she was feeling anything but.

"Yeah, me too," Lisa said and closed her eyes.

SOMETIME AFTER THAT.

Selling Christmas trees wasn't the job she was supposed to have.

In late October, she sat in the cafeteria with Lisa and Lisa's other good friend Laura, who never said much to Sita. Sita suspected that Laura was jealous, but Sita kind of liked it. No one had ever been jealous of her before.

Sitting with them in the cafeteria were a few of the guys on the basketball team, John, Brett, and Kevin. Sita didn't care for John and she didn't like Kevin that much either. They always sat back in their chairs looking for people to make fun of. Brett was different, though. He had a warm smile and talked a lot about working at his father's farm stand.

"It gets really busy in the fall," he said to them as he ate his hamburger and then took a big swig of chocolate milk, a food combination that made Sita wince. Her family wasn't kosher or vegetarian, but they didn't eat red meat at home, and the thought of chocolate milk and hamburger together made her stomach turn.

"The local farmers are pretty nice," he continued after he finished chewing. "There's this one guy, our main apple guy, who taught me how to play guitar."

"Oh cool," Sita said, and his eyes flashed toward her, since she was the only person paying attention. She tried to picture Brett playing the guitar and looked at his hands. He had long fingers with smooth clean nails that struck her as attractive. She knew the stand, just outside of town in a gravel-covered lot near a small antique shop. She had seen the displays of pumpkins, apples, vegetables, and flowers. She also loved their large tree display for Christmas decorated with rows and rows of string lights.

For the last few years, her family put up a fake white tree that they decorated with blue and silver ornaments. Her Jewish cousins thought it was strange that she had a Christmas tree, but her aunty and uncle on the Hindu side of her family, who had come to the US from India as college students, put up their own real tree bursting with decorations. They said they were taking part in an American holiday tradition, not a religious one. When Sita was younger, it seemed to her that all her friends at school and half of her family were having a really fun party that she wasn't invited to. So she begged her mom for a tree and the compromise of the white tree was okay, but secretly Sita longed for a huge green pine decked out with the works.

Brett turned toward John and Kevin.

"You guys looking for work? My dad needs to hire a few extra people for the season."

"Too many APs this semester, bro. Don't have time to help loser parents with their trees."

"Nice," said Brett sarcastically.

"Just telling it like I see it," John said.

Kevin said he was walking dogs in the neighborhood.

She thought about the red-and-black dress she had seen at the mall. If she got a job, she could buy it. She raised her hand in the air like she was giving an answer in class. "I need a job," she said and quickly put her hand down. Lisa's head whipped around.

"Yeah?" Brett said and smiled one of his big smiles. "It's pretty physical work," he said. "Gets kind of dirty, too."

She closed her fist and made a muscle. "You mean you need someone to lift all those heavy apples?" she said, surprising herself.

He laughed. "They are actually heavy when they're in crates. And soon we'll be selling trees. We have to tie them on people's cars."

"It sounds fun," she said like she'd been tying Christmas trees to cars her whole life.

"If you're serious, I'll have my dad give you a call."

"I'm totally serious," she said, and they exchanged numbers. She felt a thrill as she added him to her contacts.

"So you like Brett?" Lisa said after lunch, while they stood at Sita's locker. She seemed serious, almost mad.

"No, I need a job," Sita said.

"Sure you do," Lisa said and winked.

"I do," she said. She did like Brett, but the main reason was the dress. Whether she went to winter formal or not, she needed it. She couldn't explain why.

"You don't think he's boring?" Lisa said.

"No," Sita said. He did seem a little boring, but not as boring as Kevin and John. But she didn't say so. And he was way cuter than both of them.

"I think John likes you," Lisa said.

Sita made a grimace and shook her head. "He's kind of obnoxious," she said.

"Awww, give him a chance. He can be nice," Lisa said and then left for her class. Sita was not going to the dance with John if that's what Lisa was implying. She'd rather stay home.

A day later Brett's dad did give her a call.

"You know, it's pretty physical work," he said just like Brett. "We don't just need a cashier. Lots of lifting boxes and the trees."

"Brett told me. I'm okay lifting things."

"Well, I'm not sure what kind of girl you are, but Brett seemed to think you could handle it."

She wondered what kind of girl couldn't lift stuff.

"You're selling *Christmas* trees? Outside?" her mom said when Sita told her.

"Well, and pumpkins, apples, all kinds of things."

"Seriously?" Her mother was acting like she just had gotten a job on the moon.

"God, Mom. It's not a big deal. You're always telling me to get a job."

"But," her mom said, her forehead still crinkled with worry, "you don't even like to take walks."

"Yeah, not embarrassing family walks where you and Dad hold hands and Vik tries to skateboard. But I like being outside."

"Well," her mother said, shrugging her shoulders. "I guess it's okay."

Sita decided then and there she would be the best Christmas tree seller in all of Fairfield County. And then she'd buy the dress even if she didn't have anything to wear it to.

TWO WEEKS BEFORE THE DANCE.

Brett wasn't the boyfriend she was supposed to have. They had been working together at the farm stand for weeks now and she felt like she was in some kind of corny holiday movie. They flirted as they moved the produce crates, hands touching, taking breaks together while they microwaved hot chocolate in the heated office in back. When they sat in the small room alone, they talked about homework and vegetables and their favorite music. Then there was the kiss. She had been stirring her hot chocolate with the little plastic straw and he came up behind her. She could feel the heat of him along her back even through her jacket. He leaned over her shoulder.

"Mmmm, looks good," he said. "Can I have some?"

She caught her breath. She knew if she turned, she would be face-to-face with him, but she liked his face. She had studied it closely lately, his slightly messy brown hair that fell over his eyes, his dark eyebrows, his long nose, and strangely pink lips for a boy.

"Sure," she said, turning, trying to stay calm. She lifted the cup to his lips and he took a slow sip. He took the cup from her and moved closer, touching his lips to hers, lightly, like a question. She leaned in and they kissed, long and slow and then faster. She had never felt like this—hungry, starving. She wasn't sure if she was supposed to feel like that, but she couldn't help herself. They heard a sound, the creak of the office door, and quickly separated. She went back to stirring her hot chocolate. Brett grabbed a cup and started making some for himself.

"A new shipment of jam came in," Brett's dad said, and went over to his computer to look up the inventory. "I need you guys out there."

Brett nodded and left. Sita quickly followed, light-headed and grinning. She wondered if she had imagined it. But after that day, every time they worked together, they found five minutes to make out in the break room, Brett smelling like woodsmoke, tasting like hot chocolate. She couldn't stop thinking about the way his strong arms felt, cold from the outside, but warm under his jacket. It was a struggle to think about anything else. She didn't tell Lisa. She wanted Brett all to herself.

When the Christmas trees came with their minty pine scent, the lights strung above the stand, she felt like she had climbed inside a snow globe, one she had gazed at longingly from the outside for so long. Brett taught her how to wrap the tree in plastic netting and hoist it up on her side, using her full body weight to lift it in the trunk or up on the roof. She noticed, though, when they were in front of other people, he acted like he barely knew her. She had chalked it up to him trying to be "professional" at work. At school he was sort of like that, too, but would give her a smile when he caught her eye in the cafeteria. It was their little secret.

Brett finally asked her to the dance under the first-floor stairwell after social studies. They had walked out of class together, laughing about something strange their teacher said. He suddenly took her hand and pulled her around the corner under the stairs. She could hear the echoing footsteps of other students rushing to class. They turned toward each other and he moved a piece of hair out of her face. He put his hand on the wall over her shoulder, his other hand behind her back, pulling her closer for a kiss.

"You're so . . ." he said, pausing for a second.

"So what?" she said.

"I don't know, different." He stared at her in a way she couldn't place.

"Different how?" she asked.

He looked down. "You just are."

"Maybe you're the one who's different," she said and nudged him in the shoulder, pushing him backward.

He laughed. "That's what I mean. You're so funny. Like not in the way girls usually are."

She wanted to ask him what the hell he was talking about, but before she could, he lowered his voice and spoke.

"I want to go to Winter Formal with you," he said, then shifted his eyes away.

She wondered why she was so surprised after all their secret kisses, but she was.

"That would be amazing!" she said and then wished she had played it cooler, much cooler. The stairs above them got louder as people started to rush to their next classes. He straightened up, like he was snapping out of some trance.

"We better go," he said and moved away. He began to walk quickly ahead of her. She tried to keep up and called "bye" to him as they got to another hallway. He gave her a small wave and hurried off the other way.

That afternoon she borrowed the car, telling her mother she spilled hot chocolate on her favorite jeans and desperately needed another pair. Her mother, just getting home from work, distracted and tired, didn't ask her any questions. She drove herself to the mall, a wad of twenties in her purse because Brett's dad paid her in cash. She went straight to Macy's and to her relief, they still had the red-and-black dress. It was even on sale, reduced from $115 to $80.

"Wear it well," the saleslady said and handed her the tissue-wrapped dress in a shopping bag. Sita practically skipped out of the store. She tried it on once in her room and hung it up in the back of her closet so her mother wouldn't ask her about it. She was going to have to tell her about the dress and Brett soon, but not just yet. She sat down on her bed, still breathless, and texted Lisa.

MAJOR news!

What?? Lisa replied right away.

Brett asked me to the dance!

There were dots and then nothing. More dots, then nothing. Finally, Lisa answered.

Wow. What did you say?
I said yes!! You don't sound happy.
No I am! I'm just surprised.

Then after a few seconds,

I didn't even know you guys were a thing. Why didn't you tell me?? Laura likes Brett. I've been trying to get him to ask her. I thought you liked John?

Sita stared at her phone. She told Lisa at least three different times she didn't like John, and Lisa had never mentioned anything about Laura liking Brett before. It was true that Sita had been keeping her make-out sessions with Brett secret and apparently, he was too. More and more often Lisa questioned everything Sita did. She asked her why she wore a certain sweater or laughed in a certain way. It was like Lisa was coming to the conclusion that she couldn't make Sita anything other than who she was.

She finally texted Lisa back. I told you I don't like John. I'm going with Brett.

Okay, Lisa said and then went silent.

The next day everything changed. Lisa and Laura sat next to each other and murmured things in each other's ears that Sita couldn't hear. Brett also wouldn't look her in the eye. A few days later, Laura asked Sita where she got her jeans. Sita didn't want to say Old Navy, so she said they were vintage. Then Lisa said, "Really? They look like Old Navy to me." Then she and Laura exchanged smiles. She looked up at Brett, but he had turned away and was talking to John.

THE DAY OF THE DANCE.

It wasn't the heartbreak she was supposed to have. Sita paced around her room trying to distract herself by blasting a '90s Spotify station. She went over to her white vanity and painted her nails a bright candy red. After she was done, she looked in the mirror, staring in her own eyes until it was almost like she was staring at someone else. What did Lisa see? What did Brett see? What was she supposed to see as she stared in the mirror? She smiled, frowned, and then went neutral again.

It was only 4 p.m. The red-and-black dress hung on the corner of the door to her open closet like a ghost without a body. It seemed to be mocking her. She put it on, did her hair and makeup. She looked amazing and took a couple of selfies just to remember.

Sita had worked with Brett four days ago. He apologized and said he didn't think he could go to the dance after all, that he had to work. She stood there in the break room after he left, tears blooming in her eyes, and then quickly threw her hot chocolate away. Then she told Brett's dad she was feeling sick and needed to go home. She knew she wasn't coming back.

She also knew she wasn't going to the dance, but was somehow hoping that the way things fell apart was only a dream and she could go back into her snow globe any minute. She thought about what Brett had said two weeks ago, *I want to go to Winter Formal with you.* Maybe he was never actually asking her to the dance, but only saying what he had felt in the moment.

Lisa hadn't texted Sita since she told her about Brett. She saw on Snapchat that Lisa was going with Kevin. And today she also saw a picture of Laura getting ready and she had tagged Brett. It hit her like someone had thrown a rotten pumpkin at her. Brett hadn't posted anything, but she knew everything now. She had messed up Lisa's plan. Lisa was going with Kevin. Laura was going with Brett, and she was supposed to be happy with John. She was supposed to do what Lisa wanted her to do.

Sita turned off her music and walked downstairs, not knowing what she would tell her parents. Vik was out at swim practice again. Her parents probably didn't even remember the dance was tonight, but to be fair, she hadn't reminded them. She saw her dad, sitting on the couch reading the paper, the steam rising from his cup of masala chai, something her mother had learned how to prepare for him as newlyweds, and she often would make a pot on weekend afternoons. Sita could smell the cardamom and ginger lacing the air. She went over to the kitchen and saw some still left on the stove. She stirred it up and poured herself a cup through the tea strainer. She went over to the couch, sat down, and sipped. She could taste the bite of peppercorns, the way her father liked it.

"Why haven't we ever been to India?" Sita asked.

He looked up, alarmed.

"Why are you so dressed up?" he said.

"I just," she said, not wanting to tell the whole story. "I just bought this dress and wanted to see how it looked."

"Oh, okay. It's nice. But it's a little—" he started to say.

"Dad, stop," she said, putting her hand up. "I'm really not in the mood."

"Okay, sorry." He sipped his tea and cleared his throat. "Didn't you have a dance coming up. Is that why you bought it?"

"I don't know," she said and shrugged.

He took another sip. "Mmm, tastes like old Bombay," he said. She could tell she was making him uncomfortable.

"Why do you say that?" she said. She wasn't sure why she was feeling so angry at her dad.

"What do you mean?" he asked, looking at her over his bifocals.

"You say it tastes like Bombay as if I'm supposed to know what you mean."

Her father sat back. "Oh, I guess I do say that. It's just something you say."

"I don't say it. I've never even been to Bombay or Mumbai or whatever it's called."

"True," he said and cleared his throat. "Is that what you're upset about?" he asked.

"No. I don't really want to talk about it."

He nodded, eyed her for a moment, and returned to his reading. Another few seconds went by. Then he lowered his paper.

"I've thought about bringing you all on one of my trips, but we don't have any close family there anymore. And your mother hates flying."

"So that's the reason? Mom got on a plane to go to Florida last winter. I'm half-Indian but I've never even been there. It kind of feels like I'm sort of lying about my background. We need to go. All of us."

He glanced down at his feet, his shoulders slumping a bit. Suddenly he looked so small and sad.

"Dad, I'm sorry. I'm not actually mad at you."

He glanced back up. "You know your mom went to a hypnotist to get on that flight, but you're absolutely right."

"Really?" she said. Her father never told her she was right about anything.

"I didn't think you and Vik were that interested."

"But Dad, you never asked," she said.

"It's just somehow seemed separate, my life in India."

She wasn't sure how they went so many years without talking about this.

"Dad, how can it be separate? It's part of who I am every day."

"You're right," he said again, clasping his hands over his belly. He pressed his lips together. "Let me think about it, when we could go."

They sat another moment, both taking a sip of their chai.

"A boy asked me to the dance a few weeks ago, or at least I thought he did," she blurted out. Her father looked up, surprised. "Then he blew me off. I bought this dress for it." Tears started to form and she blinked them away. She didn't want to cry over Brett.

"Oh, Sita. I'm sorry," he said. "What an idiot that boy is. When is the dance?"

"Tonight. But he never called me to make actual plans. I just kept waiting. Then he made up some story about not being able to go, but he's going with this other girl. I'm so stupid."

"You're not the one who's stupid. So why did this idiot ask you in the first place?" her father's voice getting angrier.

"Because he," she said. She knew the answer. "He thought he liked me. He *did* like me, but he's just a coward. He didn't want to date someone like me."

"What do you mean, someone like you?" he asked.

"Different from most people at school. Not white. An Indian last name no one can pronounce, two religions that hardly anyone knows anything about. Or maybe it has nothing to do with that. Maybe it's that I'm too funny or too weird. Not the way I'm supposed to be, not cool."

Her father leaned forward and touched her knee. "Unfortunately, the world is full of cowards. Just feel lucky that you're not one. And you're cooler than anyone I know."

A NEW BEGINNING.

At the Taj Mahal Hotel the waiters started counting down to midnight.

"Ten," one man yelled out. "Nine!" another joined in, and then more people in the ballroom started to count down.

Sita's father's childhood best friend, Gobind, had invited them to Mumbai for the holidays, literally a day after Sita had talked to her dad. When they arrived, Gobind's wife, Nalini, had gifted Sita a pink and gold sari. Sita had never worn a sari before and when she put it on, she felt like she had stepped into another version of herself, a self that might have been if her mother had been Indian like her father. The shame of that thought, her mother being a different mother, made her face feel hot. She reminded herself that she had a similar thought at her cousin's bat mitzvah—what if her father was Jewish like her mother? But if these things were true, she wouldn't exist either.

Sita bumped into Vik's shoulder for a second and wondered if he ever had these kinds of thoughts about their parents. He clapped hard to the club music, the chandelier light bouncing around in his eyes. He looked so happy. Her father came by her side, her mother stood on the other, and they cheered into the lit-up room. It was funny to see her parents dancing to the loud electric beat of the music.

The energy started to build with each second. She had first planned on wearing the red-and-black dress. Now she felt like tossing it in the garbage.

She wished Brett and Lisa could see her now, dancing, happy, fully in her body, fearlessly calling out into the night. She kept trying to piece together exactly what had happened and if she had done something wrong to make them treat her the way they did. She always went back to two moments—that night Sita became upset about Lisa's ridiculous questions, and then the day when Brett asked her to the dance and how he called her "different." So was it simply that she did not act or *exist* in the way they thought she was supposed to?

"Three, two, ONE!" everyone shouted as the clock struck midnight. The room erupted with cheering and hugging as they welcomed in the new year. Sita put her arms around her parents. Vikram did the same, and they formed a circle, all four of them, moving lightly to the beat, foreheads to the center. She knew even in the sari, her American English, and the fact that she was just another tourist at the Taj hotel made her an outsider here, too. There was no fitting in anywhere, not at school in her small town in Connecticut, not in Lisa's crowd, not as Brett's girlfriend, not here in Mumbai.

The only thing left to do was to stop trying. She felt good. In fact, she felt better than good, she felt free. Maybe, for the first time ever, in this brand-new second of her life, she was exactly who she was supposed to be.

MEMORIES OF A MANGO TREE

By Sarah Mughal Rana

My life had become a series of regrets. Among the first was my grandmother.

Before I departed to the Land of Freedom, at fourteen years old, one of my last memories in Jhal—our village outside Narowal City—was of fleeing to the hills above our farmland, sobbing along the way.

"Enough crying," Nano called from behind me. My grandmother bent over her knees, pounding her chest to catch her breath. "Give me time to catch up, beti."

I went to my favorite resting spot, on a stone beneath the thick kahu and mango. Eventually Nano climbed up the rugged hill.

"Your brother said you wouldn't even take his jalebi," Nano said. Her hands unwrapped her mauve dupatta, embroidered with swirling designs of birds and wildflowers. "Take this, wipe your tears."

"I don't want jalebi." I used the corner of her scarf to dry my eyes. No matter how much my brother tried to bribe me, nothing placated my anger.

"Tell me, why are you upset?"

My eyes pooled with tears. "It was Maryam. I hate her!" I sputtered out.

"Ah your cousin." Nano nodded in pretend pity.

"No, Nano! It was Maryam *and* her mother!"

"Ah your aunty too! Such horrible people."

"Nano, you are mocking me," I scowled, wrenching her dupatta between my hands.

"Hate is a strong word for such a young child. Why do you hate your cousin?"

"She's selfish," I declared. "Aunty made her a rag doll. It's pretty. I saw it in our recitation halaqa at school. When I asked to share, she said because I don't have a mother—because she's dead—I would never have a pretty rag doll."

"And then what did you do?" Nano raised a brow.

"I threw it across the class. If I don't have a doll, she doesn't get one either. But our ustad yelled at me in front of the entire class and they laughed!"

Nano sighed and shook her head. More than my anger, her disappointment hurt most of all. Unrestful, my head bobbed, thick schoolgirl braids tickling my shoulders. I swung my legs over the stone back and forth, wrinkling the fabric of my shalwar.

"Stop moving your legs like that, it calls the shaytaan." Nano swatted my head. She turned her head over her shoulder, creased skin indenting further. "Oi, bhabi! Bring it here!"

A second later, Dur-e-Adaan Aunty brought a basket balanced on her head, of golden mangos freshly picked from our tree, placing it right under my nose. The tang of dirt and sweet syrup attracted flies. Every summer she harvested the crops of mango along the hill.

"Bring us two knives," Nano instructed her.

After she left, unable to help myself, I reached into the basket, but again Nano batted me away. "Not yet," she ordered. "You will cut all of them, first."

"All of them? Why?"

She scowled. "You are upset. Do something useful to release your anger. With time, the anger will fade."

In my childlike impatience, I didn't care the reason so long as they ended up in my stomach. "Fine."

I peered into the reed basket, fixating on a small mango tucked into the recesses between two of the fattest ones. When I fished it out, Nano sighed in disappointment.

"What?" I said defensively.

"Beti." She pulled out one (without even looking inside), skin glistening like gold. "The Pakistani mango is a delicate thing. It's equally as stubborn as its people, nothing like the mangos from India who have more merciful weather than us. So don't be fooled by its nice skin. To really see its ripeness, pull the black bud and you will tell."

At the time I couldn't point out that I didn't possess the magical gift all Pakistani elders seemed to have inherited—the ability to pick the perfect fruit. But I realized now that Nano was special; she knew from some instinct to grasp the best ripened fruit from the tree.

After my aunty brought two knives, Nano perched on the edge of the stone, watching me cut the mango. I sliced down the middle of the flesh, hitting the thick seed, and the knife slipped from my hands, but Nano's arm snapped out, catching it.

She frowned, the lines around her mouth more pronounced than before. With a pang in my chest, I couldn't help noticing how Nano seemed to have aged so quickly in the past year, taking care of my brothers and me.

She placed her hand on my wrist, shoving the knife beneath my curled fingers. "You might not have a mother, but you have your Nano. Just wait. Tomorrow make sure you sit beside Maryam and show your tiffin. You will see, God willing."

"I wish she didn't have a mother, too."

"Nāzo!" Nano gasped. "Enough. We do not curse others."

"Why? If she didn't have a mother, then . . . she would understand." My bravado made me feel self-assured in front of my elder, as nice as eating sugar.

Through a sigh, Nano inclined her head, indicating for me to follow.

She reached up to the lowest fruit. "Trees are tombs, existing long after our lives, their roots stretching and multiplying, collecting from the earth. Even when they die, those roots remain. Watch," she ordered. She guided my hand and placed it on the base of the fruit, against the branch.

"Shut your eyes. Listen to the roots of the mango tree," she whispered.

My hand slipped in the wet dripping from the fruit to my fingers, the sap sticky and hot. My eyes shut and the smell of sticky, hot sap . . . the buzz of cicadas in the lush rolling farmland, the relief of the breeze in the heat . . . A memory hit me.

For the barest second, my grandmother was no longer beside me.

"Oi Ami!" a young voice cried.

Beside me, a woman bowed over a child who sat on a wooden swing tied hazardously to the top of the tree. She waved her hand and pushed against it, embroidered headscarf fluttering in the light breeze. With each push, seven-year-old me giggled.

The memory was my mama from before, when she appeared younger, softer. Her hair braided to her hips, thick like black ropes, her cheeks light and rosy, unaffected by disease.

After another push, she stretched up to grab a mango, her fingers brushing but unable to grab it, as I urged her on in delight.

"Ay, Hania," Nano called to us from below the hill, carrying a reed basket, smiling at my laughs.

In the present, I felt my lips turning up at the unfolding memory. But when I opened my eyes, it was snatched away too soon like Mama, leaving only the scents of mango and grief.

Tears flowed down my cheeks—replaying the memory of Mama carefree, of Mama smiling. This was home.

"Do you feel better?" Nano prodded, as she went back to slicing mangos.

I blinked hard, withdrew my hands from the fruit tree, and its sweet tang that had provoked my memory, and returned to the present. Nano studied me as I stepped back from the tree, shivering despite the dry hot air.

I tried to think back to Mama and her once-soft features. The details blurred like the wisps of a dream.

Nano tapped my head. "Listen carefully, Nāzo Anāa." When Nano used my full name, she was serious, as serious as her Islamic lectures. "I come to this mango tree because I will always remember the ones I love. As will you. This tree has the roots of precious memories, of your mother, your aunty, your father, your brothers. Maryam has her doll but the doll will fall apart in a matter of days and be forgotten. This tree, this mango, this is powerful. Memories are more powerful than a rag doll." She ran her finger over the thick seed in the center. "And it tastes good." She plopped the flesh into her mouth and I smiled.

At the time, I didn't understand her words—not until it was too late.

A few minutes later, my other aunty Dur-e-Adaan brought a brown-red earthen pot.

For the next hour, we rhythmically harvested the small mangos from the swollen ones, placing the fruit to suck on the right and the fruit to cut on the left in the pot. Sneakily when Nano would be turned away, I would lick my fingers, savoring the sugary juices.

"Now bring the mangos to the dry room. Your brothers will be arriving soon."

At mid-afternoon, my brothers returned from the farmlands. The four of us sat in a circle on the floor cushions, the eating table in the center. My brothers crossed their legs, hands resting on their knees. The ritual of mango eating seemed as sacred as the act of prayer, after the ad'haan beckoned us. I mimicked their poses. Nano and Dur-e-Adaan joined us, Papa behind them.

"Now we eat," Nano said, and patted my arm before boasting, "Hania here cut all of the mangos herself!"

My grin disappeared and my brow furrowed as I realized that Nano had accidentally called me by my mother's name, not mine. But I shook away the confusion. *It's a slip of the tongue*, I assured myself. If only I'd noticed the signs before it was too late.

For the next year before I moved away, Nano would teach me how to cut and shape the mangos, and from time to time, we would reminisce memories of Mama together, falling into those bittersweet stories. Maybe we were fools clinging to grief but whatever it was—it was my reminder of home.

I was older now at fifteen years old. It was my first day of high school at an English preparatory school; Nano handed me my tiffin and tied a patterned shawl around my head to keep me warm. A month ago, Papa had finally secured our visas to America, and we moved to a rural area in Wisconsin, sponsoring us in a small town in the north.

"I don't need this, Nano." I handed back the tiffin. "I have my Eid money from last week. There's a convenience store a ten-minute walk from school. I can eat from there."

She scowled, pinching my ear. "All you do is eat junk food. You and your brothers run away from home food. Enough! In the tiffin, I put a block of panjiri. The almonds and dried fruit will make your mind smarter; your brain will work faster!"

"I hate panjiri, it tastes like dust." But at her glare, I reluctantly took back the tiffin.

Before I left, she said, "Your class fellows are ghoray. You will sound different to them; you will be upset. You'll try to change. But," her nails tapped the top of the tiffin, "remember Jhal, your village with your favorite mango trees, and your mama."

At school, in the dining hall, I found a seat at our class table, on the edge of the bench. As I unwrapped the tiffin, a small note fluttered out in curving Urdu. But I tucked that back inside the tiffin before others noticed.

I grimaced, remembering how my first class went earlier in the day. The math teacher asked me to introduce myself. At hearing my accent, she asked before everyone:

"Oh, are you South Asian?"

"I am P-Pakistan," I stuttered in English.

"Pakistan," she repeated. "You mean you are Pakistani."

"Is that in India," someone called out and I looked between the staring students, my tights itching beneath my uniform.

"No. *Pak-is-stan*." I fidgeted awkwardly. My teacher smiled and nodded for me to have a seat.

At least at lunch, I didn't have to face my teachers.

When I lifted my tiffin lid, the girl beside me coughed. I remembered her name was Katiana. "The smell is stinging my eyes," she said and peered inside.

I smiled at her, picking up the rolled paratha and achaar. "Yes." Earlier in the day, I learned in class that when people asked me questions it was easier to answer in yeses and nos.

Katiana wrinkled her nose; I was too late in realizing that she didn't find the smell pleasant.

"What are those black dots in your food? It looks like bugs."

"Kalonji," I said, which was another mistake.

"*Kal-gee*? You eat bugs?" She pinched the tip of her nose. I noticed the entire table had fallen silent, watching our exchange.

"And why do you have rotting fruit?" She glanced at the small slices of mango. The sour tang told me they weren't ripe—Nano must've bought the only mangos at the Indo grocer located downtown, out of season. Because of that, the mango flesh was green instead of bright orange.

"No," I said, in a simple answer again.

She grabbed the Urdu note from the tiffin. "Is this a prayer?

317

Cool, it's Arabic! I've seen these before. But do you have to wear it on your clothes, too?" She touched the shawl on my head, patterned in Urdu poetry.

My ears felt red-hot and I ripped the shawl off my head, embarrassed. Probably disappointed at my lack of conversation, Katiana made a point to scoot down the bench. Not before dropping the note right in my tiffin.

Remember Jhal.

My eyes burned and I turned away on the bench. Gradually other students stopped looking but for some reason, I still felt their stares.

Later at home, I recounted my first day of school to Papa and Nano, nearly in tears; frustrated that I was unable to answer most of the students' and teachers' curious questions.

Papa merely patted my shoulder in a shrewd way. "This is how Amrika is, beta," he said. "For lunch, Nano can make you an egg sandwich instead of paratha."

But our egg sandwiches were stuffed with masala and black salt. I knew the smell would be even worse. At his suggestion, I made a face and Papa sighed. Nano on the other hand seemed deep in thought, lips pursed together before she hobbled to the kitchen, leaning on her cane.

"Nano, you're quiet. What do you think of my class fellows?"

She held up the chopping knife, and my (now empty) tiffin, turning it over in her hands. "They need better taste in food," she half-grunted.

I cracked a grin. "Their food isn't so bad."

"It lacks spice," she said dryly before crossing her arms. "I have an idea. Instead of trying to change the tiffin, have them taste my food, and the mangos."

The image of Katiana crinkling her nose flashed in my mind. "I'm not sure if that's a good idea . . ."

Nano merely batted her hands and began chopping an onion expertly, a blur of steel against the wooden board. "Hania, food wins hearts! Let's try it once. If my idea doesn't work, I will make you an egg sandwich for lunch."

My mouth opened for a retort, before I bit my tongue. Again, Nano called me by my mama's name.

"I'm Nāzo Anāa," I corrected.

"What?" Nano turned her head over her shoulder.

"You called me . . ." My head shook. To distract myself, I went to grab the garlic and ginger paste from the refrigerator to help her cook. "Never mind."

The next day, during lunch, I sat next to Katiana and her friends. We sat on the edge of the dining hall, extravagant old oak benches lined against the back wall. Above us, the tall ceiling hung with decorated painted portraits of old headmasters of the preparatory school.

"What do you . . . make lunch?" I tried to form the question for Katiana.

She cocked her head at the broken English, and then showed me her brown bag, containing her lunch. A pinkish yogurt, with red berries that I'd never seen before. And two bars of granola. I frowned. Surely that couldn't be all her food . . .

"Do you still have that . . . *kal-gee* bug?" she asked.

My jaw clenched. I untied the cloth around my tiffin, removing the lid of the tray.

She gasped. I lifted it, shocked.

Nano had fried chicken kebab into the shapes of people. I couldn't figure out how she'd mastered this trick. There were two total, one taller. She'd used the meat to mold skinny arms and legs. She used flakes of minced onion to make eyes, and tomato skin to make lips. It was childish, but still a sight to behold.

Unwrapping the foil below revealed glistening ghee qeema-stuffed parathas shaped into two hearts, brimming with the minced spiced meat. In the smaller container, I found mangos carved into roses—juicy amber flowers. The scent of mustard seeds, oily onion, and peppery spices collided with the sweet scent of fruit.

"Who made that?" one of her friends asked, reaching out but I snatched the tray back.

"Grandmother," I said almost proudly. And before I could forget Nano's advice, I nudged the tiffin toward Katiana. "Please, try." I used a napkin and tore a large piece off the qeema paratha, and a chunk of the juicy, crispy kebab, folding it within a small roll of the fried flatbread.

Katiana hesitated, studying the food cradled in the white napkin.

"Please," I repeated.

She took the offering and plopped it in her mouth.

I waited.

She chewed, thoughtfully, swallowed and—"Oh God," she clenched her throat, coughing so hard, her eyes watered red. She coughed again, a deep rasping kind that reminded me of Mama when she became sick. I lurched up, looking around for water. Katiana toppled off the wooden bench, coughing on her hands and knees.

"She's choking!" one of her friends cried.

They panicked and one of them unscrewed their water bottle, forcing the cold water down Katiana's throat. The supervising teacher ran down the dining hall toward our table. People surrounded Katiana, as she sat on the floor, gulping from the bottle, the regurgitated food in a wet splatter beside her. I saw the black elachi and peppercorn before nearly groaning and turning away, flustered. I was so stupid. Nano and I hadn't thought about the spices; the hard, whole coriander seeds in the qeema; the hard elachi and peppercorns in the kebab . . .

"You—you tricked me! You tried to hurt me!" Katiana sat up farther, glaring accusingly.

"No!" I tried to say.

"Your Muslim food—I didn't even want to taste it—" she broke off, coughing again. "I was trying to be nice. You tried to kill me!"

My jaw dropped at the exaggerated accusation, and the

supervising teacher whirled toward me. "Come now. To my office."

In frustration, I slammed down the tiffin and stood up. Cheeks heated, I followed at the teacher's heels in the now-silent dining hall, avoiding the school's stares.

In the teacher's office, I was berated and lectured for sharing home food; it was apparently against school policy for hygienic reasons. And then the teacher questioned me on the food, as if it weren't food at all, saying the smell could be offensive to sensitive students. As he spoke, without realizing, my fingers gripping the tiffin poked into the mango shaped into roses, squishing the hard green pulp between my nails. For a brief moment, I shut my eyes, waiting; thinking of Jhal; of a home that once had my mama and mango trees. Nothing happened. Maybe its magic died as soon as we left Pakistan.

From that day on, no one sat next to me at lunch. They would make comments about my shawl, about my tiffin.

Later at home, I would empty the tiffin in the trash bin, along with Nano's note.

Instead, I wish I'd savored it longer.

For the next year, the cycle continued. Wordlessly, in the mornings I would take Nano's tiffin, and every evening, I would empty it into the bin. Sometimes, I attempted to throw it away at school, and the guilt of wasting food was not lost on me.

When my grandmother finally confronted me, I should've

known the day was coming.

"One of your teachers called, concerned about you and the students' behavior. For months, I've also found your lunch uneaten or in the bin. I wanted to stay quiet. But you don't even wear your scarf anymore. Remember, I made it myself." Nano hobbled into my room, leaning against the bedpost. "Tell me, jaan, what's wrong."

"Nothing is wrong."

She shook her head. "You've changed, beti. You leave your shawl at home. You try to speak in English with your papa at home, and you are mad when we don't. You never eat the food I make. You stopped going to the mosque."

"If you move someone to an American country, then they'll act American." I pretended to rummage through my school binder.

"Nāzo." Nano's disappointment made my stomach turn. "There are plenty of Pakistanis in the US. Thousands and thousands. They are fine."

I whirled around. "Nano, this isn't a big city! You don't understand what the students say. Papa put me in a private school. Our town is small. None of the students have met Pakistanis. For the past year they've played with my food; they think it smells. No one sits with me. I'm sorry. My words might hurt you but we are not in Jhal. It's— It's embarrassing. Your notes—the food, it's embarrassing."

Nano clutched her chest. "Hania." Then she took my hands in her own. "There are going to be people who don't understand you but that is all the more reason to show them why you are proud of being different. Why are you ignoring it now?"

"My name is Nāzo. Not Hania. I am not Mama. Besides, I don't want to be proud of looking and being different."

"You need a reminder or else I am failing as your elder, and I don't want this on my grave," Nano scowled, tightening her shawl. "I told you to remember our village, our tree. When you were younger, and upset, I would tell you this. It worked before, in Pakistan."

My head shook and her hands slipped from my own. "No, Nano. Where is Jhal? Where are the trees on the hill? They are not here in our town. We're in a different home. I can't keep pretending. And I'm not a little girl anymore."

Nano suddenly grabbed my arm, tugging me through the doorway.

"Where are you taking me?"

"Up the hill," Nano said, determined as she shoved her way to the doorway. "The mango tree is right there, Hania."

My anger escaped my body. "Nano." She acted as if she couldn't hear me. "Nano," I tried again, incessantly. "Nano!" I cried as she unlocked the entrance.

"What, Hania?" She turned, and her eyes were bleary.

"Nāzo," I repeated. "It's Nāzo."

Nano groaned and touched the shawl on her temple.

"Why are you both arguing? And Nāzo, is that how you speak to your elders?" Papa came from the living room, into the corridor connecting to the entryway.

"Something is wrong with Nano. She keeps calling me Mama's name. And just now, she was acting like we were in Jhal," I told Papa.

"What are you saying, Nāzo. I'm fine." Nano blinked and released my arm.

"But—"

She clutched her head and retreated sluggishly to her bedroom.

"I'll book her an appointment with the doctor," Papa said grimly.

I went to the kitchen to fill a glass of water for Nano. But my chest tightened. Something was not right.

Nano was forgetting more than just my name.

The next week, I awoke from a large noise in the kitchen at dawn. Going down, I was startled to see Nano sprawled on the ground, clutching her hip.

"Nano!"

"I'm fine," she grumbled, as I helped her up. "I was packing your tiffin."

Something was tangibly wrong when Nano turned around, her eyes seeing through me as if I was not there: "Hania, enough with this. You'll be late to the halaqa, you have your recitation test!"

I hadn't heard the word *halaqa* in two years, since we'd moved from Pakistan.

"Take this." She handed me the tiffin with the heart-shaped paratha and rose-carved mangos.

I snatched my arms back. "Nano, remember. I don't eat this," I said gently.

At the noises, Papa too entered the kitchen.

Nano smiled at him. "You can't be here, Huzaifa. The wedding is next month! A groom cannot see his bride before the wedding."

Papa's expression darkened. I suddenly realized this was more than just forgetting.

The signs had always been there—unable to recall the days, calling me Hania—my mother's name—and wandering through the house as if lost.

I'd been so caught up with adjusting in school, preparing for my extra English classes, desperate to tuck myself in the nooks of this odd country. Papa was managing an immigration law firm, to help sponsor more Pakistanis to this town. My brothers studied abroad in Qatar and the UK in colleges. Nano stayed home, alone for most of the day.

None of us had paid any attention. A deep-seated guilt rose within me.

After that day, the dementia only worsened.

Nano deteriorated before our eyes.

On the Friday of that week, we had our annual Khatam of the Quran that we did on Mama's death anniversary. I fell asleep late, but Papa and Nano stayed awake for Fajr, the dawn prayer. It wasn't until I felt a nudge on my elbow that I awoke to see Nano at my bedside, in one of her states again.

"Hania," she hissed. "Come now! Wudu!"

"Nano, it's Nāzo—"

Nano began coughing, leaning on her staff, eyes glazed feverishly.

I rushed out of bed, and forced her to sip some of my water.

"Fajr," she wheezed. "Come. Pray with me, beti."

After ablution, I followed her to the mat, my limbs awkward. I prayed here and there in Ramadan, and of course, the Khatam Quran. But Fajr was the hardest prayer because of its early timings. In fact . . . I hadn't prayed Fajr in months.

But as I studied Nano's weak stance, her bleary eyes, I felt compelled to try.

Slowly, I went through the motions. After finishing, I sat on my heels on the mat, as Nano sat on her chair.

"Hania," Nano whispered. "You must pray. After you marry, you must pray."

Instead of correcting her, I whispered back, "Why, Ami?"

She lifted her head, snatching my wrist. "Hania, when you have a child, they are your mark. My upbringing to you becomes your upbringing to them. Prayer will remind them to pray for themselves, their parents, and their parents' parents. It's a sadaqah jariyah—a legacy to leave behind. I don't want to leave this world with my children estranged to me, where they forget to pray for my grave long after I'm dead, and their children forget me as well. They will forget my upbringing, country, home, and family." Her lips trembled.

"Nano, you're scaring me. Please." I clenched the leg of her chair. "Don't speak about your death."

She ignored my pleas. "Do you promise me. Wallahi?"

"Nano, my home is here and there. It's both," I whispered.

"No," she mused bitterly. "You are forgetting." She rose shakily to her feet. "I am tired, Hania. I speak here but no one listens because no one remembers our home in Jhal. And now, you don't pray. Was this my upbringing of you? I carried you on my back in the mountains, nursed you through war, and raised you alone. Our family will live on, through your children, your children's children. Teach them our ways. Raise them well here in Jhal, so they go back and help the ones behind."

"I will," I said thickly. I felt like the worst of liars.

"Come, Hania," and she wiped her tears. "Help me to my room, I must rest."

Tears brimmed in my eyes. Jhal was long gone, a remnant of the past. I could hardly recall the details of our old village. But suddenly, I was taken back to the morning when Nano placed my hand on the mango tree. A well of guilt rose in the back of my throat.

Nano had tried to teach me, after Mama's death. I'd never listened.

Nano was bedridden. It was as if she spent whatever energy remained in her on that last prayer.

Regret twisted my insides. Before Papa left for work, I asked him to take me to the Indo grocer.

"Beta, it's an hour drive."

"Please, Papa."

By a stroke of luck, the shop had its last cart of green Pakistani mangos smuggled across the border from Canada (since Pakistani mangos were illegal to import). When he saw them, Papa seemed to understand.

At home, I brought a plate to Nano's bedroom.

When I entered, Nano gazed up at me. "Hania."

We were no longer in Pakistan, and sadly, Nano would never return. But perhaps I could bring Pakistan to her.

Carefully, I sliced the mango in wedges. Taking her rough, bony hand into my own, I brought the plate beneath her nose. The scent was strong, perfuming the room. For a moment, I was reminded of the bazaar in central Narowal, intertwining with the tang of motorbike and sweet fried desserts.

Nano inhaled, perplexed that something so familiar but forgotten had returned.

I brought her hand to the mango seed.

I shut my eyes and focused on the smell, of the memory.

I felt that memory tug itself free.

Nano stared at the mango tree, bent over, collecting fallen fruits.

"Push me, Nano!"

She tucked a stray strand of hair from my face, back into my dupatta. "Oi! Help me first! Doesn't your qari saab teach you to heed your elders."

I jumped off the swing in a tumble. "Sorry Nano-ji!" I crouched and began collecting the lemons and mangos that had fallen from the basket. Occasionally, I would lick sap from my fingers before Nano whacked my hands away.

Nano, I laughed and cried myself back into her bedroom in the present day.

Below me, Nano was smiling, eyes fluttered closed as she lived through some private memory while muttering her supplications, oneness of her faith, and remembrance.

I collected the plate and stood, to allow her to rest.

"I'm sorry that I seemed to forget," I whispered. "But I promise I won't anymore, Nano."

When I reached the door, a frail whisper froze me: "Nāzo Anāa."

It has been a year since Nano called me by my name—not my mother's. My eyes felt wet and I furiously wiped them before letting the door shut behind me.

Shortly after, in her sleep, smiling through the memory, Nano passed away.

JAHAJI

By Rekha Kuver

I

I know four phone numbers by heart. Mine, my mom's old number, my dad's current number, and this one: 810-992-5152. I think about that number all the time, even though I've never dialed it. I don't have it saved in my Contacts and I've never written it down, but if you scroll back far enough on my Missed Calls list, it's in there a bunch of times. Yet it lives in my head like an earworm from a song. Sometimes, when I'm walking to the bus stop, I say the last numbers under my breath, with my steps. *Five one five two five one five two.*

When Mom died last year, there were so many things that had to get done. One of the first things we had to do was tell people, which seems like a ridiculous thing to ask anyone to do right after a death. I sat in our dining room that night with Dad and watched him make each call, starting with our relatives. Most of them live back in Fiji, with pockets spread out from there: Australia, New Zealand, Canada, England, California, Oregon. None are here in Michigan with us. Mom kept a notepad in the kitchen drawer where she wrote down the time differences for all of these places in comparison to ours so that she could see when it was a good time to call. I thought about the pad inside the darkness of the drawer as I listened to Dad say she was gone, over and over again. He cried every time he said it, and so did I.

After the relatives, we told her friends. I offered to do some of the calls over the next few days to help out, and Dad was exhausted enough to let me. I went through Mom's phone and made a list of who to call. There were several different social circles: our neighbors, her parent friends, her college friends, her work friends at City Hall where she managed city parks. Some of them offered to reach out to others for me, which made me feel possessive of these awful calls. Shouldn't Dad and I be the ones to say these words out loud, as many times as it took? But I knew to say yes, thank you, and so I did.

Two months later in March, a voicemail pinged my phone. 810-992-5152. I let it sit there, because who even leaves voicemail? But about a week later, I listened:

"Deepa, it's Nisha Auntie. Did your mum change her number? Please tell her I'm back from my winter in Trinidad and to call me. And come for tea with her next time, beti! It's been ages!"

Fuuuuuuuuck. Mom's friend Nisha. I hadn't called her, and now eight full weeks had passed. She spent her winters in Trinidad, where she was from, and when I'd gotten to her name on my list, I'd felt sort of ill about calling. So I'd skipped her, thinking I would come back around to her at the end of the list. This was one of Mom's closest friends, but she wasn't a part of any of the other friend circles, and she was unlikely to hear this from anyone else, especially while in Trinidad.

I'm seventeen, and I know adults like to say that people my age think we're grown. In a lot of ways I do feel like a grown-up, but in other ways I know there's so much I haven't done yet. I certainly haven't done a lot of things that I think of as genuinely bad. I let Mandy, who lives across the street, copy my math homework a bunch of times in eighth grade. Lately, I sometimes tell Dad that I'm going to my best friend Daniela's house when I'm really going to Calvin's to make out. These are things I would definitely get in trouble for, which would be fair, but I don't feel super guilty for doing them. So I guess I was due for an actual bad thing. The kind where you do it, you feel horrible about having done it, but you can't seem to stop yourself.*

Not calling Nisha in January when I should have was a for real kind of bad. Even worse, I deleted her message and put my phone back in my pocket and went on with my day. And when she eventually learned the news (maybe from my dad, I still don't know) and came over with curries or casseroles a bunch of times that spring, I always made sure I was out of the house. One time she came by when I was home and when Dad called for me from downstairs, I stayed silent until I heard him apologize and say that I must be taking a nap, even though I am never taking a nap. After a couple of weeks, a card arrived in the mail addressed to me. "Dear Deepa, I'll always be here for you. Please call me anytime. Love, Nisha Auntie." Under the message, there it was again. 810-992-5152.

Now it's February. Mom's been gone for over a year, and Nisha has called me every month. She always leaves a message to say she's thinking of me and to call her back, and I always listen and immediately delete it.

There are so many things I can't stop thinking about this year. I think about Mom in her hospital bed, looking fine, like she would wake up any minute, even though the doctor had just told us that what started out as COVID pneumonia was now shutting down her internal systems and she wasn't ever going to wake up again. I think about Dad trying so hard for me, for her, for himself, for everyone, every day since. I think about whether I should defer going to U of M for a year, because how can Dad and I be apart now? I think about whether my situationship with Calvin is fair to him, given that I've been a mess and a half. And I think about the numbers that make up Nisha's phone number. But I don't think about Nisha herself. I can't think about Nisha. That's the one thing that seems like too much.

*Explanatory Comma #1

In my Media Studies senior seminar, Ms. Freeman gave us a list of podcasts and YouTube channels that we can listen to or watch and then write a reflection paper on for extra credit. I listened to one called Code Switch that talked about something called an "Explanatory Comma." They said that, whenever you stop what you're saying because you feel like you have to tack on an explanation of what you mean because what you're saying comes out of your culture or identity and so you have to explain that to be understood, that's an Explanatory Comma. When I heard that, I felt like they were talking to me. Like, when I say that ignoring Nisha for this long is bad, how do I also say that it's not just bad because it's rude and careless, but that for Indo-Fijians, disrespecting a caring elder is a special kind of bad? And that there are reasons this is so, reasons specific to us? And do you even know what an Indo-Fijian is, or do I have to do a Comma on top of this Comma?

‖

Mom was loud. I feel like if I say that, it sounds like she was brash or overbearing, but she wasn't. Her volume was in warmth and vivaciousness. She sparkled with BFF vibes. When we were done with school and work, she would greet me with a boisterous "Hello, Baby Girl!" and when we watched movies, she would make it a party. "Belle is choosing the Beast? What a rrrrip off!" she'd say to the screen, her r's rippling with that serene Islander roll.

When I was in seventh grade, my teachers kept kicking me

out of class to stand in the hall because if something hit funny I would laugh, loudly. My math teacher, Mrs. Meyers, went so far as to write on my progress report: "Laughs too much. Self-control needs improvement." This was something Mom could never be mad at. "We've got Fijian laughs," she said with a one-shoulder shrug, palm up. "Can't help it."

Mom wasn't quiet in life, but her absence is thunderous. Her empty chair at the dinner table keens at us every single day. This doesn't shut Dad and me up at all. We have always been a family of talkers, and the sad roar in the house is like a bass line that calls us to put a melody on top. We tell stories about her that make us laugh and cry. *Remember when? Remember when?* Some nights, Dad plays their favorite love ghazal records with the volume turned up.* You're not really supposed to play music in the house after someone dies, but our grief just can't seem to stay quiet. *Here, my love, today is all that is ours,* Dad would sing along in Urdu. *Today is all that is ours, my love.*

Explanatory Comma #2

A lot of times I resent the Explanatory Comma because it makes me realize how much some people don't ever feel the need to do one at all. Other times, I sort of like that I can do them because it makes me feel the specialness of myself. I think the people who don't even know that they have them because they have so much Main Character Energy are maybe missing out on knowing something about themselves. Then there are times when I feel down when I want to have an Explanatory Comma about something, but I can't because I don't know what goes in the Comma. My great-grandparents were taken from India into indentureship by the British through deceit, kidnapping, and exploitation. Many of the people on the boats were children. As they made the months-long voyage across the ocean, they bonded across different castes, regions, religions, and languages. My parents know Hindi from India and English from the colonizers and Fijian from the iTaukei Indigenous people, but how do my parents sing along to Urdu ghazals so easily? How do they know words in Nepali, Bengali, Punjabi, and Tamil? Who were the people that gave them this? Explanatory Commas are a thing, but sometimes Commas aren't what explain us. Can we make Explanatory Questions a thing too?

III

It's 9:30 on a Saturday morning and I'm sitting in Mom's car, which I guess I can start calling my car at some point, on the street in front of Nisha's house. Her driveway is a sheet of ice. About an hour ago, she texted Dad to ask him if he knew of a good furnace repair person because her heat had gone out. After responding, he put on his coat to go to work as a nurse at McLaren Hospital. "She shouldn't be in her house all day when it's this cold. Can you check on her in an hour or two? If the furnace people aren't coming for a while, she should come and stay here," he said, kissing the top of my head before leaving.

In the quiet that followed, the idea of Nisha in her house, alone, with no heat, opened something inside of me. I didn't think about the damn phone number that had been haunting me, or the shame of the unanswered messages. I finally thought about Nisha. My mother's friend Nisha. And I got myself ready and drove over there. And here I am.

Explanatory Comma #3

Mom used to tell me a story about when she was ten years old, and Cyclone Oscar crashed through Fiji. Her family and neighbors prepped their houses as the storm got closer, covering their windows with thick burlap cloth or sturdy pandanus grass mats and stocking kitchen shelves with enough food to last a few days. The storm picked up while she was in school, and parents arrived one by one to take their kids home. She remembered holding her papa's hand as they walked home, the wind already blowing her braids straight back.

"Someone needed to stay with Mumtaz Auntie, our neighbor, during the storm," she told me. "She had to stay at her place to make sure her cow stayed safe too. I asked if I could be the one to go to her. Your nana said yes, I was old enough now, and he dropped me off with her on his way home."

"How long did you stay with Mumtaz?" I always asked, even though I'd heard this story a hundred times.

"Two days, until the storm blew through," she answered.

I didn't need to ask why Mumtaz, a capable woman who lived her days by herself, needed someone to stay with her during a storm. I knew the reason why, like I knew my own name. When things get hard in Fiji, in big ways or small, no one is left alone.

IV

"Deepa! Sweetie! Come inside!" Nisha says, opening the door. She's wearing a chunky knit lavender sweater that falls halfway down her thighs, gray leggings with black leg warmers scrunched from knees to ankles. On her feet are puffy black fleece house slippers, which are already walking away from me toward her kitchen. "I'll heat the chai. You want masala or plain? Leave your coat. Do you want slippers? There are some there, in the closet."

"Auntie, your furnace," I say, stepping into her foyer and closing the door. "When are they coming to fix it?"

"Arrey, no idea. They said maybe between two and five. Come!"

I lean forward and look through the archway into the living room. The last time I was here was maybe two years ago with Mom, and because that seems like another life to me now, I'm surprised that it looks just the same. An orangey-brown sectional with lots of throw pillows, a matching easy chair, and a round coffee table with a glass top covered in arty coffee table books make a cozy scene. There's a roaring fire crackling in the fireplace, and a small altar of candles, incense, and some framed black-and-white photos on the brick hearth. I see Mom's photo among them.

"Dad and I thought maybe you could come wait for a while at our house. Maybe have lunch or something? I can bring you back this afternoon," I say, but I am already taking my shoes off and looking for those slippers she mentioned. I know how this is going to go over, and the fire is making it feel just fine in here.

"Ah, that's lovely, but let's stay here for now, eh? I have samosa! I'll put them in the oven."

I go toward the kitchen and stand in the entryway. "What can I do?"

"Baito, sweetie. Bhooja is there. Sit down."

I sit and she brings out several serving dishes of food. Why do desi houses always have food ready to go? There are samosas, gulab jamun, and doubles with channa or taro ke bhagi to go on top.

"Do you think Indians know how to do coconut taro bhagi like we do?" she says.*

The next few hours go by slowly and gently. I have this feeling like I want to absorb everything about Nisha. The soft jangle of the four gold bangles on her arm as she stirs the chai. The Trini sway in her voice as she moves from kitchen to table, table to kitchen. The easy way that her thoughts come out as stories. Like Dad, she doesn't need to raise the topic of Mom, which releases me from the task of explaining why I've been avoiding Nisha all this time. Mom is just there, woven into the conversation, not a guest that needs any invitation.

Explanatory Comma #4

A few years ago, Mom drove down to Toledo to visit her old college friend Mandisa who had just moved there from New York, and she took me along. We found a parking spot when we arrived and noticed an Indian restaurant on the corner, called Taj House. She decided to order samosas to go, so we wouldn't show up empty-handed to Mandisa's townhouse. After ordering, we sat on a bench in the entryway looking into the restaurant, which was nestled in the slow period between lunch buffet and dinner service. An elderly man with a bright white mustache was wiping the tables down. He called over to Mom in a friendly but half-hearted way: "Aap India ke hai?" Are you from India? If a person looked non-South-Asian, Mom always said yes to this question. But this time she said, "Nahi, hum Fiji ke hai." No, I'm from Fiji. A twinkle beamed from the man's eyes as he stood straight up. "Ay! Hum Guyana ke hai!" I'm from Guyana! As we left the restaurant to walk down the block, I asked why the man had been so excited. "People who come from indenture are Jahaji Bhai. Brothers of the Boat. We share something; that we're Indian, but not. We're also something else."

V

It's around 5 o'clock and the furnace repair was a success. The fireplace embers are out, the house has warmed up, and I've asked Nisha to come back with me for dinner several times anyhow. She finally agrees and we bundle up to leave.

"Do you remember anything about the day that you met me?" Nisha asks, as she zips up her boots and pulls her leg warmers over them. I shake my head. I was five when we arrived in Michigan from Fiji via layovers in Hawaii and California, and I only have vague memories of being on a plane, sitting in between my parents or snuggled on their laps for what felt like days.

"Your apartment was across the hall from mine. I couldn't believe it when Islanders showed up! When we all became friends, we would leave our doors open and you'd have the run of both. You were so cute! Big eyes and not shy. I don't know who was my friend faster between you and your mom. The first week you were there, I came over with ladoo mithai and none of you had proper winter coats! I took you all to Meijers for coats, boots, mittens, the lot. We got you a snowsuit and you picked a bright yellow one with white trim. You could speak your mind, even then."

She takes her keys off the hook on the wall and opens the door. I step outside first, putting my chin down into my coat collar against the cold.

The street is quiet and still, the wind biting our faces and stinging my eyes. I want to say that it feels like a miracle that Mom and Dad ended up all the way here, across the world in this snowy town, that they loved each other so much, that Nisha was here waiting for them, that Dad and I can say through our broken hearts *Remember when, Remember when,* and that Nisha can say, *Yes.*

We shuffle carefully down the driveway toward the parked car, side by side. Nisha starts to slide on the ice and lets out a little yelp, and I laugh and push off so I can coast a little too. As I feel myself smooth out into a slow glide, I stretch out my hand, and Nisha takes it like she knew I would reach out all along. The streetlight flicks on and we can see each other perfectly. We steady each other and smile.

RAKHI & ROLL

By Tanuja Desai Hidier

When I was with Indie, the melodies flowed like my hands were the land of milk and honey—madhu, doodh—and she always had the words to make them sing. Reel me in.

You turn my chords to chorUS, I'd told her last summer, throwing her question-mark eyes: Would she be mine? (In a non-misogynistic-ownership way, of course, as my sib Scrawl had drilled into me.) Although I was leaving in September for college, she, her gap year—and we'd only met that month— the way we riffed off each other *had* to count for more in musical time.

Indie'd eye-batted me across the park bench.

—Rafi?

All upper-case-O hope:

—YES?

—Would you like a cracker to go with that paneer?

I couldn't help but smile.

—Refrain, she'd said, laying her hand upon mine, softening my strum. But her bindiometer—that little frown line etched between her brows—had smoothed.

So I'd said it again: Cracker. Paneer.

She'd laughed outright, intertwined both my hands in her fingers, pulled them into her lap.

—Cheesy as charged, I'd agreed. But weren't so many of the good things in life? You just needed to tune them, cast a croon to them.—True blue you. Love me do. Rhyme for a reason, no?

—Sure, she'd said, arpeggio'ing my arms.—So. Chords to chorus. Porous, implore, folklore . . .

—Ecuador-us? I'd offered, grinning.

—Fauna and flor-us . . .

I'd hesitated.

—Reassure . . . us?

—Well, for starters: you never bore us, she'd replied.—And I *adore* us. Now shut up and score us.

She'd kissed me slow, her mouth a whole note.

Core: Us.

A love song, those weeks, we were living.

A swan song, turned out, too.

The open mic had been at The Elbow Room, which used to be the pizza-video rental joint.

Cheetoh—Scrawl's ex whatever from high school—had

started the night. Prolly to make people listen to his own music. But I liked Cheetoh. It looked like his nose was trying to jump from his face, but his chin was out there waiting to catch it. If people ever start using money again besides at farmers' market honor stands and after storms, Cheetoh's profile should be embossed on a coin.

As if in a Lotus Eater trance, that night, when Cheetoh'd called out my name (second time *ever* amplified; first: high school graduation a couple months prior): I'd gone up there.

And . . . turned out bedroom strumming was pretty different from standing up onstage, same guitar now plugged in, umbilical . . .

Staring down a crew of terrifyingly not-yet-drunk humans.

I'd cleared my throat—unfortunately into the mic. Lifted guitar overhead, got tangled in the strap, and then, when it had thudded onto my stomach, hung on to it for dear life.

All eyes on me now. To be fair, it *had* been a gunk-funky throat-clear; I'd just glugged a half-bottle of Nesquik, chill pill of choice, but the bunny wasn't bringing it here.

To get over stage fright, Scrawl had advised, choose one person in the audience; look them in the eyes. Sing to them alone, all the way home; they'll be your fan for life.

All anybody ever wants is to be seen.

Heard.

But looking into eyes was scary, stripping. Creepy, even. So when I'd noticed this (I think) girl (Scrawl says don't assume) leaning against the shadowy corner bar, I'd known she was the one to fake contact with.

I'd opened my mouth to sing my first line . . .

And. Nothing came out.

As in: *Zilch.*

The band, to their credit, had kept playing. Well, Cheetoh—whom Scrawl had said to *call* the band, or at least the *With Special Guest* (she'd also instructed me to say I was "debuting new material" and sub "song" for "track": make my future fans think I had an album's-worth stash). He'd kept blowing into his Pepto-Bismol pink melodica with increasing urgency, doing high-knees in slow motion.

Charybdis & Scylla: Hard place to rock. I'd turned my back to the crowd, hoping to play it more cool than fool. Nodded wide panicked eyes at Cheetoh, who'd seamlessly swapped places with me, like he'd just been waiting for this main-act moment.

I'd tiptoed through the snarly wires, shrunk myself out from under the bare bulb, and thrown myself off land's end.

(Well, hopped a couple feet down to the floor.)

At the bar, I'd pulled on my hoodie, willing myself to vanish in it.

But wasn't that kind of hoodie.

What did I have to lose? Soon I'd be splitting town, too. Still, I'd slumped over bar edge. Hunched shoulders; head down. Interlaced fingers. Found myself doing church-steeple-all-the-folks (muscle memory: no joke) . . . when—like a deus ex machina—a nip glass had landed in my clasp, accompanied by a deadpan voice:

350

—Call me the god of small things. *Goddess.*

And there she was. The girl I'd non-eye-contacted with.

She looked like Scrawl had drawn her. And Scrawl's art's sick.

The Brown world, maybe whole world, sees Scrawl as white. Me, I get mixed up for Greek, Italian, Mexican as much as South Asian.

Depends what I'm eating.

This human, though, through-and-true: Brown. Hazel eyes stretching to edges of heart-shaped face. Wavy haze of butterfly-clipped hair.

Skin.

Like mine. (Not much of that shade on *these* streets.)

My male gaze seemed to be everywhere I looked. I'd quick-shifted patriarchal pupils to her plate.

Jalapeño poppers.

Downing the shot, for a cough-syrup smack I'd braced . . .

Nesquik. She'd waggled the bottle I'd left on the countertop.

—Your favored tipple, I believe?

She'd been watching *me?*

—Dunno what happened up there, I'd finally said.—Opened my mouth and . . . *gah!*

She'd leaned back, elbows saloon-cool on the bar.

—Nobody knows the words, she'd shrugged.—So nobody knows you missed them.

She'd turned away, gifting me a glimpse of her nape, sliding invitingly up into her bonsai black-brown waves.

I'd felt almost bashful. Filmi. Like when previous generations of male gazes glimpsed ankles under saris in black-and-white Bollywood movies.

As if she'd felt me watching, she'd placed her hand on the back of her neck. She was staring down at my attempt at a merch table.

—Hmm.

Well, chair.

Courtesy Scrawl. Who'd somehow found time to hand-ink three ("limited edition") of Cheetoh's tees with a drip-trippy interweaving design (my "logo"). It matched the multicolored threads she'd throttled my wrist with earlier for Rakshaband-han (when sisters honor brothers, and brothers give them money. *Frock that chauvinistic doodoo!* she'd yipped when I'd looped them on her, too. *Although I do accept Venmo, I'm the one looking out for YOUR sorry* Kabhi *Tushy* Kabhi *Bum*).

Brown Girl with Nape from Heaven had held one of the tees over her Stop AAPI Hate tank. Swaying, half her hair free-falling, Slinky-style, from claw clip to waist.

—So? she'd asked.—How do I looketh?

I'd dared. Declared:

—Just like a . . . *devi!*

You could hear a jalapeño pop.

She'd uploaded an expression like she'd just seen roadkill.

—You did *not* just say that.

—I'm *Indian*, I'd revealed . . . ? Apologized? Had I been objectifying her? But devis weren't objects, not really, and she'd called *herself* a goddess nine seconds ago.

Maybe she *wasn't* Indian. (I could hear Scrawl chiding me: *South* Asian. *Desi: contested. Better: Brown.*) She'd raised a brow, scooting her mouth all the way over to one side of her face.

—That's even worse, she'd informed me.—No. Not worse. But not great. At least *you* should be able to tell the difference.

Between? Mere muggly mortals and one such as She?

She'd narrowed her eyes like she'd zeroed in on the pore on my face from which my brain and all of civilization were leaking. Her little frown line deepening, she'd nodded at my rakhi-ripe arm.

—Sisters?

She *was* South Asian?—Or just get friendzoned a lot? If you go around telling every Brown girl you meet they look like the cast of *Never Have I Ever* . . .

Huh?

—*Ahhh!* I'd said, getting it.—I meant devi . . . as in *goddess.* Not DEVI as in Vishwakumar.

(Though she *does* kinda look like Devi-as-in-Vishwakumar. But I did NOT just tell you that.)—And yes: one sister. Who gets carried away at Rakshabandhan. Makes them herself.

—Must be nice, she'd said. So lightly I'd held my breath, she'd rested her finger atop the tangle of gold-foil-flowered rani-pink rose-red marigold-bold threads (Scrawl's renaming of our crayons has stuck to this day).—She's quite the artist.

I'd nodded, *Go on.*

—Take your pick.

She'd scrunch-fluttered a lid.

—Are you already friendzoning me? she'd demanded.

—Hell, no! Erase and rewind?

—*If,* she'd nodded, fingers more on wrist than rakhis now.—You tell me what they were.

She made a Brown boy blush. And . . . doubt his ability to spot a Brown girl.

—They were . . . *are* . . . for this holiday where sisters tie them on brothers in exchange for their eternal protection.

Goddess of Small Things sighed; *duh* vibes.

I'd tried for sensitive-dude points.—I tie them on my sister, too.

Hint of a smile. She'd nodded stagewards.—Cool, but. I meant the *words.* That felleth not from your lips.

—Ohhh . . .

I'd felt suddenly shy. A different diffidence than onstage. *This* shy made me long to throw my arms around her world. To shy *toward,* not away from.—It's . . . new material. A track?

Pre-college reading had sparked it. *The Odyssey.* Slow-going at first, but the story seeped in like a song. (Guess that's what happens when you invoke the Muse. On line *one.*) The way those ancient Greek sea-skies were wine-eyed. Fun fact: No word for blue back then. Most ancient languages have black and white first: darkness and light. And then red: sunset? bloodshed?

Heart-led?

Those words seemed to widen the sky.

Epic; when I'd soaked up the last page, fingers had flowed from tome to strum. One go, and:

My first original song.

—Entitled? she'd asked then.

I must have looked confused. She'd clarified:—Not *you*.

Phew. I'd replied:

—"No Word for Blue."

She'd stuck out a hand.

You *know* I took it.

—Well, then. I'm your girl.

And, shaking mine with one spine-straightening well-wakening pump:

—I'm *Indigo,* she'd smiled.

So . . . that's how we met.

The sky really did look different once we did.

Turned out Indie worked just through the wall. At BNB: Books Not Borders. She'd come to town to spend time with her grandmother, who wasn't doing so well. A summer job, filling in August while the owner, Brontë (I kid you not), was away.

First time I'd stopped by BNB post our elbow intro was after my own summer gig at the Y kids' camp. The front window: festooned with even more Staff Picks than hardcovers, it seemed.

"Enigmatic and enchanting."

"A tamasha of timely and timeless storytelling."

"Aaray WOW."

The novels these index cards corresponded to were by an array of—*aaray* of, turned out—Brown authors. (I'd learn later, Indie'd given herself *carte Brown* for what merited front-window real estate: solo Staff-Picked it all.)

Jasmine. Baumgartner's Bombay. Home Has No Borders. Magic Has No Borders. The God of Small Things.

Just then, God*dess* of Small Things—Nape from Heaven glimpsable over jean-jacket back—had exited, rummaging in canvas bag.

—Hi! I'd nearly woofed.

She'd spun around, keys spangling hand.

—Hey, she'd said.—Looking for anything special?

Then:—Find-and-replace. Sorry. Autopiloted that a gazillion times today.

I'd barely met her but could tell from the slight bob of her bindiometer she wasn't totally upset to see me. So I'd gone for it:

—Look*eth*-ing *at* something special!

—Oh dear. Touch twee? We *are* going to have to work on those lyrics, aren't we?

She'd locked up, dropped keys in bag.—Too bad we just closed.

Still, we'd stood there.

—I'm open, I'd said.

We'd started meeting on purpose. In the park, on her breaks. Mirror Lake. The taco place. She wanted to be a writer! *The keeper of the story,* her grandmother called her; every family had one (*and maybe you're yours?* Indie'd added, thrillingly, *through songs?*). She'd soon shared that family, too; no time to lose. Insisted I meet this elder, Mapuji—whom I loved at first laddoo.

Me? Elated! (You don't bring in the Grands unless we're here to stay.)

We'd even WhatsApped India that day: The O-Ji—*my* grandmother—so they could face-to-face. (Soon as O-Ji'd sent her daily dose of *Good Morning* stock image quotes: sunrised doves nesting in hearts of roses.

Those who know know.)

After, the Grands had *both* proclaimed:

—*It is written!*

Blessed our conjoined fate.

And yes, Indie and me, later, alone, conjoined faces. India, America: all fragments fit, all tongue and lip, those watermelon-sugar-kissed days.

All our places.

In August, my camp counselor job laked me away. The summer-slam-dunked kids found me extra-goofy and, unanimously, great.

Love was why. S'mores-high, I'd written reams about, dreamed about Indie. To share these tunes: couldn't wait!

And Indie had been writing, too.

But by my return, I'd been cut from the page.

She was India-bound. To write her way Brown.

Too late.

Fast-forward. Here. Now. I'm back for the summer. In town.

A new August. Scrawl's fresh rainbow rakhis Pridely attest.

But can't step in the same river twice, as the O-Ji says.

Or even driveway. At Mapuji's house, a *For Sale* sign.

I guess India's home for Indie these days.

So much had changed. Yet my whole year away, however amazing (my college roommate, instant friend for life; up-hiking hours for a jaw-dropping sunrise; classes like interdisciplinary music computation *wow, what is this* life?; and yes, a girl or two who caught more than just my eye)—

A parallel universe. Zapped in a flash.

Childhood bedrooms can do that.

Upon my wall: Joni Mitchell's *Blue*. Desk: Trig; Chem; Spanish II. Those three-ring binders you buy for school (then never use).

Ms. Marvel. Dune. The Odyssey, too.

And here, semi-levitating before me, an actual human: my sister-turned-sibster. (I'm getting used to their pronouns. But that platinum buzzcut? Still astounds.) They're giving off Oracle of Delphi meets garden gnome vibes. Imperious; hilarious. There in half-squat half-lotus, on my dresser up high.

(Still stickered with Pidgey. Pidgeotto. Blu. And my all-time number one dawg: Snoopy.)

Sigh.

Across the room, my guitar's pickupping dust.

I'd been stringless in college, and no strings attached. No reverb of Indie; sounds of the past . . .

—Raffster, Scrawl says now.—Drop the kapalabhati breathing.

But a growing awareness, facing my strings:

—Without her, I . . . walk the world . . . with a ghost limb . . .

OMG, Scrawl mouths at me. They hop off the dresser, pick up the acoustic. Stride over. Curtsy.—THIS is your ghost limb. Now use it!

I accept it terrified, like a newborn baby.—Don't give up on your dreams; your music's what barely makes you *bearable*. If you insist on moaning about that ladki? Put a damn tune to it.

I strike a minor B5, tentative. Scrawl flares nostrils. Noserings.

—Dude! Resolve that maudlin shit!

Guilty as gloomed: the chord of regret. I lift hands from frets. But . . . have to admit:

Even a sad sound can shimmer, have an upbeat ring: When you sing sad *out* . . . joy weeps *in*.

I thought it might hurt too much to play. In every way. Uncalloused fingers; broken-heart-strings. But not playing hurts, too, turns out; maybe more. Like Indie'd said: not writing was harder than writing, because you still had to carry your story around. The weight of whatever you weren't expressing. Unsound.

And since all writing's rewriting, better get it all out.

—Raffling. Rakhi and *roll!* Scrawl instructs.—Enough with the blues.

A lilt lit lightbulb moment: time to change hues?

Could be it was time . . . to make a Brown sound?

Indie switched countries to kindle her words. To gather her past, and work her way past the hurt . . .

—Maybe I should move forward . . . by rewinding back? I muse aloud.—Work on a . . . South Asian-ish? . . . song?

—*Track*, Scrawl claps.—Sure. Why not? Lean-into-your-heritage shit. For eternal inspo: my Browntown playlist . . .

(Last semester, from Smith, Scrawl'd shared this diaspora mix. Anokha; Basement Bhangra: '90s watershed hits. Arooj; Anoushka. Joy Crookes. Charli XCX. *Even the British can't colonize this.*)

They're fiddling with my phone. Bluetooth speaker erupts on.

—Raff, they command, leap-trampolining my bed.—*Riff!*

And before I know it, I'm strum-thwacking along.

—*B to the E! B to the E!*

Then "Flight IC408" to Asha Puthli: *I am song.*
Sing me.

Scrawl's dimple's out in full glory. Wild, DNA; I feel my own dip in my face.

They hop off my bed, tango over my case.

—Raffling. Exit your navel—and get out your damn room! Head down to Elbow. Cheetoh's holding auditions. And his open mic's soon.

All those songs sparked by Indie, I hedged: I'm still lyricless. I had "No Word for Blue." But no words for Brown . . .

—*Yet*.

Scrawl's half-dancing, half-pacing. Eyes land on my desk.— SCREW-the-lightbulb *moment!* Try this!

She lifts up *The Odyssey*.—Haul your lyrically challenged di*ARSE*porass to BNB? On the way? Say hi to Brontë, ask for some tips. Her Jhumpa Lahiri opinion! White woke bookstore owners *live* for that shit. And since you're going there *anyways* . . .

—I am, am I?

— . . . you can pick up my book. Ordered Madhur Jaffrey in. College food's cringe. Time we learn to cook.

Return to two scenes of the crime?

They grin-yelp over the beat, as if they're reading my mind:

—Raffster. Get the frock back on the bike.

Scrawl jazz-hands out room now . . .

I unflatten the string.

Flip fear to the B-side:

Anticipation springs.

Experiencing BNB without Indie—and Elbow Room too— could be wise. At the least to say hello to Cheetoh.

And to revise my twice-shy. Regroup.

Reprise.

The last time I'd seen Indie, a near year ago now:

She'd said we had to talk.

Sidewalked. Our rhythm: off.

She'd quit her bookstore job. Thought long and hard about her gap year . . . and decided hard and fast:

She was heading for the motherland. *Grand*motherland. At last.

For her writing? I'd uttered. She'd nodded. Added, flustered:

So Mapuji could see India once again.

While she, we can.

—Okay, I'd replied. Whatever she wanted, I was in.—I'm so glad you can do that for her. Maybe she'll even start to feel better? I'll save up, see you at break. We can gather the Grands! Stay at O-Ji's place?

Indie had touched my cheek.

—This may be something I need to do alone, she'd said, softly but staunch. I was off to college and should be free for that. She was on Mapuji's timeline; didn't know when she'd be back.

She'd kissed my forehead. Staccato. Gut: sucker-punch vibrato.

I'd tried not to take it personally. Not to be the patriarchy.

Let her *breathe*. Still, I'd sought relief:

—Sure. So . . . we can still be together though . . . in a non-ownership way?

She'd blinked, then brandished one swift flinty nod.

—Cool. Let's be mature. Why not?

And then, about-facing:

—Or, actually . . . *why?*

Bindiometer a trench.—Maybe . . . let's just say bye. I mean, after all, we barely even met.

Then how did I already know she was someone I'd never forget?

Two words for blue:

Indie. Go.

She'd dodged my last-ditch hug.

Looked at me and shrugged.

Summer loving ending: abrupt.

And then she'd killed me with kid gloves:

—I'll always be grateful to you, Rafi. You got me through a cruel summer. And Mapuji too. Seeing you, us, gave her . . . us . . . a *feeling*. Of something to look forward to.

—A *future*, she'd added. Patted rakhis on my wrist, tugged a little on the string.—The best kind of fiction.

Shelved.

I'd untied one. Handed it to her, with all my good wishes.

Inside, I was shattered. Blindsided. In bits.

She'd dispatched her customer-service smile—

Then split.

Hadn't seen her since.

In love—when lover turns *over,* falling, even literally *flying,* across borders, bodies of water, *out* of it?

That's a long no-signature time.

Bluetooth off. Scrawl jams my earbuds in. Hands me my case. Now just the right weight.

Feels good, holding it.

Like I'm going places.

I don't *actually* take it. I mean, I'm not a total Ken, strumming at woke white bookstore owners. And I'm not yet ready to plug in for the world, even Cheetoh's pretty forgiving one.

But I'm ready to . . . shy toward it?

I set it down in the hall. Hit shuffle; head out. Into late slake-achy August, daydreaming beneath the covers, one eye on the clock.

Already nostalgic for itself, the way only August can be.

Or, maybe I'm emo. The problem; it's me.

Cross through Indie-eras: the park (our bench), Mirror Lake (our swim), up Soule. To Bates and Main.

Books Not Borders: on the Northwest corner.

Front window . . . a rainbow of Banned Books truths:

Milk and Honey. Doodh, madhu. *The Color Purple. All Boys Aren't Blue.*

Water Protectors. The Arabic Quilt.

The Hill We Climb. The Hate U Give.

The Bluest Eye. (And maybe this.)

Somehow they make me braver. A playlist for my eyes.

I take a breath. Step inside.

Doors bo-jangle. Like O-Ji "waking up the house"; ringing the string of bells by her kitchen temple.

The store's a magic-hat trick. Bigger on the inside than out. Like how music venues not only glow . . . but *grow* in the dark.

Floor to ceiling-sky, wall to windowed wall:

Spines. And I'm surprised to find: though I'm far from Indie, knowing I can at least hold our story . . . keeps me closer to fine.

Like just being surrounded by these tales builds, thrills, my backbone. Even the worlds I don't know make me feel . . . not alone.

A creak by the register.

And inch by inch, time-lapse human blooms from behind it:

Not Brontë, as forecast.

Rather: Like Athena springing from Zeus-head, or universe from Krishna-lips . . . or Nape from Heaven from the crawl-space storage basement . . .

She appears.

Heart in my teeth. Those eyes to the edges. Weather-report hair.

100 percent chance of Indigo. She's . . . *here?*

Galaxy of skin I can still sense, scent, on my own.

Like it was somewhere I'd always been.

Home.

Bindiometer easing as she sets down the teetering stack . . .

Then double-deepening the moment she records me. Stands back.

I miss her even more now she's in front of me.

She looks like she'd *like* to miss me. Starts organizing the books she's brought up. Too briskly.

—Wow, I say. Every emotion in my belly hyphenates: happy-sad; healed-hurt. Grief. Relief. And rising to the top?

Hope. She's noisily silent, sticky-noting names onto bags. I'm too excited to see her to be deterred.—You're . . . *back?*

Eyes averted; her tone flat:

—Filling in for Brontë. Off and on since June.

—*I'm* around, too, I say quick, thick; she never checked?— But . . . leaving soon.

—Mmmhmm.

—How *are* you? You look . . .

Like that feeling when *just* the song you need air-waves just in time.

She raises her frown line, suspicious. I try a joke. To remind her of us:

— . . . just like that girl from *Bend It Like Beckham!*

She's hard to read. An odyssey. Moving away from me. Then: without missing a beat:

—Which one?

—HA! I say a little too loud.—I swear I'm not stalking you! But it's like a sign you're here! In fact, I was just listening to Badmarsh & Sri . . .

She's unimpressed with my knowledge of *Signs*. (Featuring UK Apache.)

Should I try Monsoon's "Ever So Lonely"? *Be my friend tonight.*

I decide to hit pause on Scrawl's book pickup. Buy time in Indie's company. And work on my own lines.

— I was just coming by for some inspiration. For . . . new material.

Indie narrows eyes at me.

—Please do not say you just found it.

Paneered no cracker. I shut my trap. Then open it:

—Could you *help* me find it?

She comes out around the register. I actually have to hold my arms down to keep from hugging her.

—Course, she says.—Looking for anything special.

She's doing that thing, ending questions with periods. We once were ellipses (the mind-reading kind). Now she's full stop.

Punctuating me out.

Or, maybe . . . acting professional? This *is* her place of business.

So I try to go pro too:

—I've got this . . . *audition* really soon, I tell her.—And I'd like to write, play—*debut!*—something more South Asian than my usual?

I want her to know I can meet her in the motherland without flying. Going back to a place doesn't have to mean leaving another behind!

Bindiometer inches up. Better get to the point.

—So . . . I say.—Got any . . . Jhumpa?

She sighs those *duh*-vibes. Heads through the aisles, poking books into place as we go. Artfully arranging the candles, cards, cookbooks. I follow.

She scoops up *The Handmaid's Tale*, dramatically reshelves it in Nonfiction. I hold up a high-five *amirite* . . . but she's already coasted to Classics.

No homie Homer, white whales, anything I'm used to seeing here. She nods to the L's, per my request. Then proffers a gold-seal teal hardcover from M.

—*You'd* love this one. *Gay-Neck*.

—I'm still into *girls*, I assure her; is it the Pride rakhi?— Women. WomAN.

—*Gay* NECK.

I *do* love her nape, but. She enunciates slowly:—*The Story of a Pigeon*. First ever South Asian American children's book. Scored the National Book Award. *100 years ago*.

Mind. Blown. Something so dope *before* our Grands were born?

And: she did NOT just reference Pidgey. My room! Now feels *I'm* flying.

But she's made a break for the boxes, ripping open shipments.

—Those all look great, I say, leaning on the counter. A wing-flap of white rectangles scattered across it. I'd recognize that brown-sharpied decoy handwriting anywhere. *"Riveting and rollicking." "A keeper. One you'll return to time and again."*— But *these*. Even better.

From beneath the boings of her curls as she bends, unboxing: a smile?

—You always have the words, I add.—When you want.

She abruptly stops. Stands. X-acto brandished in hand.

—What's that supposed to mean.

Whoops.

—I meant . . . How's *your* writing going? Did you finish?

She squints at me. Gets back to unpackaging. Extra-vigorously. A bass face to make even Haim uneasy.

—I *was* working on something, she says as she shreds.—But it's a ghost story now.

And it's not really like me, but I guess now it is:

—Well, you're good at ghosting.

I surprise myself. It sounds mean off my tongue though was just woe in my throat. Guess the hurt always comes out somewhere. A tear. A zit. Vomit.

War.

Our weather: heavy. Indie's bindiometer sinks further.

I think she's going to let me have it, but—

—Better than at being South Asian, I suppose, she sighs.—You know what Brontë told me? I could be the new Jhumpa Lahiri.

Props?

—If I'd just lean into my culture a little more.

Dropped.—So I said: Then what'll *she* do? And aren't there others, too?

She gestures widely, the riches of Brown ink on (this surely by-her-curated) display.—I don't even know how to be the new *me*. Or even the *old* me. Also: Lean into *which* culture?

She plants fists in planetary hips, examines a carton's

369

contents as if her choices lie therein.—Marathi? Quote American? Gujarati? *Chobani?* I mean, we're not a frocking monolith, right?

—Preach, I grin, then wonder if I'm appropriating something, or leaving a belief system out . . . but I don't have time to go there because my whole religion is she's getting *real* with me!

I want to tell her: *Those identities all harmonize. Look at YOU. You are the* whole. *The* truth. *The living* proof.

As if on cue, I can just make out my pocket's earbud moves: Browntown slides seamless into Joni's *songs are like tattoos.*

And I'm having a lightbulb-screw, realizing maybe this even applies to *me* . . .

(And you.)

But she's off to the race races:

—This white fragility girl, woman came in the other day, a total Nosering Lululemon Blonde. Asked for a recipe for *chai tea.* From *me.*

Same pet peeve as Scrawl: that tea-tea redundancy. Who knew? The two could end up bffs.—She ordered Madhur Jaffrey's *Quick & Easy Indian Cooking.* Like: Just add ghee. I'm Brown now. Wheee.

Okeyyy. Maybe more FFS than bffs.

Scrawl. AKA: Seema from Mumbai.

They, I whisper, but she doesn't hear. I'd love to tell Indie all about my sibster. Laugh it off; she could even meet her? But mood grows dim.

She sets down knife.

—I'm sorry if I ghosted you, she says.—Maybe you got flesh and blood . . . in a whole other way? Which can feel the same.

—What do you mean? You never replied. To anything.

—You just seemed so *happy*. In those posts. College looks good on you. All those new friends.

I downplay it:

—Dunno why they keep tagging me . . .

—Rafi. Letting other people be lucky enough to know you? It's cool. Sure, it hurt a little, but I was hurting anyways. Head start on you.

I *had* sometimes, a lot of the time, been happy, I realized. But it didn't mean I hadn't missed her too. A playlist on shuffle: every mood.

—No crime in being fine, she adds, mind-reading.—Being in *life*. Something I wasn't so good at this last year, after you went your way.

—I wasn't trying to separate *your* path from mine!

—"Let's be together in a *non-ownership* way"? she replies. I'm mystified.—And I quote.

Oh. Right. Only so much you can expect someone to read between the lines.

—I didn't mean . . . open relationship stuff, I said. Too retro? Truth, though.—I just didn't want you to feel I was holding you back.

But I *had* wanted to hold her back. Keep her near. Voicing

the more generous words I'd wished I could inhabit was laying pebbles on a path. Trying to walk that walk without breaking anyone's back.—Anyways, *you* called our future fiction, right?

She sits on the last unpacked prose haul. Quizzical.

—I don't think so? she says.—Maybe I meant Mapuji's. Mine. Ours. I don't remember. But . . . isn't everything fiction till it happens?

We look at each other and we're on the same side of the pane, the page, for a moment.

And though I wish I had something more philosophical to say—a metaphor, a middle 8, to save the day—I can't help myself:

—Did you meet someone? In India?

I'm trying to smile, but did you know smiles evolved from fear? Fang-flashing to scare away danger; not a facial dance to draw someone near.

—I lost someone, she said, finally.

—Oh. I'm sorry, Indie.

And I was. For her, yes. And, well, almost as much for me. But her reply surprises:

—We didn't even go to India. We brought Mapuji back to *our* home; her health turned. But she was okay with that. Said with India, what she missed most was the *time*. That home has no borders, no sides. It's wherever love resides. It's even where love *tries*.

All summer, she went on to say, she'd been laying her grandmother's story on the page. All about India—for Indie, an unknown place. The map to its heart: her grandmother's face. Tale after tale, Indie had her relay.

—Like *1001 Nights*. Scheherazade, she said.—To try to keep her in *this* space . . .

And Indie's story becomes mine, too.

—That last time, though, Mapuji asked us for a song, she went on.—A childhood lullaby, one she'd often sung. Ayeparee? I thought of you; you'd have known how to help. Something we'd known our whole *lives* . . . turns out we'd only absorbed the opening lines. Didn't even know how to search them, spell. Sang them over and over . . . through her last breath.

I want to take her in my arms so bad they're aching, but she's sidled behind register, her earth quaking.—And now we will never know the words. And after that, all my own words got stuck, too. For what kind of granddaughter, writer, keeper of our story am I?

—I'm so sorry, Indie, I tell her, and it's true. Blue you.—I loved . . . I *love* her, too.

Her irises blur, or maybe mine do.

I step up. To the register.

—And nobody knows the words, I say softly. *And I love* you.

She looks at me. A touch of that old telepathy.

—So nobody knows, she murmurs.—How much you missed them.

I'm *literally* leaning into this heritage shit—and it's her family's, but also our own; it's her loss, and I too mourn.

Isn't that what happens when you share a story? A song?

And . . . she's leaning toward *me*.

The small miracle of which I only realize when the door jangles, making us both jump.

She shakes her head slightly, like she's jostling herself from a dream. Glances over to nod, force-smile at the gentleman who's clacked in with an umbrella-turned-cane.

I slide a decomposition notebook off the twirling rack.

She nods to it.

—Yes. At some point you have to just do the thing, right? Sorry for blathering on. Don't overthink it. *Any* sound *you* make's brown.

What I'd been wanting to tell *her!* Our synchronicity: strong. She starts ringing me up.—You got this, Rafi. You write that song.

Hearing her say my name is song enough.

Indie calls out *be right with you* to the gentleman.

I want Indie and me to be together forever, even though we're too young; we've got things to do? prove? Maybe it's too early in life. To have found someone so *nice*.

I want to pick up where we left off—but can't step in the same river twice.

Still, as the O-Ji says . . . all rivers lead to the sea.

And I know now: I'll be with Indie any way she needs. Whatever we name it: as a friend to help her through this grief. Or someone she doesn't even really see? If any thought of me can bring reprieve.

Don't get me wrong: I'd rather have her every way: word; deed (I'm greedy!). But . . . I can shift keys. If need be.

—Like a bag? she asks. Official, now that we're not alone. She's a deeper shade of Browntown, though.

—Could you wrap it please?

She nods, revolves. Tears off a sheet. Nape bared brews heart swell. She wraps up the wrap-up. Passes the parcel.

I take it in both hands . . . and offer it back to her.—You got this, too, Indie.

—A little on the nose, she says. She slides an index card across the counter. Raises me.—So . . . what time's your audition?

And today, I know: All I want to do is listen.

—I think the one I want to ace, I say.—Is this one.

Parentheses curve around her mouth. I try to bracket them.

—That is, I add.—If it's still . . . written?

She nods to the card. I flip it; a heart-skip; an epic to drink in:

"A keeper. One you'll return to time and again."

It takes just one person who loves and lives Brown: to make a Brown sound. And one person listening: to make it resound.

And home is a story. Everywhere we belong. Anywhere we tune in. For however long.

Even a moment of forever of just the right song.

Wine-eyed sky widens:

Her hand landing from outer space . . . in my palm.

—It is *rewritten,* she smiles.

It. Is. ON.

AUTHOR BIOS

FATIMAH ASGHAR is an artist who spans across different genres and themes. They have been featured in various outlets such as *Time*, NPR, *Teen Vogue*, and the Forbes 30 Under 30 List. Their first book of poems, *If They Come for Us*, explored themes of orphaning, family, the violence of the 1947 Partition of South Asia, the legacy of colonization, borders, shifting identity, and violence. Their debut novel, *When We Were Sisters*, from One World/Random House, was longlisted for the National Book Award and won the inaugural Carol Shields Prize. Along with Safia Elhillo they coedited an anthology for Muslim people who are also women, trans, gender nonconforming, and/or queer, *Halal If You Hear Me*, which was built around the radical idea that there are as many ways of being Muslim as there are Muslim people in the world. They are the writer and cocreator of the Emmy-nominated *Brown Girls*, a web series that highlights friendship among women of color that was in a development deal with HBO; and wrote and directed *Got Game*, a short film that follows a queer South Asian Muslim woman trying to navigate a kink party after being single; and wrote, directed, and starred in *Retrieval*, a lyrical short film that follows the process of a soul retrieval in the aftermath of sexual assault. They are also a writer and coproducer on the Emmy-nominated *Ms. Marvel* on Disney+, and wrote episode 5 of *Time and Again*.

TASHIE BHUIYAN is the author of *Counting Down with You*, *A Show for Two*, *Stay with My Heart*, and the forthcoming *I'll Pretend You're Mine*. She is a New Yorker through and through, and she hopes to change the world, one book at a time. She loves writing stories about gaining agency through growth and surviving against all odds. When she's not doing that, she's probably traveling, attending a concert, or bothering her cat, Zuko.

TANYA BOTEJU lives on the unceded territories of the Musqueam, Squamish, and Tsleil-Waututh First Nations (Vancouver, BC). Part-time, she teaches English to clever and sassy young people. The rest of her time, she uses writing as an excuse to eat pastries. Her debut novel, *Kings, Queens, and In-Betweens*, was named a Top Ten Indie Next Pick by the American Booksellers Association. Her second novel, *Bruised*, was selected as a Gold Standard book by the Junior Library Guild. Look for another YA novel, *Messy Perfect*, and a middle grade nonfiction book about allyship in 2025. Visit her at tanyaboteju.com.

TANUJA DESAI HIDIER is an author/singer-songwriter. Her pioneering debut, *Born Confused*, is considered to be the first South Asian American YA novel and was named an American Library Association Best Book for Young Adults. The sequel, *Bombay Blues*, received the South Asia Book Award. Tanuja has also created "booktrack" albums of original songs based on the novels. The music video for her jazz-pop ode to Bombay, "Heptanesia," was on rotation on MTV and is an MTV Indies BuzzPick, and she also produced the Deep Blue She #Mutiny2Unity #MeToo WeMix music video/PSA: an award-winning intersectionality project featuring 100+ artist/activists, mostly WOC. Tanuja lives in Maine, on Indigenous Wabanaki land, where she serves as board president of youth literary nonprofit The Telling Room, whose mission is to empower youth, including immigrants and refugees, through writing and sharing their voices with the world. Your/our story matters! Please visit ThisIsTanuja.com for more info.

VEERA HIRANANDANI is the author of the Newbery Honor–winning *The Night Diary* and the recently released companion novel, *Amil and the After*. She earned her MFA in creative writing at Sarah Lawrence College. She's also the author of *The Whole Story of Half a Girl*, a Sydney Taylor Notable Book and a South Asia Book Award finalist, and *How to Find What You're Not Looking For*, winner of the Sydney Taylor Book Award and the New-York Historical Society Children's History Book Prize. A former editor at Simon & Schuster, she now teaches in the writing for children and young adults MFA program at the Vermont College of Fine Arts. Find out more at veerahiranandani.com.

SHEBA KARIM is the author of the YA novels *Skunk Girl*, *That Thing We Call a Heart*, which made several best book lists, including Bank Street's and *Kirkus*'s, *Mariam Sharma Hits the Road*, an NPR Best Book of the Year, and *The Marvelous Mirza Girls*, winner of the South Asia Book Award. Her fiction and essays have been featured in *580 Split*, *Asia Literary Review*, *India Today*, *Literary Hub*, *Michigan Quarterly Review*, *Off Assignment*, *Sewanee Review*, *Shenandoah*, *South Asian Review*, *The Rumpus*, *Time Out Delhi*, and various anthologies in the United States and India. She lives in Nashville, where she is a writer-in-residence at Vanderbilt University.

JASMIN KAUR is an author, illustrator, and poet living on unceded Sto:lo territory. Her writing, which explores themes of feminism, womanhood, social justice, and love, acts as a means of healing and reclaiming identity. As a spoken-word artist and creative writing facilitator, she has toured across

North America, the UK, and Australia to connect with youth through the power of artistic expression.

She was named a "rising star" by *Vogue* magazine, and a "Writer to Watch" by CBC Books. Her work has been celebrated at the American Music Awards by musical icon Jennifer Lopez and shared by celebrities like Jessica Alba and Reese Witherspoon. You can find her books *When You Ask Me Where I'm Going* and *If I Tell You the Truth* at your favorite bookstores.

KANWALROOP KAUR SINGH is a Punjabi Sikh writer and civil rights attorney, born and raised in California. Her essays have been published in *Kweli Journal* and the Asian American Writers Workshop. She is an alumna of the Voices of Our Nation (VONA) writing workshop and the Interdisciplinary Writer's Lab at Kearny St. Workshop. As a radio reporter, she wrote and produced award-winning radio documentaries on Sikh communities in California and on farmers in Punjab for KALW Public Radio. She studied creative writing at the University of California, Berkeley, where she won the Yoshiko Uchida Prize in Writing. In her spare time, she loves getting lost in nature and traveling the world with her partner. Connect with her on Instagram @kanwalroop.kaur.

REKHA KUVER (she/her) is a reader, writer, and artist. Some of the writings she's the most proud of are the jokes she makes in her group chats. Her dad taught her that poetry is everywhere and her mom taught her that life is the best art medium of all. She grew up in Flint, Michigan, and now lives in Seattle, Washington, where she also works in youth advocacy and librarianship. Find Rekha on Instagram @line_sofine.

RAJANI LaROCCA was born in India, raised in Kentucky, and now lives in the Boston area, where she practices medicine and writes award-winning books for young readers, including the Newbery Honor–winning middle grade novel in verse *Red, White, and Whole*. She's always been an omnivorous reader, and now she is an omnivorous writer of fiction and nonfiction, novels and picture books, prose and poetry. Learn more about Rajani and her books at RajaniLaRocca.com.

SARAH MUGHAL RANA is a Muslim author and student at Oxford University studying at the intersection of economic policy and human rights. Her young adult debut, *Hope Ablaze*, released 2024 from Macmillan US, was librarian Mychal Threets's debut book club pick and a Junior Library Guild selection. Her fantasy trilogy, *Dawn of the Firebird*, debuts in 2026. Her books have been featured by CBC Books, Book Riot, and Indigo as best books of the year. Outside of writing, she is the cohost of the *On the Write Track* podcast, where she spills tea with her favorite authors, and she enjoys falling down history rabbit holes or training in martial arts.

ANURADHA D. RAJURKAR is the award-winning author of *American Betiya,* named a best book by YALSA, Bank Street, Book Riot, and a *Cosmopolitan* "130 Best YA Novels of All Time" selection. Raised near Chicago, Anuradha earned two degrees from Northwestern University and for years had the joy of being a public school teacher by day, writer by night. Her upcoming works include *Temporary Bodies,* a gothic thriller set in India, and a short story in *Everything Needs to Change,* a climate justice anthology. When not writing or reading, Anuradha loves creating visual stories through garden, interior, and knit design. She lives in Evanston, Illinois, with her family and a fluffy, highly opinionated rescue pup named Cleo. Connect with Anuradha at anuradharajurkar.com.

NISHA SHARMA (she/her) is a YA and adult contemporary romance writer living in the Philly suburbs with her Alaskan husband, and a plethora of animals named after characters in literature. Her books have been included in best-of lists by the *New York Times, Entertainment Weekly, Cosmopolitan,* the *Washington Post, Time* magazine, and more. Before she left the corporate world, Nisha spearheaded DEI initiatives at billion-dollar companies. She has continued her advocacy work by fighting for marginalized authors in publishing. When she's not writing about people of color experiencing radical joy or teaching about inclusivity, Nisha can be found hitting the books for her PhD in English and social justice. You can find her online at Nisha-sharma.com or @nishawrites.

NIKESH SHUKLA is a novelist and screenwriter who is currently working on a Spider-Man India comic book miniseries for Marvel as well as numerous television projects. Most recently, he released his first children's book, *The Council of Good Friends*. He is the author of *Coconut Unlimited* (shortlisted for the Costa First Novel Award), *Meatspace*, and the critically acclaimed *The One Who Wrote Destiny*. Nikesh is the editor of the bestselling essay collection *The Good Immigrant*, which won the reader's choice at the Books Are My Bag Readers' Awards. He coedited *The Good Immigrant USA* with Chimene Suleyman. He is the author of three YA novels, *Run, Riot* (shortlisted for a National Book Award), *The Boxer* (longlisted for the Carnegie Medal), and *Stand Up*. Nikesh was one of *Time* magazine's cultural leaders, *Foreign Policy* magazine's 100 Global Thinkers, and *The Bookseller*'s 100 most influential people in publishing in 2016 and 2017. He is the cofounder of the Good Literary Agency. Nikesh's memoir, *Brown Baby: A Memoir of Race, Family, And Home*, was longlisted for the Jhalak Prize. He has also written a book on writing called *Your Story Matters*. Nikesh wrote the award-winning short film *Two Dosas*, a Channel 4 Comedy Lab called *Kabadasses*, and has worked in numerous writer's rooms both in the UK and US.

NAVDEEP SINGH DHILLON spent eight years in the US Navy working as a linguist in cushy offices and chipping paint off the sides of large boats instead of going on a swashbuckling adventure in the high seas as he'd imagined. He spent his mid-twenties vagabonding across the globe, from Europe to Southeast Asia, and blew his budget on buying books at independent bookshops across the world, scarfing down delicious street food, and gulping down piping hot cups of cha. He teaches literature and creative writing in the NYC area and is cofounder of IshqInABackpack, a narrative travel blog. He is the author of *Sunny G's Series of Rash Decisions*, which received a starred review from ALA *Booklist* and was a Junior Library Guild Selection. He is a third-culture kid born in England, raised in Tanzania, Nigeria, Dubai, and Fresno, California, but is a Punjabi boy at heart. Visit Navdeep online at navdeepsinghdhillon.com and follow him on Instagram @navdeepsinghdhillon.

ACKNOWLEDGMENTS

This anthology is the answer to wild hopes and dreams Sona Charaipotra imagined years ago (Sona, we did it!), and there are so many people to thank for making this dream of a collection come true.

First, thank you to all our amazing contributors who trusted us with their gorgeous stories. Fatimah, Kanwalroop, Rajani, Jasmin, Tanya, Navdeep, Tashie, Sheba, Anuradha, Nikesh, Nisha, Veera, Sarah, Rekha, Tanuja—you are all rock stars. Your stories are brilliant and fierce, and it's been an honor to work with all of you.

Thank you, Shreya Gupta—once again, you completely blew us away with this stunning cover.

Big love to my fantastic agent, Joanna Volpe, and the entire fabulous New Leaf Team that brought this anthology to life—Suzie Townsend, Lindsay Howard, Jenniea Carter, and Sophia Ramos. I'm eternally grateful to all of you

Megan Ilnitzki, I adore you! Thank you for believing in this anthology, for sharing our vision, and for being such a champion for all these stories. Thank you also to the wonderful team at Harper and Epic Reads, especially Erin DeSalvatore, Melissa M. Cicchitelli, Danielle McClelland, Joel Tippie, Michael D'Angelo, and Taylan Salvati.

To my family, who built a home in this new world for us, and to all the ancestors who remind us of where we came from.

To Thomas, Lena, and Noah, you are the loves of my life and my inspiration for, well, everything. Home is wherever I'm with you.

And big love to you, dear reader. You are the reason this collection exists. Thank you for welcoming these stories into your heart and making a space for us in your home.

—Samira Ahmed

A hundred years ago, give or take, Samira Ahmed and I repeatedly had a What If conversation. What if we finally had the stories we wished for when we were little, the ones where kids who looked like us could finally be the heroes—where kids like *ours* could finally be the heroes. Thank you, Samira, for going on the journey with me.

And thank you to all the amazing South Asian diaspora authors who have joined us for the ride. To contributors

Fatimah, Kanwalroop, Rajani, Jasmin, Tanya, Navdeep, Tashie, Sheba, Anuradha, Nikesh, Nisha, Veera, Sarah, Rekha, Tanuja, your voices ring strong and true. Thank you so much for sharing your stories with us and the world.

Thank you to Shreya Gupta for your beautiful cover art, which truly brings the vision home.

Thank you, Megan Ilnitzki, for being an amazing shepherd and champion for both *Home* and *Magic*. These books have been a labor of love for all of us, and your unflagging energy and excitement have made them a pleasure to work on. Thank you, too, to the Harper and Epic Reads teams for everything: Erin DeSalvatore, Melissa M. Cicchitelli, Danielle McClelland, Joel Tippie, Michael D'Angelo, and Taylan Salvati.

Thank you to the New Leaf team, who are always on top of things and never afraid to shake things up: Jo Volpe, Suzie Townsend, Jenniea Carter, Lindsay Howard, and Sophia Ramos, you are all amazing and tireless!

To Mommy, Papa, Meena, and Tarun, my first collaborators. Thank you for traveling the world with me.

My favorite band of storytellers, Navdeep, Kavya, and Shaiyar—I can't wait to share your stories with the world.

And to the readers—the travelers, the immigrants, the misfits, the third culture kids. These stories are for you. May you find your home on the page.

—Sona Charaipotra